UNLOCKED

A NOVEL

ELLA KHORT

Chapter One

Hayden

The ice in the glass had melted, watering down the scotch. Hayden drank it regardless after hanging up the phone. She called. For three days he busied himself with work, wondering, though not allowing himself to hope, whether Brea would accept his proposal. It was five minutes after midnight, and Hayden's flight home to San Francisco would take off at ten in the morning. Falling asleep would be difficult. The sound of Brea's voice echoed in his mind.

He planned to postpone informing Avery about the trip to Mexico until after arriving home. It was not uncommon for him to travel with little notice if one of his subsidiary companies was in crisis, and as a result, it would be unlikely this trip would raise any suspicions. The challenge would be the following week at home, coping with the guilt of lying to Avery.

Switching on his laptop, he pulled on a clean T-shirt and fixed himself another scotch. He emailed his assistant to book his flight and draft a sham itinerary. Ashley would be discreet with no questions why he asked her to do this. Afterward, he wrote an email to his travel agent requesting she book two suites in Puerto Vallarta or Punta Mita in any available luxury resort.

Hayden paused, sipped his scotch, and pictured Brea seated at the counter of Brine several days prior. Her warm smile vanishing upon recognizing him had struck him like a bullet to the chest. He would give anything now to have her look at him as she did twenty years ago.

Though she attempted to mask it throughout the call, her strained voice revealed she was on the verge of tears. He rubbed his eyes and a wave of guilt washed over him, remembering his last night with her when he lost his control.

To have a week with Brea, hold nothing back, and to prove to her he was not the man she believed him to be, was an unforeseen gift. However insane the idea, he felt certain this trip was the only path to both help her understand the truth of that night and find her way out of her current unhappiness. Hayden stretched his neck and fixed his eyes on the ceiling. He needed to forgive himself as well, but that would only happen if he earned her forgiveness first.

Restless, he went to the patio glass doors and as he stepped onto the balcony, the damp, seaweed-scented night air sobered him. Hayden gazed at the ocean and watched the waves crashing on the sand below, finding the scene violent yet soothing to meditate on. He yanked a chair from the patio table and sank into the white wicker seat. Since seeing Brea, he had replayed in his mind their first meeting at Black Harbor Public Library many times. She never knew it, but he had seen her a week before the first time they met.

It was a Tuesday afternoon in the spring of eighth grade, and Hayden was in the car with his mother after school. While driving to her doctor's appointment before his city league baseball practice, he asked his mother for a favor. Instead of waiting an endless hour or two in an overcrowded doctor's office, he pleaded with his mother to drop him off at the public library to start on his homework, and she agreed.

After finding an empty table, he unpacked his books and set to work on his biology assignment. Twenty minutes passed, and he leaned back against the chair to stretch his neck. His eyes caught sight of a girl near his age with caramel brown hair tied into a ponytail hastening her steps to the librarian's desk. She was petite, dressed in a pale-blue oversized sweater that swallowed her whole, a pair of black leggings, and an oversized backpack in her hand.

He watched her as she spoke with the librarian, laughed and glanced over her shoulder. Hayden did not mean to stare, but seeing her face, he held his breath. She was not only beautiful, but her smile and demeanor, a gentle kindness, captivated him. After thanking the librarian, she swiveled around and, with an elated smile, rushed to the stacks.

It was not so much a question *if* he would try to talk to her, but *how* he could approach her and introduce himself. He rose from the table and, with a pounding heart, followed in the direction she went.

Spotting her several rows in, she stood hunched over, gliding her finger over the spines of the books in search of one in particular. Hayden, needing a minute to collect his thoughts, moved to the next row. He walked down the aisle until he spotted the top of her head in the fifth bay, peeking out above the third row.

"Yes, yes, yes," he heard her whisper with relief and exhilaration. Her head disappeared after she plucked the book off the shelf and sat on the floor. Hayden could not help but smile—he found her enthusiasm for a book charming.

It was a sentiment familiar to him. In sixth grade, he voraciously read through a mystery adventure series and recalled the thrill of having found the last installment at the bookstore after it had been out of stock for weeks.

Hayden crouched down and slid a book off the shelf. Pretending to flip through the pages, he raised his eyes to study her. The book covered half of her face, leaving only her eyes visible. After a minute, she lowered the book several inches and revealed a joyous smile, oblivious that Hayden watched her. Even though they had never met, he could not explain it—he felt as though he already knew her.

His heart raced, not knowing what he would say, but he needed to talk to her. He returned the book in his hand to the shelf and froze in place when he heard a voice from the other end of the aisle call out to the girl.

"Hey, we have to go. My mom's here."

The girl jumped off the floor. "Okay, I'm ready. Let me check this out. I'll be fast."

Hayden sighed—it was too late. He could run after her, but then he would appear desperate. Walking to the aisle's end, he peeked out and saw the girl take the book from the librarian. She rushed towards the entrance and left. Hayden's heart sank, frustrated that he missed his chance to talk to her. Upon returning to his table, a thought struck him—she likely came to the library often, giving him another chance to find her.

One week later, Hayden recruited his friends, Mike and Steve, to accompany him to the library on Tuesday after school. After arriving at the library, he recognized that bringing his friends was a mistake. Unknown to Hayden, Mike had invited Blair and Sarah to meet them, and their behavior at the table was nothing short of obnoxious, flirting and carrying on with loud laughter.

The group of them, dressed in their Porter Brookes Academy school uniforms, resembled an adolescent gang of over-privileged preppy misfits. Hayden fretted the librarians would demand they leave unless they calmed down.

Annoyed, Hayden rose from the table, preferring to wander the stacks of the library rather than endure another moment of his friends' puerile antics when she appeared. Dressed in a bulky green sweater and oversized pants, she hurried through the lobby, pausing at the librarian's desk before rushing off into the depths of the library. He took a step to follow her when Mike seized his shoulders from behind.

"Hayden, we're having a contest—who can guess Sarah's bra size? Whoever's closest wins and gets to keep her bra." Everyone at the table except for Hayden burst into laughter. Sarah shook her head and her dark brown curls bounced from side to side as Blair squealed.

Pressing his lips together, he searched his mind for an excuse to leave the table and a way to ensure he would not be followed while in pursuit of the girl.

"Hayden, you guess first. Sarah said she'll take off her sweater so we can have a closer look," Mike announced to the group.

"No. I won't," Sarah exclaimed with wide eyes and an awkward smile.

"I don't know, C cups," Hayden replied, irritated and disinterested. Although he wanted to tell his friends to quiet down, he knew scolding his friends in front of Blair and Sarah would backfire and expose him to ridicule.

Blair cried out with a wicked grin, "She wishes!" Mike and Steve joined in with laughter, all of them unfazed by their cruel and humiliating behavior. Hayden exhaled and sat in his chair. It would be difficult to find the girl now, and he would have to wait for her to reappear.

After twenty minutes and one warning from the librarian to lower their voices, the girl reemerged. Strolling past his table, she turned her head, and with raised eyebrows, studied them. Hayden's breath caught in his chest. Distracted by the chaotic antics encircling Hayden at the table, she did not appear to notice his eyes on her. She walked towards the adult fiction stacks, and Hayden rose from his seat to follow her.

"Hayden, help me with this math problem." Blair tugged on the sleeve of his shirt and pointed to her math textbook. She flipped her long blonde hair over her shoulder and attempted to appear demure and helpless.

Hayden bit his lower lip. Blair told Mike she had a crush on him, and although her attention flattered him, he was uncertain of his feelings for her. Many guys at school were interested in Blair, and his friends insisted he date her. They claimed that if he did not, then "*Something's wrong with you, Bro.*"

He wished pressure from his friends did not affect him, but fitting in with them, as much as he disliked it, mattered. His father caused him enough trouble at home, making school a sanctuary because his peers liked and respected him. So he chose his battles, and refusing to date a desirable girl was not a hill he would die on, but he could not shake his ambivalence.

Blair was pretty with a developed figure, but he disliked certain aspects of her personality—the most blatant being that she did not hesitate to put down other girls in his class she felt herself superior to. Drawing in a sharp breath and on the verge of sitting back down, he glimpsed the girl emerge from the stacks, holding her hand in the air as she strode across the floor at a quick pace.

"Hold on, Blair, I'll be right back." Hayden left the table—he did not want to miss his chance to meet her again.

"Hurry," Blair whined. Sarah, seated beside Blair, swatted away Mike's hand while asking if he could feel if her boobs had grown overnight, triggering another roar of laughter from the group.

Hayden followed ten feet behind the girl, clueless how to start a conversation with her, but determined to meet her—he would risk the embarrassment and improvise.

Upon reaching the bathroom door, she halted her steps and adjusted her backpack over her shoulder. Hayden stopped several feet behind her. Finding the door locked, she took two sudden steps back, slamming her enormous backpack into his chest, startling him and taking his breath away. The girl whipped around, embarrassed and with wide eyes.

"I'm so sorry," she exclaimed. Hayden could not help but smile—she apologized with sincerity as though she had mortally wounded him. He liked the sound of her voice—gentle and mellifluous.

"It's okay, I can take it," Hayden replied, musing that for such a small girl she moved with force. Glimpsing the blood dripping down her hand, Hayden pointed to it. "Are you okay?"

The bathroom door flew open, and a man stepped out. Her cheeks flushed pink. She opened her mouth, but said nothing, and with an abrupt turn rushed into the bathroom and shut the door. Hayden found her timidity adorable and, to his surprise, he no longer felt nervous talking to her. Glancing over his shoulder, he checked to ensure that none of his friends were nearby.

Leaning against the wall, he resolved to wait for her, no matter how long it took, but it was not long before the door opened. Seeing him waiting, their eyes locked for only a moment before she averted her gaze. He found her eyes marvelous—a unique shade of amber, almond-shaped and framed with long dark lashes.

"So, are you going to live, or should I call an ambulance?" Hayden teased, hoping to make her laugh.

Her smile broadened, and she let out a small chuckle. Looking once again into his eyes, she raised her hand. "I think I'll live," she said, but the paper towel had slipped and blood dripped down her hand.

"Umm, can I help you with that? You're bleeding again." Hayden, having had his fair share of sports injuries, was experienced rolling up gauze and fashioning bandages in many creative ways for awkward hand wounds.

She nodded. Hayden stepped around her to grab another paper towel from the dispenser in the bathroom and rolled it up. He paused and thought—all he needed was a rubber band, and his eyes settled on her hair.

"Could I have your hair elastic?" he asked. The girl tugged, pulled it out, and handed it to him. Hayden hesitated, distracted by the thick wave of hair falling over her shoulders, now framing her face and brightening her amber eyes. As he had surmised the first day he saw her, behind her eyes lived a kindness he never saw in anyone else—aside from his mother.

Stepping close to her, he picked up her hand to wedge the paper towel between her fingers, and then secured it with the elastic. He felt her eyes on him and raised his to meet hers, but she looked away.

"What do you think?" he asked, taking a step back and releasing her hand.

"Good. Thank you," she answered. From the manner in which she met his gaze, he suspected she liked him. Neither of them spoke for a moment.

"I think I've seen you here before. Where do you go to school?" Hayden asked.

"I'm in seventh grade at—"

The girl's face fell, pausing in mid-sentence.

"Hayden, come on, we're leaving," he heard Blair announce behind him. The girl turned away. Blair tugged on the back of Hayden's shirt and did not bother to lower the volume of her voice as he turned to face her. "Gross Hayden, talk about lowering your standards, not girlfriend material for someone like you. Let's get out of here. We're going back to Mike's and ordering pizza."

"Hold on, I'll be right there," he told Blair, before turning back to resume his conversation with the girl—but she was gone. He had wanted to ask her name and whether he could meet her again at the library. Hayden exhaled and flickered his eyes to the ceiling.

"Hayden, you have to be kidding. Why were you talking to her? If Mike and Steve see you talking to a dumpy girl like that, it will be all over school."

He did not react, finding it better to avoid confrontation. "No reason, let's go," he said. Blair smiled and led the way.

In joining his friends at the table, he resolved to return to the library alone the following Tuesday and attempt to find her again. Though he returned every Tuesday for a month, and several other days to find her—he never did.

Over the years, he thought about her from time to time, her face and eyes imprinted on his memory. He told himself if he found her again, it would mean fate brought them together for a reason—and what a thorny maze fate turned out to be. Destiny reunited them in the fall of his junior year at South Black Harbor Beach, only to cruelly separate them again with a cycle of endless obstacles.

Hayden drained his scotch and trudged to the bathroom sink to splash cold water on his face. After brushing his teeth, he lay down on the bed and replayed the phone call with Brea in his mind.

"Hayden. I'll go on the trip. We leave in one week and we stay for one week, but I have some conditions. As we had agreed, we're going to Mexico. You pick the place, but separate rooms, and we stay in public together until I'm comfortable. I'll book my flight. You said you're paying for the trip—that's fine. And if I decide I want to leave, then I'm gone—and you leave me alone—for good. Do you agree?" she said.

"I do," he responded, his heart pounding.

"And one more thing, Hayden. I need to know if what happened with us—that last night—did that ever happen to you again?"

"No, never," he answered, and it was the truth. A long pause followed.

"All right. Text me the hotel information and let me know when you arrive. You have my number now. When you text me, use Allegra's name. I'll see you in Mexico," she said and hung up the phone.

Hayden stared at the ceiling and watched the fan rotate. He doubted he would sleep much that night knowing this was his one chance to convince Brea he was not an unhinged monster. If the trip proved to be a disaster, he could lose his opportunity for Brea's understanding and, as collateral damage, he could lose Avery—but the chance for redemption was something he would risk everything for.

Chapter Two

Brea

Brea hung up the phone. After Adam had been asleep for an hour, she went to the guest room to call Hayden. It took several attempts to punch in the correct number. Her hands shook and her heart pounded holding his card in one hand while she dialed the phone with the other. Her heart lurched in her chest when she heard him exhale, relieved that she had accepted his proposal.

To slow her rapid breaths, she crouched on the floor in a tri-pod position. Inhaling through her nose and slowly exhaling helped to ground her. Lying again for Hayden was something she never imagined she would do again in this lifetime. But this time was different—to rediscover herself, and trust her mind again, she needed Hayden and the entire story revealed to her.

Brea crept through the hall and paused in her vast open kitchen, sweeping her eyes over the custom stone cabinets, stainless steel appliances polished to a high sheen, and the expansive white marble counters. She needed a drink—something stronger than wine. In the butler's pantry, Brea examined the leftover liquor bottles from the Memorial Day barbecue they had hosted. Grabbing a bottle of Grey Goose, she poured two shots of vodka into a glass of ice and left the bottle on the kitchen island counter.

After taking a generous sip, she tipped her head back and savored the warmth of the liquid as it slid down her throat. Brea moved to one of the large ivory sofas in the family room, sat on the chaise, and covered her legs with an ivory wool blanket. Drinking another sip, she let the vodka roll over her tongue before she swallowed and fixed her eyes on the earth-toned abstract painting hanging above the white fireplace mantel.

Her eyes closed with a guilt-ridden realization that this trip would be her first night away from Alex and Sophie. But pushing through the guilt was paramount as she needed this trip to achieve the most important part of this journey—to fall back in love with herself. Only then could she become stronger for her children and deliberate the future of her marriage. Still, her children were her world, and she could not help but feel uneasy being separated from them for a week.

Adam arranged with his parents for Alex and Sophie to spend the week in Santa Barbara at their estate during Brea's trip, and the children were thrilled. Her mother-in-law, Mary, after hanging up with Adam, called Brea with the Tandervon housekeeper, Alice, on the line. They had a lengthy conversation to note the list of foods needed to stock the kitchen, toys and art supplies to purchase, and current clothing sizes for the kids. Mary then asked dozens of questions related to planning for activities and outings. Her mother-in-law's excessive attention enhanced Brea's guilt, but she felt relief knowing they would be well-occupied.

Brea lay back on the sofa and as she finished her drink, replayed in her mind the last time she saw Hayden in high school. It was the last day of school and, as planned, Brea went to her job interview at Black Rose Paper Boutique. She had concealed her healing wounds with her clothing and, as expected, Hayden did not return to Harvey Slate for the last week of school.

At the interview, Brea met the owner, Trina Rose, a feisty yet kind-hearted woman in her late fifties. Her shop assistant had retired for medical reasons, leaving her short on help and Joyce, Brea's guidance counselor, a faithful repeat customer, had been in the boutique when Trina learned of her employee's retirement. Recalling Brea mentioned a desire to find a summer job at their last meeting, Joyce recommended Brea as the perfect associate for Trina. After an hour of questions and touring the shop, Brea and Trina thought highly of one another, and Trina hired her with no hesitation. Brea would start on Monday.

After exiting the shop, Brea walked less than ten feet on Black Harbor Boulevard before halting her steps—Hayden stood beside his car, dressed in a navy T-shirt and jeans, despite the eighty-degree heat, and a baseball cap and a pair of sunglasses. It was clear he had been waiting for her. Brea froze and scanned her surroundings in the event she needed to yell out for someone to help her.

"It's okay, Brea. I won't hurt you," Hayden said with a strained voice and raised his hands to show her he was not a threat. The cuts on his palms were healing, though still visible. He took a step forward. "Let me talk to you, please," he pleaded.

Her eyes grew wide, and she assumed an assertive stance—possessed by a force she did not know she harbored within. "Don't come near me, Hayden. Don't you dare touch me," she snarled.

"Brea, I won't. Please listen to me for a minute. I have your purse and shoes in the car. I just—want to explain what happened. That wasn't me, I was having—"

Brea stepped forward and interrupted him. "No! There is nothing you can say that will change my mind. You aren't who I thought you were, Hayden. If you ever try to see me again or call me—I will tell everyone what happened. I'll tell your father," she threatened.

Her last words spilled off her lips like acid. Hayden fell back a step and lowered his eyes to the ground. Brea did not care about her purse or shoes. She walked past him and did not look back as a tumultuous storm of emotions whipped through her body—fury, heartache, incertitude, and angst.

After she turned the corner, she broke into a run. It was a lie—she would tell no one about that night, much less his father. But knowing Hayden's vulnerability, she used it against him with the certainty he would dare not follow her or attempt to find her again.

Her foot, still tender from her injuries, did not slow her down, but every pounding step on the pavement caused her pain. Running as fast as she could, for as long as she could, Brea only stopped after reaching a residential neighborhood to catch her breath.

Concealing herself behind a mailbox, she lowered herself to sit on the dusty ground. Fixing her gaze on the sidewalk, she chewed her thumbnail and waited. She did not know how much time passed, whether it was five or thirty minutes, but she sat in that position until her breathing steadied, and she felt ready to walk home.

⚘

Brea woke upon feeling a hand tapping on her shoulder. Inhaling and blinking several times, she turned her head. Adam stood over, dressed in tan slacks and a light-blue linen shirt with the sleeves rolled up. His dark gray eyes bore into her. The sun had risen, and golden light filtered into the room between the slats of the plantation shutters.

"Hitting the bottle last night?" he asked, pointing at the glass and the bottle of vodka sitting on the island counter. Brea blew out a puff of air.

"Yeah, I couldn't sleep. I drank a little too much and now I'm going to have heartburn all day," she mumbled.

"That's the price you pay when you cheat," he replied with a stern expression. Any compassion from Adam was improbable as he disliked it when Brea drank too much, though it was rare she overindulged.

"It wasn't cheating. It was the only option to help me sleep," she replied, finding his choice of words jarring.

"Do some yoga next time. Just think, if the kids woke up seeing you like this—they'll think you're sick. I made a pot of coffee. Help yourself." Adam turned and strode out of the living room.

Brea lifted herself up to sit and rubbed her eyes. Her temples ached, and her mouth felt dry. She could not blame Adam for his irritation. He did not know what she had been going through in recent days, much less throughout her life. And yet, his coldness to Brea stung. It was clear now that there was neither warmth nor tenderness left in him for her. She had lived without it for years, and now, she did not know if she wanted it back.

The reality hit her—she could return home from this trip having made a drastic decision to overthrow her entire life. And further, she was betting on Hayden, blind to the odds that she would find what she was seeking. After Mexico, it was possible that all she would accomplish was a life-altering upheaval, leaving behind in its wake, destruction and desolation.

CHAPTER THREE

HAYDEN

Waking from a deep sleep, Hayden's forehead was peppered with beads of sweat. The pilot announced the plane was about to begin its descent to San Francisco International Airport. Checking his watch, he rubbed his eyes. It was a quarter after eleven in the morning. Beside him, the elderly woman on his left had made significant progress in her book and appeared to be on the last pages. Having slept little the previous night, he fell asleep just after takeoff and had a disturbing nightmare.

In his dream, Brea danced on a stage in a fire-ravaged theater amid a fog of ominous red and orange smoke. Her hair was pale blonde, and she wore layers of draped transparent black fabric around her body. If she paused to catch her breath, the cloud of smoke would consume her, hampering her ability to breathe, until she rose and danced again. Unable to sustain the relentless movements, she soon grew exhausted, collapsed, and the fiery smoke lifted her several feet off the ground only to drop her and send her sliding across the stage.

Hayden was desperate to help her, but he could not move—an invisible force bound him to the burnt red velvet seat he sat in. Seeing Hayden, Brea ran to the edge of the stage, but the smoke engulfed and dragged her across the length of the stage until releasing her, leaving her unconscious in the center. Hayden struggled to free himself and screamed, though no sound escaped his lips—there was only deafening silence. Moderate turbulence startled Hayden, and he woke up.

To this day he vividly remembered her performance at Harvey Slate over twenty years ago. Captivated, he found her performance to be both beautiful and tragic, something no one else in the audience appeared to notice. They all thought it was sexy—his interpretation had been different. Though Brea's skill and the choreography were impressive, her emotional performance profoundly struck him. Every movement she made, genuine and unforced, expressed a desperate sadness as she attempted to lure Lucien out of the cave.

That night, everything shifted—it was almost comical. Brea's character succeeded in tempting Lucien out of the cave, and in reality, after witnessing her performance, she made it impossible for Hayden to deny his feelings for her any longer. The applause erupted from the audience as she stood on the stage, radiant and out of breath, but Hayden, transfixed, was too stunned to applaud. Brea looked into his eyes from the stage, and seeing his reaction, her smile faded as the curtain closed.

Vienna jabbed his shoulder with her fist. Dazed, he turned to her, and she mouthed, "What the fuck?" with narrowed eyes and her jaw clenched tight. Opening his mouth, Hayden drew a blank—he did not know what to say. His desire to see Brea consumed him, and he doubted his capability of concealing his feelings any longer. And now, looking into Vienna's eyes, he knew their relationship was doomed.

He met Vienna at the end of his sophomore year at a Harvey Slate party, Mike, his best friend, dragged him to. They knew each other since elementary school, played city baseball together, and their families were close.

Mike was outgoing, social, and possessed a flirtatious charm in contrast to Hayden, who was more reserved and introspective. He rode on the coattails of Mike's personality throughout junior high school and their first years at Harvey Slate, though between sports and academics, Hayden socialized little outside of school unless it was to spend time with Mike or his friends from the baseball team after a game. Although interested in girls, he did not have the drive to pursue them. According to Mike, the circulating gossip about Hayden among the girls was that he was "*hot, mysterious, and picky*," enhancing his appeal to the female sex.

The reality was he felt timid and insecure around girls, unsure how to connect with them in any sense. Only when a girl showed interest and pursued him, he might date them, but these short-term relationships never lasted longer than a month as they lacked any meaningful connection.

Hayden rarely appeared at house parties and seldom drank, disliking feeling out of control and often finding himself bored. In the last month of school, Hayden relented and accompanied Mike to a party at a graduating senior's home in Tupa Bay. Everyone knew Vienna, considered the most desirable girl in school who only dated seniors. Hayden, being in the honors program and reclusive at school, had never met Vienna and never expected someone like her to be interested in him.

On the night they met, she bumped into Mike in the yard amid a conversation with several friends from the track team. Mike introduced her to Hayden, but she mis-heard Mike, believing he said, *"Hey, Ben, this is Vienna"* rather than *"Hayden, this is Vienna."*

Vienna was gorgeous with a stunning figure. That night she wore a body-hugging purple dress revealing ample cleavage, and her blonde-streaked hair spilling over her shoulders. Her eyes fixed on Hayden, sizing him up and intrigued by his handsome looks. She was flirtatious, sexy, and charming. Intimidated, he did what he knew, retreated within himself, remaining reserved and stoic, which, to his surprise, appeared to draw her in.

Hayden was hard-pressed not to be flattered that she spent most of the night chatting with him, placing her hand on his arm, and laughing at his jokes once he relaxed enough to let down his guard. There were rumors she was a lot to handle and intimidated many of the girls in school, but his perception at the time was that she was fearless and direct.

The following two weekends, Hayden went out with Mike despite the pressure of studying for finals, and when he saw Vienna at the beach or at a party, she would find her way to him, and they would flirt and chat. After some time, he realized she was calling him "*Ben*." He did not correct her until she boldly made the first move to ask him out on a date.

"Listen, Ben, I'm tired of waiting for you to ask me out. So, I'm going to ask you out. How about you take me out to dinner?" Vienna asked, seated beside Hayden at a fire on South Black Harbor Beach.

Hayden smiled and raised his eyebrows. "I have to say something first. My name isn't Ben—it's Hayden. I felt kind of awkward correcting you, but if I'm going to take you out, then I think you should know my real name."

Vienna laughed and wrapped her arm around Hayden's shoulders. He laughed as well. "I can't believe you waited all this time to correct me. This is going to be a problem. In my mind, I think of you as Ben. Can I still call you Ben until I get used to Hayden?"

Hayden chuckled. "Sure, why not?" Her confidence intrigued him. It was as though nothing scared her, and she did not hesitate to take control. The following night, he took her out for dinner.

On their third date, seated in the movie theatre, she rested her hand on his thigh as they watched the movie. In response, he briefly debated between holding her hand or putting his arm around her, but his timidity won over his courage. Once outside the movie theatre, Vienna pulled him in to kiss her, unwilling to wait for Hayden to work up the nerve to make the first move. With a suggestive smile, she invited him to come back to her house.

Vienna turned to face him in the living room after they entered her home. "My mom is out for the night. We can drink something and then go to my room." His heart raced. He had kissed and made out with several girls, feeling underneath their shirts, but other than that, he was inexperienced. The idea he had anything to offer Vienna sexually was laughable.

Hayden nodded, seated himself on the oversized taupe sofa in the living room, and surveyed the room. Long navy curtains and several grand-scale paintings of the ocean hung on the beige walls. The home reminded him of an upscale hotel lobby—luxurious but lacking any genuine personal touch or warmth.

Vienna, dressed in a black plunge tank top and a short white skirt, pivoted into the kitchen to make them a drink. Hayden's eyes followed her as she walked away. Once out of sight, he shifted his gaze to the artwork on the walls to temper his apprehension.

She soon returned, and the sound of Vienna's heels clicking on the travertine floors snapped him out his meditation. In her hand she held a bottle of tequila and in the other two shot glasses. "Take a shot with me," she said as she sat on the coffee table before him and crossed her legs. Hayden glanced at her legs and his mouth subtly opened upon noticing that her skirt had ridden up, exposing a sizable length of her upper thigh.

Vienna handed him a shot glass of tequila, filled one for herself and took it in one shot. Hayden studied the glass for a moment and then, following her lead, drank it down. He coughed once, finding the taste strong and earthy, though he concealed his displeasure. Vienna rose and outstretched her hand.

"Let me give you the tour," she said with a smile. He took her hand, rose, and followed her from room to room until reaching her bedroom. Leading him to the foot of her bed, she stepped in front of him, wrapped her arms around his neck, and kissed him with a gentle touch of her lips. After a moment, Vienna pulled back and whispered, "The girls in school think you're so hot. They envy me." A tight smile formed, and his eyes narrowed—he was not sure if he believed her considering their brief acquaintance, and his general solitary nature at Harvey Slate.

Nudging him to sit on the edge of the bed, Hayden sat, and Vienna straddled him. She kissed him with bold intensity, and as the passion deepened, with one hand, placed her hand between his legs to see if he had an erection. Satisfied he did, she smiled and stood. He did not know what to do other than to place his hands on her hips. She bent down, unbuttoned his shorts, and pulled down his zipper. "Move back onto the bed," she directed.

Hayden obeyed. After raising Hayden's T-shirt over his abdomen, she pulled down his shorts and boxers. A smile spread across her face, and she took him into her mouth. Hayden's head dropped onto the bed. The feeling of her lips wrapped around his penis combined with the suction and use of her tongue was sensational—he believed he would lose his mind if she were to stop.

He found her voracious sexual enthusiasm and confidence so arousing, he reached climax in little time, and released a guttural moan as his body was overtaken by waves of intense pleasure. Hayden often had orgasms—alone in his bedroom—but this was another level of euphoria.

After that night, Vienna became a drug he could not get enough of. The following weekend, she took his virginity. Nothing was off the table for her—she had a rapacious sexual appetite, and she got off on watching Hayden's stoic demeanor crack, even if only for moments when he climaxed. When she left for Europe on a trip with her mother and Thea for seven weeks, and Hayden travelled to Italy with his family, he went through withdrawal and soon received devastating news.

At the end of the summer, Mike informed Hayden that he and his family were moving to Chicago after his grandfather had fallen ill and his father would assume control of the family company. With his best friend having moved, Hayden found himself in the fall of junior year entrenched in Vienna's circle of friends, though he continued to limit attending parties or larger gatherings. He socialized only when he went out with Vienna, and in late October, everything changed.

Brea's arrival at Harvey Slate unleashed a brewing tempest of complicated feelings within him, alongside shining a light on the sharp contrast between who Brea was as a person compared to Vienna. Although the sexual chemistry with Vienna was phenomenal, over time, what he believed to be Vienna's sexy confidence and outgoing charm was, in truth, a mixture of arrogance, entitlement, and petty competitiveness—he doubted they were as compatible as he initially believed.

Complicating his feelings about his relationship with Vienna was that his father adored her, and for the first time Hayden could remember, his relationship with his father had improved. Having a girlfriend like Vienna illustrated Hayden's virility and, in his father's eyes, reflected on him positively.

His mother was less thrilled about Hayden's relationship with Vienna. She did not overtly interfere though Hayden, perceptive and knowing his mother, sensed her dislike of Vienna. He felt trapped and convinced himself to endure in the relationship until the problems were too great to ignore and his feelings for Brea, impossible to suppress.

Hayden's ardor for Brea became clear to Vienna over time, and his reaction to Brea's performance confirmed his infatuation with her—and at that moment, Brea became Vienna's enemy, though she would never admit it to herself. Walking out of the theatre, Vienna demanded they leave without congratulating Brea and insisted Hayden take her home to retrieve something she needed before driving to Nigel's house.

Upon arriving at Vienna's, she insisted Hayden come inside with her. Hayden, distracted and eager to see Brea, tapped his fingers on his legs and leaned against Vienna's bedroom door as she walked to her bathroom, grumbling about a specific shade of lipstick she needed.

When she exited the bathroom empty-handed, Vienna removed her shirt, revealing a sheer lace black bra. She headed for Hayden, pressed against him, and planted her mouth on his. He pulled away—the idea of touching Vienna was unthinkable at the moment.

"Vienna, not now. Let's go to Nigel's," he mumbled, averting his eyes from her. She moved her hand and placed it between his legs.

Hayden pushed away her hand, finding her touch repelling rather than arousing. "Let's go Vienna," he said louder, meeting her eyes with a stern expression. Vienna wiped the corners of her mouth and whipped around to grab her shirt off the bed's edge.

"What's wrong with you, Hayden? The past couple of months, you've turned into an old married lady, and I'm the horny husband begging for sex," Vienna snapped once dressed.

"Nothing, I'm not in the mood."

Vienna chuckled. "You're a seventeen-year-old teenage boy—if you're not in the mood to fuck me, there's something seriously wrong here."

Hayden sighed. "I'll wait in the car." He left the room, rubbing his neck as he descended the stairs. His mind was spinning, agitated and unable to block the image of Brea's facial expression as she stood on stage having witnessed his reaction to her performance.

Shortly after, Vienna climbed into the car, plastered a smile on her face and chatted throughout the drive as though nothing had happened in her room—he could tell her comportment was for show.

At Nigel's, Hayden spotted Brea entering with Jaime and his eyes followed her through the living room. Once seated on the sofa, Brea turned and locked eyes with him. Though illogical, he felt it—the energy between them had shifted and she saw him differently.

Later, when Vienna used him as an excuse to attack Brea's performance, telling her he had been *"bored,"* it triggered an instinct to protect Brea—and witnessing the hurt in her eyes filled him with an indescribable fury.

As he knelt before Brea to reassure her that her performance was phenomenal, his defenses crumbled, and he could no longer deny that his heart belonged to her. And looking into her eyes, it was unmistakable—she felt something for him, and it sparked something dangerous in Hayden—hope.

The elderly woman beside him tapped Hayden's arm, interrupting his thoughts. "Sir, the flight attendant is asking you to put your seat belt on." He apologized under his breath and fastened his seat belt.

"Are you coming home or visiting San Francisco?" she asked and returned her book to her purse.

"Coming home," he answered with a half-smile. She appeared to be a kind woman, dressed in a black blouse with a pair of reading glasses attached to a gold chain around her neck.

"That's always a pleasant feeling, isn't it?"

Hayden paused before answering. "Not this time. There's something complicated I left behind in Ocean Crest Beach. Something I need to set right, and I don't know if I'll be able to." He did not know why he said that—he could have said yes and left it at that.

"Well, when you're my age, if you're smart, you realize that every day you wake up, you have another chance to make things better or start over."

Shaking his head, he exhaled before speaking. "I don't know. I might make an even bigger mistake and wind up blowing up my life." The woman raised her eyebrows, intrigued. Hayden changed the subject.

"How was your book? Looks like you finished it. Hopefully, it was a good ending."

"That's the thing about a good story—it's never really finished. You're always left with a question, and your imagination goes further into the future beyond what the author leaves you with. But in this case, I'll say yes."

Hayden nodded and smiled. He hoped it would be the same for him and Brea.

Chapter Four

BREA

The following late afternoon, Hayden, under the guise of "Allegra," messaged Brea the hotel information in Punta Mita and details for the car service that would transport her to the resort from the airport. She responded with her flight details and that she would land in Puerto Vallarta at three-thirty the upcoming Saturday. A minute passed, and Hayden suggested they meet in the main lobby at seven for dinner. Brea typed in *"Okay,"* hesitated whether to add anything else and, deciding against it, hit the send button.

Curious, Brea opened her laptop and scrolled through the resort website. "Wow," she whispered as she scrolled through the photos. Adam's hotel and vacation tastes were lavish, but this resort was exceptional. The resort boasted access to private beaches, several pools, top-tier restaurants, personal wellness mentors, a state-of-the-art fitness center, a golf course, horse stables, yacht excursions, and a spa. Although a stunning resort, Brea struggled to imagine what they would do once they were there. What would be the point of staying at a luxurious resort? Certainly, they were not going there for an activity-filled vacation of snorkeling and horseback riding. Brea wanted answers, and once she got them, it was possible she would flee to board an earlier plane home.

With dinnertime approaching, hungry and restless, Brea shut her laptop to check on Alex and Sophie. She went to the kitchen and peeked out the patio doors. Beneath the pergola, she spotted Adam seated beside Alex on the loveseat, the pair of them reading a book while Sophie lay on a blanket on the grass and played with her stuffed animals.

A smile spread across Brea's face—an idea sparked while observing Adam ruffle Alex's hair. Tonight, she would try to reconnect with Adam and propose they make love. If she did nothing, she might come to regret not having attempted to save her marriage for her children.

"Is anyone hungry yet? I could make dinner," Brea asked as she stepped onto the patio. Adam did not look up from his book, and Sophie shook her head. Alex perked up, tossed his book on the lawn, jumped off the loveseat, and ran to Brea.

"Adam, are you ready to eat dinner soon?" Brea called out.

Meeting Brea's eyes, he hesitated a moment before he spoke, then returned his focus to his book. "No. I'm going to meet the guys for a drink tonight, remember? I'll be back later."

Brea bit her lower lip—she did not recall him mentioning an evening out with his friends. "All right, I must have forgotten. Well, tomorrow I'm planning to make sea bass with the seasoned jasmine rice for dinner, so don't be late coming home."

"Sure, sounds good." Adam's eyes flickered to Brea for a moment. His lack of enthusiasm was hurtful, though she could not expect to fix her marriage with one meal and resolved herself to remain calm and patient.

Alex tugged on Brea's elbows. "Can you make waffles, Mommy? The big round ones?"

"Of course," Brea replied with a smile. She wrapped her arms around her son and together they walked into the kitchen. "How about you help me mix the batter and you can keep watch until the light goes off?"

"Okay," he replied and pulled out a stool to sit at the counter.

While Alex stirred the mix, eggs, milk, and oil in the bowl, Brea jotted down a list of ingredients and wine she would order to have delivered for dinner tomorrow night. Also, she would call Tina in the morning and see if she could watch the kids at the park for a couple of hours to shop for a new dress and lingerie. Though Brea never initiated having sex with Adam, she would embrace change, and, to save her marriage, begin with seducing her husband.

Adam arrived home at half-past six the following evening amid Brea arranging the ingredients for dinner on the island counter. Seeing Adam enter the kitchen, she smiled. She had changed into a magenta sundress with a revealing decollete that emphasized her narrow waist. Walking past Brea, he mumbled hello and went to the refrigerator to pull out a bottle of water.

"I bought white wine—that bottle of chenin blanc you like. Could you open it and pour me a glass?"

Adam paused and turned. He walked to the counter and stopped in front of Brea. "Do you think you should drink wine? After yesterday morning, maybe you should take a break from drinking for a while."

Brea licked the corner of her mouth and inhaled. In the previous week, since Hayden had turned up in the shop, she was drinking more than usual, though it was an anomaly. After high school, Brea made a conscious decision to limit her drinking, and would drink one or two glasses of wine or a cocktail once or twice a month, if not less.

"I was only planning to have one glass," she replied, concealing her irritation over Adam's judgmental comment.

Looking into her eyes, she sensed he wanted to say something else, but he remained silent. "Sure, I'll pour you one." He turned towards the refrigerator. "Where are Alex and Sophie?"

"Working on a puzzle in Sophie's room. We made picture books while you were gone. I put them on the coffee table so you could read them. It was something I used to do when I was little. Did I ever tell you about the time I won a contest for writing a children's book when I was in seventh grade?"

Adam pulled out the cork and then removed two glasses from the kitchen cabinet. "Uh, no. I don't think so." His tone of voice betrayed his disinterest. Pouring Brea a glass, he placed it before her, filled a glass for himself and walked out of the kitchen.

Resting her hands flat on the counter, Brea dropped her head. She was too fragile, hurt by Adam's lack of interest in staying in the same room with her. Dabbing her tears with the tips of her fingers, careful not to smudge her eye makeup, she drew in a deep breath. "Don't give up," she told herself, then busied herself with making dinner.

After they ate together as a family, to Brea's pleasure, Adam proclaimed the meal, *"extraordinary."* Brea tidied the kitchen, then hurried the children into their baths and pajamas. To speed up the bedtime process, Brea promised the kids they could set up and sleep in Alex's tent. It was a special treat where she would crawl into the tent with them, read a bedtime story, and allow them to sleep on the floor of Alex's bedroom. After Alex and Sophie fell asleep, she heard Adam enter his office and shut the door.

Brea hurried to her bathroom and changed into the sheer violet nightgown with a matching lace thong and bralette she bought that afternoon. She brushed her hair and fixed her makeup. Hearing Adam enter their bedroom, she spritzed her wrists with perfume. Appraising herself in the mirror, she smiled, brimming with confidence. Brea stepped out of the bathroom and posed in the doorway with one hand touching the doorframe at shoulder level. She watched Adam unbutton his dress shirt beside the bed. Sensing her presence, he paused upon reaching his last button and turned around.

"What is it, Brea?" he asked, appearing thrown, seeing her dressed in provocative lingerie and watching him undress.

Brea smiled and pushed the hair off her shoulders. "Nothing. You look handsome tonight," she replied and tilted her head to the side.

"What are you wearing?" he asked as he studied her with narrowed eyes.

"Something I bought today, I thought it was a little—different, sexy."

Adam removed his shirt, turned his head, and walked to the dresser. Brea's eyes followed him, admiring his well-maintained, athletic build as he opened the drawer and pulled out his pajama bottoms. "It looks slutty, Brea," he said with an icy edge to his voice.

Brea dropped her arm and recoiled as though Adam had punched her in the stomach. "Okay. I—thought it was sexy and maybe tonight we could—"

Adam unbuttoned his pants without looking at Brea. "Not tonight. I have a lot on my mind. Let's wait until you get back from your trip. The rest of the week is going to be busy."

"Oh, sure. I understand." Brea turned on her heels and, once in the bathroom, closed and locked the door behind her. Humiliated, she covered her mouth with a trembling hand and stared at the white marble mosaic floor tiles. Adam, insulting her and barely looking at her, left Brea with little hope there was anything left in their marriage, aside from the children.

Her eyes, blurred by tears, scanned her pristine custom bathroom and paused on the French gray rotunda washstands flanking her vanity table. Seeing her makeup and skincare products strewn on her vanity was off-putting, as if they were mocking her, and her tears multiplied.

She hurried to the alcove bathtub and turned on the faucet, hoping the running water would muffle the sound of her crying. Seated on the toilet, she pulled out a long strip of toilet paper and wiped off her eye makeup. Holding the tissue in her right hand, she stared at the large black splotches—they resembled Rorschach inkblots.

Brea lowered her head into her hands and thought of Diane, her therapist in college. What would Diane say if Brea could share with her that her world was crumbling around her after her past had unforgivingly invaded her present? And, most importantly, ask her how she would survive the coming two weeks when she did not know what would become of the ruins of her shattered life.

⟡

Twenty years ago, several weeks after Hayden left for MIT, his father put their house up for sale, and Hayden did not attempt to contact Brea again. If ever he returned to Black Harbor, she never knew it. Brea stopped attending Harvey Slate High School parties during her senior year, focusing instead on the honors program and college applications. Her friendship with Tory and Allegra continued, though after graduating and moving to Rhode Island to attend Brown University, she lost touch with them both.

In the spring semester of her first year of college, Brea fell into a depressive episode she could not shake. Her grades were excellent, though she was plagued by trouble sleeping, anxiety attacks, and a pervasive feeling of loneliness. Her parents did not visit and only called her twice during her fall semester. Over the winter break, Brea was left with no choice but to return home as the dorms would not allow students to remain on campus, and once with her parents for four weeks, the usual dynamics resumed, each of them living in isolation under the same roof. The painful reminders of her childhood intensified her melancholy.

It was not until late February in her Introduction to Psychology course that a small beam of hope broke through the darkness that encircled her. A psychologist presented a lecture in class about child abuse and the long-lasting psychological effects it could have on survivors. What she found interesting was that not only physical or sexual harm but also emotional neglect constituted abuse.

Brea, captivated by Dr. Diane Brookenfeld's every word, felt both fascinated and saddened as the lecture described her life. Concluding the class, Dr. Brookenfeld mentioned she worked at the student mental health center three days a week to provide psychotherapy for students. The following day, Brea stopped by the center and scheduled an appointment to meet with her.

One week later, Brea sat in Dr. Brookenfeld's office, dressed in her university sweatshirt and a pair of jeans now one size too big after having lost six pounds her frame could not spare. It was a small room with large framed photographs of waterfalls hanging on the pastel blue painted walls. Brea sat on a dark blue sofa across from Dr. Brookenfeld, seated in a matching armchair.

"Call me Diane, please," she told Brea upon exchanging greetings with one another and then waited in silence for Brea to begin.

Brea estimated Diane was in her early fifties, with shoulder-length light-blonde hair and gentle brown eyes, dressed in a light-gray wool dress with an ivory cashmere shawl draped across her shoulders. Despite her nerves and shaky hands, Brea felt as though she could trust her. She attempted to conceal the tremors by clasping her hands together in her lap.

"I don't know where to start," Brea said, tapping her right foot on the floor. She scanned the room and fixed her gaze on Dr. Brookenfeld's credentials hanging on the wall behind her desk.

"Why don't you tell me what has been bothering you?" Diane asked to give Brea a starting point.

"Well, I've been having a lot of trouble sleeping for a while, nightmares, and I'm nervous all the time. It's like I can't quite catch my breath. I can do my schoolwork, but that's it. I feel—alone."

"Is this the first time you've felt this way, Brea?"

Brea thought for a moment. "No. There was a time in my junior year of high school when I struggled with feeling anxious, and I had these episodes where it felt like I couldn't breathe."

"That must have been scary. Can you think of anything that triggered your anxiety?"

Brea sat in silence, uncertain of how much to reveal. "I don't know. Things were far from perfect in my life. I was far from perfect, and I screwed up a lot of things." She was not ready to talk about Cylis or Hayden, worrying Diane would judge her for cheating on Jaime and bringing upon herself what happened with Cylis.

"It sounds like you're pretty hard on yourself. Why?"

Brea let out a breath. "I guess I was odd as a kid. My parents weren't like everyone else's. I'm an only child, and they had little interest in me other than the expectation I did well in school. It was lonely in my house, and as I got older, I became pathetic and obsessed with finding a boyfriend. But with any guy I dated, I either screwed it up or I wound up in situations with boys who weren't who I thought they were."

"Hmmm. From what you are saying, you wanted to be loved." Diane commented, then paused for Brea's reaction.

Brea twisted her fingers and winced in pain when she pinched her skin too hard. "Of course, don't we all?"

"Exactly, Brea, we all do. So why are you so hard on yourself for wanting love as though somehow that was a bad thing? Wanting something your parents couldn't give you does not make you pathetic—it makes you human. And now you find yourself alone again after a major life change, coming to college. I can see why that could be difficult."

Brea nodded and reflected for a minute before speaking. "How do I fix all of that?"

"Well, we'll start by learning more about you, the experiences you've had, and how you cope with stress. It will take time to explore what made you who you are today. But I hope over time you'll learn some healthy ways to cope, understand yourself more, and be kinder to yourself."

"How long does that take?" Brea asked, wiping her eyes with the back of her hand.

"I can't answer that. It depends on a lot of things. Some people feel better after a few weeks, and for some, it takes a lifetime of work. I'm going to learn a lot about you, Brea. And while we work together, I'll do the best I can to help. What I ask is that you're honest with me and don't hold back. You don't have to tell me the right answers or pretend with me—that won't help you."

Brea let a few tears fall down her cheeks and leaned over to pull out a tissue from a white lacquered box on the end table. "That may be difficult. I had to pretend a lot, almost my whole life—because I didn't think anyone would like the real me."

"We'll take it slow, Brea. Be patient with yourself, and I'll be right by your side to help."

Blotting her eyes, and then blowing her nose, Brea felt a slight reduction in the heaviness in her chest. She did not know if she could trust Diane to share all of her painful memories, but it was a beginning.

CHAPTER FIVE

HAYDEN

Hayden called Avery to tell her he would leave for Mexico on Saturday, then directed his driver to take him to the office to catch up on work, and, truth be told, to avoid Avery. At eight o'clock, he arrived home. As he walked into the foyer, he heard the television on in the living room. He drew a breath and ambled down the hall. Avery, seated on the sofa with a glass of wine in her hand, did not raise her eyes from her phone when Hayden entered the room.

After dating for one year, Avery proposed they move in together—he hesitated. He had few relationships in the past lasting longer than six months, and though Avery was attractive, intelligent, and uncomplicated, he debated whether he was ready to take that step with her.

Hayden had been transparent with Avery regarding his disinterest in marriage. He enjoyed being in a relationship with her, but he did not want her to have expectations he could not honor. After several long discussions, he agreed to living together once assured they were in alignment and, further, reckoned it was time he committed in some fashion to a woman. As a result, six months ago, Hayden purchased a three-bedroom condominium in Pacific Heights in a newly constructed building. The interior showcased the particular aesthetic Avery desired—window walls in the vast living room, a balcony, beautiful morning light, and a modern-style kitchen and bathrooms, with natural oak hardwood floors.

"Hi, Babe." Avery greeted him with her eyes fixed on the screen, typing a message on her phone. She wore gray sleep shorts and a matching tank top with her long blonde hair pulled into a loose bun atop her head. "Did you eat anything? I've got sushi in the refrigerator if you want it."

"Hi. No thanks, I'm not hungry," Hayden replied, clutching his suitcase, carry-on bag, and house keys. Avery raised her eyes and studied him with a puzzled expression.

"What's up with you? You look tense. Was it a rough day?"

Hayden dropped his gaze to the floor—a wave of guilt washed over him. He turned, placed his bags on the ground beside the dining room table, and returned his keys to his pocket. "Yeah, sort of." He went to the kitchen, straight to the refrigerator, and took out a cold beer.

"Do you want to talk about it?" she asked, watching him from the sofa.

"Not really." Hayden paused and took a long sip of his beer. "How was your meeting about the benefits crisis with that company?" he asked, vaguely remembering her describing an urgent project she was involved with on the phone two nights ago. Avery worked as a human resources executive for a large national bank—a job she enjoyed that kept her busy. Because of her demanding career, she forgave Hayden's late-night meetings, working on the weekends, and frequent traveling.

Avery began a long rehash of the meeting that Hayden half listened to as his mind derailed to thoughts of Brea. Last month, he never could have imagined that his and Avery's mini-vacation tacked onto a brief business trip in Ocean Crest Beach would upend his life.

"After you change, should we put on a movie?" Avery asked once finished with her recount of the work-related crisis.

Hayden searched his mind for an excuse. "I'm going to take a shower and get some sleep. I think I'm fighting off a virus."

Avery pursed her lips and studied Hayden standing at the kitchen counter. "You're drinking a beer and you think you're getting sick?"

Hayden glanced at the beer in his hand. Shit. "It's better than a sleeping pill," he replied with a tight smile, then left the kitchen to walk into the bedroom.

Seated on the edge of the bed, Hayden removed his shoes, slacks, and unbuttoned his shirt. He had only been home for ten minutes and was already raising red flags. Resting his elbows on his knees, he dropped his head in his hands and inhaled a deep breath. He could not help but second-guess himself and this trip.

Having proposed the idea was one thing, but Brea accepting, and now the reality of spending an entire week with her, unloading his past and explaining what happened that night, was daunting. Like Brea, Hayden told no one what happened with her at his house, though he could never forget about it, nor her.

Lifting himself off the bed, he went into the bathroom and turned on the shower faucet to the hottest setting. Once full of steam, he stepped under the searing hot water, braced himself against the wall, and dropped his head for the water to hit his neck, shoulders, and back. Tomorrow morning, he would go to the gym for a workout. He had neglected his usual routine over the week, and it never failed to help him feel better when on edge.

After turning off the water, he wrapped a towel around his waist and stepped into the brisk air—it felt good. While brushing his teeth, Avery opened the bathroom door and leaned against the door frame. Her face, wholesome and pretty, watched him in the mirror.

"Are you feeling any better?" she asked with a charming smile.

"Yeah. I'm going to get into bed in a minute," Hayden answered, avoiding eye contact with her.

"Hayden, are you okay? You've been a little off. I didn't want to say anything before you left, but, seeing you now, you don't seem like yourself, and you're going away again next week. I don't know if I'm being paranoid, but I just wanted to check in," she asked, her intuition spot on.

"Yeah, I'm good. It's just stress, and I haven't worked out all week. Now, with another trip coming up, I just want to rest this week and take it easy." Hayden met Avery's eyes with a reassuring smile. Before going into the bedroom, he planted a brief kiss on her lips.

"That's all I get? It's been a few weeks since we've had sex. Maybe I can get into bed with you and help you deal with some of that stress?" she offered with a suggestive raise of her eyebrows.

Hayden lowered his eyes to the floor—he was not in the mood, but he did not know how to navigate his way through rejecting her offer without wounding her. There was no other option other than to lie with an enormous cliché.

"Could you get me a glass of water and some Tylenol? I think I'm getting a headache, maybe even a fever, and then when I feel better, let's do that," he said, forcing a smile onto his face.

Avery's face softened, believing Hayden, which made him feel worse. "Of course. Why don't you get in bed, and I'll be right back."

She dimmed the lights before leaving the room. Slipping into a pair of boxers and a T-shirt, Hayden climbed into bed under the comforter and closed his eyes. The memory of the first time he and Brea kissed on her porch flashed through his mind, followed by the memory of her eyes, panicked when she realized it was Hayden standing in the shop—it was a look he hoped never to see again.

Hayden thanked Avery when she returned with the tablets and a glass of water in hand. After drinking half the glass, he squeezed her hand, then rolled over to lie on his stomach. Avery rubbed his back for several minutes before rising and returning to the living room.

❦

Hayden asked Ashley to clear his schedule for the following week, then briefed his CFO, Braden, on the software company he was contemplating for acquisition. Following several late nights in the office, he took Avery out to dinner at a restaurant she wanted to try for months. But he could not bring himself to have sex with her that night—his guilt and something else he could not put his finger on held him back. Again, he made up an excuse and told her he had a migraine.

On Friday, Avery went out with girlfriends for dinner and to see a play, leaving Hayden alone for the evening. Since Avery believed he would be on a business trip, aside from lounge wear and a swimsuit, he packed professional attire. It mattered little, as earlier in the week he instructed Ashley to order resort clothing and arrange delivery to his room with the concierge. After placing his bags in the rooms corner, he picked up his phone and scrolled through his messages, convinced he would see one from Brea backing out last minute—there were no messages from her.

Hayden pressed on their message thread. *I'm leaving in the morning. I'll see you tomorrow,* he typed and sent. He waited several minutes, staring at the screen. No response. Tossing his phone on the bed, he went into the kitchen, fixed himself a sandwich and poured a bottle of beer into a glass. After eating, he could not shake his unease and carried his drink with him to the balcony. He sat on a cushioned chair and watched the sun setting over the Golden Gate Bridge.

The beautiful view reminded him of the night he and Brea had left the diner and, upon stepping out into the frigid night, they looked up into the sky filled with a breathtaking spread of stars. In the city, you could never see the stars like you could in Black Harbor, and he wished he was back there, feeling connected to something bigger than himself.

Finishing his beer, he returned inside, and settled on watching a movie until ready to fall asleep. While in the kitchen, his phone chimed. His heart stopped beating—he knew with no doubt it was Brea replying to his message.

Placing his glass in the sink, he walked into his bedroom, certain she was cancelling. On the lock screen, he saw Brea's number on the notification. Picking up his phone, he pushed on the thread and read her response. *"I'll see you tomorrow at seven in the lobby."* A faint smile touched the corners of Hayden's mouth—he had his chance, and there was no turning back.

CHAPTER SIX

BREA

As Brea ran last minute errands throughout the day before leaving for Mexico, she had second thoughts about the trip. At the library returning books, she nearly texted Hayden to call it off—not because she did not want to go, but because she struggled with the part of herself that wanted to continue hiding from her past. Clutching her phone in her hand, she told herself she would take another hour to decide.

When she arrived home, Brea briefly greeted her children and Tina in the kitchen and then headed into her room to pack for the trip. Walking down the hall, she checked her phone and saw there was a message from Hayden—it was as though he sensed her ambivalence. She held off replying and paced her bedroom until the tender memory of her and Hayden sleeping in his car at the beach flashed through her mind—tomorrow she would board the plane and see this trip through. Following her reply to Hayden, she connected her phone to the charger and, after a deep breath, unzipped her suitcase to begin packing.

During the week, Brea kept busy preparing the children for their trip to Santa Barbara, as well as shopping for herself. As they were staying at an elegant resort, she splurged and purchased new sundresses, sandals, and bathing suits.

Once packed, she rolled her suitcase to the corner of her bedroom and returned to the closet to see if there was anything she forgot. Scanning her closet, her eyes fixed on her memory box, a dark blue shoebox on the shelf above her coats. She could not remember the last time she opened it. Using her wooden step stool, Brea stepped onto it and stretched her arms until her fingers snagged the corner of the box. Giving it a few nudges, she pushed it far enough to grip it with one hand and pulled it down.

Seated on the stool, she lifted the lid off the box and rooted through its contents. Inside were a stack of photographs, playbills from high school shows, copies of poems, and jewelry, including the gold necklace Jaime gave her on the night of Tory's party. Her eyes landed on a beaten-up red cardboard box at the bottom. Pressing her finger to her lips, she hesitated to open it, knowing what the box contained—the blue butterfly brooch Hayden bought her in Sicily decades ago.

The last time Brea opened the box was while packing her apartment to move to Los Angeles. She had burst into tears and cried for an hour on her bedroom floor. After pulling herself together, she returned the brooch to its container, and buried it in the shoebox. For an inexplicable reason, she could never throw it away or donate it. Brea pulled out the red box and packed it in her suitcase—she dared not open it, but felt compelled to bring it on the trip.

Brea went into the kitchen to help Tina with dinner, and planned to usher Alex and Sophie into the bathtub as soon as they finished eating. She wanted to spend as much time with them as possible before they fell asleep and, of critical importance, she promised they would make pillow forts with the sofa cushions before bedtime.

Upon seeing her children's faces light up as she entered the kitchen, her heart ached, reminding her she would be away from them for an entire week. Making silly faces and running up to them to smell their hair, she sprinkled them with kisses as she extolled how much she would miss them while she was gone.

Tina, a twenty-one-year-old attractive college student, stood beside the stove, beaming as she witnessed the display of motherly affection towards her children. Often, Tina would comment on Brea and Adam's seemingly perfect life and express her hopes to one day have a similar home and marriage. Brea would meet her eyes and plant a forced smile on her face. If Tina knew the truth about her marriage and her dark and complex past—what then would she think about Brea's life?

CHAPTER SEVEN

HAYDEN

Arriving at the resort at two o'clock, Hayden had ample time to check into his room and rest before meeting Brea in the main lobby at seven. Earlier that morning, he booked a reservation at one of the more casual hotel restaurants for seven-thirty, knowing Brea would arrive on a later flight and have less time to settle in before dinner.

At the front desk, Hayden declined the bellman's services and verified that his and Brea's oceanfront casitas were adjacent to one another. He hoped Brea would not mind, as they were still in separate accommodations. Entering his casita, Hayden slipped out of his footwear and stripped off his slacks and button-down shirt. Without bothering to put on a bathing suit, he opened the glass doors, stepped onto the patio and descended the steps into the private plunge pool in his boxers.

The afternoon weather was hot and dry with a cloudless blue sky. He dunked his face in the water, leaned back, and closed his eyes. For the first time in weeks, he felt as though he could catch his breath and relax—the feeling did not last long.

Anticipating seeing Brea, an onslaught of memories flooded his mind. With the sun warming his face, he replayed the last time he saw Brea after her interview at Black Rose Paper Shop—one of his worst lifetime experiences. He wanted to believe, to hope, that this week he could prove to Brea that what happened that night was an aberration, a series of errors and the cruel hand of fate that had conspired to keep them apart for reasons he would never understand.

Less than a month after having left for MIT, while studying in his dorm room, Hayden's father called to inform him he planned to sell their house in Black Harbor. A tumultuous upheaval of emotions washed over him, though he knew he needed to walk a fine line in reacting to his father's news. Perhaps foolish, he hoped that in the future his path would cross with Brea, and after time had passed, she would hear him out and forgive him. If they sold the home, the odds of that happening were infinitely smaller.

"Dad, are you sure? Can't we wait for a while, maybe a few years?" he asked, betraying no emotion or weakness in his voice, which his father would have found insupportable from his son.

"Hayden, there is no reason to keep that big house for the two of us. The real estate agent viewed it today, and I signed the agreement. You're in college now, and it's best we let it go. I'm going to move into an apartment until I figure out the next steps." Hayden dropped his head into his hands. Any disagreement risked angering his father.

"You'll need to come back to the house to pack up your room. I'll book you a plane ticket for next weekend."

"Dad, can you have the movers pack for me? I want to stay here and focus on my summer program." Returning to Black Harbor the following weekend, where endless reminders of Brea lurked, was the last thing he wanted. The vivid memory of her eyes, laden with fear and fury, still haunted him.

"Hayden, you will come home next weekend. We're not discussing it," he replied in a stern tone of voice.

"All right, Dad." Hayden knew one did not argue with Gavin Botero unless you were prepared for a battle. Seated at the desk in his dorm room, Hayden leaned back and looked at the ceiling—his throat tightened. It was the only home he knew, steeped in memories of his mother.

The following Saturday, Hayden dutifully boarded the plane and arrived at the airport in the late morning. Exiting the lobby, he spotted his father's black BMW parked in the arrivals pickup lane. After climbing into the front passenger seat, his father greeted him with a neutral air, and they drove to the house.

"Angela prepared some meals for you. She will be at the house all day to finish up cleaning, and then will clear out your mother's things. I asked her to set aside a few boxes for you if there are things of hers you would like to keep. I'm going to spend the afternoon in the office, but I'll be home for dinner. No friends this weekend. I want you to focus on packing up, all right?"

"Yes, sir," Hayden grumbled.

"What's that?" his father asked with a hard edge to his voice.

"Yes," Hayden replied, attempting to conceal his hostility.

"Don't fuck around with me, Hayden. I'm not having it," he barked and banged the steering wheel with his fist.

"I'm sorry, Dad, I understand," Hayden said in a conciliatory tone of voice. It could go either way—it would either appease him or set him off.

"Good." They drove the rest of the way in silence. His father pulled into the driveway and, once parked, Hayden opened the car door and sprang out to retrieve his bags. Angela's white Volkswagen sat parked by the curb. Hayden rubbed his forehead and dragged his feet on the walkway to the front door to let himself into the house. Dropping his bags on the ground in the foyer, he scanned the living room. Everything was the same except their housekeeper, Angela, had stacked a dozen boxes along the wall with either "Donation" or "Storage" written on the sides in thick, black marker.

"Hayden, my baby," Angela called out as she entered the living room from the kitchen. "You look too skinny," she exclaimed in her familiar Portuguese accent. She was a petite woman with a full head of dark shoulder-length hair, and Hayden never saw her dressed in anything other than black leggings and a brightly colored T-shirt. Angela never failed to amaze Hayden with her boundless energy as she flew about from room to room. In her arms, she carried a bundle of clothing in a basket.

"Hi Angela. It's because I'm too busy to eat and I miss your cooking," Hayden replied with a warm smile. Angela had been a constant presence in his life, working for his family since he was four years old. Now, with the house for sale and priced aggressively, she too would soon be gone from his life.

"I have food made for you. Come into the kitchen and I'll heat it up for you," she said and beckoned with her hand as though trying to lure a puppy into her arms.

"Great. I'll stop in my room for a minute and I'll be right there." Hayden picked up his bags and walked down the hall. Ever since that night with Brea, he felt ill at ease in his bedroom. For days, he would find pieces of glass embedded where the mattress met the headboard or on the floor. Staring at his bed, the memory of stripping off the blood-stained bedding made him sick to his stomach.

He placed his hands on the desk and lowered his head, suddenly overwhelmed by a vivid memory of Brea, distraught and crying out that Cylis had hurt her—perhaps his father selling the house was for the best. It would make it easier to forget Black Harbor and, over time, the guilt that tormented him.

Hayden opened his eyes. Although his complexion did not burn easily, he did not want to tempt fate by staying in the plunge pool for too long without sunscreen. Climbing out, he grabbed a towel off the rack and watched the ocean. While drying off, he thought to himself that Brea made a good choice twenty years ago, choosing Mexico as the destination for their trip. It seemed fitting to be by the ocean—the setting would mirror Black Harbor.

Once inside, he took a quick shower. Wrapping a towel around his waist, he grabbed a cold bottle of sparkling water from the minibar and drank it as he gazed out the glass patio doors. He thought of his mother, recalling how much she loved to stay in a room where you could hear the waves of the ocean crashing onto the shore at night. As a child, she would often take Hayden to South Black Harbor Beach, whether it was a wintry day for a picnic or a hot summer day to swim in the ocean. She would shield her eyes from the overhead sun, point to the water, and tell him the ocean was "*magic.*"

"*Hayden, when you look out at the ocean, remember it's magic. Life came from it, and it's bigger than everything else on earth. The ocean holds secrets that people will never know or understand, but it draws us to it because it is part of us. Beautiful, violent, healing, frightening, and misunderstood. Just like us.*"

After shutting the curtains, Hayden stretched out on the bed and set the alarm for five-thirty. Too tired to dress or unpack, he threw his towel on the floor and covered himself with the white bed sheet. He turned to lie on his side and stared at the slivers of light that snuck into the room from behind the edges of the curtains until his eyes closed and he fell asleep.

CHAPTER EIGHT

BREA

Within weeks of working at Black Rose Paper Boutique, Brea and Trina developed a strong bond and Brea continued to work as a part-time sales assistant throughout her senior year. As Brea always planned, after six months of working she saved enough money to buy a used Toyota Camry. The faded and scratched blue paint revealed the car's age, but it belonged to Brea, and the day the title transferred to her filled her with immense pride.

Irritating to Brea, though her mother and father offered neither financial help nor advice while searching for her car, they did not hesitate to express their disapproval of her choice. She cared little—it was hers and hers alone. When she drove to work, Brea parked her car on Black Harbor Boulevard and rushed into the store, calling for Trina to come and see it.

"Well, isn't this something?" Trina extolled as she slapped her hand down on the hood. "Brea—she's a beauty. Now I can have you run all of my errands too!" she joked with a hearty laugh.

Trina, having grown up in Texas, never lost her Texan accent. Daily, she wore her salt-and-pepper hair in a teased mass of curls set atop her head and a flawless face of makeup. Trina, always in a bright and cheerful mood, could warm up a gray, stormy day with her smile and her ability to draw you into a lively conversation.

Though Trina found Brea to be a tough read, their relationship had become quite close. It was difficult to draw Brea out to talk about herself unless the topic of discussion involved her love of writing and school, and Trina found it strange that for such a pretty young woman she did not appear to have any interest in boys. A couple of her girlfriends would pop into the store on occasion to say hello and chat with them when the shop was slow, yet finding out more about Brea's personal life was difficult. Brea's introverted nature aside, her inherent goodness was undeniable to Trina—a gentle soul, although she likened her to a timid doe.

"Well, I'm so proud of you! What an accomplishment. Hey, I just got hit by lightning! Why don't you take me for a spin after we close up tonight, my dear, and I'll treat you to a cheeseburger," Trina offered.

"Sure, thank you, Trina. It would be nice to celebrate, right?" Brea replied with a sentimental smile spreading across her face—moved that Trina was proud of her. They returned to the store, arm in arm.

At seven o'clock, Trina closed down the shop. She preferred to close later on Friday nights in the event there were last-minute odds and ends a working parent may need for a birthday party or a special occasion the following day. It was true to Trina's nature—intuitive and kind.

Brea drove Trina to Eddie's, a local restaurant, not much to look at, but without fail served Black Harbor's best burgers and French fries for decades. The secret of the French fries was that they used beef tallow for the frying and then salted them to perfection, but no one could ever figure out their well-guarded secrets for the juicy beef patties.

Seated in a worn wooden booth near the bar, Trina jumped up to greet several locals. She asked Brea to order her a soda and would return in a moment. Brea scanned the menu. Having a good appetite and in a celebratory mood, she settled on ordering a bacon cheeseburger and a side of cheese fries when she heard a male voice bellow, "Cy, over here!"

Brea dropped the menu. In a panic, she slumped into her chair, panting. Her fingers trembled as she gripped the edges of the table. It was not possible he could be here—she heard from Tory that Cylis had moved across the country to Seattle in the summer.

"Brea honey, what's wrong?" Trina crouched down beside Brea and touched her forehead. With her complexion ashen and sweat beading on her hairline, Brea stared ahead with a blank expression. "Honey, look at me," Trina pressed.

"Si—Simon, you old fool, come here!" Brea heard the voice say, attempting to flag down an older man at the bar.

Catapulting into the present moment, Brea blinked several times and then turned her head to look at Trina. "Oh, I'm so sorry. I think—I forgot to eat lunch today, and I felt dizzy," she rambled with a wavering voice.

Trina studied Brea's face—she did not believe a word that came out of her mouth. Feeling dizzy was a possibility, yet Brea had been as terrified as a buck looking down the barrel of a gun.

"Okay, sit up, honey. Marshall, get me two Cokes right now and something from the kitchen—make it snappy," Trina called over her shoulder to the barman. He gave her a salute, grabbed two glasses, filled them up with ice-cubes and cola, and then hurried over to the table.

"Drink this honey," Trina said. She pulled the paper off the straw, stuck it in the cup and held the drink up to Brea's lips.

After a few sips, Brea waved her hand. "I'm fine, Trina, I promise. I just didn't feel well for a moment."

Trina slipped back into her seat across from Brea and studied her face. "What happened, honey?" she asked with her eyes locked on Brea's and a determined resolved not to let Brea off the hook until she told her the truth.

Brea shook her head and searched her mind for a way to either change the subject or think of a plausible lie. Her mind blank, and observing Trina's concerned expression, she knew she would see through her attempt to hide behind a distraction or a half-baked lie.

After releasing a sigh, Brea told her as much of the truth as she could manage without sharing too much. "I thought someone I never wanted to see again came in. It wasn't him—but I panicked."

"Hmm. Did he hurt you?"

"Yes."

"Does this happen to you a lot? Getting scared like that? Brea, you looked absolutely shook-up, honey."

"Not a lot, but it's happened before. I don't think about him—it's better that way," Brea answered with an edge to her voice.

"I'm not a doctor, but I think maybe you should talk to someone and get some help. You can sweep the dust under the rug, honey, but that doesn't mean it's gone. It just piles up and gets really dirty under there."

"Thanks Trina. I know—but I'm okay." Brea raised her eyes and thanked Marshall as he placed a basket of fries and ketchup on the table. After they ordered, Marshall took the menus and returned to the kitchen. Brea grabbed a handful of French fries and ate them, one after another, to settle her stomach.

"How about your parents? Do they know what happened?" Trina asked.

Brea scoffed and rolled her eyes. "No, no way. They are not normal parents, and I know a lot of kids say that about their parents, but mine are on a whole different level of abnormal. They don't hit me or anything like that, but they live their lives and I'm alone. I have to figure everything out myself."

"You're right—that doesn't sound normal." Trina replied. Scrunching her lips together, she inhaled a deep breath and rapped her fingers on the table. "I'll tell you something, honey—we live in a fallen world. People are flawed, and some do horrible things. It's difficult to see it, but there is always a path forward, and there is so much love out there—and sometimes that love finds you when you least expect it. I promise you it will find you, and you're not alone—you have me. You just keep living and you'll see what happens."

Brea nodded. Sitting up straighter, she drew in a deep breath through her mouth.

"Can I help you, honey? Anything I can do?" Trina asked, reaching over the table to take Brea's hand.

"You already help me, Trina," Brea replied with a smile. "Just being you is helpful. You mean so much to me."

Trina sat back in surprise. "Well, that may be the nicest compliment I ever heard. Brea, listen to me. If you need something, you tell me, okay? A day may come when you may struggle to deal with this by yourself. If you ever want to talk or you need help—you promise me you'll come find me?"

Brea nodded. "I will. I promise."

Trina slid out of the booth to sit beside Brea. She wrapped one arm around Brea's shoulders and squeezed her in close. Marshall returned to the table and set down their cheeseburgers. They ate, side by side, in silence, and Trina did not remove her arm from Brea's shoulders until it was time to leave.

The plane touched down on schedule, arriving in Puerto Vallarta at three-twenty in the afternoon. Brea wiped her eyes. Four years ago Trina passed away from breast cancer, and she missed her. They kept in touch by phone and Trina came to Brea and Adam's wedding, visited after Alex was born, and sent him Christmas and birthday presents every year until she passed away. Brea would often cry, remembering her kindness and the love she held for Brea.

Without Trina, Brea would not have had any faith left in humanity the summer before her senior year at Harvey Slate. Trina's tenderness and unwavering support helped to push Brea through the last year she lived in Black Harbor.

As the plane taxied to the terminal, Brea wished Trina were still alive—she would have called her after seeing Hayden last week. And Trina was right—one day she would have to face the past. Staring out the window, Brea prayed for astral advice from Trina's spirit, or for a divine sign telling her she made the right choice in meeting Hayden in Mexico.

Once the plane came to a full stop, the passengers unbuckled their seatbelts, and the pilot announced overhead that they were free to deplane. If there had been a sign from the universe, Brea missed it, and she would need to trust her own mind from that point forward.

CHAPTER NINE

BREA

The resort website did not do the property justice—it was spectacular. Once checked in, Brea strolled through the luxurious lobby overlooking an expansive view of the ocean beyond the open-air wall. Animated guests engrossed in lively conversations and drinking cocktails occupied the white upholstered seating on the terrace.

On her right, her eyes swept over an elegant cocktail lounge with black leather seating and blown glass pendant lights hanging from the ceiling. The bar was ebony marble and on the walls, black and gold shelving with built-in warm-toned lights. A bellman cleared his throat to attract Brea's attention and informed her the golf cart was ready to drive her to her casita. With a nod, she turned to follow him, eager to freshen up and rest.

Brea entered the casita at a quarter to six, leaving her an hour before she would need to return to the lobby to meet Hayden. Her eyes widened as she surveyed the one-bedroom lodging—Hayden had spared no expense for the trip.

The impressive living and dining area comprised ivory stone floors, a light-gray built-in wooden credenza table with a refrigerator and minibar, a spacious ivory sofa, and a six-person gray marble dining table set. Teal and gold abstract paintings decorated the ecru walls, and pocket glass sliding doors overlooked the beach. On the patio, Brea saw two cushioned lounge chairs and a large private plunge pool.

Brea peeked into the bedroom. The ivory furniture consisted of an upholstered king-size bed made up with light-gray and white linens, and on its left, a chaise lounge beside another set of ocean-facing pocket-sliding doors. Across from the bed sat a modern-style desk and chair.

After tipping the bellman, she closed the door and strolled through the casita. Brea slid open the living room pocket doors and stepped onto the patio—she felt as though she had crossed into an alternate dimension where only peace and tranquility existed. The air, warm and perfumed with sea salt, wrapped around her body and, for the first time in two weeks, she felt as though her agitated mind had stilled and she could draw in a breath with ease.

Remembering she was short on time, she returned inside and hurried into the bathroom to unpack what she would need to prepare for dinner. A wide smile blossomed as she scanned the space, seeing a large stand-alone tub and an immense shower large enough to fit several people inside with gray slate tiling and two shower heads. After turning on the shower, she unpacked her suitcase and selected a strapless ivory jumpsuit and a pair of gold high-heeled sandals to wear for the evening.

Brea had lingered in the hot shower, ecstatic to have no obligations other than to take her time to dress and make up her face. Satisfied after appraising her reflection in the mirror, she checked the time. Her heart thumped in her chest seeing it was six forty-five and she would need to leave for the lobby. Brea inhaled a deep breath and clasped her hands together. Grabbing her clutch, she headed out to meet Hayden.

Nearing the entrance to the lobby, Brea slowed her steps and veered to the left of the glass doors. She scanned her surroundings. Now that the sun was setting, the resort lights along the paths and posts were switching on, creating a lovely ambience. Brea shook out her hands and ran her fingers through her hair.

Composed, she entered the lobby and paused. Twenty feet away, Hayden stood with his back to her, dressed in a long-sleeved navy button-down shirt and both hands tucked in the pockets of his gray slacks. Beyond the open-air wall, he watched the sunset, a breathtaking vista of a blue ombre sky with streaks of orange and pink on the horizon.

Brea lowered her eyes to the floor, overwhelmed by a flood of mixed emotions. She rubbed her forehead and raised her eyes—Hayden had turned and was watching her. Neither of them smiled. They held one another's gaze, uncertain what to say or do next. Hayden took the first step forward, and Brea followed until they met in the center of the lobby.

"I have to admit, I've been standing here for twenty minutes trying to figure out what I should say when you walked in. I came up with something good, but as soon as I saw you, I went blank," he confessed and exhaled an audible breath.

Brea nodded with understanding. "I'm—repeating over and over in my head—I can't believe I'm here, wondering if I've lost my mind. This is all a little too—real, I suppose." They exchanged awkward smiles and averted their eyes from one another.

"You look great. Your hair is back to its natural color," he offered as a compliment.

"Thanks. I was due for an appointment, and I wanted a change—to feel more like myself, I suppose." Brea smoothed down her hair and pushed it off her shoulders. "You look great too, although that's not an outfit I would expect to see on someone at a beach resort. Perhaps at a business meeting or something." Brea fumbled her words, embarrassed she had complimented his looks.

Hayden looked down at his pants and dress shoes. "Right. Well, Avery thinks I'm on a business trip."

Brea nodded. "Of course. So, what now?" she asked, surveying the lobby.

Hayden checked his watch, noting it was only five minutes past the hour. "Our reservation is at seven-thirty. I booked us a table at a restaurant just down the path. Should we have a drink here first?" Hayden pointed over his left shoulder to the lobby bar behind him.

"Yes," she replied, eager for something to ease her tension. Brea took a step forward, as did Hayden, and they nearly collided with one another. They both stepped back and smiled.

"Should we try that again?" Hayden said, gesturing for Brea to walk first.

Walking beside one another, neither of them spoke. There were available tables and seats at the bar. As they had little time, Hayden led Brea to two stools at the bar, and they sat down. The bartender appeared before them with a smile, greeting them first in Spanish and then in English. Hayden gestured for Brea to order first.

"I'll have any cocktail you recommend with tequila. Please surprise me," Brea requested, finding it difficult to decide.

"The same for me," Hayden said.

The bartender nodded. "Two Palomas, perfect for a night like this." Brea looked out at the ocean to glimpse the sunset. Her eyes settled back on Hayden, watching her.

Shifting his eyes to the bar, Hayden cleared his throat. "I'm sorry for staring. I've thought about seeing you again so many times, and what I would say when we had the chance to talk, and now I don't know where to begin."

"Hayden. One thing I'm going to ask is that we don't talk about that night right away. I think it would be better if we eased into everything." Hayden nodded in agreement.

She continued. "Last week after I saw you, I went back and thought about everything I could remember from those years. I thought about my family, Jaime, the time we spent together, and everything else in between. It was—difficult. There was so much I willed myself to forget. One thing in particular struck me—I knew so little about what you went through with your parents. You always stopped yourself from telling me more details. I don't blame you for it—if anyone would understand, it's me."

Hayden placed his hands on the bar and drummed his fingers before speaking. "I'm not planning on hiding anything from you this week. Whatever you ask me, I'll answer. It's all on the table, no matter how difficult it might be for me to tell you, or for you to hear."

The bartender arrived with their cocktails, set them down on square-shaped black napkins, and then gestured at the glasses to present the drinks to Hayden and Brea.

"Two Palomas. Tequila, lime, red grapefruit juice, agave nectar, and sparkling water. Please enjoy." The bartender nodded and left them to attend to another guest.

Hayden held up his drink and waited for Brea to do the same, both tasting it at the same time. It was delicious, crisp, and refreshing. After setting his drink down, Hayden tapped his fingers on the bar before speaking again.

"Brea, I have to ask. Are you still afraid of me? Like the way you were when I saw you last week. I know I deserved that reaction—but I want to explain before we start—that would never happen again. If I could, I would give anything to go back and fix that night."

Looking into Hayden's eyes, full of regret and remorse, she felt in her bones he was sincere. "Mostly, no. The logical part of my brain says I shouldn't be after I went back and remembered everything, how traumatic it was losing your mother and everything you must have lived through with your dad. But, when I remember that night, it was so frightening to see you that angry, and I lived with that fear and confusion for so many years. I have to be honest—I waffle a little."

"Fair enough." Expecting her to be completely at ease with him after fifteen minutes would have been unrealistic. "How's your suite—or casita, I mean?" he asked, changing the subject.

"Stunning. If this were a normal trip, I would call up Hannah, my best friend, and gush about it, but somehow it doesn't seem appropriate. The guilt I'm stuffing away in my brain won't let me surrender and embrace it all just yet."

"I know what you mean." Hayden thought a moment, and a slight smile played on his lips. "How about this—what if we consider this week more of a self-help experience that we both deserve instead of consuming ourselves with guilt? True, we lied about the purpose of this trip, but we've done nothing wrong otherwise."

Brea tilted her head to the side and considered Hayden's suggestion. "So, this is like—lying to the world about spending a week in a hotel recovery center to get plastic surgery? However, in our case, we are going to exorcise the past in secret and reemerge psychologically cleansed?"

"Right—exactly," Hayden confirmed. They both smiled at one another and lifted their drinks to take another sip.

"Hayden, did you plan team-building exercises and ice-breakers too?"

"Not exactly. But I think by the end of the week we should try to figure out our spirit animals," he joked, finished his drink, and then checked his watch again. The tension having eased, they both laughed.

"Let's walk over to the restaurant." Hayden signaled to the bartender for the bill. Brea finished her drink and studied Hayden as he signed the check. His eyes met Brea's. "Are you ready to get started?"

Shaking her head, she covered the lower half of her face with her hand. "I don't know about 'ready,' but we're on a moving train. There's no turning back now."

Hayden tapped the bar with his hand and stood, held out his arm to gesture for Brea to go first, and then followed her out.

Chapter Ten

Brea

A light breeze blew in the temperate night air as Brea and Hayden walked side by side down the path to the restaurant. Brea studied Hayden's profile and raised her eyebrows. Hayden, sensing her eyes on him, turned his head.

"What is it?"

"Nothing, it's only you look so much older," she replied.

"Ouch," he said with a light laugh.

"Not like that, I'm sorry. It's just going to take a little time getting used to it. I bet I look a lot older too."

Hayden opened his mouth to reply, but Brea prevented him from speaking. "Say nothing. It's better not to say anything to a middle-aged woman about how old she looks. Let me spare you the fallout."

Hayden pressed his lips together. "I appreciate the warning, Brea, but I already told you when I first saw you at the shop, you look the same today as you did at seventeen." They both laughed. The soft glow of the lanterns against the lush landscaping cast a tranquil atmosphere as they continued along the path.

"Have you kept in touch with Allegra over the years?" Hayden asked.

"No. I made up a story about her inviting me to a bachelorette party here. By the way, I told Adam I would text his mother pictures to show the kids, so you're going to need to hire some women for me to sit with on the beach drinking margaritas."

Hayden chuckled. "We'll figure something out. Did you call him after you arrived?"

"Nope, I sent him a text to tell Alex and Sophie I love them with a picture of myself at the airport. He never replied. It's my first time away from them, and it's odd. In a way, I'm happy to have a break and time to think, but I also feel like a piece of me is missing." Brea felt a tug on her heart, picturing Alex and Sophie, probably in the bathtub or reading books now.

"How about you? Have you kept in touch with anyone from Harvey Slate?" Brea asked as Hayden opened the restaurant door for her. After informing the hostess they had arrived, they paused their conversation, and she led them to a corner table overlooking the ocean. The restaurant décor was informal but charming with dark wood tables and chairs, etched tile flooring, candle fixtures mounted on the walls and wrought iron lamps hanging from the ceiling.

Once seated, Hayden answered. "Not really. Trevor reached out to me a few years ago. He's a music producer in Los Angeles. Sadly, he told me that Aaron died in a car accident about six years ago and forwarded the obituary to me. He was a lawyer and left behind his wife and two boys."

Brea's face fell upon hearing the tragic news. She did not have any social media accounts, nor had she kept up with anyone from Black Harbor, other than Trina. And having lost her husband before she retired, Trina closed her shop ten years ago and moved back to Texas to be closer to her sisters.

"I'm sorry to hear that." Brea sighed, thinking to herself how in a moment your life could turn upside down. After scanning the menu, she selected what she would order with little deliberation as she had not eaten since earlier that morning. Their server appeared to greet them. Hayden ordered a draft beer and Brea a glass of white wine, followed by their entrees.

Hayden hesitated, but needed to ask. "What about Vienna? Did you ever reconcile or see her again—like at a family reunion?"

Brea laughed. "The Staxons do not have family reunions. Until recently, I hadn't thought about her for years. I don't even speak with my own parents that much, maybe twice a year. The last I heard anything of her was around ten years ago when my father told me she married someone from Canada and moved to Montreal. And speaking of her, I'd like to hear more about what it was like dating her and also why she felt threatened by me."

Hayden took a sip of beer. "I'm going to need to finish my drink before I go there—she was something else."

"No way. It's been twenty years. Keep drinking and tell me." Brea gestured with her hands to encourage Hayden to talk.

Hayden leaned back in his chair and told Brea the story of how he met Vienna to the night of Brea's performance. She sat and listened, refraining from making any interruptions. When Hayden reached the night of Brea's performance, he continued on.

"After I left Nigel's, I followed her out, and I drove her home. She apologized and told me this long sob story that there had been years of competitiveness between the two of you, resulting from her grandmother having pitted her father against yours. And she claimed her father emotionally abused her and reminded her all the time that you were so much more intelligent and capable than she was. She said she felt as though she could never measure up to you in her father's eyes."

Brea's mouth gaped open. "Hayden, that is ridiculous. I met her two weeks before I saw you with Jamie at the beach. My Uncle Pax did no such thing."

Hayden shook his head. "Well, and you know a bit about my relationship with my father, so when she told me that, it struck a chord. I wanted to believe her. She claimed that your appearance at Harvey Slate devastated her, because everyone said you were 'a better version' of her."

With a slight laugh, Brea replied, "Well, that part was true, or so I heard from Jaime."

Hayden continued. "My feelings for you over time became obvious, and it was clear after the performance that me and Vienna were wrong for each other. And then, the night I drove you home from the campsite, when you said she told you not to 'cross her,' I realized she had lied. I wanted to break up with her, but I felt trapped. My father loved her. He treated me better while dating her, and I had this fear that if I did, he would take it out on my mom."

Brea dropped her chin into her hand and sighed. Though bizarre, it was satisfying to hear explanations for the things she wondered about decades ago.

"But it was a nightmare staying with her after that night at the campsite. We fought all the time. If she thought I looked at you a certain way or if your name was mentioned near me, she would lose it, and then accuse you of trying to steal me. Then, the night we broke up, she threatened me, saying if she ever found out we were together, she would make your life miserable—crazy things, like telling the school you were doing drugs, having sex with teachers, and even call up your parents and tell them you were having sex with boys at school for money. That was about a week after the party, when you wore that dress with the giant blue butterfly on the side."

"It was a blue flower, Hayden, but go on," Brea interjected. Upon reflection, this explained his thoughts of her in Sicily when he saw the blue butterfly brooch.

Hayden smiled and laughed. "I missed that, although to be fair, I was focusing on you in the dress, not the dress itself."

Hayden cleared his throat and averted his eyes from Brea after having let that comment slip out.

"Anyway, that night was the final straw. I couldn't take it anymore and told her if she went after you or made any trouble with your family, I would tell everyone a secret of hers that she didn't want anyone to find out. Although I hoped it would work to keep her silent, I couldn't trust that she wouldn't try to burn it all down to the ground if we wound up together."

Brea closed her eyes as Hayden's last words absorbed into her brain. "Well, it makes sense now. Why she hated me so much. It was such a mess back then. Wait—what was her secret?"

Hayden shook his head. "I'm a man of my word. It goes to the grave with me." Brea snapped her fingers. The petty teenager that still lived inside her wanted the dirt on Vienna.

He continued. "I beat myself up for years that I should have handled things differently, but I was just a kid. You didn't want Jaime to find out, and I didn't want you to get hurt. A part of me also worried that Vienna would spread some crazy rumors about me too that would get back to my father. I know that wasn't very heroic, but there it is."

Brea licked her lips. She felt compelled to tell Hayden her regrets. "You know, you brought up something I realized when I fell down the rabbit hole of my memories. We were just kids. I mistook your reserved personality for someone who was unbreakable, and it wasn't fair. You went through so much with losing your mom, and—"

The server arrived with their food, and they paused until he placed their plates down and with a nod, left the table. Raising his eyebrows, Hayden signaled for her to continue. Brea reconsidered venturing down the path of bringing up that night after she had been the one to request they postpone that discussion. She cleared her throat. "Hayden, you and your dad. What was he like? You said he was angry, and you didn't want to leave your mother alone. I knew only that. You don't have to tell me everything, but maybe something to help me understand more about what it was like for you growing up." Hayden nodded and rubbed his temples.

Brea picked up her fork to eat her lobster enchiladas. The mouth-watering fragrance made her stomach grumble. "Why don't we eat first so our food doesn't get cold, then tell me over dessert."

Having been lost in Brea's words, he blinked and agreed. They ate without talking, hungry and eager not to waste time, as they were both tired from traveling. After they finished and put down their utensils, Hayden wiped his mouth with his napkin and then clasped his hands together.

"He was volatile, rigid, difficult to live with, and violent. I always feared him, but I didn't understand that he abused me and my mother until I started middle school. I had a best friend, Mike, and our parents were also good friends. Mike's dad was so proud of him, and they had a father-son relationship I envied. But I needed to be smart, perfect—what my father wanted me to be for survival. Let me share with you an example of what I'm trying to say." Hayden cleared his throat and began.

CHAPTER ELEVEN

HAYDEN

"Hayden, focus. Keep your eye on the ball," Gavin Botero yelled from the stands while Hayden was up at bat. With two strikes and three balls, a full count, Hayden, twelve years old, tried to tune out his father—his intrusive parental coaching distracted him rather than helped to boost his confidence.

To other parents, when Gavin argued with the umpire or called out unsolicited advice to Hayden, their impression was that he was an involved father and devoted baseball fan supportive of his son. However, they were not privy to witnessing the aftermath in the car or at home after the game.

"Come on, you got this, Hayden," he heard Mike call out from the dugout, though all Hayden could think about were the mistakes he made in the game. He was one of the best outfielders in the junior league, but in the top of the ninth inning he missed the ball and the Sea Crest Cardinals scored a run to tie up the game seven to seven. Fortunately, they tagged the kid out at second as he ran for third. Hayden's team, the Black Harbor Bluejays, were now up at bat.

The Bluejays had two outs, and if Hayden blew this pitch and struck out, they would go into another inning and could lose the game. All he needed was to get on base to get Mike up at bat, one of the league's best hitters. If Mike could score a run, they would take the game.

Hayden did his best to focus, inhaled a deep breath, then positioned his feet with his knees slightly bent, coiled, stacked his hands, and relaxed his grip on the bat. If he struck out, the best-case scenario after the game would be enduring his father's lengthy rehash of the game followed by a list of Hayden's needed improvements. Worst case, his father would unleash relentless criticism until dismissing him to his room while shouting, "*I'm sick of looking at your face*." Then he would shift his attention and lay into his mother. Once that happened, it was impossible to predict how long the berating would last.

Hayden watched the pitcher shake off the catcher's first call, wind up, then release the ball—a high curveball diving fast towards the plate. Hayden did not swing.

"Ball." The home-plate umpire called a walk, sending Hayden to first base. There was not much glory in a walk for Hayden, but it set up Mike to get on base, or to score a home run. From first base, Hayden looked into the stands at his father—he stood with his arms crossed and his chin in his hand, disappointed.

Mike walked to home plate, focused and confident. Hayden fixed his eyes on the ball and prepared his stance, ready to react once he could see the trajectory of the ball if Mike hit it. First pitch and Mike slammed it, an obvious home run. Hayden took off to second base, and just as he hit the bag, the announcer called it. "Home run—a walk-off win!" The announcer announced it again while the crowd cheered and chanted. He slowed his run and, when making it to home plate, turned to wait for Mike as he completed his victory run for a high five.

Hayden craned his neck to look back again into the stands after Mike crossed home plate. Chewing gum and clapping his hands with little enthusiasm, his father held his gaze on Hayden. It did not matter that Hayden helped his team to win the game.

Mike had the glory of the game-winning run and, according to Gavin Botero, that meant Hayden failed.

Gavin rubbed his eyes as Mike's parents congratulated Hayden and praised his performance on the field. Mike went in for another high five with Hayden and then took off with his family. Mike's parents extended an invitation for the Boteros to meet them for pizza, but Hayden's father declined and ushered Hayden to the car.

Under his breath, his father cursed several times. "That asshole was gloating about Mike, as though he's the only player on the damn team." He slapped Hayden on the back, knocking him a bit off balance. "If it weren't for you, Mike wouldn't have gotten up at bat and the game would have gone into another inning. But all that matters is that he won the game with that run—he stole it all from you. That's all anyone will remember—that he's the big winner. I don't know why you fell apart out there, Hayden. There's no reason you couldn't get a run tonight."

"My head wasn't in the game. After I missed that ball, I couldn't focus." Hayden admitted.

"I don't understand that excuse, Hayden. That's bullshit. You make a mistake, then you do better, work harder." Hayden's father halted his steps upon reaching the car, flushed and agitated, and pulled Hayden back by the shoulders to look him square in his eyes. "You don't fall apart, okay? That's what a little girl would do, not a man. You don't want to be a little girl, do you?"

"No, sir," Hayden replied, not daring to break eye contact, knowing it would make his father livid. He considered it a sign of weakness not to look a man in the eye when speaking.

"Don't let Mike be the hero all the time. In a few years you will both be in high school, and you don't want him to overshadow you. If you don't stand up and take what you want, you'll spend the rest of your life as the guy on the sidelines who lost out on the best job and the best girl. You don't get anywhere by being a nice guy. If you want to get what you deserve and be like your dad, then listen to me."

Hayden nodded his head and replied, "Yes, Dad."

Later at home, Hayden's father's anger escalated after drinking a bottle of beer and finding fault with the dinner his mother had prepared. Mid-meal, he threw his plate on the ground when Hayden's mother announced that she "*was proud*" of Hayden upon hearing that his walk to first base helped his team win the game.

They froze in their seats. His father rose, slammed his hands on the table, and rattled the plates. Startled, Hayden knocked over his glass of water. Pointing his finger in Hayden's mother's face, Gavin shouted, "Tell your son to get the fuck out of here and go to his room."

Hayden looked to his mother with tears forming in her eyes—she whispered, "Go, Hayden."

He ran out of the kitchen to his room, worried that if he did not move fast enough, it would further anger his father. Hayden listened at the door of his bedroom while his father carried on for twenty minutes, shouting and blaming his mother that "*Hayden is too soft*" and "*It's your fucking fault.*"

After the storm passed, and Hayden heard his father stalk through the living room to his parents' bedroom, he crept down the hall into the kitchen to check on his mother. Crouched on the floor, he watched her pick up the pieces of the broken dinner plate. Sensing Hayden behind her, she turned her head, and he saw her left cheek was pink. Meeting his eyes, she placed a finger on her lips, warning him not to make any noise.

Upon his death, Hayden's maternal grandfather, Hayden's namesake, left his small aircraft manufacturing company to Gavin Botero. Hayden did not remember his grandfather, who had passed away when he was two years old. Hayden's father, though, had looked up to him and called him *"the greatest man I knew,"* having lost his own father in a factory accident one month before he was born.

After Gavin's father died, his mother, a recent immigrant from Southern Italy, refused to return to her native country, dreaming that in America her son would have endless opportunities for a better life. After several years of working various jobs in textile factories and as a maid, she married a security officer who, according to Hayden's father, was *"a piece of shit of a human being."*

Hayden's father told him little about his childhood other than money was always tight, and he could only depend on his own efforts to push himself into a better life. Thirty years later, after Gavin's stepfather passed away, his mother moved back to Italy to care for her ailing sister.

Though Gavin had a rough childhood, he was brilliant, worked two jobs and put himself through college to study aerospace engineering. After graduating, Hayden Evans Clarke hired him to work as an associate test engineer for his aircraft manufacturing company and, claiming Gavin reminded him of himself at a young age, took him under his wing. One year later, he introduced Gavin to his youngest daughter, Clara.

Hayden's father was a tall man with an olive complexion, dark hair, hazel eyes, and a formidable athletic build. Considered handsome, he never lacked for attention from women, though it was not until he met Clara Clarke, a radiant beauty with chestnut hair and light-blue eyes, that he considered marriage. Her composure, elegance, and education were clear.

Marrying her would open doors for him, though his interest in her was not only for professional gain—he believed himself to be in love. Hayden's mother would often tell him his father *"swept in and stole my heart"* at nineteen years old. It would not be until years later that she would see the darker side of him emerge.

One night in eighth grade, not long after Hayden met Brea in the library, he worked up the courage to ask his mother about his father's anger.

"He wasn't always like this, Hayden. When we first married, he was charming, full of ambition, and he laughed a lot. Everywhere we went, he drew attention to himself, and my parents adored him. But for years I had trouble getting pregnant, and he struggled with that. Your grandpa Hayden pushed us a lot, not understanding why he didn't have a grandson from us. Sometimes I was successful in getting pregnant, but I couldn't hold on to the baby. Then, after many years of trying for children, we had you, and your father was over the moon. Things went well for a while, but then your grandpa Hayden passed away, and your father took over the company. There was a lot of pressure on his shoulders, and he always felt the need to shine brightest. He loves us, Hayden. But some people can't handle the world without a fight."

"Mom, sometimes he scares me," Hayden confessed.

Wrapping her arms around Hayden, she replied, "He won't hurt you, I promise."

"But he hurts you, and I'm worried—that you're going to leave." Hayden searched his mother's eyes. What he wanted to ask, though he did not dare, was why they could not leave and find a new place to live—only the two of them.

A tight-lipped smile formed on his mother's face. "I'm okay, Hayden, I promise. I'm not going anywhere. The only thing that could hurt me is if I weren't here with you while you had to live in this house. One day you'll be free, Hayden, and you'll make a life for yourself, just the way you want it."

"What if I become like him?" Hayden asked, staring at the floor.

His mother's mouth opened, and she drew in a deep breath. "Hayden, I see you. I know you inside and out. You have a gentle heart and a kindness inside you—bigger than that massive brain in your head. Never could you be your father. I promise you that."

Hayden nodded, though her reassurance could not banish the worry from his mind. Nearing high school, he knew his father's anger was abnormal. When he was home, the air in the room felt heavier, and Hayden and his mother walked on an endless tightrope, never knowing what minor issue could set him off.

Moreover, his father's expectations set an unattainable standard for Hayden. He even insisted as a child, Hayden start school a year later to have a one-year academic and athletic advantage over the other students. As the years passed, the pressure Hayden felt from his father became difficult to cope with. By the end of his freshman year, the constant stress, studying, and hours spent playing baseball exhausted Hayden, but he pushed himself to continue on.

Having his father's approval was not something he desired but a necessity to help shield his mother from his father's anger and constant criticism. If Hayden did not perform to his perfectionistic standards, his mother was the prime target of his father's anger.

Hayden's father did not beat him, but when furious, he could get rough with his hands, especially if Hayden attempted to intervene when he targeted his mother. It was not uncommon for him to shove him, push his face with his hand, or grab him by the shoulders, which often made his mother cry and escalated the situation. Despite Hayden's efforts to overachieve, his mother could not escape Gavin's physical abuse, though she would deny and attempt to hide any injuries she sustained.

Growing up in this environment, Hayden's personality developed so that he became adept at lessening the chance he would be a target of his father's anger. Besides staying at the top of his class and playing sports, he remained neutral, stoic, and displayed a calm, confident demeanor.

Unbeknownst to him in his youth, he had also developed an unintended superpower as well—he could pick up on subtle cues, shifts in mood imperceptible to others, changes in body language, and see what someone hid behind their eyes. The one thing Hayden could not figure out was how to save his mother from his father's fault-finding and violent outbursts.

Hayden hid the abuse he endured at home from everyone—neither Mike nor Vienna ever suspected or discovered the truth about the type of man his father was. With effortless poise and charm, Gavin Botero captivated family, friends, and colleagues. It was not until Hayden met Brea that he felt he could share the truth about what life was like for him at home—and even then he held back so much.

Following his last night with Brea, he lived with the fear of becoming his father. It took him many years to trust himself again and convince himself that he was the man his mother believed him to be—nothing like his father. Now, after twenty long years, he had the opportunity to prove it to Brea.

CHAPTER TWELVE

BREA

Drained from traveling and the emotional anticipation of the trip, Hayden and Brea slowed down. When Hayden finished telling her about his father, she closed her eyes and swallowed, saddened and horrified to learn of the severity of the abuse he and his mother endured.

"Hayden, I can't imagine what that was like for you. Suffering with your mother, alone with no help or someone to talk to. Did he realize what he had done to you and your mother? Do you have a relationship with him?"

"No, there was no remorse or apology. Several years after my mother died, he remarried and built a new life. He paid for college and business school, and I saw him on the holidays for a while. Now, we talk on the phone once a year, but it's more of a formality rather than his having any genuine interest in my life." Brea rested her chin in her hands, tilted her head and exhaled. Hearing Hayden's story had been more taxing and disturbing than expected. Both of them needed a break and a full night's sleep.

"Maybe we should get some rest," Hayden suggested after a pause.

Brea nodded. "Good idea. I'm going to stop at the front desk and have the cart drive me." Brea averted her gaze from Hayden as she continued. "I'm more comfortable with that than you walking me back to my room—at least for tonight." Hayden nodded his head. "That's okay, I get it."

"Well, what about tomorrow? What are we going to do?" she asked.

Hayden drew in a breath. "I haven't thought that far ahead. I'm going to wake up early to work out at the gym. Would you like to meet me?"

Brea smiled. "I admire your dedication to fitness, but maybe tomorrow I'll sleep in and go to the gym on Monday," she replied.

Hayden chuckled. "All right. How about we plan on meeting at the beach? I'll call your room in the morning."

"Sure." Brea rose from the table and paused, searching her mind what to say next.

Hayden stood and placed his hands in his pockets. "Goodnight, Brea."

"Right. Good night, Hayden." With an awkward wave, she turned to leave the restaurant.

Outside, the night air had cooled and a light breeze blew, carrying with it a faint smell of seaweed. The paths were lit with lanterns, and the night sky, filled with stars, was breathtaking.

As she walked, Brea pondered the question Hayden asked himself for years. "*Was he destined to be like his father?*" That thought crossed her mind many years ago, but now as she strolled down the path, and even though they had only spent a few hours with one another tonight—she knew in her body that Hayden was nothing like his father. His voice, their history, and his eyes—humbled and gentle—spoke to her bones that his mother had been right.

The following morning, Brea opened her eyes and stretched out her arms with a broad smile. The luxurious cotton bed sheet, soft as feathers, felt incredible wrapped around her skin, and the gentle breeze from the overhead fan blew over her neck and shoulders like a whisper. She slept through the night undisturbed, and woke tranquil and refreshed.

Brea rolled over, checked the clock on the nightstand and saw it was nine. Sitting up, she rose from bed, ambled to the patio doors and pulled open the curtains—she exhaled seeing the ocean and the clear sky, a shade of electric blue.

On the beach, she watched scattered couples strolling with coffee cups in hand and radiant smiles on their faces—the collective positive energy infused her with serenity. The hotel phone rang, interrupting her peaceful meditation. Brea hurried to the desk to answer the call.

"Good morning, how are you feeling?" Hayden's voice greeted her on the other end.

"Actually—fantastic. I rarely sleep this well, even when my kids are sleeping with me. How about you?"

Hayden blew out a breath. "I slept so well I was confused when I woke up. I didn't remember where I was for a moment."

Brea smiled. "So, are we going to the beach today?"

"Yes. I booked a private cabana and brunch service. They also talked me into booking a kayak excursion for us this afternoon—with a group. What do you think?"

"Sure. So, this trip is going to be like summer camp, huh?" Brea commented.

Hayden chuckled. "How about we meet at ten-thirty on the resort beach? The hostess will bring you over to our cabana for the day."

"Okay, see you then." Brea hung up.

Recalling the oversized stand-alone tub, Brea pranced into the bathroom. She opened the faucet and added a squirt of shampoo to make bubbles. When full, she climbed into the tub and the delicious warmth of the water enveloped her body and penetrated deep into her muscles. Brea hummed and the vibration from her nasal passages lulled her into a delicious state of quietude. Diane taught her that trick to help her relax when she felt anxious. Her thoughts drifted to the time she told Diane about Cylis, or at least as much as she had been willing to reveal.

❧

For two months, Brea met with Diane once a week. Now she slept through the night and had accomplished a better understanding of the severity of emotional neglect she endured throughout her childhood. Diane explained to her that, for some children with that form of abuse, it could leave the child with a profound sense of loneliness, difficulty setting personal boundaries, and a desperate need to seek the love denied to her as a child from a romantic partner.

"I don't think I read people very well, Diane. Someone I thought I could trust hurt me a couple of years ago, and I'm wondering, how could someone pretend to be a good person but turn out to be someone else?"

Diane shifted in her seat and nodded. "Well, sometimes a person hides a certain side of themselves, but often there are clues. I think I need a little more context to answer your question, Brea. Could you share a little more?"

"After my relationship ended with Jaime, I fell in love—well, I thought it was love. His name was Cylis. I thought he cared about me, that we were perfect for each other, but he turned out to be—evil. And one day—he trapped me in his house after giving me a drug. He wouldn't let me leave, and he—I'm sorry, I can't. It's too difficult."

"It's okay, Brea, if you aren't ready to talk about it. So, Cylis, he changed, and you were blind-sided?"

"Well, not exactly. I suppose I missed the warnings signs. Someone else—a friend of mine—tried to warn me about Cylis. I say he was a friend, but it was more complicated than that. Anyway, I thought I knew him and that I could trust him too. I had felt safe with him until he turned into someone else one night—it was terrifying."

"Can you tell me what happened?" Diane asked.

"It was right before my junior year ended. His mother died, and I was over at his house. He found out to an extent what Cylis did to me and lost it—angry, screaming, and then threw a glass jar at the wall."

Brea inhaled a deep breath. "All I remember seeing was blood—he had cuts on his legs and hands. When he left the room, I ran away, ran until I made it home. I refused to see him again after that night."

"Brea, I can see why that frightened you. After experiencing trauma, such as the one with Cylis, your body could be very sensitive to anything it perceives as danger. Did this boy realize he scared you?"

"I remember him apologizing, but it was like my brain shut down. All I could think about at the time was running. The point is, everything was my fault. I put myself into those situations, and I'm still so angry and confused."

"Brea, it wasn't your fault—though that is an unfortunate belief shared by many victims, for reasons we'll work on together. Cylis is accountable for his actions—no one else can take the blame for what he did. You mentioned this other boy's mother died. Do you know any more details about what happened?"

"Only that he found her dead in his living room coming home one morning after we had been out together. He wouldn't talk about it with me."

Diane paused and reflected before speaking. "Brea, I wasn't there and I know nothing about this boy, but I can say that for a young man or a teenager, to find his mother dead would have likely been a tremendous trauma. Sometimes people bury their trauma, live their lives, but when something stressful happens, they fall apart. There is no excuse for violence, but it's possible—to answer your question—someone may develop a post-traumatic stress disorder and have anger episodes, panic attacks, nightmares, or even dissociate. It's like when you aren't in your body or you can lose control. There could be many reasons."

Brea shook her head. She harbored too much anger and confusion to consider that idea. It would let Hayden off the hook.

"What are you thinking, Brea? Does that resonate with you, or maybe do you see some of those symptoms in yourself?"

Brea wiped her eyes. "I don't want to talk about it anymore."

Diane nodded. "Sometimes the mind isn't ready to process trauma, and we don't want to push. When you're ready, you'll know. It's different for everyone."

"What if I'm never ready, Diane?"

Diane smiled. "Well, you keep going. You can't predict when or what your path through the trauma will be. Sometimes it's gradual and takes time, or a switch flips and you're ready. Don't think about time. Let's focus on today and take things step by step."

Brea nodded and exhaled—but in her mind, she resolved to try harder to push her memories of Cylis and Hayden away, hoping they would never resurface.

Dressed in a light-blue one-piece bathing suit and a navy-colored silk sarong knotted around her waist, Brea stepped off the path onto the beach. Scanning from left to right, she spotted the hostess kiosk for the cabanas. Reaching the stand, the hostess greeted her.

"Good morning. I'm meeting Hayden Botero. He reserved a cabana for today. I'm Brea."

"Of course, Mrs. Botero. Please follow me."

Brea blinked twice and shook her head. "No, I'm Brea Tand—I mean, Staxon. I'm his guest, or a friend—not his wife."

"My apologies, Ms. Staxon, please follow me." With raised eyebrows, Brea followed the hostess to the cabana furthest from the stand on her right. Though a benign error, being mistaken for Hayden's wife left her unsettled.

"Mr. Botero ordered the brunch service. We have an assortment of pastries and fresh fruit arranged on the table, and we will serve a variety of hot dishes over the hour. Could I offer you coffee or a mimosa?"

"Coffee, please, for two," Brea replied with a smile.

The hostess nodded and left Brea to settle in. The white curtains, tied on the poles of the cabana, offered a full view of the beach and the water. For now, she was in shade and comfortable, though soon she would need to untie the curtains as the sun continued to rise.

The cabana housed two cushioned lounge chairs, a high-top rectangular table with juice, water, fruit and pastries in the rear, a small square table to set their food and drinks on, and a towel rack draped with plush white-and-blue striped beach towels.

Brea dropped her beach bag on the floor beside the lounge chair and surveyed the pastries on the tiered serving stand. Choosing a croissant, she bit off a large bite and her eyes fluttered. "Oh, amazing," she proclaimed, savoring the flaky pastry melting in her mouth. Seating herself on the edge of the lounge chair, she watched the waves and devoured the remaining croissant. While brushing off the flakes that had fallen on her lap with both hands, Hayden arrived.

"Good morning," he said, watching Brea as she wiped the crumbs off her lap. "Did any of that make it into your mouth?" he teased.

Brea chuckled and studied him dressed in a white T-shirt and black swim trunks. Placing his sunglasses and room card on the small table, Hayden went to fill a glass with orange juice. Upon his return, he sat across from Brea in the opposite lounge chair.

She smiled and let out a sigh. "You know what, I think there's something about being here, sleeping by the ocean. It's like—magic."

Hayden stared at Brea and held his glass suspended in mid-air.

"What? What did I say?" Brea asked with wide eyes.

"Nothing, just—that's something my mom would say about the ocean—that it was magic."

"Oh," she replied, lowering her eyes and slipping her feet out of her sandals. "Hayden—"

The server entered the cabana with their coffee, placed a tray with a carafe, cups, cream, and sugar on the table between the loungers and then poured them each a steaming hot cup. After introducing himself, he informed them that an assortment of French toast, bacon, sausages, roasted breakfast potatoes, eggs, and quiche would arrive in fifteen minutes. Brea and Hayden thanked the server and with a nod, he turned and left them to enjoy their coffee.

Both Brea and Hayden drank several sips before Hayden spoke. "What did you want to say before?"

Brea reclined on the lounger and pulled up her legs to make herself comfortable. "I'd like to know more about your mom. Also, if you can tell me, what happened to her—how she died."

Hayden turned his head to gaze at the ocean. "It's difficult to talk about."

Brea nodded. "I know you said you wouldn't hold back, but I understand if you can't talk about it."

Hayden turned to face Brea and clasped his hands between his knees. "I'm ready. Her name was Clara, and she was—a lot like you, Brea."

CHAPTER THIRTEEN

HAYDEN

"Come sit next to me on the sofa, Hayden." It was the night of Jasmine's party, but Hayden was not in a particular rush to leave the house. He planned to drive himself, and his only motivation for attending was to keep an eye on Brea. Several days prior, their paths crossed in the courtyard at school, and she mentioned that Tory and Allegra had convinced her to celebrate with them at the party after the SAT.

His mother, dressed in her pajamas and a robe, sat on the sofa in the family room flipping through a culinary magazine. With his father out for the night to entertain an important client, it left him and his mother to enjoy the evening alone. His father's absence provided a welcome relief from the tense energy that clung to the air when at home.

"How are you feeling, Mom?"

Giving Hayden a wink, she smiled. "I'm all right—but I wish I had your energy." Hayden sank onto the sofa beside his mother, and she wrapped her arm around his shoulders. "So, what are you up to tonight? A party or a date? It's been a long time since you've had a steady girlfriend."

Hayden glanced at his mother with an awkward grin. "Mom, I don't want to talk about girls with you."

"Okay, I understand," she conceded with a laugh. "But I would love to be around for you one day, when you're married and have children. You are so big now—I don't know how the time went by so fast, and soon you'll be leaving for MIT."

Hayden winced. He disliked it when she referenced the future and implied she might not be around for it. Her doctors could not give her a definitive prognosis, but with treatment, they hoped she could have decades to live—albeit with a questionable quality of life. Lately, the doctors were considering the possibility she could have an undiagnosed overlapping condition, and one mentioned that stress could be a contributing factor to her rapid progression—and that worried Hayden. Every day, living in their home with his father was stressful.

"Mom, I don't want to leave you alone with Dad. Maybe it would be better if I went somewhere closer to home. I could withdraw from MIT and start another school in the spring."

Hayden's mother pulled her arm back and turned to face him. "Look at me, Hayden—no. The only thing that would break my heart is knowing you gave up this incredible opportunity for me. It's your time to leave and I want you to be free, okay? You promise me?"

Hayden broke eye contact with his mother and stared at the scar on his knuckles, a consequence of his father finding out Hayden received a B on his chemistry final the previous year. From his bedroom, he heard his mother pleading with his father to calm down in the hall on his way to Hayden's room.

Hearing an awful thump against the wall in the hallway, Hayden burst out of his room and saw her lying on the ground, holding the back of her head. Running to help her, his father blocked his path, but for the first time, Hayden fought back. At eighteen and the same height, he nearly equaled his father's strength. Bypassing contemplation, and with the element of surprise on his side, he grabbed his father's shoulders and pushed him aside.

When Hayden stepped forward, his father attempted to grab him on his left shoulder to spin him around, but Hayden evaded him and pushed his father into the wall. His father recovered and lunged at him with tremendous force, knocking Hayden into the opposite wall. Then, grabbing Hayden's right arm, he slammed his hand against a hanging picture frame. Hayden's hand cracked the glass, and a broken piece sliced the skin over his knuckles.

Seeing Hayden's bloodied hand, his father backed off, allowing Hayden to help his mother off the floor. Two nights later, Brea noticed his injured hand at the party after Jaime's big win at the Lacrosse All-Stars game. To this day, Hayden remembered in vivid detail first seeing her that night, dressed in the sultry ivory dress with what at the time he believed was a blue butterfly across her torso. Consumed by desire, he near lost his mind and strode over to kiss her in the middle of the room.

"Hayden, do you hear me?" his mother repeated. Hayden's mind shifted back to the present.

"I don't want you to get hurt, Mom."

His mother smiled and wrapped her arm around him again. "I'm tougher than you think, kiddo. You have a big heart, and you put yourself second too much. I will not let you do that for me. Promise me you'll fight for yourself, all right? I know you're going to have a wonderful life. I know it." Hayden nodded.

"All right, give me a hug—a big, fat Hayden hug." Hayden chuckled. His mother used to say that to him when dropping him off at elementary school and before tucking him into bed at night when he was little. It had been many years since she last spoke those words. Hayden embraced her, careful not to squeeze her as she had lost a significant amount of weight over the previous several months and, although irrational, he worried he could break a bone if he held her too tight.

"I love you, Hayden. Always remember that you have been the light of my life," she whispered in his ear.

"I love you too, Mom."

"Okay, get out of here. Go find love, your soulmate—it will make me smile." Settling herself back on the sofa, she shooed Hayden away with her hand and watched him walk out of the room. Turning back to look at his mother, he smiled and waved. He could not help it—he would still consider withdrawing even if his father went crazy on him for it.

Later that night, parked on the private beach with Brea, he woke up and watched her as she slept. Never had he felt such contentment, and in that moment, he decided he no longer wanted to be without Brea nor leave his mother at home alone with his father—he would withdraw from MIT. But before telling his father, he would need to devise a strategy to protect his mother from the fallout.

After dropping Brea off at her house, he brimmed with optimism and hope. He would call Brea later that afternoon and tell her he would do whatever it took for them to be together—confront Jamie with the truth and protect her from Vienna. If he could convince Brea that together they would overcome any backlash from Harvey Slate, then he would bring her over to meet his mother. He knew she would adore Brea and, after meeting her, understand his decision.

Hayden climbed out of his car, bounded up the walkway to the house, unlocked the door, and slipped inside quietly not to wake his parents. He walked through the living room towards the kitchen for a glass of water, replaying the events of the evening in his mind, in particular the part when Brea kissed him in the supermarket parking lot. Dropping his keys on the floor, he swung around to pick them up. As he straightened, he noticed his mother lying across the sofa with her arm and one leg dangling over the edge.

Hayden froze. "Mom?"

He took a few steps closer—she was still. Approaching her, a sense of unease crept into his body. Once several feet from her, he studied her face and seeing her lips parted and eyes slitted open, he rushed to her side.

"Mom," he shouted. Hayden dropped to his knees, shook her arm and touched her skin—her lips had a blue tinge, and there was neither warmth nor life in her body.

"Dad," he screamed. Hayden did not know what to do. "Dad," he screamed again and clasped his mother's icy hands in his. His father burst into the foyer, dressed in his pajamas with a bewildered expression on his face.

Hayden continued his efforts to rouse her, shaking her shoulders and hands in a futile yet desperate attempt to revive his mother. She was only sleeping—the alternative was not possible. Locked in a state of disbelief, he told himself he was only having a nightmare and that he would soon wake up.

Gavin hurried to the kitchen and called for an ambulance while Hayden wrapped his arms around his mother's frail body. "Mom, please," he repeated, holding her. "Mom, wake up." A profound sense of dread consumed him as the devastating reality set in—this was not a dream, and she was dead.

In shock, Gavin reentered the room and stood behind Hayden until hearing sirens approaching the neighborhood in the distance. Walking to the door, Hayden's father unlocked it and waited on the porch, leaving Hayden with his mother in his arms beside the sofa.

The police officers entered first, and a moment later, the EMTs rushed inside. An officer placed a hand on Hayden's shoulder. "Son, you're going to need to move aside. The paramedics need to examine your mother."

Hayden would not move and shook his head. "No," he whispered through his tears. "Please move aside," the officer repeated.

"Hayden, get up," his father barked.

The officer placed another hand on Hayden's other shoulder. "Hayden, please move so we can take a look and help."

He squeezed Hayden's shoulders with a gentle touch. Hayden pulled back and looked into the officer's face, a middle-aged man with a dark mustache and bright blue eyes, his expression soft and sympathetic.

"Please, son," the officer repeated. Hayden let go of his mother, stood up, and took a step back. His father placed his hand on Hayden's shoulders, but he stepped away, finding his father's touch unnerving.

The officer gestured to his partner to join him, a younger male officer with short blonde hair. "Officer Mills, can you please take this young man into the kitchen?" The officer looked to Hayden's father. He nodded and pointed in the kitchen's direction.

Officer Mills went to Hayden. "I'll help you to the kitchen. I'm going to take your arm, okay?" Hayden did not respond and allowed himself to be led away.

The officer pulled out a chair for Hayden at the table. Numb, he sat down and rested his hands on his legs. "What's your name again?" Officer Mills asked.

"Hayden," he answered.

"Hayden, I'm going to ask you a few questions." He glanced at the officer and nodded.

"Can you tell me what happened?" Hayden detailed everything he could remember after walking in the front door.

"You said you came home a little while ago. Where were you all night?"

"At a party, then at the beach."

"Were you alone or with someone at the beach?"

Hayden answered without hesitation—he did not want the police to go to Brea's house to question her. "Alone," he replied. "I drove to a private beach in Tupa Bay. I go there sometimes to watch the water, and I fell asleep."

"Was the door locked when you came home?"

Hayden nodded. "Yes, I used my keys to unlock the door."

"Do you think anyone would try to hurt your mother?"

Hayden shook his head. He would say nothing about his father's anger or abuse as he did not think it possible that his father could have killed her—it was unthinkable. "She has Parkinson's disease, sees a lot of specialists, and takes many medications."

Officer Mills jotted several notes in his pad, nodded, then stepped out of the room. Hayden did not know how long he sat at the kitchen table, staring out the window into his backyard. At some point, he felt his father's hand on his shoulder.

"Hayden. Angela is on her way over to prepare some suitcases for us, and then we're driving over to your Aunt Isabella's house. If you want to take a shower, do it soon, and if you want to bring anything in particular with you, you'll need to get it."

Hayden looked at his father, searching his eyes for any guilt, remorse, or sadness—but he saw nothing—they were blank. Lowering his eyes to the table, he nodded.

Ten minutes later, Angela burst into the kitchen, flew to Hayden, cradled his face in her hands and looked into his eyes, murmuring in Portuguese. She knelt before him and wrapped her arms around him. Hayden did not cry—he sat still, unable to move or react.

"Hayden baby, I'll pack for you. I will get your books for school, clothes, everything. Then I'll make you food to take with you. Don't worry about anything." Angela kissed the top of his head and hurried off. Hayden continued to stare out the window into the backyard.

Several days later, Hayden overheard his father share with Aunt Isabella the preliminary results of the autopsy. She died of respiratory and heart failure, and there were several drugs detected in her body that may have contributed to her death.

Hayden's father suggested that his mother could have been confused and overdosed unintentionally, though there were no large quantities of missing pills when the police had searched through her prescriptions. But Hayden's mother had accumulated many old containers of muscle relaxers, pain and anxiety medications that were only used on an as-needed basis with various quantities in the bottles. The autopsy did not reveal any injuries to her body.

His father had told the police he returned home at ten o'clock and she was alive, reading on the sofa, and told him she would come to bed once finished with her magazine. He had fallen asleep in his bedroom, awakening only upon hearing Hayden calling for him in the morning.

Hayden could not return to the house for over a month and stayed with his Aunt Isabella, his mother's older sister. His father spoke with Headmaster Carter at Harvey Slate, and they agreed it would be best for Hayden to finish the year through home study and take his finals in a private room during finals week.

While staying with his aunt, Hayden isolated himself. Other than studying and completing his school assignments, he ate little and slept. He never cried—rather, he felt numb and weighed down with guilt, believing he could have prevented her death if only he had begged her to leave his father. Every day he thought of Brea, but could not bring himself to charge his phone and call her. If he heard her voice, he feared he would lose himself in grief, weep, and never recover.

Almost a month passed, and Aunt Isabella entered his room and sat on the edge of his bed. She was worried and on the cusp of calling her doctor to recommend a psychiatrist for Hayden.

"Hayden. I need to talk to you. You don't have to talk, but I need you to listen."

Hayden slept in his cousin Arie's room, who was finishing his spring semester at an out-of-state college. Lying on the bed, he rolled over to face his aunt, but he did not have the energy to sit up.

"I loved Clara so much. It hurts—every day I wake up and remember that she is gone. I want her back too. I don't know why we lose people we love, good people who are young, and kind and wonderful down to their toes. It's going to hurt, like a knife in the gut—for a long time, honey. But I know your mom—she did everything for you and sacrificed so much to give you the life you deserve. She had a hard life with your dad, and she tried to hide it from me—but I knew. You are going to keep pushing forward. Do it for her and honor everything she did for you. Maybe she should have left your father, but you have to know you couldn't have saved her. I know you, and it breaks my heart to think you might blame yourself. And I know you'll be okay—I know it. But, if you don't start eating at least two meals a day and spend at least an hour outside of this room starting tomorrow, I'm calling a psychiatrist."

Hayden nodded. Aunt Isabella leaned down and kissed him on the cheek. Hayden felt tears forming in his eyes, but still, he did not cry. She picked up his hand and sat with him until he fell asleep. He did what his aunt asked of him, and one week later, he returned home with his father.

Two days after arriving home, he called Brea. He needed her—she was all he had left. Relieved he would see her on Saturday, he exhaled after hanging up the phone and sat down at his desk. He would have to study for his physics final for the rest of the night. Tossing his phone onto his desk, his eyes fixed on something odd.

In the middle of a stack of books on his desk, sandwiched between an atlas and an astronomy book, was a children's book. Hayden pulled it out. His lips parted slightly when he saw the cover—The Velveteen Rabbit. It was the book his mother read to him every night when he was in elementary school.

Searching his mind, he did not know how it got there. He opened it and saw writing on the flyleaf—it was his mother's handwriting. He read the words. "*I love you, Hayden. You were the magic in my life. Live every day with joy, find love, and don't let it go. You are free, and I will always be with you. Love, Mom.*"

Hayden pushed his chair back from the desk and clutched the book in his hands, knowing what his mother had done to set him free. He doubled over and bit his hand so that his father would not hear him sobbing. He cried for his mother, her life's pain, her selfless love, and her sacrifice. But it was not only grief that consumed him—something else woke deep within him—anger.

Chapter Fourteen

BREA

Hayden paused and looked out at the ocean. Brea wiped her eyes. A heavy ache sat in her chest, unable to imagine the depth of Hayden's grief after not only losing his mother but discovering she had taken her own life.

"What you went through, Hayden, though I felt so bad for you—I was so wrapped up in my world, I didn't see how much you were struggling."

He rubbed his forehead. "You couldn't have known. I never told you. I should have, but I kept it all in."

They sat in silence until Hayden continued. "The crazy thing is she knew I wouldn't listen to her and would withdraw from MIT. Maybe it wasn't crazy—she just knew me too well. I know she was suffering and her illness was progressing, but I have to admit, sometimes I'm still angry with her for taking her own life. I know it's selfish, but I wanted her with me—instead, she left me alone."

Brea shook her head. "Wanting your mother isn't selfish—it's human. Everything you felt was and is normal. I don't know if this will help, but being a mother, I understand what it feels like—willing to do anything to help your children. Even sacrificing yourself if it meant you could save them." Brea paused and continued. "I wish I could have met her, Hayden. It sounds like she was a wonderful mother and such a brave woman."

Hayden sniffed and met Brea's eyes. "I think—she would have loved you."

Brea's lips parted, uncertain how to reply. Hayden continued. "I told no one about finding that book. It was our secret, me and my mom's. But—I always knew if I would tell anyone, it would be you."

Brea sat upright and faced Hayden. Leaning forward, she reached out and placed a hand on Hayden's hands, clasped together between his knees. Hayden looked down, then into Brea's eyes, surprised she touched him.

Clearing her throat, she pulled away her hand, and scanned the casita. The hot dishes sat untouched, and the food was now cold on the table. "We should eat something, Hayden, all this food is going to be thrown away if we don't."

Hayden glanced over his shoulder. "Would that be the worst thing that could happen?"

Brea replied with an air of exasperation. "Yes, Hayden. There are people starving all over the world. I don't waste food in my house, and we will not waste food here."

"Yes, ma'am," Hayden replied, holding up his hands in surrender. A smile spread across his face, amused by Brea's passion.

They stood to fill their plates and then returned to their respective lounge chairs. Hayden squinted and eyed the cold food on his plate, and then looked up at Brea. "Do I have to eat the whole plate?"

Brea pressed her lips together. "Fine, at least half."

Hayden dropped the fork on the lounge chair, picked up a piece of French toast and, using his fingers, topped it with scrambled eggs and a piece of bacon. Slapping on another slice of French toast, he made a breakfast sandwich. Surveying it first, he took a bite.

Brea's mouth gaped open, but after a moment of consideration she said, "You know what? That's a great idea." After making her own sandwich, she took a big bite, chuckling as bits of egg dropped onto her plate.

Watching one another as they ate, they laughed, both admitting they could not stomach anymore after several more bites—it was too cold and unappetizing.

"I'm going to get in the water," Hayden said, dropping what remained of the sandwich onto the plate. Wiping his hands on a napkin, he asked, "Do you want to join me?"

"Soon. I want to read for a little while. It's been at least three months since I've read a book."

"Okay, nerd," he replied with a smirk. Hayden removed his shirt, threw it on the lounge chair, and grabbed a towel off the rack. Brea averted her eyes and stared at the cover of her book—she did not feel comfortable looking at him without his shirt on.

"Hayden, aren't you forgetting something?" Brea asked without looking up. Hayden turned to her with a puzzled expression.

"Brea, I'm not eating more of the cold food," he said, holding up his hands in protest.

"No, sunscreen. You don't want to get burned."

"Wow, you are such a mom. I already put it on in the room."

Brea, embarrassed, chuckled. "Oh, right. Just a mom habit."

"It's nice to know you care, though," he said with a grin.

Brea sighed and nodded. "Okay, go. Enjoy your swim."

Hayden laughed and ventured out onto the beach. Brea lowered the back of her lounger and opened her book, a romantic novel she bought over a year ago and never read. With a smile, she turned to the first chapter, eager to lose herself in the story.

Brea woke up, covered with a beach towel and the cabana's side curtains were now drawn to block out the sun. Hearing a server moving about the cabana behind her, she turned and a woman was setting up a soft drink bar.

"Señora Staxon, I have a menu for you to choose what you would like for lunch. Mr. Botero had to take a phone call in the hotel and asked that I not disturb you and let you sleep. This is for you." The server held a note in her hand.

Brea yawned, thanked the server, and took the folded piece of paper from her hand. "What time is it?" she asked, having left her phone in the casita.

"Twenty minutes past twelve. Your reservation for the kayak excursion is at one-thirty," the server replied.

"Oh, all right." Brea flipped open the note and read it. "*I'll be back by 12:30. Order me what you're having for lunch.*" Brea picked up the menu, scanned it, and ordered two salmon salads.

"Could I bring you a drink?" the server asked.

"Yes, a lemonade or whatever you have set up would be great."

The server set to work. In making a lemonade, she took her time, fussing with various ingredients as though concocting a magic potion. After placing the glass on a tray, she offered it to Brea.

"Wow, this looks great," Brea remarked after thanking the server. The glass contained mashed green leaves and fresh berries. Taking a sip, her mouth dropped open. "Oh my, this is fantastic! This might be the best drink I've ever had. There's no alcohol in this, right?" Brea sucked down half the glass through the straw.

"No alcohol. It's fresh lemons, sugar, basil, mint, macerated blueberries and strawberries."

"It's amazing. Could you make me another one after I finish this? Oh, and one for Hayden when he comes back, please."

Brea chatted with the server while she fixed Brea another lemonade. After several large sips, Brea stood up to stretch. It was hot, and after sleeping under the towel, her chest was damp. Ready to swim, she headed out of the cabana.

Feeling the blistering hot sand on her bare soles, Brea quickened her pace to reach the water. She stepped in as a wave broke on the shore and the water, refreshing and cool, submerged her feet. Looking to the horizon, she closed her eyes, then extended her neck back. The scorching sun penetrated her skin, enveloping her with soul-reviving warmth.

She waded in further, laced her fingers together behind her neck, and stopped when the water depth reached her hips. The waves nudged her back, but she remained balanced and steady. Lowering her arms, her fingers grazed and danced on the surface of the water, lifting her up and down as her body cut through the waves—she felt connected to the earth, grounded and content.

In the short time on this trip, she had to admit that she did not miss Adam—she felt relief. Capturing a piece of seaweed with her fingers, she played with it and thought back to a law firm dinner they attended two months ago.

Brea knew all the guests, and although they socialized well with one another, it was an exhausting effort to fit in with the wives of Adam's law firm partners. They were women with high-profile professional careers and bold, outspoken personalities. Before arriving at the restaurant, Brea felt insecure and hurt. Adam, cold and distant throughout the evening, failed to acknowledge the effort Brea had put into her appearance that evening, dressed in a body-hugging teal cocktail dress and silver high heels.

Seated across from Brea and Adam were Courtney and James, the couple they often spent the most time with at these events. They were both polished and accomplished, but competitive, condescending, and rather opinionated regarding the correct way to raise children, even though they had none.

"Brea, I hear you're still working at that interior design studio. Good for you," Courtney said between bites of her sea scallops. She wore an austere black cocktail dress, fire-engine red lipstick, and had styled her dark brown hair in a tight knot at the nape of her neck.

"I am, though it's actually a beach-themed home décor boutique. And I've started some restoration work on small pieces of furniture. I've sold every piece I've completed so far, and I'm thinking of working on larger items—dressers, coffee tables, and such. We don't have extra help or space in the shop for now, but I was thinking maybe I could rent a small artist's studio and put in some extra time now that Sophie is getting older. Maybe even start a small business if I become skilled at it. There's something so satisfying about working with my hands and seeing the finished project."

"That sounds wonderful. I'll have to come by one day and see your work, though our taste is contemporary rather than shabby chic beach décor," Courtney replied with a politician's smile.

Adam cleared his throat. "Well, don't encourage her. She's gone so much already. I'm worried our children will soon call our nanny 'Mommy'."

Brea lowered her eyes and gripped her fork tighter. "I work three days a week, not that much. And my friend Hannah owns the shop. She's very understanding when I can't work if Alex or Sophie is sick."

Courtney and James exchanged a glance. James smoothed his slicked-back blonde hair and chimed in. "I don't know Adam. It's concerning how women nowadays are making the choice to have kids and then outsource raising them. Brea should think about cutting back—three days a week is a lot. Especially when your children are so young."

Brea swallowed, insulted that James spoke to Adam as though Brea was only an appendage and had no mind of her own.

Adam nodded in agreement. "You have a point, James. Brea, what's more important, old furniture or the kids? There's an obvious choice there." The three of them laughed and fixed their eyes on Brea.

Brea managed an awkward smile. "Of course, my children, they are the most important. But it's nice to have something for myself—it was only a thought." Brea wanted to stab herself in her leg with her fork as Adam turned away from her with no consideration for her feelings. Be polite, be compliant—that was the message.

Now gazing into the vast ocean, she embraced the host of emotions she felt, knowing the tension and pretense of needing to be neutral, calm, and pleasant she had left behind at home. Today, she could be impassioned, morose, petulant, sarcastic, and there would be no need to conceal it. It was liberating, and Brea had an epiphany—one she never considered before. Maybe her feelings were not the enemy?

Brea jumped up and allowed herself to fall into the water, abandoning herself to the will of the ocean as it pushed her towards the shore. The salty water enveloped her body and it was as though she had been reborn and welcomed back to another part of herself that she buried for decades. Washing up on the shore, she would stand and run back into the water, repeating her high-spirited water play until her hair was in knots and her body covered in sand. She felt a long-lost feeling—pure, unfiltered joy.

Chapter Fifteen

Hayden

When Hayden returned from his swim, Brea was asleep with her book on her chest. Hayden held his breath upon seeing her voluminous caramel brown hair spread over her shoulders and a bare leg visible where her sarong had opened. He did not want to allow himself to think it—but he could not ignore how beautiful she appeared.

The hostess entered and informed him that his administrative assistant was trying to reach him to join an urgent meeting in the hotel conference room. "Thank you, I'll head over in a minute," he replied. To break his trance, he averted his gaze from Brea, covered her with a beach towel, and departed the cabana.

One hour later, Hayden exited the conference call. An urgent issue had required his presence at an emergency meeting with his product manager and software development leadership team. Leaning back in his chair, Hayden stared at the ceiling. His cell phone rang. "Shit," he whispered, seeing Avery's name upon checking the screen—he forgot to call her last night. After several rings, he answered, knowing it would be unwise to avoid her.

"Hi Avery."

"Hayden, I was getting worried. You said you would call me last night. What happened?"

Hayden rubbed his forehead. "Nothing. After checking in, I fell asleep, and I had to get up early to drive to a meeting. I had a break just now."

"Okay," she replied, then paused. Neither of them spoke for a moment.

"How was your morning?" Hayden asked to break the silence.

"Fine. I'm about to meet Michelle for lunch. You know she's planning her wedding, and she always has a hundred things she wants my opinion on."

"Sounds great. Look, I have to hang up. I'll call you tonight if you're still awake."

"Okay, I miss you."

"You too, bye." Hayden closed his eyes—lying to Avery felt terrible. He left the conference room, strode through the lobby, and followed the path to the beach. In his note to Brea, he wrote he would be back by twelve-thirty, and it was now twelve-forty.

Reaching the cabana, he found it empty. Brea's bag sat on the ground beside her lounge chair, and her book on the table. Opening the curtains, he peered out to the shore and spotted Brea in the water. He put on his sunglasses and stepped onto the beach to watch her.

A grin spread across his face, witnessing Brea splashing and jumping in and out of the water like a child. She still wore her sarong, now wet, and it had bunched up and clung to her hips. Her body was beautiful—healthy and lean, but with curves she did not have as a teenager. The smile on her face, her abandonment of any self-conscious inhibition, brought him back to the nights they spent together in Black Harbor when she would tease him and make him laugh. Seeing her this carefree and joyful already made the trip worth it.

Observing her at this moment was a stark contrast to the day he followed her to the Museum of Natural History with her family two weeks prior. He wore a baseball hat and tracked them throughout the museum, careful to keep his distance. Within twenty minutes of following them he recognized a dire problem with her marriage. Adam was detached and cold towards Brea, and her face and body language would change when they spoke to one another—that is, with what little they interacted with each other.

At one point, Brea excused herself and rushed out of the butterfly hall. Hayden followed her. She clutched her purse and hurried to the bathroom, disappearing inside for several minutes. When she emerged, she wiped her eyes and her nose several times. Hayden knew intimately what Brea looked like when she cried, and he knew she had fallen apart in the bathroom.

When they ate lunch as a family, Brea played with her children, concocting a dinosaur battle with chicken nuggets her children found hilarious. At one point, she tried to recruit her husband to play with the kids, but he waved her away, engrossed in his phone. Brea attempted to conceal her distress from her children, smiling and roaring with her kids, but Hayden saw her turn her head, place her chin in her hand, and squeeze her eyes shut.

He knew Brea, no matter how many years had passed—she was struggling and unhappy. The universe brought them back together for a reason, against all odds, and he could not turn his back on her. Most would consider what they were doing together in Mexico to be deceitful, but now, he felt certain bringing her here had been one of the better decisions of his life.

After rinsing herself off once more in the water, Brea crossed the sand back to the cabana and paused upon seeing Hayden on the beach watching her. With a self-conscious smile, she smoothed down her sarong over her legs and attempted to untangle her hair with her fingers.

"Is everything all right?" Brea asked upon reaching him.

"Yeah, fine. Just a snag in a program we're developing. You ready to eat?"

"Yes, I ordered us a salmon salad."

Hayden smiled. "Sounds good. I'm starving."

"And a bread basket. Just in case the salad wasn't filling enough," Brea added.

"Perfect, thanks," Hayden replied with a smile. Brea had read his mind.

Together they returned to the cabana, walking beside one another. "You were having a lot of fun out there," he commented. "I wasn't sure if you were bonding with the dolphins or what."

Brea laughed. "Yeah, it's going to be hell trying to comb my hair later. Oh, our server said our kayak reservation is at one-thirty, so we have to eat fast." Hayden nodded, seeing the food had arrived, set on the table between their lounge chairs.

"Hayden, try Margaretta's lemonade—it's amazing. The best drink I've ever had."

"Who is Margaretta?" Hayden asked with furrowed brows.

"One of our servers. She's working here to put herself through nursing school, and she has seven younger brothers and sisters. Margaretta is lovely and deserves a big tip," she whispered.

Hayden smiled at Brea's sincerity. Margaretta returned, and seeing Hayden, went to fix them a glass of her special lemonade. Brea grinned as Margaretta presented the drinks to them on the tray.

"Thank you, Margaretta," Hayden said, aware that both women studied him to glimpse his reaction as he drank. Taking a sip, Hayden nodded and raised his eyebrows. "Incredible," he proclaimed and then took another sip. The two women exchanged smiles.

"Enjoy your lunch." Margaretta nodded and exited the cabana.

They ate and exchanged stories of their life-changing events over the previous decades. Brea shared with Hayden what it was like having her children and revealed more details about her pregnancies and childbirth than Hayden needed to know. Regardless, he listened and laughed alongside her, impressed with how brave and tough women were birthing children. Hayden then described to Brea how he founded and developed his software company. The time passed, and the moment arrived for them to set off on their kayaking excursion.

CHAPTER SIXTEEN

BREA

New to kayaking, Hayden and Brea embraced their need for laughter, patience, and a bit of fumbling for them to find their rhythm. To their mutual amusement, they nearly capsized but managed to remain upright. They did not speak of the past, or much at all, but enjoyed the tranquility of the ocean. In the distance, they glimpsed a dolphin, and Hayden teased Brea that after watching her swim earlier, that was her spirit animal.

"Nope. It's too soon. Do more research," she declared.

"Okay, fair enough," he replied and chuckled.

It was not until after five o'clock that they returned to their rooms to rest and freshen up before dinner. Before leaving the cabana, Hayden asked the hostess to book them a reservation at one of the resort restaurants, and they agreed to meet in the lobby at six o'clock.

Strolling along the path to her casita, Brea noticed the strap of her bag chafed the skin on her shoulder. "Oh, no," she mumbled—she had forgotten to reapply sunscreen after her swim. Entering her room, she hurried through the casita to examine her body in the bathroom mirror. Sure enough, her arms, shoulders, and chest were pink. Fortunately, she had worn a hat, protecting her face.

If she acted with speed, she could ease the swelling using a personalized skincare plan that worked for her children when they had sunburns. Rooting through her toiletry case, she plucked out her ibuprofen gel capsules and a small tube of aloe vera gel.

Brea filled up the bathtub with cool water, swallowed two pain relievers and submerged herself under the water for fifteen minutes. After patting her skin dry, she cracked open several of the pain relievers and spread the gel on the pink-tinged areas. It was five-thirty and her shoulders were still tender. She would not tolerate the chafing of any straps or fabric on her body that evening. Groaning, she picked up the phone and punched in Hayden's casita number.

"Brea?" Hayden answered.

"How did you know it was me?" Brea asked with surprise.

"Just a guess. I don't think anyone else would call me on this line."

"Right. Look, I got a sunburn. It's not terrible, but it hurts, and I can't wear a shirt or anything on my shoulders. If I do my regimen tonight, soak in a cold tub again and lather on aloe every thirty minutes, I should be fine in the morning. So, I'll have to stay in rather than meet you out for dinner."

"Well, didn't the universe just bite you in the ass today? 'Oh, Hayden, didn't you forget something'?" he mocked Brea with glee.

"Shut up. I put on sunscreen, but I forgot to reapply it. You just had to get one over on me—I'll get you back for that," Brea proclaimed.

Hayden laughed. "I'm sorry. Okay, tell you what. Do whatever you need to do, and the least I can do is send you room service. I'll return the favor since you ordered lunch for me."

"Thanks. If I'm better in the morning, I'll go to the early yoga class. I should be back around eight if you want to make plans for the day."

"Join me in the gym after yoga. Otherwise, I'll call you when I'm back from working out."

"Maybe. Goodnight, Hayden."

"Goodnight, Crispy," Hayden teased.

"Oh, shut up." Brea hung up on Hayden before he could say anything further. Looking out the patio doors, she chuckled, remembering what a smartass Hayden was.

⁂

One hour later, there was a knock on the door. "Room service, Señora Staxon."

Brea opened the door. Her eyes widened in surprise at seeing two members of the hotel staff at her door—one with a tray of food and another with a cellophane-wrapped gift basket with a silver ribbon. "What is all of this?" she asked as she waved them into the casita.

The server replied, "Courtesy of Señor Botero." Brea watched the server arrange a bowl of chicken soup, a grilled cheese sandwich, and a teapot with an assortment of tea, honey, and lemon on the dining table. Brea laughed. "What is this? I don't have a cold," she mumbled to herself and laughed, but it was a sweet gesture.

The hotel staff turned to wish Brea a good night, then left her to enjoy her dinner and sort through the gift basket. Inside, she found a large bottle of aloe vera gel, a box of pain relievers, various bottles of sunscreen, disposable cold packs, and half a dozen packages of cookies and candy bars—Brea bit her lower lip and smiled.

Once seated at the table, she dipped the grilled cheese sandwich into the soup and took a bite. "Oh, damn," she said and moaned. The thick, buttery slices of fried bread soaked in the salty broth, combined with the thick layer of cheddar and gruyere cheese, transported her into culinary nirvana. "Maybe he's the smartest man alive," Brea said out loud as she devoured her dinner. After finishing her meal, Brea refilled the tub and climbed back in to soak in a cold bath for her next round of water therapy.

Chapter Seventeen

Brea

Upon awakening in the morning, Brea pressed her fingers on her chest and shoulders and sighed in relief. The pain had diminished, but she would need to be extra careful to limit her sun exposure for the day. Checking the time, she picked up the casita phone and called the concierge to double-check the yoga schedule at the wellness center. There was a class starting in thirty minutes. Brea sprang out of bed, changed into a black yoga top and matching leggings, and slathered on a generous layer of aloe and sunscreen.

She stepped outside, and although it was early, the temperature was well over eighty degrees. Regardless, she felt invigorated, basking in the beauty of the early morning light that cast a golden glow across the resort. Brea arrived at the wellness center in time and rushed into the studio. A dozen people, both men and women, were stretching or talking beside the windows or on yoga mats.

"Good morning, I'm Manny, your instructor this morning. Buenos días a todos." The instructor invited everyone to take their places on the mats to begin. Starting with a series of gentle stretches and sun salutations, Brea focused on her breaths and body, surprised at how easily her mind could empty itself and surrender to an hour of yoga and mindful meditation.

Concluding the class, they greeted the day with an affirmation, welcoming whatever gifts or challenges the day would bring them. Brea strolled past the fitness center, remembering Hayden planned to work out and had invited her to join him. Full of energy, she shrugged her shoulders. "Why not?" she said to herself.

Brea scanned the gym. There were several guests in the middle of their workouts, either on cardio machines or lifting weights, but she did not see Hayden. The aesthetics and size of the fitness center impressed her. The large windows overlooked lush green landscaping and let in a robust amount of natural light. Brea spotted the treadmill and smiled. It had been over two weeks since she went for a run. She grabbed a disposable pack of headphones and sauntered over to the treadmills, having her pick as they were all unoccupied.

Plugging in the headphones, she scrolled through the various channels offering workout music mixes, settled on hip hop, and began her warm-up. Several minutes passed, and out of the corner of her eye she saw someone climbing onto the treadmill on her right. Turning her head, she saw it was Hayden. He gave her a small wave. Brea returned the gesture and then refocused her attention in front of her.

Hayden cranked the treadmill to four and a half and took off with a jog. Brea looked at him as he met her eyes with a wink and a smile—it tweaked Brea a bit. Yesterday she looked away when Hayden removed his shirt, but now, dressed in a loose gray tank top and black athletic shorts, she could not help but see he was in excellent physical shape. Her eyes locked onto his muscular arms, and she raised her eyebrows. Observing the powerful form he maintained as he jogged, Brea felt an inexplicable urge to go faster and cranked up her speed to match Hayden's.

Side by side, they jogged until a minute later, Hayden raised his speed to five and a half and smiled at Brea. Was he challenging her? Brea changed her speed to five and a half, now nearly at a sprint. Hayden appeared comfortable at his speed. After increasing the volume of her music, she focused on her breathing. Brea's face perspired as the song ended. A high-intensity rap song that Brea loved began as Hayden further raised up his speed to six and Brea followed.

"It's not a race," Hayden shouted over her music, amused.

"Now it is," she yelled back, running to keep up with Hayden.

"Fine," he replied. Brea would not back down, and she would do whatever she could to keep up with him. Blowing out loud breaths, she focused straight ahead, keeping her pace. It was childish and unnecessary—but she felt the need to show him she was strong, that she could beat him, and that she would keep going even if it killed her.

Hayden, though now breathing faster, had no trouble keeping pace with Brea as they fell into synchronous strides. Brea persevered as if nothing mattered more than continuing to run. Once the song finished, Brea had nearly reached her limit at that speed, and Hayden sensed it, judging by her flushed face and her rapid breaths.

He lowered his speed, and Brea followed. They continued jogging side by side until fifteen minutes later, Hayden slowed down to a walk. He caught her attention and signaled for her to pull out one of her earphones.

"I'm moving over to weights. Find me when you're done." Brea, out of breath, nodded as Hayden slowed to a stop and hopped off the treadmill. She slowed her speed to cool down, inhaling through her nose and exhaling out of her mouth to slow her heart rate.

Hayden dropped a towel on her railing and placed a cold bottle of water in the cup holder. Grateful for the towel, she blotted her face and switched on the treadmill fan. After another five minutes, she slowed and stopped. Turning around, she spotted Hayden at the bench press.

"Looks like your magic treatments worked last night. You're only a little pink, or maybe it's the 5k you just ran," Hayden said with a grin.

Brea picked up her left ankle to stretch her quadriceps, and then switched to her right leg. "It helped. I can wear a shirt today, so that's good news. Thank you, by the way, for the dinner and the gift basket. I think I'm set with sunscreen until next year."

"I just wanted to do my part so you would be more responsible in taking care of your skin," he teased.

"Ugh, lay off me." Brea shook her head, though more amused than annoyed with Hayden teasing her. She took a sip of cold water, then gestured to the bench press. "Do you want me to spot you?"

Hayden sat up straighter and raised his eyebrows. "That depends—are you planning to hurt or traumatize me?"

Brea pursed her lips together. "The thought hadn't crossed my mind, but now that you mention it. I owe you one," she replied with a serious expression.

Hayden lowered his eyes to the floor—he appeared wounded, and it was clear he did not find what she had said amusing.

"I'm kidding, Hayden. I meant that about the crispy comment from yesterday, not—that night—bad joke, sorry," she apologized and redirected the conversation. "So how much can you lift?"

"My max is two-seventy-five, but I won't lift that today. I'll bench up to two-twenty-five," he answered, shaking off his reaction after misunderstanding Brea.

"Wow, that's a lot. Actually—I'm not sure I'm the best person for the job," she said and waved her hands in front of her as she second-guessed her strength. She scanned the gym to see if there was anyone more qualified to help Hayden out.

"It's okay. I won't fail completely. You need to help me out only if I'm struggling. But don't start looking out the window. Keep your eyes on me." Brea nodded and chewed the inner corner of her mouth.

"Come here, stand behind me, and if you see that I'm struggling, help me pull the bar up to the rack," Hayden instructed as he lay down on the bench. He worked through five reps, adding weight until he reached two-twenty-five for the final two.

"All right, your turn." Hayden set the bar on the rack.

"No way. I haven't done this before," Brea replied, shaking her head.

"Start with just the bar. It's forty-five pounds and I'll spot you." Hayden rose and wiped down the bench for Brea. She stood fixed in place with her arms crossed over her chest.

"Isn't part of this week about trusting me again? I won't touch you. I'll do what you did."

"Okay," she conceded and sat on the bench. Hayden removed the plates from the bar one by one and then positioned himself behind her head.

"Feet flat on the floor and arch your back a little. Tuck in your elbows. Now grip the bar with your thumbs wrapped around it."

"Like this?" Brea asked.

"No, move your thumbs under, so it's more secure." Brea readjusted her thumbs.

"Good. Move your hands a little less than shoulder-width apart. Keep your wrists over your elbows—straight. Now lift and bring it down to the lower part of your chest at a bit of an angle. Elbows out a little, but not too much."

Brea completed one rep. It was not very challenging. After all, she spent the last few years lifting a toddler and a child throughout the day. "Again?" Brea asked.

"Yeah, let's go for four more."

Brea finished three reps with modest effort. On the final rep, her fatigued muscles struggled to press the bar back up. "I'm going to help Brea," Hayden alerted her, then placed his hand in the middle to help her regain control and kept it in place to help rack the bar.

"That was good. Ready for squats?" Hayden threw out the challenge to Brea. Grabbing her towel again, Brea wiped her neck and shoulders.

"I think I'm done for the morning. I'm going to head back to the room."

Hayden nodded. "All right. Last night, I booked us a tequila tour in Puerto Vallarta for lunch, and there's an art gallery the concierge recommended we visit.

"That sounds like fun," Brea replied.

"Meet me in the lobby at ten-thirty. We can have breakfast and coffee before the car picks us up."

"Sure. I'll see you there soon." Before leaving the gym, Brea grabbed another bottle of water to drink on the walk back. Glimpsing herself in the mirror near the exit, she rolled her eyes. Her hairline was wet from perspiration, and her complexion bright pink, with a few streaks of white sunscreen around the edges of her face. Though her appearance was ragged, she reminded herself that it did not matter—after all, it was Hayden.

Eager to soak in the tub before needing to dress for the day, Brea picked up her pace to reach her casita, hoping to hear her kids' voices before freshening up. Once inside, she grabbed her phone and called Mary. Ecstatic to talk to their mother, Alex and Sophie told her about their trip to the beach the previous day followed by a trip to the toy store.

Relieved that the kids appeared to be having a great time, Brea hung up with Mary and the children, then debated whether to call or text Adam. Shaking her head, she reminded herself that he had not tried to reach out to her. Brea exhaled and opted against it, as she was enjoying the space from Adam. Instead, she redirected her focus to enjoying a luxurious bath.

CHAPTER EIGHTEEN

HAYDEN

As Brea exited the gym, Hayden's eyes followed her. Even though she said it was a joke, her comment still bothered him. He wondered if there was any truth to it—did she harbor anger towards him, hoping for revenge? Shaking his head, he needed to dismiss the ridiculous thought. It was his own guilt and paranoia commandeering his mind. Massaging his neck with one hand, he knew he needed to stop dwelling on that night. Tonight, he would ask Brea if she was ready for his account of the events that transpired at his house twenty years ago.

Perhaps once she knew the complete story, she would forgive him and they could—no. Hayden held back from imagining their future relationship. It would be too dangerous to travel down a tunnel of imagined scenarios as it would drive him insane with hope and expectations. Moving over to the dumbbells, he selected his weights to finish his workout.

Beginning a set of squats, Hayden paused and chuckled to himself, replaying the image of Brea, earnest and intense, sprinting next to him on the treadmill. He could have further increased his speed, but he wanted to run next to her as long as possible. There was something about them once again, side by side, that lifted him up.

Hayden blinked several times to refocus on his workout. Rather than dwell on his thoughts, it would be better to direct his energy into exercise, then return to the casita to shower and dress.

Entering his room, Hayden's eyes landed on the boxes and garment bags set on top of the dining table with the resort clothes Ashley had ordered for him. She knew his taste, and his only request had been that she avoid selecting anything with a print or pastel colors.

Flipping off the lids to the boxes, he found an assortment of casual linen long-sleeved lapel shirts, shorts, pants in an assortment of neutral colors, and several V-neck cotton T-shirts in various shades of blue. In the garment bags hung two pairs of formal slacks and a dinner jacket. The final three boxes contained a pair of leather dress sneakers, beach sandals, and slip-on casual shoes.

He selected a pair of light-gray pants and a navy lapel shirt, opting for a more formal ensemble, as they would tour several celebrated high-end restaurants for lunch. After a shower, he forewent shaving for the second day in a row as he was on vacation and found himself more relaxed than he had felt in years.

Hayden entered the lobby on time and within moments, spotted Brea, seated in the lounge, gazing at the water and appearing to be in a state of deep reflection. She wore a sleeveless ice-blue wrap summer dress with the hemline hitting just above the knees, and her hair was styled in a side ponytail. A pair of sunglasses sat atop her head. Reaching her, he cleared his throat.

"Hi. You ready?" he asked. Brea turned her head and raised her eyes to meet his—her expression softened and a smile formed on her lips. Picking up her camel-colored leather handbag from the table beside her, she rose from the chair and they turned to walk to the cafe. "What were you thinking about over there? You looked pretty serious staring out into the ocean."

Brea sighed. "I was thinking about how I regret giving up writing after I graduated college because it triggered too many feeling—I didn't want to stir up a hornet's nest. But after I saw you in Brine, that nest exploded, and I wrote something last week—a poem. Maybe I'm just high on vacation energy, but now I'm considering writing a collection of poems and, if I'm bold enough, trying to publish it."

Hayden listened. "I thought what you wrote back in high school was brilliant. Maybe this hornet's nest we've stirred up will win you a Pulitzer."

Brea laughed and nudged Hayden, pressing her shoulder into his arm. "Yeah, maybe." Hayden stopped and looked at Brea—she had touched him again.

She halted her steps and searched Hayden's face. "What is it? What did I say?" She did not realize what touching him meant—hope that her fear of him had faded and her trust in him restored.

Hayden blinked, walked again, and shook his head. "Nothing, I just had a shooting pain in my head. I need coffee. Are you still drinking tea?" he asked, trying to divert her attention.

"I do, but I'll join you for a coffee. A hot latte with cinnamon would be amazing," she replied as they entered the crowded cafe. It was elegant, decorated with walnut wooden tables and Parisienne bistro cafe chairs over herringbone wood flooring. A dozen glass-covered cake stands filled with fruit tarts, croissants, cookies, muffins, and various fruit-filled turnovers sat upon a long L-shaped white marble counter. Joining the line to order, Hayden picked up two menus and handed one to Brea. "This place is fancy," she commented, eyeing the crystal chandeliers that hung from the ceiling.

"Only the best for us," Hayden quipped and glanced over the menu. After his workout, he had a good appetite, though he did not want to fill up before the tequila tour, which promised the best seafood in Puerto Vallarta.

"What would you like to eat? I'll order, and how about you try to grab us a table?" he asked, noticing the tables filling up quickly.

"Sure. I'll have the oatmeal bowl with berries," she replied and then held out the menu for Hayden to take from her outstretched arm.

Hayden scrunched up his nose. "Gross."

"What are you, five?" Brea exclaimed with wide eyes.

"No—it's just a childhood thing. Never could stand it."

"Is this something where if I order it, you wouldn't be able to sit at the table with me?" Brea asked through narrowed eyes. With her children, if she ate any food they hated in front of them, it would end with her children refusing to eat and Brea squeezing her eyes tight in frustration.

Hayden raised his eyebrows and shrugged his shoulders. Brea sighed. "Fine, I'll have the berry yogurt parfait and the latte. Is that on your approved food list?"

"Yes, good choice," he replied with a satisfied smile.

Brea muttered as she walked away, "Such a baby."

Hayden laughed—it was fun to get under her skin. Looking over the menu, he decided on an omelet with a side of fresh fruit and a black coffee. After he ordered, he scoped Brea seated at a table beside a window overlooking a bronze fountain and a small courtyard. He carried with him two glasses of water and, reaching the table, sat across from her.

"So, if you write a book of poetry or a novel, what would you write about?" he asked and leaned back against the chair to settle in.

"Being here, the past, us—everything that happened over the past couple of weeks. What you told me about yesterday."

Hayden looked into her eyes. He did not know what to say in response, though he took what she said as another good sign. Something was breaking through to Brea, and she was waking up. "Do you have what you need to write—a laptop or a tablet?"

Brea smiled. "All I need is a pen and a few napkins."

"Should I get some for you?" Hayden offered, uncertain if she was serious.

"No, it's all right. I'll wait until I have it fleshed out. A couple of lines or a phrase will pop into my mind, and when I can't stop thinking about it—then I'll go with it."

"Hayden," the barista called out.

Hayden rose from his seat to pick up their coffees and passed the server with their food orders on the way to their table. Returning with their drinks, he observed Brea eating her food with enthusiasm. After placing their coffees on the table, Hayden checked his watch. They had fifteen minutes to eat before the driver would arrive, having opted to hire a chauffeured car service so they would have a comfortable ride and flexibility throughout the day.

Brea swallowed a large sip of her latte and smiled. "I'm excited for today, Hayden."

Hayden watched Brea resume eating her yogurt bowl. He felt a long-forgotten feeling resurface—something he could only describe as akin to joy.

Chapter Nineteen

Brea

Upon arriving at the first stop on their tour, Alonso, their chauffeur for the day, opened Brea's door. With traffic, the trip took one hour, and as they drove, Hayden explained they were to visit several of the best restaurants in Puerto Vallarta to sample various dishes, tequila, and cocktails.

Beneath the sign of the first restaurant stood a polished gentleman roughly the same age as Brea and Hayden, dressed in a stylish navy suit. He held a black leather portfolio tucked under his arm and an impressive watch on his wrist.

"Mr. Botero and Ms. Staxon, welcome. My name is Antonio, and I will be your guide this afternoon. I've selected three of our most stellar restaurants for your tour. Please, follow me this way."

He opened the door for Hayden and Brea and, once inside, Antonio shared with them a brief history of the restaurant, the chef bio, and from where they source their ingredients. If one only had seen the exterior of the nondescript white stucco restaurant, they would not have considered it extraordinary, however, the interior was an elegant mix of dark wood, hanging lanterns, and a large multi-panel glass skylight within a dark wooden frame. Soft celestial light bathed the space and on the walls hung Mexican folk tile artwork in vivid shades of teal, orange, gold, and yellow.

Brea and Hayden admired the atmosphere and décor as Antonio ushered them through the restaurant. "Would you prefer bar or table seating?" he asked. Brea looked to Hayden.

"Your choice, Brea," Hayden said.

"The bar," she determined, in the mood for a more casual setting.

"Before we begin, please alert me to any food allergies, preferences, or other details I should know before I speak with the chef." Antonio took a step back and opened his portfolio with a pen in hand to take notes.

Brea shook her head. "Nothing for me. But Hayden hates oatmeal—the sight of it will offend him," Brea conveyed to Antonio with feigned seriousness.

"Of course, sir." Antonio took Brea's words at face value and noted it as though Brea had told him Hayden was allergic to penicillin. Suppressing his laughter, Hayden shook his head and rubbed his chin.

"Any other concerns?" Antonio inquired.

Hayden smiled. "No, we're open to anything else. Let's start with some drinks. Oh, and Antonio, we do not want to decide anything today. We are in your hands—surprise us."

"Excellent, sir." Antonio signaled to the bartender, then hurried away after pulling out Brea's bar stool for her and gesturing for her to take a seat.

Brea scanned the empty restaurant. When Hayden told her this was a private tour, never would she have imagined that they would open the restaurant only for them. This tour would cost a fortune. "Hayden. This is all incredible, but how are you going to hide this from Avery? What if she sees all this on your credit card statements?"

"She won't. My assistant and accountants handle my bills," Hayden replied. Regardless, snooping was not Avery's style—she trusted him, though he did not deserve her trust.

"Okay. You know, when you said you were paying for everything, I didn't expect you to go all out like this. I would have been fine with a regular hotel, as long as it had air conditioning and a pool."

"Well, let's just say I wanted everything to be simple and easy so we could focus on us."

"Hayden—nothing about any of this is simple. I thought poor Antonio was going to have a stroke when I told him about the oatmeal." Brea lowered her voice as she finished, finding it impossible not to laugh with Hayden. A young man behind the bar, dressed in a white dress shirt and an orange tie, interrupted them.

"Mr. Botero and Ms. Staxon, my name is Santiago. I will be your mixologist and bartender while you visit with us. To begin, I have prepared a flight of our best mezcal to taste while our chef is preparing a three-plate sampler of our finest dishes."

After greeting and focusing their attention on Santiago, he pointed to the tasting glasses one by one, describing each sample in succinct detail and highlighting the various subtle differences in the flavors they could expect. Once they finished enjoying their flights of tequila, the first dish appeared—a small portion of seafood stew with fish, plump mussels, jumbo shrimp, and scallops in a fragrant tomato-based broth. Brea moaned after she swallowed the first spoonful. The broth had body and depth, and the tender seafood was so fresh that someone likely caught it that morning and stewed it to perfection.

"Hayden, how are we going to make it through three restaurants?" Brea whispered as the server brought out the next dish—a savory crusted steak in two small filets over a creamy version of a cornbread. To accompany the dish, Santiago served a half-portion of a spicy margarita with fresh slices of jalapeno peppers. Brea could not help but finish every bite on her plate.

"Don't eat it all, just taste," he stated plainly.

"It seems like a waste of food," she replied and shook her head. You could not take Brea's upbringing out of her. She imagined her mother seated beside her, berating the staff for the wasteful excess. While Hayden and Brea ate, they sipped their drinks and chatted about favorite movies they had seen over the past twenty years. Antonio checked in, pleased to hear Brea's lavish praise, and then quickly withdrew into the kitchen.

Upon finishing the delectable last course, a sweet marquecita with Oaxaca cheese piped into a crispy crepe served with a caramel sauce drizzled on top, the chef stepped out of the kitchen to greet and talk with Hayden and Brea as they sipped one last cocktail sample. After ten minutes, Antonio informed them it was time to move on to the next restaurant. And as much as Brea was enjoying this experience, she was eager to pick up the conversation where she and Hayden had left off the previous afternoon.

They followed Antonio out the door and settled back into the car. Brea turned to Hayden and whispered. "So, when are we going to talk about—everything else?"

Hayden met her eyes. "Whenever you want to. Ask me anything." Brea leaned her head to the side and pointed at Alonso and Antonio, seated in the front seat. He thought for a minute. "Right. How about we enjoy the tour and then after the gallery we can talk at the resort? I'll have Alonso call the concierge to set up a private fire for us on the beach after dinner."

"Agreed," she replied with a satisfied smile. Antonio shared a concise history of the city as they drove. Brea listened and gazed out the window, enjoying the view and anticipating the second restaurant.

CHAPTER TWENTY

HAYDEN

The subsequent two restaurants were equally impressive. Cautious not to overeat, Brea restrained herself and only tasted several bites of each dish. And to avoid imbibing excess alcohol, she took conservative sips of each cocktail, though she drained the last one, a generous-sized chocolate caramel tequila martini. Animated, Brea insisted that Antonio taste her martini and then showered him with profuse praise for his *"exquisite"* taste and attention to detail on the tour. When the time arrived for them to part ways, Brea pulled Antonio in for an embrace.

Hayden stood by and rubbed his eyes. Antonio, caught in a tough spot—not wanting to offend Brea by refusing—could not help but notice the expression on Hayden's face, conveying to Antonio he should back away from her as soon as possible.

Once in the car, Brea chatted with enthusiasm throughout the drive to the gallery and even provided Hayden with an entertaining impression of how she would describe the dishes they ate if she were writing in the style of Ernest Hemmingway. Hayden suppressed a smile—it was clear Brea drank more than she realized. As she rattled off other memorable meals from past vacations, Hayden tried not to notice that the skirt of her dress had hiked up her thighs—but he noticed.

Arriving at the gallery, Alonso sprang out of the car to open Brea's door and offered his hand to help her out, recognizing that the afternoon's libations had gone to her head. Hayden made a mental note that they would stay away from any daytime drinking the following day.

Stepping ahead of Brea, Hayden opened the door for her. Her lips parted upon seeing the gallery, a minimalist space composed of concrete flooring, white walls, and suspension-mounted lighting to highlight the bold and vibrant colored abstract canvases.

Scattered throughout the room sat an extensive selection of sculptures—busts, torsos, and full-body pieces perched on pedestals. They strolled side by side into the gallery's center, pausing when the gallerist greeted them. She introduced herself, summarized the art on display by various local artists and shared a brief history of the gallery.

Hayden trailed several steps behind Brea while she studied the art—it appeared as though the paintings could speak to her in a language only she could understand. Now and then, her lips moved, whispering something under her breath. Though Hayden admired art, he could not claim to understand it or translate what he thought about it into something intelligent to share.

In contrast, Brea would proclaim a particular piece extraordinary and explain her reasoning, referencing her knowledge of art history and technique. It was clear she had studied art over the years, in particular, early and mid-twentieth-century European and American artists.

"Hayden, come here," Brea called out not long after he had ventured off on his own to examine a painting he found interesting.

Following the sound of her voice, he found her standing before a marble sculpture of a woman, seated with her legs angled to the side, the lower half of her body draped in fabric, and her arms raised at her sides with her palms facing the ground.

"Look at this—it's amazing. I almost think she's going to move. She's like a butterfly—trapped before but now she's free."

Hayden studied Brea's face, thoughtful and absorbed in the beauty and meaning of the statue. "Like you," he said.

Brea turned to face him and met his eyes as the corners of her mouth turned up. "Yes, I think so," she replied. Fixed in place, they looked at one another.

Breaking his eyes away from Brea, Hayden drew in a deep breath and checked his watch. It was five o'clock and it would take an hour, if not longer, to return to Punta Mita. "We should go. Our reservation for the fire is at seven."

She nodded and turned to lead them out of the gallery. Hayden picked up a card and placed it in his pocket before exiting the door, hoping to return one day. Once seated in the car, Brea struggled to secure her seatbelt and fumbled with the buckle. Hayden took the seat belt from her hands and clicked it in for her. Slapping Hayden's knee, she giggled.

"Thank you. My fingers aren't working anymore." Opening a bottle of water, Hayden handed it to Brea.

"Drink this," he said, trying to distract himself from the aftershocks of Brea's touch on his leg. Brea turned her head and accepted the bottle of water.

"I'm not drunk, I'm tipsy. There is a big difference in case you forgot," Brea mumbled and then yawned.

"Sure, there is," Hayden replied with a smile. After she drank half the bottle, he took it from her and signaled to Alonso to take off. Brea laid her head against the headrest and closed her eyes. Hayden pulled out his phone and saw there were two missed calls from Avery.

"Damn," he muttered under his breath. Again, he forgot to call her last night. Waiting until it appeared Brea was on her way to falling asleep, he pressed call and Avery picked up after two rings.

"Hayden?" she answered with an edge to her voice.

He licked his lips. "I'm sorry, I wound up getting pulled into a late conference call, and then I had an early meeting this morning. I'm heading back to the hotel now. How are you doing?"

"Hayden, I'm confused. I don't think I'm being crazy here, but you sound odd."

"How?" he replied with a steady voice.

"I don't know, Hayden. I can't describe it—I just sense it."

He glanced at Brea. "Listen, everything is fine. I'll call you back in a couple of hours." Hayden paused, waiting for Avery to respond.

"Fine. I want to talk to you about something, so I don't care if you're tired or you have another headache. Call me back," she said in an assertive tone.

"Okay, bye," he replied and hung up. Gripping his phone in his hand, he pressed it to his chin and shut his eyes. Brea mumbled something inaudible. Her head rolled onto her right shoulder, then dropped to her chest.

Hayden unbuckled his seat belt and slid next to her. Picking her head up with his hands, he wrapped one arm around her shoulders and then held her head against his chest with his free hand so it would not flop over again. Tipping his head down, his nose grazed the top of her head, and he inhaled—her hair smelled of flowers and vanilla.

He leaned his head back. Holding Brea, he felt the familiar ache of desire and tenderness consume him. Her skin, her scent, and her body in his arms felt right. It was as though he had been living in a dim room and someone turned on a light, bringing him back to life.

A hollowness formed in his chest, and he worried he might have made a grave mistake bringing Brea to Mexico. Perhaps all this trip would accomplish was a reawakening of his dormant feelings for Brea, but now she was a married woman. He would not confess what he felt, place her in an awkward situation, and repeat history. There was nothing to be done about it, and the reality of the most probable outcome struck him—he would suffer the torture of his unrequited feelings for the rest of his life.

"Alonso, could you call the hotel and have them cancel our reservation for the fire?" With a nod, Alonso pulled out his phone to call the resort. Brea would not be in any shape to rouse herself for the rest of the evening. It would be best for her to sleep, and for Hayden to return to his room and consider in solitude whether he should call off the rest of the trip.

※

After arriving at the hotel, Brea would not stir other than to mumble several incomprehensible words despite Hayden's efforts to rub her cheek with his thumb and coax her to open her eyes. Hayden would have to carry her to the casita and put her to bed. He knew she would not want him entering her room, but he had no other choice. In her purse, he found her room key and stuffed it into his pocket before handing Alonso her handbag.

As he picked her up, he told Brea to put her arms around his neck and, once confident he held Brea secure in his arms, asked Alonso for her purse. Alonso handed it to Hayden with a nod and a smile in solidarity with all men who have at one time faced this romantic and amusing task.

Hayden returned the smiles of miscellaneous staff members witnessing him pass by. It was a tender scene of a man carrying a woman, who they figured was his girlfriend or wife, through the lobby. Hayden could not help but worry about how Brea would react when she woke up in the morning, finding herself in her bed. She might panic, wondering how she wound up there. If she called the police—rather than enjoying an afternoon of leisure tomorrow with Brea—he would need to call his lawyer to meet him at a Mexican jail.

Reaching her casita, Hayden waved the key card, trying not to drop Brea as he pushed down the handle to bring her inside. After entering the bedroom, he set her purse down on an empty chair, and laid her on the bed.

She rolled onto her side, facing Hayden, and stretched her arm towards him. He covered her with the folded blanket at the base of the bed, knelt beside her, and took her hand in his. Tipping his head down, he held her hand against his forehead for a moment, then abruptly stood to leave.

Chapter Twenty-One

Hayden

Overwhelmed, Hayden had not expected that he would be the one considering whether to abandon the trip early. With clenched hands, he went to his casita, then halted at the door. The memory of holding Brea and her scent would haunt him all night—he needed a drink.

Whipping around, he strode up the path toward the main lobby. It was only six-thirty in the evening, and the idea of pacing his room like a caged animal tortured by a torrent of conflicting emotions, lacked appeal. Entering the lobby, he saw the lounge crowded, though there were empty seats at the bar.

After catching the bartender's eye, he asked for a scotch neat, bartender's choice. Hayden dropped his head into his hands and rubbed his temples. Failing to ease his tension, he slapped his hands on the bar, contemplating perhaps it would be wiser for him to go to the gym and run on the treadmill for an hour to exhaust himself.

"Is it a woman?" he heard a man's voice ask beside him.

Hayden looked up—it was too cliché to be true. "Excuse me?" Hayden asked the older man seated on his left, two barstools down from him.

"Is it a woman? I know that look," the man repeated. He was an American, dressed in a green lapel short-sleeved shirt and a khaki Panama hat. Hayden estimated he was in his late seventies.

"Yes," Hayden admitted with a polite, yet half-hearted smile.

"You want to talk it through? I've been there before. There's nothing more that can make or break a man than a woman."

Hayden studied the gentleman and then extended his hand to him. "I'm Hayden. What's your name?"

"Henry. I'm here on vacation with my wife, but she was tired, so I came here for a drink. Something tells me I made the right choice leaving a beautiful woman in bed to come here for a martini." Henry rose from his stool to sit beside Hayden.

Hayden raised his eyebrows and shook his head. "I don't know. I may not be worth the trouble."

"Well, those are the words of a suffering man. You're a young, good-looking guy. You could have any girl you want, I bet."

"Yeah, except one."

"Exactly!" Henry confirmed. "Can make or break you, am I right?" he said as a statement rather than a question. Hayden nodded in agreement and thanked the bartender as he placed his scotch in front of him. Lifting his glass to his lips, he took a sip.

"Tell me the story. What's she like, this woman?"

Hayden's eyes flickered to the ceiling, and he exhaled. He did not want to talk about it, but there was something about Henry that invited him to let down his guard. "I wouldn't even know where to begin," he replied and wiped the corners of his mouth.

"Tell me. Sometimes it's helpful to talk, man to man. I don't know if your father is one to help with these things. Mine wasn't. He was too drunk and angry to help me with my problems."

Hayden nodded. He appreciated Henry's candid and genuine demeanor. "Mine too—the angry part at least—and I've rarely spoken to him over the past ten years." Henry nodded for Hayden to continue. "Well, I've known this woman, Brea, since we were kids, and I screwed everything up twenty years ago. It's a crazy story, but she's here with me now, and I have the chance for her forgiveness." Hayden paused and swallowed. "But it doesn't matter if she forgives me—it's too late."

Henry picked up his martini and took a sip before replying. "It's never too late. Not until you're dead and buried. You love this woman?"

Hayden chuckled. "I don't know what it was between us. I just—it's been so long since I last saw her, and one night I lost it, scared her after she already had a rough life. It's complicated."

"It's not complicated. People complicate things—love isn't complicated."

Hayden laughed to himself. "I feel like I'm in an old black-and-white movie right now."

"Of course you do. History repeats itself—boy meets girl, they fall in love, it falls apart. But if they are lucky, they have a chance to fix it. It's classic, human, and the only thing we've got worth anything in this world. You don't give up on it—you fight like hell for it."

Hayden looked into Henry's eyes. "Is that what happened to you?"

Henry smiled. "In a way. I was one of the lucky ones, though. I found Willa when I was nineteen-years old, and I almost lost her, but I won her back. That's a story for another night. We've been married for sixty years. And speaking of her, I'm going to call it a night."

Henry rose and extended his arm to shake Hayden's hand. "Hayden—that's your name, right? You seem like a good kid. Your father—maybe never let you know that. Don't give up and don't be afraid to let that girl know how you feel, all right?"

Hayden nodded and watched Henry stroll through the lobby until he disappeared from sight. Returning to his drink, Hayden reflected on Henry's words and resolved to stay in Mexico to finish what he had set out to do.

Once he finished his drink, he signaled for the bill—it was time to call Avery back. He took his time walking on the path from the lobby to his casita, enjoying the clement night air. Upon reaching his door, he pulled out his phone and, with a deep breath, entered the casita and pushed the button to call her.

Avery picked up after the first ring. "Hi, Hayden."

Hayden sat on the bed's edge and inhaled. "Hi, I'm back in the room. Sorry about last night. It's been busy."

"Hayden. I'm going to get right to it. Something is going on, and you're not telling me. I talked about it with Michelle, and she brought up an interesting point. She thinks that perhaps moving in together without being married was a mistake. Maybe we haven't made a true, solid commitment in our relationship, and we're taking one another for granted."

"What are you saying, Avery? Are you telling me you want to move out?" Hayden exhaled and rubbed his eyes. At the moment, he was not in the right headspace to have this conversation.

"No, that's not what I'm saying, Hayden. I love you. But I have been thinking, and I would like to revisit the topic of marriage."

Hayden felt his chest tighten—this was not what he expected to hear from her. He thought that, if anything, she had uncovered the truth about his trip or suspected he was cheating on her with another woman.

"Hayden, what do you think? Maybe we should get married. We love each other, and we live together. Why wouldn't we think about it?"

"Avery, this is not a good time to talk about this. We should talk when I come home."

"Hayden, I need to talk about this now. I know I've said that I didn't care about marriage, but seeing Michelle yesterday planning her wedding and talking about it with my parents, I think I've changed my mind. We're throwing something wonderful off the table because of some half-baked reasoning that we don't want to be conventional."

Hayden lowered his eyes to the floor and pressed his fingers to his mouth. He pictured Brea in the gallery, her eyes bright and her lips parted as she studied the marble statue of the woman.

"Hayden?" Avery said to see if he was still on the line.

"Avery, I will not change my mind. I won't," Hayden replied with frank honesty. He needed to be fair to Avery and end the relationship. Brea back in his life made it impossible for him to go on like this.

"That you won't marry anyone or you won't marry me?"

Hayden closed his eyes—he could not lie to her. "That we won't ever get married."

Avery blew out a forceful exhale. "Hayden, do you still love me?"

"Let's talk about this when I get back. I care about you, Avery, but we should talk in person." He wanted to end the relationship with the respect Avery deserved. Hayden rose, went to the patio doors, and fixed his gaze on the beach.

Avery chuckled. "This isn't about work or being tired. Something has changed this past month. Do you want to be with me at all anymore? Wait—Hayden, are you seeing another woman? Answer me, and no—we are not waiting to finish this conversation."

"No, not the way you're thinking, but there is someone from my past back in my life, and everything is different. I'm sorry, but I can't continue like this, and I have to be fair to you. Things have changed, and I won't be able to find my way back to you. You don't deserve to be with a man whose heart belongs to someone else."

"Fuck, Hayden. You don't want to get married, and now you're saying it's over? You're leaving me for another woman?"

"In all honesty, I don't know what will happen with her. But I know I can't be with you, Avery. Stay in the condo for as long as you need to, and when you're ready, I'll put it on the market. When I get back, I'll stay somewhere else and have Ashley help you find a realtor."

"No, Hayden, I don't need you to do that. I don't want to stay here, and I don't want you to help me. I'll be gone by the time you get back, and I'll arrange for my stuff to be moved out."

Hayden sighed. "All right. Let's meet when I come back."

"That's unnecessary. And Hayden, I have a feeling you're going to wind up broken and alone. So good luck with all of your 'changes' and when you wind up old and with no one, you'll deserve it." Avery hung up.

Hayden tossed his phone onto the sofa and threw up his arms. "Damn it," he muttered. He had not wanted to hurt Avery, and their relationship had been good, but he could not deny something critical—the relief he felt rather than devastation of losing her spoke volumes.

After grabbing a bottle of water from the minibar, he returned to the sofa and stared at the gray abstract painting on the wall. A jolt of unease hit him—Avery could be right. He may end up alone, and there would be no one to blame but himself.

Chapter
Twenty-Two

BREA

Upon opening her eyes in the morning, Brea was thankful for the drawn curtains and the dim room. Her mouth was dry, and her body damp from perspiration. Disoriented, she rolled onto her side and scanned her surroundings. Her handbag sat on the chair by the desk. "Oh, no," she mumbled, seeing she was still in the dress she had worn the day before.

Searching her mind for the last thing she could remember from the previous afternoon, she recalled marveling over the sculpture at the art gallery with Hayden. Brea closed her eyes and rubbed her aching head. "Oh, no," she said again as the memory of her animated drunken chatter and carrying on in the restaurant about her tequila martini replayed in her mind.

Moving to the edge of the bed, she sat up slowly and paused until she felt ready to stand. Lightheaded, though in desperate need of sugar and caffeine to perk her up, Brea walked with slow steps to the minibar and pulled out a can of soda. Drinking down the entire can, she then reached for a bottle of sparkling water and hobbled to the bathtub. Brea sat on the tub's edge after turning on the water. Her hangover could be worse—she had not vomited, nor did she feel nauseous.

"No alcohol today," she declared as she stood to take a pain reliever from the bottle on the bathroom counter. After her bath, she slipped into a hotel robe, returned to bed and ordered room service. She groaned with embarrassment as she picked up the phone to call Hayden's room.

"Brea, I'm amazed you're up so early considering you drank half the tequila in Puerto Vallarta," Hayden teased, knowing it was Brea on the other end of the line.

"Oh no, this was your fault. You booked the evil tour with amazing food and cocktails. I am holding you responsible," she replied, her voice hoarse.

"Okay, fifty-fifty for the blame," Hayden replied and chuckled.

Brea bit her lip. "I'm sorry if I embarrassed you. This is not the impression I want to make—that I'm some kind of binge drinker who gets sloppy drunk and acts like an idiot."

Hayden replied, "Brea, anyone but me, okay? I just hope you remember all of your ideas for the book you're going to write about the food in Mexico. It was rather entertaining the way you impersonated Hemingway."

Brea winced and mumbled, "Oh, no."

Hayden laughed. "It was cute. I'm looking forward to buying the hardcover. So, I'm assuming you're not up for a boat cruise today, but I booked one for tomorrow unless you have an iron stomach and could handle the ocean while you're nursing a hangover?"

"No way. I will stick to the land today. How about spending the day at the pool? I can handle sitting under an umbrella and swimming after I eat the breakfast I ordered."

"Sure. Let's meet at the infinity pool around eleven. I'll see if I can reserve a cabana."

"Great." After a pause she asked, "Hayden, did you carry me all the way to my room and put me in bed?"

"Yes, that's why I couldn't make it to the gym today—it was a long walk," Hayden teased.

Brea laughed. "I'm humiliated, but thank you."

"Forget about it. I'll see you soon, Jose Cuervo, or should I call you Tipsy?"

"Okay, that's enough. I'm hanging up." Brea chuckled. After hanging up the phone, she pressed her fingers into her temples, hoping the pain reliever would soon kick in.

Half an hour later, her breakfast arrived. Brea ate her omelet and hash brown potatoes, then sipped her black tea with cream as she lounged on the patio and watched the ocean. She was not a hundred percent, but improved enough that she could leave her room and take part in the day's activities. On the hotel notepad, she jotted down a few lines for a poem that had popped into her mind during her bath. A knock on the door interrupted her.

"Delivery, Señora Staxon," Brea heard as she rose to walk to the door. A bellman presented Brea with a modest-sized white gift box with a wide, dark blue ribbon wrapped around it and tied into a bow.

"Please wait a moment so I can give you a tip," Brea said as she stepped back. "Unnecessary. Mr. Botero already left one." He smiled and turned to walk up the path.

"Thank you!" Brea called out after him. She carried the box to the sofa and held it in her lap for a moment before untying the ribbon. Lifting the lid, she saw an ivory envelope on top of the tissue paper. *"You'll need these, Hayden,"* she read from the card.

Flipping open the flaps of tissue paper, a broad smile stretched across her lips, seeing a box of pens, mechanical pencils, and several notebooks in an assortment of colors. She picked up the black notebook, opened it to the first page and ran her fingers down the paper.

Brea rose, taking the notebook and hotel pen with her to the patio. With her legs extended, she sat on the lounge chair and, pressing the pen to her lips, thought for a moment. She wrote, "Marbled Women." Her idea was to write a short story inspired by Hayden's mother and the statue she had admired in the gallery. Bringing pen to paper, she wrote, losing track of the time until checking her phone. It was half past ten and time to slip into her swimsuit to meet Hayden at the pool.

Chapter Twenty-Three

HAYDEN

After hanging up the phone with Brea, Hayden called the concierge to confirm that Brea's gift was ready to deliver, and to reserve a pool cabana and a private beach bonfire for later that evening. Once showered and dressed in his swim shorts, he ventured onto the patio to stretch out on a lounge chair and drink his coffee. He smiled, knowing that as soon as Brea's gift arrived, she would engross herself with writing.

Over the years, he always wished he had a copy of "Stolen Night," the poem she had written about their first night together. It would have been heartbreaking to read, but it would have been something tangible to remember her by. Although hesitant, perhaps before they parted ways he would work up the courage to ask her if she would send him a copy. On dark days, he wondered if she had ever written anything about their last night together, though he doubted he could read it—it would be too painful.

At a quarter to eleven, he left the casita to meet Brea and, during the walk, settled on withholding the news of his breakup with Avery. Brea might not take it well, believing he might try to make a move on her now that he was single. He would also need to conceal his resurfaced feelings for her as he could not dare to hope she could one day be free. And even if her feelings for him returned, the odds of a happy ending for them were not in his favor.

Reaching the top of the hill, Hayden surveyed the landscape. The expansive pool sat against the edge of the overhang and beyond it boasted a majestic view of the ocean. On the pool patio sat a series of cabanas, flanking both ends of the pool, and two rows of wooden loungers with taupe cushions lined its length. Behind the seating was an upscale bar and grill restaurant with high-top tables. Hayden greeted the hostess, and she informed him that Brea had already arrived.

Brea met Hayden's eyes as he entered. She wore an ivory one-piece bathing suit with gold detailing, a pair of white shorts, and her hair knotted into a loose bun and secured at the nape of her neck. Hayden grinned, seeing the visible streaks of white sunscreen on her shoulders.

"I'm happy you applied a bottle of sunscreen this morning," he commented, seating himself on a lounge chair and pointing to her shoulders.

"Yes, courtesy of my generous benefactor. And thank you for the notebooks. It was one of the most thoughtful gifts anyone has given me."

Embarrassed, Hayden lowered his eyes. Perhaps he was trying too hard, and the gift made him appear desperate to win her over. But searching her eyes, she betrayed no awkwardness, only appreciation.

"You're welcome. I also booked a bonfire for tonight. We can eat dinner here at the bar and grill and then head down to the beach at seven to watch the sunset. And if you're ready, I'm hoping that we can talk about that night."

Brea inhaled and looked out at the pool. "I'm ready," she answered, then turned back to look at him again. After a pause, she spoke.

"Hayden. I want to ask you something?"

"Of course, open book," Hayden replied.

"Why have you never married or had children? Although—maybe you have in the past. I didn't think to ask you that before." Brea pulled up her legs on the lounger to sit cross-legged.

Hayden furrowed his brow. It was uncanny that of all mornings, she would ask that question after his breakup with Avery last night. "It's not that I never wanted children, but I decided a long time ago I did not want to father biological children. With my mother having early onset Parkinson's, the doctors said there isn't a test to see if I could get it, but there is a higher genetic risk. I wouldn't want to have children and put them through that or pass it on to them. So, I had a vasectomy." Lowering his eyes, he continued.

"And as for marriage—I suppose it would take feeling a level of certainty to make that type of commitment to a woman. And something always held me back once I was at an age to consider it." Hayden met Brea's eyes, withholding the truth—he never felt with another woman what he did with Brea.

"Can I ask you something too?" he asked after clearing his throat, though uncertain he wanted to hear Brea's answer. Brea nodded. "Why did you marry Adam? I know I'm speaking out of turn here, but when I followed you in the museum, it's obvious there was something serious happening in your marriage."

She sighed and lay back on her lounge chair. "I wanted to have children, take a shot at having a normal family and a beautiful home filled with love. I felt flattered and honored that he chose me to marry him. And looking back, I was afraid of the world—making decisions or of making mistakes. Adam, being so confident and stable, took control and took care of me. But now, it's like my life isn't my own and he doesn't know me. I don't even think he loves me anymore. I'm the woman who raises his children, dresses up, and smiles to show the world that he has the perfect life."

Hayden nodded and felt compelled to ask her another question. "Do you think you'll work it out?"

Brea shook her head. "I honestly don't know. I was desperate to see if there was any hope of fixing things. Before I came here, I humiliated myself and practically begged him to make—"

Hayden looked away—he did not want to hear any more about Adam. Brea picked up on his discomfort and paused.

"I mean, I'm thinking about whether there is anything left to save. Alex and Sophie are my priority and I have to do what's best for them. I can't pretend everything is fine and fake happiness. They're too smart and I can't fool them. No matter how difficult it may become for a while."

They sat in silence after she spoke, lost in their respective thoughts. Hoping to lighten the atmosphere, Hayden tapped his fingers on his legs and asked, "Do you want to swim or hang out in here for a while?"

"I need about three more glasses of water, a trip to the bathroom, and then I think I'll be ready to swim. I brought the book I just started. Do you have anything to read?"

He had packed a book but did not think to bring it with him. "Nope, I forgot."

Brea smiled. "Should I read out loud? You could listen?"

Hayden narrowed his eyes. "It depends. Is it a chick book?"

She nodded. "Yes, and it's the best. Lots of feelings and hugging."

"Then hell yeah, go for it," he said, laughing.

Brea opened to the first chapter to start from the beginning, not having made it very far on the beach before she had fallen asleep. The server popped into the cabana for their drink order. They asked if it would be possible to order Margaretta's lemonade. Familiar with the drink, she hurried off to prepare a pitcher.

After the server left, Hayden reclined in his lounge chair and turned his head to face Brea. "Okay, read to me so I can surrender my man card at the front desk when we check out." Brea laughed and read.

CHAPTER TWENTY-FOUR

BREA

Hayden seemed different that morning, though Brea struggled to find the reason that made her think so. He sported a three-day beard, and though it suited him, that was not it. Maybe it was her, feeling more relaxed now on their third day together and a sense of ease and familiarity had settled between them.

Reaching a steamy sex scene in her book, Brea felt her face flush. She paused and glanced at Hayden after reading several lines detailing the male love interest's abdominal muscles as he removed his clothing.

"Keep reading—this is getting good," Hayden teased with a wide grin.

Folding the top corner of the page and closing the book, she placed it on the table. Brea cleared her throat. "I'm ready to swim now. You can borrow the book to see how it ends."

He laughed. "I have a pretty good idea of how it's going to end." Hayden rose and removed his shirt, leaving him only in his black swim trunks. Brea's lips parted, and she held her breath, seeing his well-toned upper body with a light amount of chest hair. She blinked several times to stop herself from staring and stood to slip out of her shorts. Halfway down her hips, she paused and pulled them back up. Hayden looked at her with a perplexed expression.

"Hayden, I'm almost forty and I've had two children. I will not parade around quasi-naked in front of that group of twenty-one-year-old girls over there. Some things just don't bounce back after losing baby weight and breastfeeding." Brea pointed to a group of six college-age students—a mix of men and women—drinking cocktails, talking, and laughing with contagious enthusiasm.

"Brea, you're gorgeous. Give me a break. Who says you need to look twenty-one forever?"

"Uh, the entire world, Hayden. I mean, please, look at you. You look so—good." Brea's cheeks flushed. She looked away and crossed her arms over her chest to deflect from her admission.

Hayden shook his head. "Do what makes you comfortable, but I think you're being ridiculous. Who cares what they think? Just be you."

Brea sighed, removed her shorts, and then wrapped a towel around her waist. "But I'm wearing this until we get in the pool."

Hayden raised his eyebrows. "After you."

Once in the pool, Brea submerged herself under the water. The lovely sensation of weightlessness and the rush of warm water sheathing her skin soothed her. She swam to the edge of the pool after several laps and folded her arms on the edge to gaze at the ocean. Hayden joined her a little while later.

Her gaze unwavering, she spoke. "This is incredible. I mean, I love the view from my house, and I see the ocean every day from a distance, but there is something about this place that's like—"

"Magic," Hayden said with Brea at the same time. Hayden studied Brea's face as she stared at the ocean. Drops of water dripped from her hair onto her cheeks, sparkling in the sunlight.

"Brea, this is difficult for me to ask, but before we talk tonight, I think I need to know. Would you tell me what happened with Cylis?"

Closing her eyes for a moment, she turned to look at Hayden. "How much do you want to know? I can't take it back once I say it out loud. You may see me differently, like I'm damaged."

"You're not damaged, and nothing you say will change how I think or feel about you. It's up to you how much you can tell me, and if you can't talk about it, I understand," he replied.

Turning to look back at the ocean, she took a deep breath. "That Saturday, days after we fought in the library at school, I went with Cylis to the museum. You were right that there was something wrong with him—he was sick. He talked me into taking ecstasy and invited me back to his house while his parents were away on a trip." Brea inhaled and wiped her face.

"I was easy prey, trapped in his house alone in the woods. He changed, became aggressive, taunted me cruelly, and then raped me several times, in various ways, over the course of the afternoon and night. And that terrifying day left me humiliated, afraid, ashamed, and I blamed myself. He made me think I wanted it, even though I begged him to stop and let me go."

Hayden gripped the edge of the pool and dropped his head, his demeanor shifting as though a tidal wave of guilt consumed him. "I'm sorry, Brea, that I couldn't protect you from him—and I only made everything worse. There were so many things I should have done differently."

Brea turned to face Hayden. "There was no way you could have protected me. And yes, what happened that night at your house scared me, but I have to believe that everything that happened in the past happened for a reason." Hayden did not move and Brea continued. "Hayden—you need to know you aren't like your father—I don't even need to hear your story about that night to know it."

Hayden swallowed, raised his head to meet Brea's eyes and then drew in a sharp breath. She continued after a brief pause. "Look, I've stopped myself—many times—from walking down the road of things I should have or should not have done because it went nowhere other than to hit a dead end of helpless despair. Stop yourself from doing that because all we can do is move forward or we'll drive ourselves crazy. And for myself, when I get home, I'm ready to face what Cylis did to me. I'll need help though, a therapist to start with, because the idea of giving up any more time to avoid my past is unthinkable—I'm done with that."

"Can I help?" he asked.

Brea continued to look into Hayden's eyes. "Yes. I never saw Cylis again after that day. I want to know where he is and anything you can find out about him."

Hayden wiped the drops of water dripping into his eyes from his forehead. "I can do that. Do you want to know everything I find out? Even if it's difficult to hear?"

Brea turned her head to look back at the ocean. She crossed her arms over the edge and placed her head on her forearms. "Everything."

Side by side, they watched the ocean in silence for several minutes when a ball landed behind Brea and Hayden, splashing them. They both startled and whipped around. Two of the college-age guests had begun a game of water volleyball.

"Hayden picked up the ball and volleyed it to them."

"Thanks. Hey, do you want to join us? Guys versus girls?" one of the young men asked. Hayden looked at Brea, uncertain if she would be in a mood to play or needed some time after their heavy, emotional discussion. Brea smiled and nodded.

The pool staff switched on the music, and the atmosphere and energy livened as more guests entered the pool with cocktails. Brea and Hayden stuck to soft drinks and remained in the pool for two hours, swimming after playing several rounds of volleyball. Every fifteen minutes, Hayden teased Brea to reapply her sunscreen. Over time, she could no longer take it anymore and would attempt to jump on Hayden's back or push him under the water whenever he brought up the sunscreen.

"Are you kidding me? I'm twice your size, Brea!" he would remind her. With ease, he would fling her off his back or flip her around, then toss her into the water. It was playful, childish, and the most fun either of them had in a long time.

Chapter Twenty-Five

Brea

Late afternoon, Hayden and Brea returned to their casitas to dress for dinner. After a hot shower and applying her makeup, Brea lay on her bed in the hotel robe and watched the overhead fan spin in slow circles. She had checked on Alex and Sophie, overjoyed to hear their exuberant voices as they took turns telling her about their day at the zoo. Upon hanging up with Mary and the children, Brea pressed her hand to her chest and inhaled. It was time to call Adam. The phone rang four times before he picked up. Brea's shoulders and neck tensed upon hearing his voice.

"Hi Brea," Adam answered, making no attempt to hide his annoyance with the interruption.

"Hi, I just checked on the kids with your mom. They sound like they're having a great time."

"Yeah, she's doing a great job with them," he replied, his tone indifferent and distracted.

"How are you?" Brea asked.

"Fine. Busy at work. I should go." Adam cleared his throat.

"That's it, Adam? You don't want to talk to me at all after I've been gone for days?"

Adam sighed, exasperated. "What are you looking for here, Brea? Just tell me."

"How about, are you enjoying yourself? How's your trip? I miss you. You're a great mom, Brea. You're my wife, and I want to know what's going on in your head. Something other than dead icy silence and a brush off," Brea spouted off into the phone, unleashing the fury she could no longer suppress.

Flustered and taken aback by Brea's eruptive anger, Adam exclaimed, "Are you high, Brea? What are you talking about?"

"Adam, I'm not drunk. I'm only waking up from a dead sleep I've been in for the past decade. I love our children, and I love the home we've built, but I'm not sure you like me very much. Do you?"

"Brea, go sleep it off. You sound crazy, and I can't do this right now. We'll talk tomorrow," Adam said and hung up the phone.

Her mouth gaped open, astounded. "That's it? He blew me off?" Brea cried out. Over nine years, she had seldom raised her voice, and now, sharing valid reasons for her distress, he assumed she was drunk and deranged.

Furious, she slipped into a pair of linen shorts, a t-shirt, grabbed a cream-colored cable-knit sweater from the closet and bounded out the door to meet Hayden at the poolside grill for dinner. Outside, she flew down the path in wide strides, shaking her head and occasionally muttering to herself. The guests she passed on the path gave Brea a curious side glance as she passed them by.

Arriving at the bar and grill, she spotted Hayden seated at a high-top table with a draft beer. Focused on the menu, he did not notice Brea until she reached the table and slammed her hands down. Startled, Hayden sat back, uncertain if her anger was directed at him or someone else.

"I am so—pissed off," Brea exclaimed as she yanked the chair back to sit down.

"Okay. At me?" Hayden asked, pointing to himself.

Brea looked out at the horizon and sighed. "No, of course not."

"Do you want to talk about it?"

"Not really," she answered.

The server appeared with a beaming smile. "Good evening, could I offer you a cocktail or a glass of wine?" Hayden glanced at Brea with raised eyebrows.

"A virgin mojito, please. The memory of the tequila is still too fresh." Brea dropped her head in her hands to compose herself. She sucked in a deep breath and picked up the menu. Hayden lowered his eyes to continue scanning the menu and raised them again when she spoke a moment later.

"Why are relationships so difficult? Or maybe I should ask, why are they so damn difficult for me?"

Hayden hesitated, unsure how to respond, knowing full well he was in no position to give Brea advice on her marriage, considering how conflicted and biased he was. "Are you asking for my perspective or are you only venting?" he replied, hoping she would confirm the latter.

"Yes, your perspective would be great. You're in a seemingly functional relationship."

"Brea, a disclaimer is necessary before I begin. I have not had many relationships, and most of the women left me because they felt I couldn't commit—and they weren't wrong. And don't forget about Vienna. Do you still want my advice?" Brea groaned and dropped her head onto her arms folded on the table.

Hayden searched his mind for something helpful to say. "Well, there was this guy I met once, Henry, a wise older man." Hayden cleared his throat, trying to remember what Henry had said at the bar the other night without giving away that he had been in a crisis over Brea. He continued, "Love isn't complicated—people complicate it."

Brea lifted her head, and meeting Hayden's eyes, attempted to suppress a smile. "How is that advice? It's a fucking fortune cookie, Hayden, but—thank you."

Hayden laughed. "Hey, I thought it made sense, and I warned you I would be useless."

Brea shook her head. "You know, on the phone, Adam said he thought I was 'high' and he hung up on me. I just wanted to talk, you know, unleash 'the Brea' on him."

"The Brea? Now you're referring to yourself in the third person—like a whole other entity. She sounds terrifying. I'd be afraid of her."

Brea and Hayden laughed. The server returned with Brea's drink, and they both ordered grilled mahi-mahi taco plates with cilantro rice and frijoles con elote. As they ate, to change the topic of conversation, Brea told Hayden about her friendship with Hannah and a disastrous trip to Paris they had taken together in their senior year of college.

After dinner, they walked to the beach. Reaching the shore, the hostess led them to their tent and fire pit. Flanking them on either side were half a dozen other bonfires set twenty feet apart. On a rectangular high-top table in the tent sat an assortment of soft drinks, a hot cocoa bar, and the ingredients for smores. Brea collapsed into one of the white Adirondack chairs and picked up a folded woven blue blanket off the small table beside her. A soft smile spread on her lips watching the sunset. The sky was transitioning with thick, blended strips of pink and violet above the horizon.

"Brea, do you want a drink?" Hayden asked.

"A bottle of water, thanks. Hayden, look at this. It's like we're sitting in a painting." Hayden handed Brea a bottle of water and sat in the chair beside her.

"Do you ever paint? You seem to know a lot about art," he asked.

Brea smiled. "No. I'm drawn to it because it expresses an idea—something painful, hopeful, or chaotic without words. I find it fascinating that lines, colors, or something representational taken from one moment in time can make you feel something. My mother went through a phase when she painted—obsessively painted. It was strange, but it was the only time in my life that I felt a connection to her. Maybe that has something to do with my interest, now that I'm thinking about it."

"What do you think happened to your mom to make her the way she is? You used to describe her as cold and unpredictable," Hayden asked.

Brea rubbed her lips together. "I know little about her childhood since she shared no stories or talked about my grandparents very much. I didn't know it when I was younger, but my therapist in college thought she had some kind of mood disorder, probably bipolar. She would have these extreme episodes, sometimes high and sometimes low. Some days, she wouldn't stop talking, and she would follow me around the house for hours. I would have to hide in the garage to get away from her so I could have an hour or two of peace."

"The mouse den, you mean?" Hayden said.

Brea laughed. "Yeah. You were a good sport about it, though."

Hayden fixed his gaze on Brea. "I would have gone to hell to be with you that night."

Brea turned to look at him. A wave of bittersweet sadness hit her, remembering how peaceful she had felt when Hayden held her. And now, after spending these past few days with him, the familiar sentiment that they belonged to each other had resurfaced. They averted their eyes from one another when a server came by to light the fire and offered to bring them a drink from the bar, which they both declined.

They watched the sunset together in comfortable silence, lost in their own thoughts. As the sky darkened, Brea's attention shifted to the fire, fixing her eyes on the bewitching flames vacillating in the evening breeze.

"For a long time, seeing fire made me anxious. It reminded me of Cylis. He had this tattoo of the Greek god of fire on his back."

Hayden inhaled. "Brea, I found out something about Cylis. I messaged my attorney while we were at the pool, and he got back to me a little while ago."

Staring into the fire, Brea swallowed. "What did you find out?"

"He's dead. Died of a drug overdose ten years ago. It will take a little more time to find out if he had a criminal record and other details." Hayden studied her face as she continued to gaze into the fire.

After a moment, Brea wiped her eyes. "This is the last time I'll cry over him, and those weren't tears of sadness." She let out a breath and looked into the sky. Mostly, she felt relief that he was gone and could never hurt her or anyone else again. But a part of her also felt anger—she would never receive an apology, nor know if he ever experienced any remorse for what he did to her. Regardless, it mattered little.

"Are you okay?" Hayden asked.

"Yes," she replied, and she meant it. "Thank you. Not just for finding out about Cylis, but again for convincing me to come on this trip. I think I would have stayed stuck in my life until I became an empty shell of a person if you had not come back to talk to me."

"Brea, you know you're stronger than you think. Look at everything you've been through, and you kept going. You have two amazing kids, and you can change your life. A wise man once told me we always have the chance to fix our mistakes until we're dead and buried."

"Let me guess, your friend Henry told you that?"

Hayden smiled. "Yeah, I'm not deep enough to have come up with that one."

Laughing, Brea unfolded the blanket to cover her legs. "Hayden. Can you make me a smore?"

"I thought you'd never ask," he replied and stood to bring over the tray of ingredients. Once seated, Hayden placed a marshmallow on a stick and handed it to Brea.

"Do you lightly toast or let it burn, Hayden?"

"What do you think?" he asked.

"Burnt. Charcoal. Black as hell."

Hayden smiled. "So do you."

"Yeah," Brea confirmed.

Waiting until their marshmallows lit on fire, they waited until the perfect moment to blow them out. Hayden fixed the smores, then handed one to Brea on a plate. They bit off a sizeable chunk and moaned as they savored the mélange of delicious flavors. Brea joked again it was as though they were teenagers at summer camp, and Hayden laughed.

Though humorous, Brea felt a pang of sadness. In a few short days, they would leave, and she would need to face the complicated decisions that awaited her back in Ocean Crest Beach. Stealing a glance at Hayden, she wondered if maybe there could be a place for one another in their lives, or would they pretend as though this week never happened?

"Hayden, are you ready to tell me now?"

Hayden finished his last bite. Taking Brea's plate from her hand, he brought them back to the tent and returned with another bottle of water for each of them. Handing it to Brea, he sat and leaned forward, staring into the fire.

"I am," he said. He gazed into the flames, intensely focused, as though he could conjure the past to replay before them.

Chapter Twenty-Six

Hayden

Parking in the driveway, Hayden found it remarkable how comforted he felt by Brea's presence. After discovering the copy of The Velveteen Rabbit among his books, he struggled to sleep and experienced episodic waves of anxiety accompanied by hand tremors. Two nights of insomnia had made him desperate to find a solution.

Earlier in the week, knowing his father and Angela had yet to clear out his mother's belongings, Hayden snuck into his father's bedroom in search of her old sleep medications. On the bathroom counter, her toothbrush and face cream remained in place, which he found both comforting and disturbing. He checked the medicine cabinet first and slammed it shut—someone had removed her old prescription pill bottles. Cursing under his breath, he ran his fingers through his hair to think.

Returning to the bedroom, he checked her nightstand drawer but found only books, hand cream, and several pens inside. On her nightstand lay a stack of magazines and her glasses, and on the dresser sat her jewelry box and a bottle of perfume. He opened the top drawer and rummaged through her socks until, in the far back, he glimpsed an orange plastic container.

Pushing aside the socks, he pulled out the bottle and placed it on the dresser. He searched through the remaining drawers and found two additional bottles. One by one he read the names and the instructions—one was a muscle relaxer, another a narcotic for pain, and the last a bottle of sleeping pills he recalled she used when she felt anxious or could not sleep.

He read the label for the sleeping pills. There were five left in the container, and the instructions said to take one pill at bedtime. Slipping three of them into his pocket, he left the bedroom and slept for the following three nights.

Hayden and Brea strolled to the front door and entered the house. Brea spoke first. "So, should we start? I think I'm going to propose we partner up like in science lab. That way, we can only blame each other if something explodes or your house burns down."

He smiled—he had missed her sense of humor and their playful banter. "You know your way around after snooping last summer," he teased, then gesturing with his arm, invited her to step ahead and lead the way into the kitchen.

Brea's mouth dropped open seeing the abundance of boxed cake mixes and frosting containers set upon the kitchen island countertop. Earlier at the grocery store, the checkout clerk eyed him with a smile as she rang up the items.

"Someone is going to have a nice birthday," she commented.

Hayden smiled. "Nah, just trying to impress a girl," he replied.

The checkout lady raised her eyebrows. "Well, in that case, you need sprinkles. That's the best part. Go grab some. I'll wait for you."

Brea picked up the colored sprinkles and smiled at Hayden. He would have to hug the checkout lady the next time he shopped at the grocery store.

"It's only going to be us, right? I mean, I think I can eat two, maybe three cupcakes at most, and I'm done for the night," Brea remarked.

"Well, there isn't much food in the house, so I figure I can live on the leftovers for the rest of the weekend."

"Yikes. Okay, I need to borrow one of your mom's aprons. I bought this dress today, and there is no way I want to smear chocolate all over it. Where does she keep them hidden?"

A vivid memory of him sitting at the counter on his tenth birthday, watching his mother bake birthday cupcakes, hit him like a gut punch. That night, having left the dirty bowls and spoons in the sink for too long, his father screamed at his mother for not having cleaned up the kitchen to his standards.

"I'm sorry, Hayden," Brea said. "I wasn't thinking. That slipped out."

"Um, sure, my mom kept them here," he replied. After pulling the apron out of the drawer, he saw the shame on Brea's face.

As he walked toward her, she watched him, her eyes over-filled with chagrin and sadness, and on the verge of apologizing again. "It's fine. Please don't worry about it. I forget she's gone sometimes too," he said and placed the apron beside Brea on the counter. He picked up the box to check how many eggs they would need.

"If you don't want to talk about her tonight, I understand. If you do, I'm here for whatever you need, all right? I wish I only knew what to say. I had no one close to me die before."

Hayden focused his eyes on his hands—his tremors were starting again. He did not want to spoil the night. "No, I'm good. I don't want to talk about it," Hayden replied, forcing a slight smile on his face. "Let's do this one," he added and handed the box to Brea.

While Brea focused on the instructions, Hayden turned to shake out his hands and drew in a breath to slow down his heart rate before opening the refrigerator for the cold ingredients. Returning to Brea's side, he exhaled, grateful she was there, and he hoped that touching her might calm him down. After setting the eggs and milk on the counter, he placed his hands on her shoulders—the touch of her skin and proximity to her tempered his unease.

"Do you want a drink? There's some wine in the refrigerator," Hayden offered.

"Yes, good idea," she answered. He did not enjoy wine, though he recalled there was a bottle in the refrigerator and hoped it would ease his tremors and calm his anxiety. He poured them each a glass, handed one to Brea, and then mixed the batter after she pushed the bowl to him.

As he used to do with his mother, Hayden licked the spoon and then handed it to Brea to have the rest. Watching her lick the spoon, Hayden felt the desire to pull her into his arms and kiss her, but he held back.

"This is better than the wine," she exclaimed. Hayden picked up a small measuring cup to fill one of the cupcake tins with batter. His hand shook, and he had trouble keeping it still enough to pour in the batter. He made a mess, filling it up too high and chocolate batter dripped over the sides of the pan and onto the counter.

"I'll take over with that—this needs a woman's touch," Brea teased and bumped him with her hip to move him aside. As she worked to fill up the remaining tins with batter, an idea came to him—he could return to his mother's dresser and take half a pill to ease his anxiety.

"You can eat the monster cupcake," Brea remarked as she stepped back, showing him her handiwork. Hayden chuckled and carried the pan to place in the oven, hoping that with his trembling hands he would not drop it.

"They need to bake for twenty-two minutes," Brea read off the instructions and then pulled herself up to sit on the counter.

With the alcohol, Hayden's anxiety diminished, and they fell into a conversation about used cars. Automobiles were one of the few topics that Hayden could have a neutral conversation about with his father, and his knowledge was extensive. Brea smiled and listened as Hayden gave her his top five list of used cars and everything she should ask before considering buying one. In particular, what to pay attention to on a test drive. It was not long until the oven timer sounded and Brea jumped off the counter.

Hayden grabbed an oven mitt, removed the cupcakes from the oven, and placed them on the counter to cool. "Let me have one." Brea reached out her hand to pull one out of the tin. Hayden, feeling playful, knew it would drive her nuts if he stopped her, and he loved to get a rise out of her.

"Nope, we have to wait until they are cool before we frost them. It says so on the box." Hayden smiled and stretched out his arm to prevent Brea from reaching for the cupcake. Her persistence surprised him, but she was no match for his height and strength. When she grabbed his arm, he felt the impulse to wrap his arms around her and kiss her when she swung out her other hand and nearly grazed the pan. Hayden did not want her to get hurt. "Stop. You're going to burn yourself," he exclaimed, laughing at her relentless efforts to get the darn cupcake.

"Fine." Brea let go. Her eyes sparkled when she pretended to pout and crossed her arms over her chest.

Knowing how much she loved desserts, Hayden smiled, glad he had stopped by the bakery. "Look, in exchange for your patience, I'll take out what I bought from the bakery this morning."

After cutting the ribbon and opening the box, Brea surveyed the pastries and with wide eyes proclaimed, "I'm going to gain two pounds tonight." He raised his eyebrows, thinking to himself she could stand to gain five to ten pounds, she was that lean.

Hayden checked his hands—they still trembled, though less. The effect of the wine was not enough to eliminate his anxiety. "Why don't we bring this into the family room and pick out a movie?" He closed the box and carried it as he led Brea to the family room.

Leaving Brea to search through the movies, he hurried to his father's bedroom and opened the dresser drawer. After retrieving the bottle, he struggled to open it and it slipped out of his hand, falling to the ground just as he unscrewed the top. The remaining two pills scattered across the floor. Kneeling down, he searched the floor and under the dresser, but he could not find them.

"Shit," he whispered—they were gone. He groaned and with firm pressure rubbed his neck. After standing up, he returned to the dresser drawer and hoped one of the other medications could help him. In handling each bottle, he read the indications on the label.

Hayden knew it was dangerous to mix alcohol with pain medication. His mother had given up alcohol for that reason. Returning the pain medicine to the drawer, he picked up the other bottle, chewed his lower lip and read the bottle's instructions: "*Take one to two tablets as needed for muscle spasms.*" Given his tremulous hands, it appeared to be a reasonable option. Opening the container, he removed two tablets.

Brea would wonder where he had disappeared to. After burying the bottles under the socks, he placed the tablets in his mouth and swallowed them with water from the bathroom faucet before dashing to the kitchen for the plates and napkins.

"Please eat at least three desserts or I'll wind up sick by Monday," Hayden joked as he returned with the plates and napkins. Brea held up a movie he had seen dozens of times, but never tired of watching. After turning on the television and loading the disc, he turned to face Brea as she spoke.

"Hayden, you need to taste this. It's so good." Brea held a rainbow cookie. He leaned down and ate it out of her hand. She laughed. "What are you, a dog?" Her laughter fluffed his male pride, and the touch of her fingers on his lips filled him again with the desire to kiss her.

He would need to find the right time that night to have a serious talk with her. Now that Harvey Slate knew the truth about them, nothing prevented them from being together other than his leaving for MIT the following month. And assuming that was the only problem, he felt confident they could maintain a long-distance relationship until her graduation from Harvey Slate.

Brea stretched out on the sofa. He considered picking up her legs and placing them on his lap, but thought against it, opting instead to give her space so she did not feel crowded. They settled down to watch the film.

An hour into the movie, he felt something unusual—a heaviness in his body though his mind felt stimulated and amped. It was odd. He paused the movie after glancing at Brea, appearing tired and on the verge of dozing off to sleep.

"Should we decorate the cupcakes?" he asked. Brea blinked several times and yawned. She nodded, stretched her arms and legs, and then sat up.

"Sure. I don't think I can eat more than one now, but we can decorate them and, on the way home, we can throw them at stop signs."

Hayden smirked. "Not going to happen. I'm not interested in going to jail tonight," he replied as they returned to the kitchen.

After dividing up the cupcakes to frost, Hayden found his hands would not cooperate with his brain and his motor coordination was off. They were not shaking, but he struggled to manipulate the knife.

Brea appeared amused. He was faltering, and although he always enjoyed her playfulness, now he felt strangely annoyed. The pills were not helping and he considered returning to his mother's dresser or searching the closet to see if there were other hidden bottles of medication.

"Hayden, that does not look appetizing. I think you had too much wine, and you lost your motor skills," Brea teased and scrunched up her nose as she pulled herself up onto the counter.

"Hey, I'm not a girl," he exclaimed to defend himself, concealing his irritation.

"You know, there are famous pastry chefs and bakers all over the world who are men," she pointed out with a snarky smile.

Hayden looked at her with a side-eye, irritable for an inexplicable reason. Brea extended her hand to the cupcake he held to scoop up a little frosting on her finger. He attempted to move it away before she could swipe any frosting, but she moved swiftly and succeeded.

She would not get away with it. He dropped everything he held in his hands and grabbed her wrist before she could lick the frosting off her finger. Brea froze. Meeting her eyes, he saw both surprise and desire behind them. He pulled her hand to his mouth, opened it, and licked off the frosting. Brea's lips parted, and she wore an expression that he was intimately familiar with. Hayden needed to kiss her—he did not want to wait any longer.

"Hayden, what are you doing?" she whispered. Holding her wrist, he stepped in front of her. "You're leaving for school, and after everything that has happened this year, I should be alone, no more boys for a while. I want you to kiss me, but this isn't a good idea. It's too complicated."

Holding her gaze, he let go of her wrist. "This is the best idea," he whispered and leaned in closer. Hayden paused. He would kiss her only if she wanted him to. Uncertain of her next move, his heart raced. Brea leaned in and kissed him, and for the first time since his mother died, he felt it possible that he could find happiness once again.

He pulled her close, and she wrapped her legs around him. Feeling the touch and warmth of her skin against him, the sentiment that there had been a void in his life vanished. Lifting Brea off the counter, they continued to kiss and he did not want to let her go—not even for the walk to the bedroom. Tonight, there would be freedom from guilt and the fear of discovery—they were together as it should have been from the beginning, and it was exhilarating.

Inside his room, he removed his shirt and untied Brea's top. It was too soon for them to have sex, and he did not want to rush anything. All he desired was to feel her close, to please her, and to experience the night with no obstacles standing between them.

Hayden carried Brea to his bed, laid her down, and positioned himself over her. When he kissed her breast, she arched her back and moaned. Hayden slid his hand up her inner thigh, and reaching her panties, touched her. He wanted to bring her to climax and watch her lose herself as pleasure spread throughout her body. But it was difficult to feel comfortable as the shorts he wore felt awkward and constricting. Hayden stood to remove them but kept on his boxers so Brea would not assume he was pushing to have sex. He lay back down over her, kissed her neck, and then with his lips, traced down her chest. She whispered his name, and he interpreted it as a passionate expression of her desire for him.

"Hayden," Brea said, louder. Taken aback, he paused and looked at her. Her eyes were closed. Perhaps having paused in pleasuring her between her legs had frustrated her, though he wanted to take his time tonight.

"What is it?" he asked, then lowered his head to kiss her chest.

"I'm sorry, Hayden. We can't. We have to stop. I can't breathe. Let's go finish the movie, and when you're ready to drive, take me home." Stunned, he paused and looked at her. Her eyes were open, and she appeared panicked.

"Get off me, Hayden, I can't breathe," Brea shouted.

Alarmed, Hayden rolled onto his side and sat up. She would not look at him, and appeared frightened. "Brea, what's wrong?" He pulled the top of her dress up to cover her bare chest and sat beside her. Brea scooted back to the headboard, sucking in rapid breaths while tying her top. She closed her eyes and would not answer him.

"Brea, talk to me. What's going on?" he asked, bewildered.

"It's—it's Cylis." Hearing Brea say his name was a painful blow—his heart pounded and anger filled him. Turning away from her, his mind raced. He could not believe it—she still had a fixation on that asshole. "You still love him? Are you seeing him?" He could not control the contempt in his voice.

"I'm sorry. I can't. I'm sorry," she whispered.

"You love him? Did you lie to me, Brea? Have you been seeing him the whole time?" If Brea confirmed she was still seeing Cylis, he would not be able to suppress his indignation. But beyond his outrage, he did not understand Cylis's power over Brea. She did not answer him.

"Are you seeing him? Don't lie to me, Brea. Tell me the truth." Still, she did not respond. Her silence bolstered his exasperation, and he sprang off the bed. Unable to calm himself, he paced.

"Everyone knows about us, Brea. It doesn't matter anymore about Jaime or Vienna—we both know it was supposed to be us, always. I don't understand what is so damn special about Cylis. Why do you still want to be with him?"

She remained silent, and he could not look at her. He continued to pace the length of the bed. "After everything that's happened between us, I can't believe you would still choose him," he exclaimed, stunned that after two years they had the chance to be together and her infatuation with Cylis lived on.

Brea cried out, "No, I don't love him. Hayden, he trapped me in his house and hurt me."

He froze—her words hung in the air as though the world came to a standstill. No—it better not be what he thought. His entire body tensed. Slowly, he turned his head to look at Brea. Tears streamed down her cheeks—the look in her eyes confirmed his worst fear. He did not need to ask, but he had to.

"What did he do to you, Brea?" he asked through gritted teeth and on the edge of losing himself to his anger.

Brea shut her eyes and shook her head. Hayden swallowed. "I can't say it out loud. I can't. It was my fault what he did to me."

Red. There were no thoughts—only rage, and he lost any sense of reason or control.

He did not realize what he had done until his mind rejoined reality, seeing Brea, her mouth agape and numb with shock, seated on the bed. Surrounding her were shards of glass, pens, and coins. He raced to her, repeating her name to snap her out of her stupor and instructing her not to move.

Adrenaline surged throughout his body as he knelt beside her on the bed, and he felt no pain as pieces of glass sliced into his knees. "Don't move," he repeated, his voice panicked.

Hayden held her arm to hold her still while he picked off pieces of glass in her hair and on her dress. Failing to think with a clear head, he brushed glass shards off the comforter, accumulating cuts on his hands and leaving smears of blood behind on Brea's arms and dress. He would look into her eyes periodically. The manner in which she stared ahead with a blank expression frightened him.

"Brea, I'm so sorry. I wasn't thinking. I didn't mean to scare you—I would never hurt you. Please don't move, or you'll get hurt. Stay here. Don't move."

Needing to find a broom and dustpan to clean up, he slid off the bed and stepped onto a sharp piece of glass. Though it hurt, he did not remove it until reaching the hallway. He bent down to pull it out, ignored the splotches of blood on the floor and continued on across the living room.

In the utility closet he found a garbage bag and a dustpan. He set them aside on the floor and then rooted through the cleaning supplies. Finding several rags and paper towels, he shoved the items into the garbage bag to carry back with him to his room.

"What the hell happened?" he mumbled to himself as he hurried down the hall to his room—he had never lost control of himself before. His heart raced, and his hands shook wildly—something was wrong with him. Before reaching his door, a thought came to mind—the way he felt could be from the pills in his mother's dresser.

Entering his room, he froze—Brea was gone. He raced to his bathroom and, finding it empty, spun around and saw the curtains pushed aside and the glass doors open. He ran outside into the darkness, but there was no sign of her, and it was impossible to know in which direction she ran. Unless she scaled the fence at the rear of the property, she would be stuck in the backyard. He reasoned it was more likely she fled towards the front yard.

On the verge of running to find her, his state of undress, wearing only boxers, and seeing his knees and hands bloodied gave him pause. His thoughts twisted in his brain in a relentless frenzy. If he found Brea, she might scream, and someone could call the police—but it was a risk he had to take—he could not leave her outside alone. He would have to find her, apologize, and coax her back into the house.

Hurrying inside to dress and find his car keys, a profound wave of nausea overtook him. Bracing himself against the wall, his whole body trembled, and he became lightheaded. As he slid to the floor, he attempted to inhale several deep breaths, but it was difficult. Black patches clouded his vision, and then everything went dark.

Chapter Twenty-Seven

BREA

Hayden rubbed his eyes and covered the lower half of his face with his hand. "I woke up in the morning on the floor. At first, I thought it had only been a nightmare. Then I saw my knees and hands—I can't describe what I felt. I tried to call you that morning, but your father picked up the phone, and I hung up. Then that night, I drove by your house and I saw your bedroom light on, but I froze and sat in my car for an hour before I left. And when I tried to talk to you after your interview, you were so angry. The way you looked at me—I knew I had lost you." Brea wiped her eyes. She could not find her words.

"I hated myself and accepted that I deserved to lose you. It wasn't until years later that a friend of mine in college told me about a similar reaction he had after taking a muscle relaxer. He became angry, agitated—it was what I suspected happened to me that night, but until then I wasn't certain. Losing my mom, finding out about Cylis—it broke me, and that medication was like throwing gasoline on a fire. I'm so sorry, Brea. I can't imagine what that was like for you, after everything you have been through."

Brea turned her head and stared into the flames of the fire. The curtain had lifted now that Hayden revealed the missing piece of the story. She closed her eyes. Her thoughts and emotions, chaotic, whipped around in her mind, but she could tease out the most prominent feeling—guilt.

"Hayden, I was so lost and wrapped up in myself back then. I knew you were grieving, but I missed all the signs of how much you were struggling. Or maybe I didn't want to see it because I was too afraid. I always thought you were so strong because you were there whenever I fell apart."

Hayden ran his hands through his hair and wiped his eyes as he continued to gaze into the fire. Brea rose from her chair, went to Hayden, and knelt before him. "I'm so sorry I gave up on you. All this time I thought you hid some evil part of yourself from me. But I turned my back on you when you needed me most."

"No, I was too stubborn to ask for help and it was my fault. I don't know if I'll ever be able to forgive myself for what happened—scaring you like that when you were alone and needed me to be strong for you."

Brea shook her head. "You don't have to forgive yourself today—but you have to know I forgive you, I swear I do." Brea lifted her arms and with her hands cradled Hayden's face. Looking into his eyes, she nodded. "Okay. Hayden?" She lowered her hands to his shoulders, and Hayden embraced her, pulling her in tight against him. "We don't apologize for that night again—it's gone forever," she whispered.

After several minutes they pulled back, looked into one another's eyes and smiled in relief, knowing that with the gift of forgiveness, the curse was lifted, and they were now free.

"Hayden?" Brea whispered.

"Brea?" Hayden replied.

"Maybe we should make another smore? This was very intense, and I really need one."

Wiping his eyes and the corners of his mouth, he laughed. "Yes. I'll make us another smore."

⁂

Strolling beside one another on the resort path, they paused to look at the night sky before splitting off to their respective casitas.

"Hayden, do you believe in fate?"

"You know, I stopped believing in fate until I saw you in the shop last month," he replied.

"I know what you mean. What were the odds that we met again at Harvey Slate years after meeting in the library and then twenty years later after high school? It couldn't have been just coincidence. Anyway, even though this trip was a 'crazy idea,' I'm glad you came back to find me." Brea turned to face Hayden. "You know me better than I know myself."

The edges of Hayden's mouth lifted. "You know yourself. I think you only have to practice trusting yourself and accept that you don't have to be someone else to be loved. Let's stop by the resort shop tomorrow, and I'll buy you a giant sweatshirt to help put you back in touch with your seventh-grade self—she was pretty cute."

Brea smiled and chuckled. It was the best compliment she had heard from a man. Looking into Brea's eyes, Hayden's smile faded. He lifted his arm and placed a hand on Brea's cheek. She wrapped her hand around his forearm as Hayden tilted his head down and paused inches from her face.

Conflicted, she did not know what she wanted in that moment, but his touch and tenderness, she craved. Her lips parted, and she held her breath. His scent and the touch of his hand overrode her mind, and she did not want him to move away or for the moment to end. The pace of his breaths quickened, though he neither moved nor removed his hand from her cheek. Closing her eyes, she held her breath.

"Brea?" he whispered. Opening her eyes, she searched Hayden's face. It was difficult to read his expression.

"Let's go to sleep. We have the cruise tomorrow at ten. I'll come to your room at nine."

Brea averted her eyes, pressed her lips together and nodded. She took a step backwards, and a torrent of emotions filled her—desire, guilt, relief, and disappointment. "Goodnight," she replied.

She hastened her steps and would not look back at Hayden, afraid of what had woken inside her. In her mind she repeated, *"I am married, and Hayden has Avery."* And she would repeat that to herself as many times as it took tonight to get the idea out of her mind that Hayden had nearly kissed her, and more important, that she had *wanted* him to kiss her.

In her casita, flushed and restless, Brea tore off her sweater—she needed something to snap her out of her state of mind. Grabbing a hair elastic from the desk, she tied up her hair, slipped off her shorts, and walked to the patio doors to step into the night air. With no ambivalence, she went to the plunge pool and descended the steps to submerge herself.

The cool water tempered the physical tension in her body, though her mind continued to race, replaying the evening with Hayden. Leaning her head back, a heart-sinking thought surfaced. Fate had repeatedly brought her and Hayden together, only to cruelly separate them time and again, like some sick joke.

"It isn't fair," she whispered to herself.

Sleeping tonight would not be possible with the storm of thoughts whipping against every corner of her mind. She stood, climbed out of the plunge pool, and grabbed a towel. Once inside, she dried herself off and changed into a pair of underwear and a cotton tank top.

Grabbing her notebook and pen, she stopped at the mini-bar to grab a soda, then collapsed on the sofa. She could not focus on writing something comprehensible, so she wrote anything that came to mind—words, phrases, and the fleeting emotions that swarmed within her like a deranged hive of bees.

It was an exorcism of her pain, cathartic and true, and an attempt to reclaim what she had never allowed herself to have—her own voice and power. Brea read aloud her stream-of-consciousness scribbling and sighed. She knew what she needed to do in the morning. It had been a long time coming, and she was no longer afraid.

Chapter Twenty-Eight

HAYDEN

Hayden watched Brea as she turned and walked to her casita. It had taken all of his restraint not to kiss her a moment ago. Every part of his body wanted her, but he had vowed not to insert himself between her and her husband for his own selfish desires.

If she were free and chose him, only then would he allow himself to kiss her—no secret friendship or stolen nights. He wanted her for himself and to make a real life together. To have only a taste and let her go again, he could not imagine what that would do to him.

"Damn," he murmured, loath to return to his room with the bubbling unrest that now consumed him. He knew where he needed to go. Hastening his steps, he bounded into the lobby and went straight to the bar, pausing once his eyes locked on the reason he came there.

Henry, dressed in a dark blue collared shirt with his Panama hat set atop the bar, sat on the same stool as the previous night with a glass of scotch in front of him, chatting with the bartender. Hayden approached him, gripped the back of the vacant stool beside Henry, and dropped his head down.

"We've got to stop meeting like this," Henry said. Hayden chuckled and nodded.

"Yeah, well, I came looking for you, Henry," Hayden admitted.

"Have a seat. Javier, McCallan 18 for my friend here. Looks like you need the good stuff tonight." Hayden pulled out the barstool and sat down. Javier appeared and set down a tumbler of scotch before Hayden.

"Thank you, Javier. I'll pick up Henry's as well."

"Not a chance. Put it on my tab, Javier. Son, it's an old man's job to pick up the check for a man as troubled as you."

Hayden nodded with appreciation. "Thank you, Henry."

"Tell me, how is it going with your lady friend? Wild guess, but I suppose not well?"

Hayden exhaled and glanced at the ceiling. "Honestly, I can't believe how well it's going. She forgave me—it's better than I could have imagined. And I think she wanted me to kiss her tonight."

Henry cried out, "So what the hell are you doing here with me?"

Hayden shook his head, picked up the scotch, and took a long sip. "Damn, that's good, Henry."

"The day my company went public, I bought my wife a new dress and took her out for a steak dinner. I got to talking with the bartender before our table was ready, and he poured me this on the house to congratulate me. It's hard to go back to something else when you've had a little taste of heaven." Henry studied Hayden a moment and lifted his hands off the bar in a gesture of incredulity. "So now what's the problem?" he asked.

Hayden continued to hold his drink and tapped the glass with his finger. "Well, that's my problem. This woman, Brea, is like this scotch. We took this secret trip here to get closure on our screwed up past—and we did that tonight. But now, it doesn't feel like that's enough. She's married, and from what

I can tell—and I'm not wrong—to an asshole. And I lost my girlfriend yesterday because she wanted me to propose and I said no. With Brea back in my life, I couldn't go back home to Avery." Hayden rubbed his temples and avoided eye contact with Henry—saying it all out loud was embarrassing.

Henry inhaled and then chuckled. "What I said before about love being simple, I take it back in your case. That sounds pretty crazy." He lifted his finger into the air. "But not hopeless. Crazier things have happened in this world, mark my words." Hayden raised his glass to take another sip.

"So, did you tell her how you feel?" Henry asked.

"No. I can't put her in another difficult position. We did that years ago, in secret, and everything got screwed up."

"Do you love her?"

"Love is—I mean, I don't know. We haven't seen each other for twenty years, but when we were kids, I couldn't stay away from her. I wound up throwing a rock at her window at midnight to get her downstairs to tell her how I felt, even though she had a boyfriend who would have kicked my ass if he had found out. And now, who am I kidding? Since she came back into my life, she's all I can think about."

With a shake of his head, Henry picked up his drink. "What do you mean you don't know? Did you fall on your head too many times? You love her. Tell her."

Hayden slapped his hands on the bar. "I can't do that to her again—try to convince her to throw her life upside down for me after twenty years. She only forgave me an hour ago."

"Oh, you're so sure, huh? Maybe you don't need to convince her. Maybe you just put on your big-boy pants and tell her how you feel? If it doesn't go your way, you know, then you move on. But if it does—then you win big. You get the girl, and your life changes."

Hayden looked at Henry. "You have a real, simple way of putting things, Henry."

"Hey, you live to be my age, you learn a thing or two, and the least I can do is pass it down. Let me tell you about how I almost screwed things up with Willa. Told her I needed to make more money, impress her father before we could get married, and she almost married someone else. The worst months of my life, and I did a twelve-month combat tour in Vietnam in sixty-five. You got some time, kid?"

"Yeah, plenty, Henry." Hayden lifted his scotch and shifted his body to face Henry. He did not know what to do about Brea. They had three days left together, and laying everything he felt on the table felt impossible. But the alternative—to let her go without a fight, and this trip being the end of their story, would be devastating.

Chapter Twenty-Nine

Brea

S prawled out on her bed with her notebook and a pen beside her on the mattress, Brea woke. It was eight in the morning. Sitting up, she rubbed her eyes and reached for her phone. She called Adam before she could talk herself out of it.

"Good morning, Brea," Adam answered in a condescending tone.

"Hi, what do you love about me, Adam?" she asked, bypassing small talk to ask the meaty questions she needed answers to.

"Hold on, give me a minute here," Adam paused, and she heard shuffling in the background. "Brea, I had hoped after you slept you would be back to normal. Are you and your friends on some kind of crazy bender over there? You're a middle-aged woman and a mother, not a sorority girl on spring break."

"I wasn't drinking yesterday, and I am dead cold sober right now. Adam, answer my question," Brea said with conviction.

Adam sighed. "I don't want to get into this right now. Let's talk when you get home."

"No. No, Adam. I need to know right now. For the past few years—even longer than that—we have not been happy, and we can't ignore it anymore. I'm wondering if we were ever happy, or we got married because I'm a complacent trophy wife. Thinking back, I have been a walking shell of myself, and being here without you, I am the happiest I've been in years. That says something."

"Brea, I don't want to talk about this. You're having some sort of mental crisis right now."

Shaking her head, Brea pressed on. "Adam, listen to me. When we're in the same room, I feel more alone than when I'm actually alone. True, I have not been my full, genuine self with you. I've spent the better part of nine years trying to be calm, happy, and ignore the things I need and deserve. And you need to know that I have also spent two decades pushing away my painful childhood as though it never happened. I'm ready to tell you all about it now—no more secrets. But I need to know if you're in it with me. Do you love me enough to discover with me who I really am? I've made mistakes, others have hurt me, and I have a dark side. I never told you this, but I went to Harvey Slate because I wrote intense sad poetry that freaked out my high school English teacher. Is this person someone you want to go all in with for the rest of our lives?"

"Brea, I'm worried about you. I think you're having some kind of breakdown."

"Adam, I am not crazy—just answer me. Do you love me enough to fight for this marriage?"

"Brea—"

"Don't lie to me because it's easier, Adam. Be honest with me—I need it now more than ever." Brea raised the volume of her voice to let Adam know she would not relent.

"I've been seeing another woman for the past year."

Brea stopped breathing. Her mouth opened, but she remained silent, stunned. Adam waited a beat before he spoke.

"Did you hear me, Brea?"

"I'm in shock. I was not expecting to hear that." Brea felt as if the world had imploded. "Were you ever going to tell me? Does this mean you want out?"

"We have the children, a life together, Brea. We're going to do the right thing and stay together." The manner in which Adam spoke, as though the only option was to stay in a loveless marriage for the sake of the children, astounded Brea.

"Adam, do you have any love left for me?" Brea asked in a slow, controlled voice.

"Brea, this isn't about romance and love. We have children and my family's reputation to consider. It isn't about feelings. This is the responsible thing to do. When you come home, we'll go back to normal, and I will break things off with Kaylin."

"I need to hear it, Adam. Do you love me? I might get over 'Kaylin,' but I need to hear you love me. I need to know that you would go to hell with me if it was the only way you could be with me?"

"What are you talking about, Brea? That makes no sense. I'm not answering that. Come home, let's move on, and things will be fine."

Adam's words and demeanor, detached and cold, felt as though Brea had plunged into a pool of ice water—she was now wide awake.

"I have to go, Adam. I'll talk to you later."

"Brea—"

Brea hung up the phone and pressed it to her chin as she reflected. The late nights, the frequent trips, the descent into living together as roommates who tolerated one another's presence—the signs were there for years, but Brea had buried her head.

Stumbling to the minibar, Brea opened the refrigerator and removed a bottle of sparkling water. In a daze, she placed it on the table and went to the patio doors. She slid them open and stepped outside. On autopilot, she crossed the patio to the gate and climbed over it. Whipping around, she eyed the neighboring casitas, remembering Hayden's was to the left of hers when facing the front door. Quickening her steps, she hopped over his gate and crossed the patio.

Raising her arm, she knocked on the bedroom pocket doors. Rolling her eyes, she thought to herself he was likely at the gym, working on his incredible physique. A moment later, to her surprise, the curtains opened several inches and half his face appeared. He blinked several times in surprise before pulling the curtains further apart and sliding the door open.

"Brea, what are you doing? Why didn't you come to the front door?" he asked with a perplexed expression, still half-asleep.

"Adam's fucking another woman, and he thinks we should just—go back to normal for the sake of the kids."

Hayden's mouth opened for a moment then closed, uncertain he had heard Brea correctly. "Um, come in. Are you okay? You seem oddly—calm or maybe a little crazed, I can't tell." Hayden stepped aside.

"He told me after I pressed him if he still loved me. In a five-minute conversation, my marriage turned completely upside down and exploded." Brea fixed her eyes on Hayden, dressed only in his boxer briefs. She turned her head and felt the blood rushing to her face. Seeing her reaction, he went to the dresser to put on a T-shirt.

"Um, Brea, you're—in your underwear," he pointed out. Brea glanced down and saw she wore only her white tank top and a pair of nude boy short panties. She raised her eyes to the ceiling. Hayden suppressed a grin, pulled a pair of boxers from his dresser, and tossed them to her. She caught them in her hands.

"Oh my God," she mumbled and slipped into them.

"So, are you telling me you have to leave? To go home?" Hayden asked, his brow furrowed as he sat on the bed's edge.

Brea shook her head. "No, I'm not leaving. If anything, I need time to figure things out. This happened five minutes ago. I'm sorry I woke you up. I don't know why I came here, but I should take a shower and—I need a drink."

Hayden nodded. "We have the cruise today. Should I cancel—"

"No," Brea cried out, holding up a finger. "Absolutely not. That is what I need—the ocean and a drink. Get ready and meet me back at my casita."

Hayden rubbed his forehead. "Brea, let's not go off the rails today. I don't want to carry you off the boat throwing up. Let's take a deep breath and enjoy the day, but not recklessly."

Brea nodded, though avoided eye contact with Hayden. "Sure. Of course. I'll see you soon." She whipped around and exited through the patio doors.

"Do you want to maybe—leave through the front door?" Hayden asked and pointed to the bedroom door.

"No, I don't have my key. Just get ready." Brea waved to Hayden as she crossed the patio to return to her casita.

Her thoughts looped in circles as she walked. Once inside her bedroom, she scanned the closet for something to wear and her eyes landed on a short ruffled white wrap dress with a deep V-neck. Today, she aimed to prove to herself that was still sexy and attractive. And if Adam no longer found her desirable—there were plenty of other men who would.

CHAPTER THIRTY

HAYDEN

Rising from the bed, Hayden followed Brea to the glass doors, watched her climb over the gate and turn with a brisk pace to her casita. This was unexpected, and now everything was more complex and tangled. Grabbing a bottle of water from the minibar, he drank it down while waiting for the shower to warm.

Before falling asleep, he settled on telling Brea what he felt for her over dinner, but this piece of news shattered his plan. Her husband had been unfaithful, her head was spinning, and although Adam had done serious damage to his marriage, it was still possible Brea would decide to work things out with him. He did not want to confuse her and make things more complicated by confessing his feelings.

Hayden called the concierge to order bagels and coffee to pick up at the front desk upon seeing they were running short on time. Knowing that Brea was in shock and planned on drinking once they boarded the cruise, he wanted to make sure there was something in her stomach before they left. Hanging up the phone, he wondered what advice Henry would give him, considering this development. *"Put on your big-boy pants and go with it,"* he thought to himself with a chuckle.

Stepping into the hot shower, the memory of Brea in his bedroom invaded his mind, dressed only in her tank top and panties, with her bare, sexy legs and messy hair flowing over her shoulders. Shutting his eyes, he rubbed his neck with a firm pressure to distract himself, or rather the lower half of his body, from responding to the image of her breasts, barely covered by the thin material of her tank top, burning into his mind. He groaned and switched the water to the coldest setting.

Half an hour later, Hayden knocked on Brea's door. When she opened it, he stood speechless—she looked incredible, dressed in a short white sundress highlighting the curves of her breasts that peeked out of the neckline and the ruffled skirt hitting mid-thigh. If there were an effective type of torture in this world to crack the toughest of men, she was it.

Hayden blinked and cleared his throat. "You look ready. I ordered food. Bagels and coffee for us. All the good stuff," he rambled and trailed off.

"Great," Brea said, holding his gaze as she stepped past him.

Hayden closed the door of her casita and turned to face her. "Did you bring a bathing suit? The cruise docks on a beach for a barbecue, and we can swim."

"In my beach bag. I figured I could change on the boat."

Having packed a change of clothes for dinner, Hayden wore his bathing suit and a white T-shirt. He planned to propose they eat in Puerto Vallarta after the cruise, having hired Alonso once again for the entire day.

Walking beside Brea, he briefly studied her face. She appeared more composed than earlier. "How are you after everything from earlier this morning? Do you want to talk about it?"

"No, I don't. But I need to say that if it weren't for you, Hayden, I don't know if I would have found out." Raising her hands, palms up, she shook her head in disbelief. He did not know how to feel about that comment. Although part of this trip had been for her to delve into the root of her unhappiness, the reality was now startling. The end of her marriage could be his fault, and perhaps today she was appreciative, but what about in a week, or a month from now? She could wind up hating him for it.

Entering the lobby, they stopped at the concierge desk. "Señor Botero, Señora Staxon, for you." With a smile, he handed them each a coffee cup and a white paper bag containing their toasted bagels with cream cheese.

"Thank you, Alejandro," Hayden replied. After pestering him with a multitude of tasks, he had become rather friendly with Alejandro and tipped him generously for his efforts.

"Enjoy your day. Alonso is waiting outside, but you have time to enjoy your breakfast in the lounge for ten minutes if you prefer." Alejandro gestured to the seating area. Brea smiled and sauntered over to an empty set of chairs with a small table.

Hayden's eyes fixed on her legs as she crossed the lobby. He exhaled and looked at the ceiling, admonishing himself for his weakness. To survive the day, he needed to get his head straight.

Joining her, he seated himself in the opposite chair. Brea spoke. "Hayden. You seem kind of tense. I'm sorry I intruded and woke you up this morning."

Shaking his head, Hayden let out a breath, amused by her lack of awareness as to the extent her sudden appearance in her underwear had thrown him this morning. "It's fine, you were—in shock."

"In my panties, so embarrassing," Brea laughed.

"Yeah, well. You're dressed—now—in that." Hayden faltered, cleared his throat, and turned his head to feign surveying the lobby. He battled with himself to ignore the fantasy playing out in his mind—unwrapping her dress and watching it fall to the floor. Hoping to banish the thought, he covered his face and closed his eyes.

Brea raised her eyebrows and glanced down at her dress. Self-conscious, she tugged her skirt down an inch and took a bite of her bagel. Hayden followed suit and stuffed his mouth so he would not have to talk, then drank his coffee. After ten minutes, he checked his watch.

"All right, let's go or we're going to miss the cruise."

They exited the lobby and, seeing Alonso, joined him at the car. Alonso greeted them, and while exchanging pleasantries, unburdened them of their bags to store in the trunk. After settling in their seats, Alonso informed them that the traffic was lighter than expected and they would arrive on time. Brea sighed and glanced out the window before turning back to face Hayden.

Hayden tapped his leg with his fingers. "Brea, what about your kids, now that you found out about Adam having an affair?" he asked.

Brea shook her head. "I can't deny that it would be easier to live with Adam as we are for the sake of Alex and Sophie, but I don't know if that's possible." She shut her eyes and rested her head on the seat.

Hayden nodded and turned his head to gaze out the window. Her reply confirmed what he worried might happen—she could decide it would be better to stay with Adam for the sake of her children. They sat in silence throughout the drive, navigating their thoughts. As difficult as it was, he had to accept the likelihood his future would not include Brea—at least not the way he wanted her in it.

Chapter Thirty-One

Brea

"Honey, you look beautiful," Trina proclaimed, embracing Brea in her wedding gown. Brea wore a lace cap-sleeved gown with a square bodice and a full princess skirt, a dress that Adam's mother insisted would "put a smile on Adam's face." Though the style of dress inspired at best, luke-warm feelings, Brea had acquiesced as she aimed to please Adam and her future family.

She stood before the window in the bridal suite of the rented luxury home in Malibu. Peering down, she gazed upon the two hundred guests milling about the property on the cliff's edge overlooking the ocean. The vast majority of guests were from Adam's side of the family as Brea had invited only her parents, Trina, Hannah, and friends from work.

Trina stepped away to pour them a glass of champagne. Drawing a deep breath, Brea turned from the window. The hairstylist was nearly done with the final touches to Hannah's hair, and the ceremony would begin soon. Trina beckoned Brea to join her on the chaise for a toast.

"To good fortune and a long, happy life," Trina said, raising and clinking her glass with Brea's.

Several months prior, Brea learned of Trina's breast cancer diagnosis. The doctors were optimistic, having caught it early, and with surgery and chemotherapy, informed her she had a good chance of survival, but Brea still worried.

Dressed in a short beige cocktail dress with her hair styled in a voluminous updo, Trina resembled every inch of the doting surrogate mother of the bride she had been to Brea, serving as Brea's sounding board for any details that Mary tasked her with for the wedding—selecting Hannah's maid of honor gown, her choice of colors for the flowers, and the gift registry. Brea's mother had been vocal that she had no interest in being involved in any wedding planning and now, preferred to wait in the living area of the rented home, rather than prepare with Brea so she could "rest before the ceremony."

Brea exhaled and dabbed a tear from the corner of her eye with a tissue. The entire morning, she felt uneasy, though continued to remind herself it was only wedding jitters. In her mind, she replayed an incident that happened at the wedding breakfast. Having joined Adam while in conversation with several guests, she slipped her arm around his waist. With a swift motion, he removed her arm and continued to speak as though he had brushed aside an intrusive fly. Though it felt like a slap in the face, she smiled and pretended as though nothing happened.

"Honey, what is it?" Trina asked, placing her glass on the table.

"Jitters. I was so excited to get married, and Adam is handsome, smart, and he'll make a wonderful husband. But now I'm scared. I thought on my wedding day I'd be sure, with no doubts." Brea wiped away another tear.

Trina took Brea's hand in hers. "What are you afraid of?"

Brea sniffed and looked out the window. The memory of looking into Hayden's blue eyes in the library when she was twelve resurfaced. She shook her head to push the image from her mind. "That I'm wrong. That I'm making a mistake. I don't know if I trust myself."

"Well, honey, we can't be certain about everything. But I'll tell you something. You know what the best part of life is?"

Brea met Trina's eyes, kind and full of love. "What?" Brea asked.

"Surprises. We never know what or who is down the road. You can have another chance if you make a mistake. No matter how hard or how hopeless it may seem, there's a choice and, if you're lucky, another day. So, you make the best choice you can today. Because who knows what's down the road?" Trina placed her hand on Brea's cheek. "What do you want to do, honey? I've got a rental car out there, and if you need me to carry you out and hide you in the trunk, I'll do it."

Brea squeezed Trina's hand and laughed. She was on the verge of getting everything she wanted, and she would not ruin her chance for a stable, secure life. "No, I'm getting married today."

"You trust yourself, honey, okay? No matter what happens in the future, it will be all right. And if you fall, pick yourself up, have a good cry, and then make another mistake. Do it again until you get it right."

❦

Alonso sprang out of the car and opened the door for Brea. Lost in her memories, she opened her eyes. Stepping into the bright sun, she pulled her hat from her bag and set it atop her head. Hayden put on his sunglasses and joined Brea. Alonso handed them their bags.

"I'll be waiting here when the boat docks at six o'clock. Enjoy the cruise," Alonso said with a nod and a warm smile.

"Thank you," Brea and Hayden replied and turned to check in at the welcome kiosk. Upon boarding, Brea smiled, impressed by the size of the white yacht boasting a two-level upper deck with a bar, teak wood flooring, beige cushioned seating, a DJ booth, and a large white dining table set with a spread of hot and cold appetizers. Six other couples were milling about, holding cocktails.

As Brea and Hayden crossed the deck, several of the couples smiled and greeted them. Seeing a set of empty chairs, they settled in to wait until the yacht pulled away from the dock. Across from them, a married couple celebrating their twenty-fifth wedding anniversary from Michigan, Greg and Julia, introduced themselves.

"How long have you two been married?" Julia asked, pointing to Brea's wedding ring. Brea's eyes grew wide and she looked at Hayden. They had not thought to create a backstory in the event they spoke with other people.

Hayden coughed. "Oh, no, this is my—sister, Brea," he replied.

Brea snorted and then cleared her throat. "Oh, excuse me, I think a bug flew up my nose," she said with a strained voice.

Greg and Julia smiled. "Oh well, isn't that sweet, a family reunion trip, I love it," Julia said and fluffed her shoulder-length blonde hair. She wore a vivid orange strapless sundress and coral lipstick. Greg, bald, wore a white polo shirt and tropical printed swim trunks.

Hayden stood up from his chair. "Um, sis, do you want a drink?"

Brea rose. "Yeah. I'll go with him to make sure he doesn't put something gross in my drink. He did that once when I was ten. I still have nightmares about it."

Turning to walk to the bar, Brea jabbed Hayden in his side. "Your sister? That's twisted, Hayden. Couldn't I have been your friend?"

Hayden lifted his hands. "I don't know. I was on the spot. It popped into my head." Brea glared at him. "What? Okay, order your drink," Hayden said, placing his hand on her back, and giving her a gentle push to move her closer to the bar.

"I'll have a mojito, and he'll have an apple juice. He's my brother, and he has terrible irritable bowel syndrome. If he has anything too acidic, or any alcohol, he'll be in the bathroom for the whole cruise," Brea informed the bartender with a serious facial expression. The bartender glanced at Hayden and then Brea, perplexed and uncertain if he had heard her correctly.

Hayden tipped his head back with an incredulous smile. "I'll be fine. I'll have a draft beer." With a mischievous smirk, Brea swiveled around and chuckled.

"Brea, you don't want to play this game with me," he challenged.

"Hayden, I do. I really do," Brea laughed louder and jabbed his arm with her elbow. The bartender served their drinks, and they returned to their seats across from Julia and Greg.

Greg lifted his glass in the air. "To a wonderful afternoon," he said. Brea and Hayden grinned and raised their drinks. "So, Hayden and Brea, what do you both do for a living?" Julia asked in a chipper voice.

Before Brea could speak, Hayden answered. "I'm a hedge fund manager, and Brea is an exotic dancer in a gentleman's club in Miami. After she loosens up with a few drinks, she could show us the latest routine she's working on. But without the goat, we won't get the full experience of the performance."

Brea widened her eyes and then smiled. "Yes, it's an upscale club that is very popular. Hayden used to go there all the time until he got kicked out for scaring the customers and harassing the dancers. He would sit at the table and cry all the time. But you're better now, Hayden, right—after I paid for all of that therapy with my tips."

Brea patted Hayden's shoulder twice before he brushed off her hand. Greg and Julia exchanged a curious glance.

"Well, that's nice—to hear," Julia replied with a tight-lipped smile while nodding her head.

Hayden coughed. "That was after you left rehab. It only took, what? Six tries? She was getting arrested all the time for stealing to support her cough syrup addiction. And then you got that rash all over your body. The doctors kept saying scabies, but none of the creams worked."

Brea pressed her lips together. "Yup," she replied. Hayden grinned at Brea. They both turned to smile at Julia and Greg.

"Well, we should get another drink. We're just so excited to be here—and we'll see you both later." Julia and Greg rose from their seats and hurried away.

Brea's mouth opened, staring ahead. Hayden lost it and laughed. "I hate you," Brea said, shaking her head.

"Come on, let's have some fun today," Hayden said and nudged Brea's shoulder, knocking her slightly off balance.

Brea rubbed her forehead. Looking into Hayden's eyes, she smiled. "Fine, it's on." Laughing, they clinked their glasses and moved on to the next couple.

"Hi, we're Hayden and Brea, from Miami. Hayden just got out of prison, and we're looking to meet some new friends today?" Brea exclaimed, holding out her hand to a bewildered couple.

After another round of drinks and working the cruise to greet the other guests, Brea and Hayden grew tired of their game. It was not surprising most of the other guests avoided them, leaving them to enjoy most of the upper deck to themselves until they docked at the beach.

Brea changed into her light-pink bathing suit and knotted a white silk sarong around her waist. After lathering on sunscreen, she strolled across the beach and joined Hayden, seated at a table near a covered outdoor bar with two glasses of iced-tea and a bowl of chips and salsa.

"I'm a little worried the boat is going to leave us behind. I may have gone too far when I told Sarah and Denis about the sexually transmitted disease you caught traveling abroad last month the doctors can't identify," she said, seating herself opposite Hayden.

Hayden shook his head and laughed. "I can't believe you said that. I almost threw you off the boat."

Brea smiled and dipped a chip into the salsa. "Maybe we should come clean and admit we were just messing around."

"No way. You created one hell of a reputation for me. Nobody's going to fuck around with me today."

"Well, except for me," Brea replied and raised her eyebrows. Hayden chuckled and grabbed a few chips out of the bowl. "Hayden, I'm having fun. Real fun—down to my bones fun." Looking into Hayden's eyes, she remembered all those years ago when she discovered he had a sense of humor after many months of avoiding conversation with her.

"Me too," he replied with a smile, though Brea picked up on a hint of sadness in his expression as he lowered his eyes to the table.

"I don't want to be strangers after this trip. We can stay in touch, right?" Brea asked, hopeful he felt the same way. Finding him again, and after last night, the idea of never seeing him again would be tragic and unnecessary. Raising his eyes to hers, he hesitated a moment.

"Of course," he replied. It was what Brea wanted to hear, though as they held one another's gaze, a part of her wanted more. She did not know what she wanted him to say, but something more. The scent of the smoke from the grill permeated the air, and Brea's stomach growled. She picked up the paper menu on the table and read aloud that they were to enjoy a lunch of shrimp, lobster, and carne asada tacos.

"Tell me more about your kids, Brea," Hayden asked when she had finished reading the menu.

"Well, Alex is serious. He reads, builds, and has a mind that loves to focus on the details of what makes the world and life possible. I think he's going to be a scientist or a doctor. And Sophie has the biggest heart. She is so kind and sensitive, which means she can have big feelings, cry at the drop of a hat or if she sees someone suffering or upset, she gives them a big hug. I think she'll do something creative. Maybe she'll be an artist or a writer."

"Does she hug you all the time?"

Brea frowned. "You know what—she does. Naturally, I thought it's because I'm her mommy, but maybe that isn't the only reason. Actually, one of the turning points for me that played a big role in my decision to come here was after she told me I was 'sad all the time' and it made her sad." Brea turned her head to survey the beach and sighed. A merchant stopped beside the table, carrying a large box of souvenirs, miscellaneous beach toys, and sunscreen for sale.

"Oh, no thank you," Brea replied, though Hayden scanned the products and pointed at a deck of cards.

"Five dollars," the merchant said. Hayden did the math and dropped in two hundred pesos, double the price, for a generous tip. "Gracias, señor."

"What game did you have in mind?" Brea asked.

Hayden smiled. "What can you play?"

Brea did not want to let on, but she was an excellent poker player. In college, she and Hannah would host poker nights in their apartment, and Brea could reliably clean out the table if she was in the mood.

"Blackjack, Gin Rummy. But I've always wanted to play more poker. Maybe you could remind me of the rules?"

"We have nothing to bet." Hayden turned around to see if there was anything they could use. "I have an idea. Hold on." He stood up and went to the bar. Several minutes later he returned with a large plastic jar filled with bottle caps and held them up, victorious.

Greg and Julia passed by the table with an awkward wave. Brea called out after them. "Greg, Julia. Do you want to join my brother and me for a game of strip poker? I play with Hayden all the time."

Hurrying away and pretending they did not hear Brea, she chuckled and looked back at Hayden, who had lowered his head and covered his eyes with his hand. "Okay, now you have to stop, Brea," he exclaimed through his laughter.

She laughed. "No way, I'm having too much fun. Deal the cards."

Brea feigned attention to Hayden's review of the hand rankings and general rules of Texas Hold'em and then played the first six hands conservatively while observing him—he was not mindful of hiding his tells. If he tapped his fingers on the table, he was holding onto a good hand and would ask Brea a question to distract her. If his hand was garbage, he would blink several times or shift in his seat. Once confident she had his game down and pattern of betting, she flipped the switch and played to her skill level.

After bluffing Hayden out two rounds and winning a high pot with three of a kind, Hayden sat back in his seat. "I think you hustled me, Brea."

Brea grinned. "I don't know—maybe it's just beginner's luck, bro."

Hayden shook his head. "Oh, it's on. No holding back now."

For the following half hour, Hayden and Brea went head-to-head until a young newlywed couple, Advik and Mira, introduced themselves and asked if they could join the game. The four of them played, and after several rowdy hands, attracted an audience. They paused only for a quick lunch when Hayden and Advik offered to bring the food to the table.

With an hour left on the beach, the foursome decided on one last hand to have time for a swim before needing to board their respective boats. Brea had amassed the most bottle caps, with Hayden and Advik tied for second, and Mira the least amount. Mira folded after the second round of betting. Hayden, Advik and Brea checked on the third round, but when the final community card was dealt, a king of hearts, she held a flush, and she spotted Hayden blinking as he studied his cards.

He was bluffing. Brea went all in, and the surrounding crowd whistled and cheered. With an arrogant smile, Brea looked into Hayden's eyes. "Advik?" Brea asked.

"I'm all in," Advik replied with confidence.

Hayden did not break eye contact with Brea and exhaled. "You sure you want to do this, Brea?"

The crowd let out an "ooh" at the challenge.

Brea nodded, "Absolutely."

Hayden smirked and pushed in his caps. "All in."

Everyone cheered, then quieted down as Brea picked up her cards, smiled, and flipped her two cards over, one by one, to show her king-high flush of hearts.

"Ooh," the crowd bellowed. Advik groaned and showed his cards, losing to Brea with two pairs. Mira frowned and wrapped her arm around Advik to comfort him as everyone shifted their focus onto Hayden, still staring into Brea's eyes. He pressed his lips together and picked up his cards. Brea held her breath as Hayden turned his cards over—with his king and ace of diamonds, Hayden had a full house, aces full of kings.

The onlookers hollered in disbelief, carrying on and creating a scene as Advik jumped out of his chair with his head in his hands and cried out, "Holy shit." The only two who remained calm were Brea and Hayden. Composed, she sat with a smile on her face as Hayden placed a finger across his lips with his chin in his hand, continuing to hold Brea's gaze. Brea was not angry. She was impressed, and she could not help but think—he looked sexy as hell.

Chapter Thirty-Two

Hayden

Playing poker with Brea, Hayden did not know how he made it through the game. He found her intense focus, sharp wit, and confidence alluring. If not for the crowd of people surrounding them, half of whom thought she was his sister, he would have made a move to kiss her, and all the complications and Adam could go to the devil.

"Good game, Hayden," Brea conceded and offered him her hand. The other guests, staff, Advik and Mira congratulated Hayden and waved goodbye to Brea, dispersing either to swim or to order one last drink from the beach bar. Hayden took Brea's hand and shook it.

"I can't believe you had a full house—I saw your tell," Brea exclaimed and shook her head in disbelief. "I really thought I had you."

"Well, I had to fool you. Once you revealed yourself as a skilled player, I knew I had to be ruthless."

"I'm getting in the water and after we dock, you're taking me out to a club tonight. I want to dance."

Hayden shook his head. "We're old, and I don't dance."

"We're not that old, and I want to go to a club. You owe me after the public humiliation. And you told that couple over there I used to operate a kitten fighting ring. I've caught them glaring at me with hostility, and I'm worried they're planning a beating."

"Wait, I'm the poker winner. Don't I get to pick what we do tonight?"

"Tomorrow night you can take me out for dinner at five o'clock, followed by a riveting game of bocce ball, but tonight—it's a club."

Hayden held up his hands. "Fine. But if I'm asleep in a booth at ten, don't wake me up."

Brea laughed. "Do you want to swim?"

"In a minute. I'm going to bask in the glory of my victory, and then I'll join you."

Brea turned around and muttered, "I can't believe you had a full house."

Hayden chuckled and watched Brea cross the beach to the shore, then test the temperature of the water with her feet. He could not take his eyes off her, captivated by her long hair left loose down her back and the white silk sarong whipping around her legs in the breeze. "Her husband is an idiot," he mumbled to himself.

Allowing his mind to wander, he smiled, remembering the night his mother taught him how to play poker when he was twelve. When his father would travel out of town, after Hayden finished his homework, he would play card games at the kitchen table with his mother. These were some of his fondest memories with her.

"Okay, Hayden. I'm teaching you how to play poker tonight. I think it's the most interesting card game because it's not only about the cards in your hand. You need to learn when to push, when to pull back, and the way you learn that is by knowing the player across from you."

Hayden squinted his eyes. "So, is it like cheating?"

His mother smiled at him. "No. It's more like you are figuring out their secrets—the ones they don't want you to know. Those are their giveaways. Are you familiar with the expression 'put on your poker face'?"

"Yeah. You're not supposed to smile, so you don't give away that you have great cards."

"Right, but it isn't just about smiling. Some people are fantastic at hiding what they don't want you to see. But if you're good at the game, you look for everything—if they hold their breath, open their mouths, scratch their ears, or talk too much. That can help you decide how you play—if you bet, fold, or go so big, you risk it all."

"Mom, that sounds hard."

"Well, Hayden, you're already good at it. You can always tell when I'm worried about something or if I'm sad, right?"

"Yeah. But that's because you're my mom."

"That may be part of it. But you're good at it with many people. You can see when someone is struggling. Do you remember the time the woman at the grocery store had a little boy who kept running away from her?"

"She couldn't shop, and she looked like she was about to cry," Hayden replied.

"Right, and what did you do? You took the little boy's hand and ran around the store with him so she could finish her shopping. Because you knew it would help her, not because you asked, you could just tell. That's a gift Hayden, not everyone can do that."

Hayden thought for a moment. He had always been that way—it seemed natural. "So, you think I'll be a good poker player?"

"Yes. I also know you'll be able to use that skill in life. I think there will be times when you'll need it to make an important decision. Sometimes you won't know if someone is saying something true or lying to you based only on their words."

"Okay, so are we going to play poker now?"

His mother smiled as she shuffled the cards, hoping that though her son did not grasp the entirety of her lesson, she had planted a seed, and someday he would understand.

Brea rotated at her waist and gestured for Hayden to join her. He rose, relieved she had enjoyed the afternoon despite having received some of the worst news someone could hear earlier that morning. Although devastating, after living with Adam in a failing marriage for years, perhaps she did not know how to extricate herself, and this was the needed push.

Hayden rubbed his forehead in frustration. This was conjecture—a theoretical outcome of what he *wanted* to happen, and dangerous ground to tread on. Staying out of it was the only way to help Brea, as her friend, until she made her choice with a clear head. In a less complicated world, he might take Henry's romantic advice, but how he navigated the rest of this trip could make or break the chance he had to keep Brea in his life. If he screwed up, she could disappear forever—and it would be intolerable.

Chapter Thirty-Three

BREA

In need of a tranquil pause, Hayden joined Brea in the water. They ventured deeper, drifting apart and then swimming back to one another, enjoying the cool temperature of the water and the gentle waves pulling their bodies towards and then away from the shore.

Grateful to be with Hayden, Brea watched him as he bobbed in the water, gazing out into the ocean at nothing in particular, and she wondered what he was thinking about.

A hollow ache settled in her chest, wondering if he was thinking about Avery. Brea had avoided asking Hayden questions about her. In the beginning, out of guilt, but now if she were being honest with herself—because of envy. Although immature, she felt it would be better to pretend Avery did not exist. The thought that he would return home to her, make love to her, and maybe even marry her one day left her unsettled.

Her thoughts turned to Adam. The possibility of spending decades with him, carrying on in the marriage with no changes, weighed on her heart with a crushing sadness. The old Brea would try to convince herself that she did not deserve the love she wanted, but that part of her needed to die—she deserved love as much as anyone else.

Being with Hayden these past few days brought back her longing and desire for him, though her feelings were irrelevant. He had Avery, and Brea was older now, a mother, and likely Hayden was no longer attracted to her. Brea groaned, remembering when Hayden told her to "*go to sleep*" after the beach fire. Briefly, she imagined he had wanted to kiss her, but it was all in her head.

For all she knew, Avery was the love of his life—beautiful, smart, and young without all the baggage that Brea towed behind her. And regardless, even if Hayden's feelings returned, she would have to push aside her desire and focus on her children. Falling back into a pattern of having Hayden as a secret lover, history repeating itself, would be the last thing she needed in her life. If she and Adam were going to divorce, Alex and Sophie would need stability and trust that Brea would be consistent and there for them—not sneaking off for a secret sexual liaison.

Once they boarded the yacht, Brea and Hayden changed and met on the top deck. Brea wore her white dress, and Hayden a pair of ivory linen pants and a slim-cut black linen button-down shirt. He waited for Brea on a cushioned chair facing the water. Joining him, he met her eyes and smiled.

"Are you sure you wouldn't prefer heading back to the resort after a quiet dinner and playing a board game?" Hayden asked.

"No, I'm looking forward to that excitement tomorrow. But instead of a nightclub, I'm willing to compromise. We can go to a lounge with music and be back at the resort and in bed by midnight."

"I'm glad you've become more reasonable over the past hour," Hayden replied with a playful grin. They enjoyed the cruise and chatted until nearing the port, Greg and Julia popped up behind them.

"Hi. We were talking, and we realized you were both just pulling our leg, with all those stories. Spicing up your marriage and being—kinda crazy and woo-hoo," Julia said with Greg standing behind her, nodding and wagging his finger.

Brea and Hayden exchanged a glance and laughed. "Yes, we were just messing with you, having a bit of fun," Brea confessed.

Greg shrugged his shoulders and wrapped his arm around Julia. "Hey, we need to do fun stuff too to keep things fresh. How long have you two been married?"

Brea shook her head. "No, we're not together. We were secret lovers twenty years ago, but now I'm married with children and he's in a relationship. He found me two weeks ago and asked me to come on this trip with him so we could fix a huge misunderstanding from the past and get closure."

Greg and Julia exchanged glances and looked at Hayden. He nodded in agreement and after a beat, Julia laughed. "Oh, you two are hilarious—so much fun! Enjoy your vacation. You almost fooled us again." They turned and strolled away. Brea and Hayden laughed until Brea's tears trailed down her cheeks.

Near the check-in kiosk, Alonso waited by the car for Hayden and Brea. In greeting them, Alonso relieved them of their bags. Hayden opened the door for Brea and chatted with Alonso, inquiring if he knew of a well-regarded restaurant and a nearby lounge he would recommend.

While she waited in the car, Brea touched up her makeup. Joining Brea, Hayden informed her that Alonso had suggested a local restaurant serving the best empanadas in the city and nearby, an upscale lounge where one of his friends worked as a bouncer, and could secure them a last-minute table for a generous tip. Brea agreed, and Hayden asked Alonso to make the arrangements for the lounge as they drove off.

"Hayden. What do you do for fun when you're not working?"

"Working is my fun."

"I'm serious, Hayden," Brea said, nudging his arm with her elbow.

"So am I."

Brea tipped her head to the side. "Don't you play? Goof around? I always say my kids keep me young. They make me crank up the music, have dance parties, play on the playground, and there isn't a craft project in any retail store I haven't made yet."

Hayden pressed his lips together and thought for a moment. "Well, as you know, I read a lot. I play golf, although more for business than pleasure. Baseball—but now that I'm thinking about it, it's been a while since I've gone to a baseball game. I have a suite for the season, but often, I give the seats to employees and investors."

"What about with Avery?" Brea did not want to, but she felt compelled to ask.

Hayden hesitated a moment before answering. "I don't know about fun—that's not the word I would use. Hey, we're here. That was a quick drive." Hayden leaned over to look out the windshield when Alonso stepped out to open Brea's door.

Brea glanced out the window. It was obvious Hayden was not keen to talk about Avery with her. Relieved he had diverted off the topic, she dropped the subject. Learning about Hayden's relationship with Avery would only be uncomfortable and, although immature and spiteful, make her despise Avery.

They stepped onto the sidewalk in front of a modest-sized restaurant near the beach with a vibrantly painted blue and purple stucco exterior. Entering the building, a host seated them on the second-floor balcony overlooking the water. "Everything looks delicious. I don't know what to order," Brea muttered while scanning the menu.

"I'll order for you to take the pressure off deciding. If you like it, you'll be impressed and think I'm a genius, and if not, you can blame me all night. I think that's something you would love to do since I handed your ass to you today at poker," he replied with a broad smile.

Brea shook her head and laughed. "You like getting under my skin, Hayden. Wow."

"Yeah, I do. It's fun," he teased.

"Let's add that to your fun list when you're not work-ing—torture Brea."

"Yeah, top of the list." Hayden laughed. "So, do we have a deal? You order for me and I'll order for you."

"Okay, deal," Brea accepted, then returned her attention to the menu.

The server greeted Brea and Hayden and took their drink orders, and both ordered a margarita on the rocks. After turning to Brea for her dinner order, Brea gestured with her hand to Hayden. "The gentleman will order for me."

Hayden cleared his throat and paused, intending to build anticipation. "The lady will have the beef empanadas with the avocado salad," he said and handed the server the menu.

Brea nodded and smiled. "A solid choice. And he will have the Camarones a la Diabla, extra habanero, please. He's tough—he can take it."

Hayden grabbed the menu out of Brea's hand to read the description, then handed the menu to the server and raised his eyes to the ceiling. "You're going to pay for this, Brea."

"Oh, Hayden, I'm just doing my part to make sure you have extra fun tonight," Brea replied with a feigned expression of sincerity. Hayden narrowed his eyes in response.

As they sipped their margaritas, Brea envisioned Adam having sex with a faceless woman. Brea clicked her tongue, and her eyes flickered up to the ceiling. The reality of Adam's affair ebbed and flowed into her consciousness throughout the day and, though her love for Adam had died a slow death over the recent years, she now felt her anger escalating to a new level.

For someone who glorified commitment to familial duty and reputation, Adam was a hypocrite. And if he had been unapologetically unfaithful, maybe she should have sex with someone else. In fact, that might solve the problem of helping her to survive the subsequent decades—an open marriage where they stay together for the kids, and she could assume a lover.

Shifting her gaze to Hayden, she observed him picking up his drink. Meeting her eyes, a half-smile formed on his lips, and he raised his eyebrows, expecting Brea was on the verge of saying something. She sighed and averted her eyes, eliminating Hayden as a potential candidate as a lover for reasons she had previously thought of.

"What? What are you thinking about?" Hayden asked before sipping his drink, having perceived the abrupt shift in her demeanor and exasperation.

"Hayden, what do you think about open marriages?" Brea asked, staring into his eyes with bold intensity.

Hayden choked on his drink and coughed.

Chapter Thirty-Four

HAYDEN

"Brea, I'm not an expert, but I think it's a terrible idea, for obvious reasons," he replied. His heart raced, uncertain of where Brea was going with this. Though every part of him desired to make love to her, he had to draw the line. He knew what he wanted, and he would not settle for being only her lover.

"What are the obvious reasons from a man's perspective?" she pressed.

"Jealousy. Wanting to murder the guy who touched your wife. Not to mention your wife could get jealous, and it could traumatize your children if they found out. Is this something you're seriously considering?"

Brea shook her head and dropped her head into her hands. "No, not really, I don't know. I can't get over the fact that Adam was so cavalier about having an affair—and he didn't even apologize. And it bothers me he hid it and didn't have the nerve to tell me until today. It's as though my life, my feelings, and what I want from a marriage don't matter. He believes our marriage was just a contract and that my role is 'wife in name, and mother to our children.' So now why not? I have carte blanche to wrap my legs around the next guy I see."

Hayden rested his hands on the table. "I think that would be the worst thing you could do, Brea. To get involved with someone out of revenge—would that really make you feel better?" He could not believe he was having this conversation with Brea, and given his bias, the last thing he would encourage her to do is to be with another man.

The food arrived, interrupting their conversation. "Wow, this smells amazing," Brea exclaimed.

Hayden examined his dish with a creased brow, eyeing the shrimp bathed in a fiery red sauce. He wondered whether the odds favored scorched taste buds beyond repair or excruciating heartburn for twelve hours. With one hand on his chin, he used the other to lift his fork. Glancing at Brea, he glimpsed her eating her dish with enthusiasm.

"Hayden," she proclaimed after she swallowed a mouthful. "Great choice. This is delicious. What a great idea to order for each other." A playful grin spread across Brea's face. "Aren't you going to try yours?"

Of course, he would never entertain shirking the challenge. Piercing a shrimp with his fork, he lifted it to his mouth, smiled, and ate it. To his surprise, the heat from the habanero pepper was rather mild. In triumph, he pierced another shrimp and ate it, maintaining eye contact with Brea.

"Not spicy. Sorry, Brea," he boasted.

Brea shrugged her shoulders, disappointed her attempt to fluster Hayden failed to yield much of a reaction. Hayden ate another shrimp and set his fork down. He did not particularly enjoy the flavor of the dish, though he was hungry. Raising his hand, he caught the server's attention.

"Could you bring me the beef empanada plate? The same as hers," Hayden requested. The server nodded and strode away. A moment later, he coughed—an intense heat bloomed in his mouth. "Damn, now that's hot," he said, followed by an escalating fit of coughing. His mouth now felt as though it were on fire.

"Hayden?" Brea said, studying his face. "Are you okay?" she asked, seeing his face flushed. "Here, have some cold water! Oh, no!" Brea swiveled in her chair and called out across the balcony to a server standing beside a table. "Milk, leche, can you get us a glass of milk fast?"

"Yes, right away," the server replied and hurried off, observing Hayden coughing.

Hayden was not worried—he could breathe, but the overwhelming heat in his mouth was uncomfortable and had triggered his cough reflex. He wiped his eyes, now tearing, and drank a gulp of his margarita.

"Hayden, I'm so sorry. I'm such a jerk." Brea waved her hands as though she could conjure a glass of milk out of thin air in desperation. The server appeared, placing the glass of milk in front of Hayden. He grabbed it, drank half the glass and signaled to the server to bring him another glass.

Brea held her hands over her mouth and nose, repeating how sorry she was. With the pain abating and more composed, Hayden lifted his hand. "It's fine, Brea, I'm okay. That was just intense."

"I'm so sorry, Brea said, rising from her chair to rush to Hayden's side, though he held up his hand to stop her.

"I'm fine. Sit down. But I'm not finishing that," he said, pointing to his dinner plate. "And I will never let you order for me again." Brea nodded and wiped her eyes, worried she had hurt him. Hayden reached across the table to grab her hand. "Look at me, I'm alive. I may not speak to you for the rest of the meal, but I'm fine."

"Okay. One more time. I'm so sorry."

"Give me one of your empanadas, and we'll be square."

Brea handed one over to Hayden. Taking it out of her hand, he took a large bite, then washed it down with another large gulp of milk.

"You have a little milk on the corner—"

"I don't care." Hayden said, cutting Brea off. He took another bite of the empanada and then finished the glass of milk. Brea watched him to ensure he was indeed recovering and beyond any further coughing fits.

Hayden was neither angry nor embarrassed. All he could think about was that if he could, he would pick her up over his shoulder and carry her into the restroom. Placing her down, he would press her against the wall, then touch the most intimate places of her body to torture her in the most exquisite ways he could think of to teach her a lesson. Of course, after having another glass of milk and allowing another thirty minutes to pass.

"Brea?"

"Yes, Hayden?"

"You know, I'll get you back for this."

"Okay," she replied, humbled, and picked up her fork to eat her salad. Hayden tipped his head down and raised his eyebrows. Brea glanced at him, smiled and pressed her lips together. Continuing to look at one another, they chuckled softly, though soon their laughter escalated, drawing stares from the nearby tables.

Chapter Thirty-Five

Brea

Buckling their seatbelts, Brea turned to Hayden. "If you want to go back to the hotel, I understand."

"No, I'm going to be awake all night while my insides roast, so let's stick with the plan."

"Really? It still hurts?" Brea's hand flew to her mouth as another wave of guilt washed over her.

"No, I'm fine, just messing with you." Hayden smiled and nudged her arm with his elbow.

Alonso drove off to the lounge. It was nearby, and they would arrive within several minutes. While they ate dinner, Alonso had called his friend to reserve a table for Brea and Hayden near the dance floor.

Brea stared out the window. Though Hayden was fine, she feared she had gone too far and hurt him. It was a panic similar to when Alex fell off the top of a slide at the playground last year and when Sophie at three-years old nearly choked on a piece of cantaloupe.

The car slowed to a stop in front of a modern standalone building with large stained-glass windows, a sign in blue neon lights, and large planters flanking the door. A line of people outfitted in smart attire waited behind a red velvet rope.

Alonso exited the car to inform his friend they had arrived, then jogged back to open the door for Brea. The bouncer waved them over and let them in ahead of the crowd. A few men in line groaned and raised their arms in frustration as Brea and Hayden passed them by.

Inside, the hostess escorted them through the lounge to a reserved booth with a polished black table and leather seating overlooking the dance floor. The interior was modern and distinguished, with dark-gray walls, sculptural metal light sconces, and mounted shelving holding flameless candles.

Brea felt underdressed, observing that many of the women wore form-fitting dresses, stiletto heels, and meticulously applied makeup. But the energy and ambience of the lounge overshadowed her concern once they sat down. On the table sat champagne glasses and an ice bucket.

The waitress appeared holding a bottle of champagne, presented it to Hayden, then opened it once he signaled his approval. "Would you like something else to drink?" Hayden asked Brea, raising his voice over the music.

The cocktail waitress placed her hands on the table and leaned in. She had a voluptuous body, dressed in a fitted black tank top dress and platform nude sandals.

"No thanks, champagne is fine," she replied, eyeing the cocktail waitress, who fixed her gaze on Hayden with a coy smile and leaned in close to him for his order.

After rolling her eyes, Brea scanned the dance floor. She had not been to a lounge or nightclub in years. With Adam, they socialized solely with friends or attended law firm parties, either in restaurants or in elegant homes. Brea moved her head and shoulders to the music, finding it lively—a blend of Latin and American dance music.

"Hayden, are you sure you never dance? Not even at weddings?" Brea asked.

Shaking his head, he replied, "No. I can manage a slow dance, but with music like this, it wouldn't be pleasant to watch. Trust me, I'm better off watching from the sidelines."

"I bet if you were drunk enough, you would get out there."

Hayden smiled. "Brea, I don't get drunk. I know my limit, and I don't like the feeling."

Their waitress reappeared. Brushing Hayden's hand, she placed a cocktail napkin on the table and smiled, gazing into his eyes. Ignoring Brea, she held the glass of scotch in front of him, hovering it over the cocktail napkin with a seductive smile. Hayden nodded, and with a polite smile, took it from her.

Brea raised her hands in the air, astounded that the waitress had no regard for the fact Hayden was sitting next to a woman wearing a wedding ring. How could she know they were not married?

"Hayden. That waitress is hitting on you. Did you see that?"

"No, she isn't. She's looking for a large tip, Brea."

Brea squinted her eyes and smirked. Was Hayden that naive?

"We could be married. She doesn't know that we aren't." Brea held up her hand and pointed to her wedding ring.

Hayden changed the subject. "You don't wear an engagement ring. Why not?" he asked.

She shrugged her shoulders. "It was Adam's grandmother's—I didn't love the stone or the style. But not wanting to appear ungrateful, I didn't make a fuss about it. So, the day we got married, it went into a jewelry box, and that's where it lives."

Observing the crowd on the dance floor, Brea felt the palpable sexual energy radiating throughout the space, and she yearned to join in. "You know what? I'm taking it off," she proclaimed. Brea tugged on her ring to wiggle it off her finger. It would not budge. She took a sip of her champagne and then placed her finger in her mouth while Hayden watched her with astonishment. Brea succeeded, liberating her finger from the wedding ring and dropped it into her clutch.

"Not a good idea, Brea," Hayden warned. "What are you angling to accomplish tonight?" he asked, tilting his head to the side with a disapproving look. She toasted Hayden with her champagne glass, then drank a large sip.

"Brea, in a place like this, not wearing a wedding ring on your finger is an open invitation for every guy in here to hit on you."

She leaned in close to Hayden and met his eyes. "Good. I need the distraction, and I owe Adam one."

Hayden's mouth opened, but Brea pressed her fingers over his lips to stop him from talking. She picked up her glass and drained it. "Kindly refill my glass, please. I'm going to dance. If you get bored, you know where to find me."

A popular Latin song played. Brea slipped out of the booth and turned to wave to Hayden as she joined the modestly populated dance floor. Brea let her mind empty as she moved her hips and raised her arms over her head. She did not want to think about her marriage or the future. All she desired in the moment was to feel connected to herself—sensual—to run her hands along her body and believe herself worthy of passion. It had been over a year since her last orgasm—and she was certain it happened during a sex dream.

Following thirty minutes of dancing, Brea returned to the table for a quick break. Thirsty, she plopped into her seat and drank half the glass of champagne. "Are you going to join me now?" Brea asked, her face damp and her heart racing from the exertion.

After picking up his drink and taking a sip, Hayden smiled and shook his head. "Hayden, you aren't old, you're boring," Brea teased. Draining her glass, she slipped out of the booth once again to dance. As she walked away, she spun around once more to beckon him onto the dance floor. Hayden sat with his gaze fixed on Brea, lifted one arm over the top of the seat, propped up his head with his hand and shook his head.

Shaking her head, she mouthed "boring" to him, then cheered with the crowd, hearing a favorite dance song begin—a sexually charged song perfect to make love to. In fact, now that champagne bathed her brain, Brea mused on her next task—find someone to have sex with to this song. She danced provocatively, dragging her hands up her thighs, lifting her skirt and then letting the fabric slip through her fingers just as the hem reached where her thighs met her bottom. It was not long before she attracted a friend beside her.

"Hi, you look amazing out here. I had to say hello. Can I dance with you?" He was an American, likely in his late twenties, tall, with a pleasing face, and dressed in a pair of jeans and a blue short-sleeved button-down shirt. Feeling high and desirable, a seductive smile formed on her lips.

With no shame, she wrapped her arms around his neck. This was not about payback for Adam—she felt sexy and alive, embracing yet another part of herself that had awakened, having lain dormant for decades, buried beneath the idea that her sexuality was something to be ashamed of. Tonight, she craved a man's touch on her body, and she did not need permission to embrace the feeling of desire.

Brea turned and pressed her back against his chest. Rolling her hips, she raised her arms and with her hands, piled her hair atop her head and then let it fall over her shoulders. The man placed his hands on her hips and pressed his fingers in to hold her with a firm grip. Moving his face against Brea's cheek, he then slid his hands to her abdomen and placed them flush against her ribcage below her breasts.

Another man appeared in front of her, seeking her interest. Her current partner pulled her back a step and turned her away from the other suitor. They continued to dance, and the man pushed aside Brea's hair and grazed his lips across her neck.

Brea laughed. Encouraged, he lowered his hands to her legs and scrunched up the skirt of her dress.

"You're so hot. Come back with me to my hotel," he said. Brea smiled and brought his hands back to her waist. Despite the champagne having gone to her head and her earlier bold assertion that she wanted to have sex—she would only dance and flirt tonight. Under no circumstances would Brea consider going to a hotel room with a strange man.

Hayden appeared on the dance floor beside them. Taken aback, Brea did a double take. "Brea, come back to the table with me," Hayden said, yelling over the music. Her dance partner tightened his grip on her waist and pulled her away from Hayden. Brea waved at Hayden, signaling to him she was fine. With a stern expression on his face, he stepped in front of her.

"I'm not asking her—she's coming with me," he declared. Hayden was not playing, and his assertive eye contact with the man communicated that he would use physical force if needed. Brea narrowed her eyes and clenched her jaw. Hayden's gaze flickered to her, then back to her dance partner. Brea brushed the man's hands off her waist and took a step forward. Hayden took her hand and pulled her off the dance floor.

Returning to the table, Hayden would not look at her. He signed the bill on the table, threw down the pen, and grabbed Brea's purse from the seat. "Hayden, what is your problem? I'm dancing, I'm having a good time," Brea yelled out over the music.

"Let's go. We'll talk in the car." She huffed and snatched her purse from Hayden's hand. He placed his hand on her lower back to guide her out. Brea, incensed by his audacity, planned to unleash her displeasure with his paternalistic overstepping once they exited the building.

CHAPTER THIRTY-SIX

HAYDEN

Upon witnessing Brea remove her wedding ring and tuck it into her bag, Hayden found himself thrust into a horrific predicament. Knowing her well, Adam's infidelity could drive her to desperate measures to soothe her wounded pride, and she was on the verge of succumbing to her impulses with a reckless disregard for the consequences.

Hayden endured the torture of watching Brea on the dance floor until she danced in such a suggestive manner that many men watched her and several fixed to home in on her. He knew their intention—to seduce her, and he would do everything necessary to prevent that from happening tonight.

Exiting the lounge, Brea took off, stepping off the curb and striding across the street in the beach's direction. "Brea. Wait here. Alonso will be here in five minutes," Hayden yelled after her.

"No, do not follow me, Hayden. I'll wait by myself," Brea shouted over her shoulder.

"I'm not leaving you alone out here. It could be dangerous," he shouted back and took off after her. Catching up to her, he reached out to grab her arm. "Hey, stop and look at me."

Brea halted her steps and whipped around. "You are not my brother, Hayden. I am a grown woman now. I do not need

'Hayden the rescuer' coming to save pathetic, sorry Brea from herself."

"That's not it. I just—I couldn't watch you in there." He swallowed and paused, knowing he needed to be careful with what he said to avoid confusing her.

"Hayden. I have been a walking zombie for years, and I found out today that my husband has been with another woman. I needed something tonight to make me feel sexy and desired. If you can't understand that, that isn't my problem." Brea turned and continued walking down the sidewalk.

He raised his voice. "Brea, stop." She halted in place. Reaching her, he stepped in front of her.

"You don't even know what you're going to do about Adam. An hour ago, you were talking about having an open marriage, and now you're tearing off your wedding ring and dancing with strange men who only want one thing from you. You were about to make a big mistake, letting that guy put his hands all over your body and who knows what else." Hayden locked his eyes with Brea's, trying to get through to her.

Brea studied Hayden, held his gaze, and took a step closer to him. She pressed herself against his chest, took his hands, and placed them on her hips. "Do you want to make a big mistake with me tonight, Hayden?"

Taken aback, Hayden's mouth fell open as he drew in a stunted breath. Feeling the pressure of her breasts against his chest, his heart began to pound and desire surged within him. "Brea, come on," he said in a low voice.

"Don't you want to put your hands all over my body, Hayden?" she whispered, moving her hands to his biceps and pressing in her fingers.

With his hands on her hips, Hayden could not move or breathe, and he felt his entire body tense. He only needed to lean down several inches and he could kiss her, but his determination to do the right thing and commit to his resolve held him back.

"Let's go. Time for people over thirty-five to go home," he replied, averting his eyes from hers to see if Alonso had arrived with the car.

"What happened to no rules, Hayden?" Brea whispered. She placed her hands on his chest and slid them down to his abdomen. Slipping a hand under his shirt, she hooked one finger under the waistband of his pants. It was too much for Hayden to bear—his resolve was on the verge of shattering. Taking an abrupt step back, he turned away from Brea, and covered his mouth to regain his composure.

He whipped around to face Brea. "Let's go," he said and then exhaled, seeing her face and posture brimming with humiliation and devastation at his rejection.

Brea pressed her fingers to her forehead. "I'm sorry, Hayden. That was so inappropriate of me. You're with Avery, and I forgot myself."

"I'm not with Avery. We broke up a couple of nights ago," Hayden replied and lowered his eyes to the ground. He did not know what else to say—if he confessed what he was feeling, it would only confuse Brea more.

Brea's eyes widened, incredulous. "Really? So, it's me? I'm too old, and you don't want me. I get it. Let's go." Having spotted Alonso waiting beside the car, she took off across the street.

"Brea, come back here. Let me explain," Hayden yelled after her, though he was clueless how to climb out of the hole he had fallen into.

"No! You sit in the front. Do not sit in the back with me or I'll find a taxi home," she shouted.

Alonso hurried to open the door for Brea. Before Hayden could reach the car, Brea slammed it shut. Throwing his hands in the air, he stopped walking. "Fuck," he muttered. With an empathic glance, Alonso opened the front passenger door for Hayden, having heard the heated exchange of words.

"Thank you, Alonso," he said with an awkward half-smile. Alonso nodded, once again in solidarity with men all over the world who had found themselves in this situation before.

Once seated in the car, Hayden turned to Brea. "Brea, can you be reasonable and listen to me?"

Brea ignored Hayden. "Alonso, could you please turn on some music and make it loud enough so no one can talk?"

"Of course." Alonso turned up the music and exchanged a glance with Hayden. Brea stared out the window and Hayden sighed, shaking his head.

⁂

Hayden opened his eyes when they pulled in front of the lobby entrance. He turned in his seat, attempting to speak to Brea.

"Alonso, could you give us a minute?" Hayden asked as Brea fumbled with unbuckling her seatbelt.

"Of course, sir." Alonso opened the car door.

"That's unnecessary, Alonso, thank you. If you could hand me my bag, please." Brea opened the door and sprang out of the car. Hayden groaned and threw his head back on the headrest.

He opened the door and jumped out to follow Brea as Alonso opened the trunk. "Brea, stop. Let me talk to you. I'm trying to do the right thing here."

With an abrupt motion, she swung around and folded her arms across her chest. "Hayden, why didn't you kiss me last night?" she asked, looking into his eyes, composed yet direct.

"Brea, let's go inside so we can talk," he replied, gesturing to the lobby doors.

"I'm curious, Hayden. I've been thinking the entire drive back, and I want to know why you didn't kiss me?"

"B. Sorry, Brea." Hayden corrected himself. "This is all so complicated, and after everything we have been through, the smart thing to do—"

"Hayden, what about 'what happens on the trip stays there' and 'Brea, I don't know what we are.' So why didn't you?" Brea had attempted to mimic Hayden's voice, which sounded nothing like him, or at least in his opinion.

"Brea—"

"I'm not attractive anymore—that's it. Adam married me because I was pretty and compliant, but now I'm aging and un-desirable unless a younger man finds older women attractive—I get it now. Thank you for the education. Now I can consider plastic surgery and start lying about my age."

Her direct confrontation caught Hayden off guard. "Look, the last thing I want to do is say something wrong here. The position I'm in is complicated, and whatever I say could worsen things. I don't want to mess everything up again."

"I don't understand you. You pulled me out of the lounge, where someone on this planet found me attractive, and dragged me back here. You might as well be my brother Hayden," Brea exclaimed at a thunderous volume, startling the valets into si-lence.

Brea grabbed her bag from Alonso, standing on the curb attempting, yet failing, to ignore Brea's dramatics. With a smile, she thanked Alonso, then glanced back at Hayden with a hostile expression.

"Brea, you're being irrational," Hayden called out after her. Turning back to Alonso, he took his bag, thanked him, and strode into the lobby after her. "Brea," he called out after her once again.

"Leave me alone, Hayden," she yelled over her shoulder and marched through the lobby. The surrounding guests paused and stared.

Hayden dropped his bag on the ground and threw up his hands. What could he do? If he told her how he felt, then he would place her in another difficult situation, and she could hate him for it. When he did the right thing, attempting to act as a gentleman, she hated him for it. He shook his head and fixed his eyes on the floor.

"Kid, she loves you. Don't stand around here like an idiot. Go after her." Hayden looked up to see Henry beside the concierge desk with an elderly woman, clearly his wife, Willa. Hayden exhaled, scanned the lobby, and hesitated. Raising his eyebrows, Henry gestured in the direction Brea had passed him by.

Rubbing his forehead, Hayden nodded, grabbed his bag, and took off after Brea. Stepping outside, he hastened down the path but did not see her. Reaching his casita, he paused in his steps. What was he going to do—bang on her door and demand she let him in? Pulling out his room key, he swiped it, and entered his casita.

After tossing his bag onto the dining table, he paced the room for several minutes before grabbing a bottle of water. He cracked it open and, after taking a sip, picked up the hotel phone and called Brea's room—she did not answer. He tried her mobile phone, but it went to voicemail. Frustrated, he threw his phone onto the bed.

Remembering what Henry said, he shook his head. There was no way Henry could tell that Brea loved him by observing her stalk through the lobby, yelling at Hayden to leave her alone.

Reasoning it would be better to let her cool off and talk to her in the morning, Hayden opted to take a shower. After turning the handle, he stripped off his clothes and attempted to diminish his agitation with the aggressive brushing of his teeth, but it was useless.

Once under the stream of hot water, the highlights of the day replayed in his mind and despite his unrest, he laughed, recalling some of the ridiculous stories Brea had created on the cruise to embarrass him. Then, the vivid memory of her dancing in the lounge invaded his mind—showing off the spectacular curves of her legs just below her bottom as she slid her hands up her thighs and lifted her skirt.

Hayden groaned, slapped his hands on the tiles and dropped his head. Turning off the water, he grabbed a towel to dry himself, entered the bedroom and dressed.

He needed air, ventured outside onto the patio, and sat on a lounge chair. Closing his eyes and listening to the sound of the ocean, it did not take long for him to realize what he needed to do—but he needed help. Hayden returned to the bedroom and picked up the hotel phone.

CHAPTER THIRTY-SEVEN

BREA

When the hotel phone rang, Brea ignored it and picked up her cell phone to shut it off. She knew it was Hayden calling, and at the moment she could not stomach his rejection speech. There was no question in her mind that she would apologize to him for her ridiculous outburst, but not tonight. Wrapping her head with her hands, she fell back onto the sofa.

She wiped her eyes and blew out a forceful breath, knowing full well her anger had been unreasonable and childish in retrospect. How could she have expected Hayden to surrender himself to her as a sexual object to cope with her confusion and anger? He had fulfilled his end of the bargain—shared his side of the story and helped her uncover the root of her unhappiness.

Still, having Hayden back in her life stirred buried feelings deep inside her, and now everything felt convoluted, catapulting her back to her sixteen-year-old self at Harvey Slate. Shutting her eyes, she ran her fingers down her neck and collarbone as she recalled the feel and pressure of Hayden's chest against hers outside the lounge.

Lifting her legs and dropping her forehead on her knees, she wished she could knock the acceptance into her head—Hayden did not want her, and she needed to focus on what to do about Adam. The question she needed an answer to was whether Adam wanted to find his way back to loving her, her true self, and if so, perhaps she owed him that chance regardless of what she felt for Hayden.

"Ugh." Brea smacked herself on the forehead with her hand. It was too much to think about now. Rather than drive herself insane, she pulled out a nightgown, tossed it on the bed, and went into the bathroom to take a shower.

Stepping under the hot water, she settled on calling Hayden in the morning to apologize for her appalling behavior, then booking an earlier flight home. She had ruined any chance of their being friends, and nothing was more unattractive than a woman begging a man to take her to bed, and then throwing a fit when rejected.

After dressing in her nightgown, Brea carried a bottle of mineral water with her to the dining table along with her notebook and pen. Dimming the lights, she placed the tip of her thumb between her front teeth, opened to a clean sheet, and wrote.

"Desire, like wild-tongued flames, licked the curves of her body
Fingertips like feathers, she could not brush away
Everything she felt, spoilt on the ocean's shore
Ground to dust, against the stubborn will of fate"

Brea paused and reread the lines. It was a start—not quite right. A sound startled Brea, and she sat up straight. Something hit the glass patio doors. Frozen in place, she debated whether to call security. The sound repeated, and Brea realized what it was—there was only one thing it could be. Suppressing a smile, she smoothed down her nightgown and rose from the chair. Reaching the patio doors, she pulled back the curtains to peek outside.

Hayden stood outside the patio gate. Brea let out a stifled laugh when he lifted his hand, opened it, and a fistful of pebbles dropped onto the ground. Hayden hopped over the gate as she slid the pocket doors open and rushed out to apologize. "Hayden, I'm so sorry. I had no right—"

"No, listen to me." Hayden placed his hand over Brea's mouth. "That first night, years ago, when I came to your house, I should have fought for you. I should have demanded that you break up with Jaime—done whatever I could have to be with you. It's my biggest regret. And our last night together all those years ago—that's what I had planned to do. I was going to win you over and tell you everything I felt, but fate screwed us over. I don't know why so many things happened, and the universe kept us apart, but it did." Hayden removed his hand from Brea's mouth and placed his hands on her shoulders.

"When I came back to find you in the shop, I told myself it was only to help you, but I'm an idiot—I want everything now. I broke up with Avery because everything changed once I saw you again. The reason I didn't tell you is that I didn't want to confuse you or for you to think I was trying to manipulate you into leaving Adam. I don't want us to be secret friends or lovers who meet in a hotel once a month. I want you for myself, every day—out in the open—in real life."

Hayden moved his hands to Brea's face. "For days, all I have wanted to do is kiss you, on your mouth, your body. You're beautiful, and every time you touch me, it drives me crazy. And I don't care how old we are—you will forever be the skinny little girl in the library swallowed up in a sweater three sizes too big for you, even when you're one hundred years old. And if I have to go to hell and back to win you—I'll do it. But Brea, I can't do it, and I won't do it until you make a choice, and you have to be sure."

Brea exhaled, ashamed of her insecurities yet relieved and elated to hear Hayden's words that echoed her feelings. "Hayden, after my humiliating attempt to seduce you tonight, I don't want you to think that all I want is sex and a secret affair. For weeks, remembering our story and spending time with you again made me realize something about us—how right we are for each other, and everything I felt then and feel for you now. You have been the one man in my life who cared about me for who I am—all of me. But now there is so much more. I have Alex and Sophie. I come with two little children who are crazy, wonderful, and exasperating. Life with me will not be a luxury vacation in Mexico, and you would need to think long and hard if this would be something you want in your life."

"I want all of you, Brea. Sophie and Alex included. I understand that, and we could figure that all out. That doesn't scare me—not being with you scares me." Hayden searched her eyes. "And I am not asking you to choose today. I don't care if it takes you a year or longer, because I won't run away or give you a deadline. Take all the time you need to be sure."

Brea shut her eyes to center herself before she spoke. "All those years ago, I was so confused, and I left a mess in my wake. But when I look back, my best decisions were the times that we were together. I wanted you too, but I was too scared and lost, and I wound up denying myself the one thing that was right and made sense—being with you. But I need to decide about Adam. The last thing I want to do is hurt you because I couldn't live with myself if I did that."

Hayden pulled Brea close to him. Wrapping their arms around one another, everything around them erased, having been two lost people at last finding one another with their truth.

As they continued to hold each other, Brea spoke. "Hayden, I want you to stay with me tonight. Not for anything physical, but if it's all right with you, could you sleep next to me like we did in the car that night on the beach?"

Hayden pulled away and took a step back. "I don't know. I'm not sure I can trust you to keep your hands off me." He cracked a smile.

"I think I can handle it. Worst case, we have the plunge pool outside. That could be the 'go to jail' spot if either of us gets too fresh," Brea teased.

Hayden chuckled. "Let me grab a few things and lock up my room. I'll be back in ten minutes. And please—put on a bathrobe or a few layers of clothing over your nightgown."

Brea laughed, "All right, deal."

Hayden paused, and then added. "And Brea, never apologize for trying to seduce me—I almost cracked tonight. We were thirty seconds away from an arrest for public indecency, and I'm really looking forward to your next attempt."

Brea smiled and chewed her bottom lip. "Okay, okay. Go grab what you need and get back here."

✤

Hayden knocked. Brea opened the door, dressed in a bulky sweatshirt and sleep shorts, with her hair tied up in a high ponytail. He wore a sweatshirt and pajama bottoms, and with him, he carried several candy bars from the minibar and his toothbrush.

Brea wondered if they had been hasty with their certainty they could keep the night platonic. They were adults, and they had self-control, but knowing one another, it would only be a matter of time until either of them did something that would drive the other crazy and spark the desire to touch one another.

Hayden's eyes widened seeing Brea. "Couldn't you put on a garbage bag and one of those green face masks, or something?

You accomplished only to look sexier and more attractive," Hayden said as he entered the casita.

Chuckling, Brea replied. "Nope, not unless you want to break into the spa tonight."

Hayden grabbed the remote control. "Funny you should mention that. I have something planned for tomorrow night, and I asked the concierge to set you up for a day at the spa so I can prepare."

Smiling, she replied, "Hayden, that's sweet, but we can hang by the pool or go to the beach. I don't know if I should be at the spa all day—alone."

"Are you saying you'll miss me, Brea?" he asked with a sexy grin.

Brea licked her lips and looked up at the ceiling. "Maybe. Okay, fine. I haven't had a massage in years."

"I also need you to lock yourself in the bathroom for five minutes so I can snoop around. It's for the surprise I have planned."

"Now?" she asked.

"Yes, please," he replied, then gestured for her to go. Obliging him, Brea grabbed a soda from the minibar and went into the bathroom, intrigued.

✺

Once Hayden gave Brea the all clear, she saw Hayden had arranged a pile of snacks and candy bars on the bed. Brea flopped onto the mattress and lay down on her stomach. Hayden joined her, and they searched the guide for a movie.

Hayden unwrapped a Twix bar and handed one to Brea. As they ate, they argued over which movie to watch. He blackballed the romance films and, Brea, anything in the horror genre. On the cusp of giving up, they saw an action film on the guide, and after a high five, switched to the channel.

"Brea, I have to work out tomorrow morning. I can't eat all this and expect to keep this figure," he joked, unwrapping another chocolate bar to share with her.

"Well, the habanero pepper kicked up your metabolism twenty percent, so it offsets your Twix bar," she replied.

"I have to think of something fantastic to get you back for that." Hayden shook his head, still in disbelief at what Brea had done to him.

"You can try, but that is going to be difficult to top," Brea replied with a playful grin.

Hayden tickled her under her arm. Brea swatted his hand away. "Hey, no physical contact. Your rules, Mr. Botero," Brea exclaimed.

"Apologies." Hayden replied. "Maybe we need to have a jar. Every time there is unapproved touching, we have to put in fifty dollars."

"Fifty dollars? Now I know you're super rich. In my house, it would be a dollar, five tops." Brea sat up to lean against the headboard, grabbed two pillows, and handed one to Hayden. To get a rise out of Brea, Hayden placed the pillow between them rather than using it to prop himself up.

They made it halfway through the movie until they were both too tired to continue watching. Seeing Brea's eyes closing, Hayden turned to her. "You ready to go to sleep?"

Scooting down the bed, Brea rested her head on the pillow and rolled onto her side to face Hayden. Her hair fell over her cheek, and she laughed. Hayden pushed the hair off her face. "Illegal contact—that's fifty dollars in the jar," Brea muttered.

Hayden smiled. "I'm going to brush my teeth. Don't forget to brush yours."

"Okay, Dad," Brea whispered.

While Hayden brushed his teeth, Brea dragged herself into the bathroom and grabbed her toothbrush.

"Brea, how much money do you spend on cream and make-up per month? I've never seen such a collection. Do you really need all of this stuff?" he asked.

"A thirty-seven-year woman has a lot of skin care needs. I don't look this beautiful by only washing my face with soap." Brea looked up and smiled—toothpaste covered her lips and dribbled down her chin.

Hayden tossed a towel into her face. "Hey," she exclaimed, then wiped her mouth.

After rinsing, they returned to the bedroom, and Brea switched off the light. Lying on their backs, they stared at the ceiling.

"Hayden?"

"Yes?"

"Thanks for sleeping over."

"No problem."

"Hayden. You're not planning on drawing on my face with a marker while I'm asleep, are you?"

"Of course, I am. I'm just waiting for you to fall asleep."

"Okay. Only checking." Brea whispered, and they laughed.

"Hayden?" Brea whispered again.

"Yes?" Hayden murmured, close to falling asleep.

"I'm worried. No matter what happens, it will be hard on my children. I brought these amazing kids into the world, and now I might hurt them, or scar them for life."

Hayden reached over and took Brea's hand. "They'll be fine. If you're unhappy, that can't be good for them. Being miserable and torturing yourself, although maybe noble, is not the best choice. They'll be okay."

Brea sighed, and Hayden held her hand until they fell asleep.

Chapter Thirty-Eight

BREA

That night, Brea dreamt she stood in a vast field of white ferns under a cloud-covered sky, dressed in an ivory sundress. In the distance, she saw her old house in Black Harbor. She turned away to walk through the endless field on what felt like an interminable journey. A breeze blew through the ferns. Brea pivoted in a circle and looked into the sky. The sun peeked out, and the clouds thinned and dissipated.

Brea smiled, welcoming the sunshine that wrapped around her body. Looking down, see now stood in a field of pale-pink peonies. With her fingertips, she grazed the tops of the flowers and, on occasion, plucked a petal to bring to the tip of her nose and lips. Brea reached a river—magnificent and dark blue, stretching left and right for miles.

She tilted her face up to the sun, uncertain which direction to turn. Straining her ears, she heard a voice in the distance, almost a whisper, though she could not make out the words. Upon stepping into the river, a long gold snake appeared, swimming and weaving around her feet, but she was not frightened. Content, she sat in the shallow water, lay back against the smooth pebbles and allowed the cool water to rush over her body in peaceful surrender.

Brea woke up. It was morning, but the drawn curtains rendered the room dim. Rolling over, she saw Hayden asleep next to her, having removed his sweatshirt and now in a white tank top. Warm, she sat up to remove hers, lay back down and watched him sleep. She outstretched her arm to touch his hand lying flat on the bed near his chest. He appeared to be in a deep sleep, with his breaths evenly paced.

With a light touch, she brushed the back of his hand, then traced the length of his arm with one finger. Her eyes flickered to his face to see if he stirred. She smiled. Bolder, she moved her hand to his face, touching his cheek and then placing one finger on his lips. From his lips escaped a soft moan, and she retracted her hand. Picking up her left hand to scratch her forehead, she saw something drawn on her wrist in ink. Her eyes focused on the drawing—it was a heart with an arrow drawn through it.

Brea smiled and glanced at Hayden. He was awake and watching her. "That's really sweet, Hayden," she whispered, holding up her wrist.

"Hmm. Well, you don't want to see what I drew on your face."

Brea chuckled. "Are you going to the gym soon?"

Hayden rolled onto his stomach. "Later. This bed feels too good. I like you in it too."

Brea's hair was a mess. Sitting up, she pulled out her elastic, ran her fingers through her hair, and lay back down while pulling the blanket up to her shoulders.

"What are you going to do while I'm at the spa this afternoon?"

"I'll keep myself busy. Don't worry about it," he replied.

"Are you going to tell me about the surprise tonight?"

"Do I need to remind you what the word surprise means?"

Brea sighed. "Fine, I'll be good and surrender despite my curiosity. But I need coffee."

Hayden mumbled. "What else? I'll order room service. Unless you kick me out, I don't think I can get out of bed for another thirty minutes."

"Let me think. Pancakes with blueberries, butter, syrup, and hot coffee."

"And bacon," Hayden added.

"You're a smart man," she said with a smile and yawned.

To reach the phone, Hayden rolled on top of Brea, squashing her. "Hayden, I can't breathe." Brea laughed and tried to push him off, but he was too heavy. Hayden sat up on her legs. Once room service picked up, he ordered.

"Don't forget orange juice," Brea whispered.

"And orange juice," Hayden repeated into the phone, then hung up once room service confirmed the order.

Hayden grabbed the remote control, rotated, and continued to sit on Brea's legs while searching for a news channel.

"All right, get off me. I need to use the bathroom, and then we can brush our teeth." With a chuckle, Hayden rose from the bed and held out his hand to help Brea up.

They took their time to freshen up. Hayden lifted each of Brea's creams, asking her what each bottle or jar claimed to do before he would let her grab her toothbrush. Standing beside one another, they brushed their teeth and took turns bumping one another to spit and rinse in the sink—even though there were two sinks.

"Hayden, I think you're still a little boy, so immature," Brea teased, dried her mouth with a towel, and then used it to smack Hayden's bottom.

Hayden spun around with a grin. "That was illegal sexual contact—a direct violation of our agreement. And you know what that means."

Brea squinted, searching her mind to remember what he was talking about. Hayden looked at the patio doors.

"No, Hayden, no way," she pleaded.

Moving fast, Hayden lifted Brea and placed her over his shoulder. "Hayden, put me down," she squealed through laughter as he carried her onto the patio.

"Your rules, Brea!" Hayden stepped into the plunge pool. "Are you going in with a fight, or do you accept your fate?"

"Okay, okay, just do it, but I'm taking you with me," Brea exclaimed, laughing with tears rolling down her cheeks. Hayden descended the steps, sat, and settled Brea onto his lap. Finding the water warm and pleasant, she splashed Hayden, and he returned the playful gesture. Wiping their faces and looking into one another's eyes, their laughter slowed.

Their faces drew closer to one another, arresting within an inch of making contact, and Brea gripped Hayden's upper arms. He placed his hands on her lower back, scrunched the fabric of her wet tank top with his fingers, and a breath escaped her parted lips. She then laid her head on his shoulder and grazed his neck with her lips.

"Brea, that feels—"

"So good," she whispered. Lifting her head, Hayden's lips brushed against her cheek, then her ear. With a feather touch, he grazed her earlobe with his lips and, moving his hands to her outer thigh, pulled her closer to him.

Brea moaned and traced his upper arms with her fingertips. "Hayden," she whispered. Her mind was on the brink of abandoning itself of reason and succumbing to her desire for Hayden.

Hearing voices and laughter in the distance from the beach, they froze for a moment, then pulled back from one another.

Brea suppressed a laugh. "Did any of that count as illegal contact?"

Hayden smiled and shook his head. "Nope, all of that was acceptable per the terms of our contract."

Swatting his arm, Brea stood up. "Let's dry off and change. The food should be here soon. I still have your boxers so you can change into something dry." Brea rose to exit the plunge pool first.

She peeled off her wet shorts, hung them on the rack and turned to face Hayden. Standing before him, braless, in a wet ivory tank top and her underwear, he dropped his head in his hands. "Brea, come on, give me a warning, at least."

"Sorry," she said, flashing a smile and returning inside.

Grabbing a towel, Hayden pulled off his pajama pants and tank top, laid them out on the lounger to dry, then draped a towel over his shoulders. There was a knock at the door. Hayden called out, "Just a minute." He wrapped the towel around his waist and went to the door to let the room service staff in to set up their breakfast.

While Hayden dressed, Brea sat at the table and poured herself and Hayden coffee. She lifted the cover from her pancakes and inhaled. Peeking at the dish Hayden had ordered, she glimpsed the veggie omelet and helped herself to a bite.

"If you eat any more of my breakfast, I might have to pick you up and throw you in the ocean next," Hayden teased, joining Brea at the table.

"Okay, so what about today? Any more details I need to know that won't spoil the surprise?"

"You need to be at the spa at eleven, so I'll hang out here for another hour, and then I need to take care of a few things," Hayden replied.

Brea smiled. "After we eat, I'm going to write. In light of recent events, I may try my hand at writing a sonnet."

Hayden raised his eyebrows. "Will it be about me?"

Brea shrugged her shoulders. "You'll have to read it to find out."

"If we keep going like this, maybe you should write a book about us." Hayden smiled and Brea laughed. It wasn't a bad idea—with their history, she could write a series.

"Maybe you should write something too, Hayden."

Hayden swallowed the food in his mouth. "Like a poem?"

"Yes, or even just write words on a page. Allow what's on your mind to flow onto the paper."

"It might be too dirty," Hayden said with a grin.

Brea laughed. "Of course, but maybe I wouldn't mind."

Hayden dried his mouth with a napkin. "Okay, I'll give it a shot."

They finished eating their breakfast and moved to the sofa. Brea brought over two notebooks and pencils. She handed one of each to Hayden, and he opened the notebook to a blank page.

He exhaled. "I don't know about this. I'm not a wordy type of guy and, you can't laugh, my fragile ego wouldn't be able to take it."

"Never, I promise. My goal is only to foster your artistic inner child. And no naked pictures in there. I remember your yearbook story," Brea said, pointing her pencil at Hayden as he chuckled.

"I'll try." Hayden lifted his legs onto the coffee table and placed a pillow under the notebook. Brea did the same. She checked the time. It was nine, leaving them an hour to write.

Brea set to work on "Marbled Women," having an idea for a section inspired by her dream. After writing several paragraphs, her phone chimed. Checking her message, she smiled seeing it was from Hannah, asking if she was having a good time in Mexico. Brea replied she would call her in a little while and debated whether to tell her about Adam and Hayden. Though if ever she needed advice, this was the time in her life to ask for it.

Peeking at Hayden, she saw him focused on his paper. He crossed something out, then flipped to a fresh sheet. Another twenty minutes passed, and her phone rang—it was Adam. She declined the call and responded via text message she would call him in half an hour.

Hayden turned his head to Brea. "Do you need to pick it up? I can go back to my room."

She shook her head. "No, it's Adam. I'm not ready to talk to him. I'll call him back in a little while." Returning her attention to her story, she wrote another sentence. Her phone chimed again. It was Adam. "*Call me now,*" the message said.

Brea sighed. "He wants me to call him now."

Hayden nodded. "No problem. I'm going to take this with me, and I'll keep working on it. And be back in your room at six o'clock. No earlier or later than that or you'll spoil the surprise."

Brea raised her eyebrows. "I am intrigued, Hayden. I promise I'll be good and stay away until six."

Hayden nodded and rose from the sofa. Moving about the casita to collect his things, he turned to say goodbye before he headed out the front door. Just as the door closed behind him, Adam called again.

She answered after taking a deep breath. "Adam, you couldn't wait?"

"Brea, I've been thinking and talking with my parents—you need to come home. I don't like the way you've been acting. My mom is saying the kids miss you, and I don't want you in Mexico anymore. You're my wife, and being around those girls is putting some crazy ideas into your head."

"Adam. Did you think at all about what I said to you yesterday?" Brea asked, ignoring his order that she return home.

"Brea, come home—right now," Adam repeated.

"Adam, listen to me. I will give you all the time you need to get to know who I really am, but will you walk with me on this journey and see if you can love this authentic version of myself? And I don't want you making all the decisions any longer—I want a seat at the table in my life. I want to work more in the store and start writing again. I can't be the pleasant and accommodating wife without a soul—it isn't who I am."

There was no response on the other end of the line from Adam. Brea exhaled. "Adam, do you love me, and can you love who I really am?"

"Brea, don't start that up. Get on a plane and come home—now."

"No."

"No? Are you fucking kidding me?" Adam repeated, his voice now hostile.

"No, I've been sleepwalking for the past decade, and now I'm awake. It took me way too long, but I see it now. Adam, you can never give me the love I want or what I deserve to have."

"Brea. You are acting like a child. You've lost it."

"I have never felt clearer or more certain about anything in my life. Adam, I want a divorce. When I come home, you need to find a place to stay. After I find a lawyer, we can arrange for a temporary custody arrangement."

"Brea, I am not leaving my house. Have you lost your mind?"

"Adam, I'm not in love with you, and you're certainly not in love with me. There is nothing left to save in this marriage." Brea sighed—it was the brutal yet honest truth.

"Brea, you're not well. Do you think I'm just going to let you leave? You don't even have money for a lawyer. Everything you have—I gave to you. Your friends have warped your mind."

"I'm not here with friends. I lied to you, Adam."

"You did what? Are you even at that resort in Mexico? Are you alone?"

"Yes, I'm at the resort, but I'm not alone. I'm here with a man, a friend. And to be clear—I never cheated on you, although I wanted to last night. But this isn't about him. Everything that has happened this week is because who I really am is back. It took me a very long time to find where I buried her, and he helped me. I'm not going back into the cage, Adam."

"Brea, you can't at random one day say you want out of our marriage and think I'll be fine with it. We have my family name to consider, our position. Some strange guy weasels his way into your life, and you think I'll let you walk away with nothing to say about it? You have lost your mind, and you need help."

"Adam. Our marriage has been over for years, not even considering the fact you had an affair. I was just too numb and scared to admit it. For Sophie and Alex, staying together would be the biggest mistake we could make. I wanted a life opposite of my parents, and somehow, I wound up in a marriage just like theirs, and it has been slowly killing me. I am grateful for our children, and we had some good years together, Adam, but that's not enough to keep us together."

"Brea, get on a plane and come home."

"No, I'm coming back as planned on Saturday. Hannah's picking me up at the airport, and I'll see you at home. Goodbye Adam."

Brea hung up the phone and exhaled. Although her hands trembled and her heart raced, the exhilaration of making a choice and taking control over her life was one of the best feelings she had known. Tears of relief streamed down her face. Brea tossed her phone on the couch and opened the patio doors. A warm breeze blew across her face as she inhaled the salty air.

A thought interrupted her victorious meditation—upon returning to Ocean Crest Beach, if Adam would not move out, then Brea would need to find a place to stay. "Hannah," Brea whispered. Picking up her phone, she saw Adam was trying to call her back. She hit ignore and called Hannah.

"Brea, my love, how is Mexico? And by the way, I won't pretend I'm not offended that you've blown me off for years about taking a girl's trip," Hannah said after picking up the phone.

"Hannah, I have to tell you something, and I need you to listen to the entire story. Don't react until I'm done. I'll need at least twenty minutes." Pausing for a moment, Brea scrunched her eyebrows—the irony of history repeating itself did not elude her. Over twenty years ago she had the same conversation with Allegra about Hayden, and now round two with Hannah.

"Oh, shit, Brea. This is going to be good. Let me close the shop." She heard Hannah shuffle through the store, then slam the door to Brine. "Okay, I'm ready," Hannah announced. Brea began from the day she met Hayden at the library in seventh grade and ended with telling Adam she wanted a divorce.

"Hannah?" Brea said once finished. There was silence at the other end—she repeated in a louder voice, "Hannah?"

"Brea, why didn't you tell me everything before? I always figured you had a tough childhood from the little you shared, but I never imagined it was that bad."

"For years I thought it was because I didn't want to be seen as this damaged person, but the truth was, I couldn't face it all, for many reasons. I suppose I needed time—and Hayden to wake me up."

Hannah chuckled. "You know what? It's strange, but true. The quiet ones have the most interesting stories. So now what? What are you going to do?"

Brea tapped her fingers on her knee. "Hannah, could I stay with you when I get back, with Alex and Sophie? I'll sell some jewelry to pay for a lawyer—and a therapist. But I'll need some time to get set up with a place to live because the money will be tied up for a while."

"Of course! Anyway, I was tired of having sex on my kitchen table every night. I'll clean it up, and now it can become an arts and crafts table."

"Hannah, I did not need to know that."

"Brea, what about Hayden? I mean, it's all so unreal. What are you going to do about him?"

"I don't know yet. Nothing has happened. Well, something almost happened—a few times. He's not pressuring me to decide anything right now, and he said he'll wait for me, if and when I'm ready."

"When was the last time you had sex?" Hannah asked.

Brea dropped her head into her hand and with a sheepish tone replied. "Once or twice this past year."

"And Adam thinks staying together is the best option!" Hannah cried out

"Well, don't forget he had Kaylin on the side for the past year," Brea replied.

"Brea, stop using your head, get out of it and let Hayden get on top of you—at least two or three times before you get on that plane," Hannah commanded in an authoritative tone.

"I don't know, Hannah. I should get everything straightened out first with the kids. It's too soon. What would people say?"

"Brea! It's been over twenty years! You're leaving Adam, and you've waited long enough for Hayden. I'm just saying. And for the love of everything—stop caring about what people think. Do what feels right to you, all right?"

Brea placed her hand on her chest and inhaled. "Hannah, you're the best. I have to go to the spa. Hayden needed me occupied for a surprise he planned, and I have to head over there or I'll be late."

"Okay, I love you. I'll see you at the airport on Saturday at four to pick you up. In the meantime, I'll ready the house with kid shit—chicken nuggets and diapers."

"Hannah, Alex is seven and Sophie is four. They don't need diapers."

"Well then. I'll just stock the fridge and hide my porn. Enjoy and don't think—just do—him."

"Bye." Brea hung up laughing. It was a quarter to eleven, and Brea needed to hurry. Slipping into her sandals and grabbing her phone and handbag, she raced out of the casita. On the path to the spa, she peered into the sky. It was clear, blue, and inspired within her a refreshing rush of optimism. Looking forward to an afternoon of repose, she hastened her steps and promised to surrender herself to an indulgent afternoon.

Chapter Thirty-Nine

Hayden

After spending an hour at the fitness center, Hayden returned to his casita. Having revealed how he felt and his hopes for the future with Brea, he had needed an outlet to clear his head. He smiled to himself, remembering waking in the middle of the night to remove his sweatshirt, and then lying back down to watch Brea as she slept. Though the devil in him wanted to get her back for the habanero, instead he opted for a romantic gesture.

Grabbing a pen from the night table, he switched on his cell phone flashlight and propped it up on the mattress. He took the cap off the pen with his teeth, pulled up her sleeve, and drew the heart on her wrist. It was saccharine, though genuine. A remarkable feeling of contentment filled him, waking up beside her, and he wanted to repeat it every day. But keeping to his word, he would give her the space and time she needed to decide her future, no matter how difficult or devastating her choice might be.

Hayden checked the clock after taking a shower and dressing. He had half an hour until Alonso would arrive to run several errands, and feeling restless, he grabbed his wallet and phone to take a short walk along the beach.

While walking down the path, he felt an eerie sense of his mother's presence, paused, and memories of her birthdays surfaced in his mind. As a boy, his tradition had been to build something to gift her—a car built from Legos, a birdhouse, or a box for her jewelry. His mother would embrace him and proclaim it the best gift she had ever received. After, without fail, she would then tell him, *"But I need nothing, Hayden, only you."*

Over the years, his gifts would become more sophisticated. Hayden knew his mother—regardless of her protest, it moved her he attempted to outdo the previous year's present. For her forty-sixth birthday, six months before she died, Hayden bought her a sterling silver rope chain bracelet with two letter charms for her initials.

They stayed home that Friday night, ordering takeout for dinner and playing poker on the couch. His father was out for the evening, entertaining his board of directors, and would not return home until late.

"Mom, why don't you open your present?"

Smiling, his mother reclined on the sofa. "Hayden, every year you give me the most wonderful gifts, and every year I tell you that all I want next year is a hug. Will you ever listen to me?"

"Nope," Hayden replied and stood to retrieve the gift from his room while his mother laughed. Returning with the jewelry box in hand, he sat down and handed it to her.

"Hayden, I think you went over the top," she said, eyeing the elegant box.

"Mom, open it, come on," Hayden said, eager to see her expression when she opened the gift.

She untied the ribbon with difficulty. Her tremors had progressed over the previous several months, making it more challenging to write and use her hands, yet she was stubborn and would not ask for help unless she felt hopeless to manage on her own. Struggling to grip the corners of the box, she handed it to Hayden. He lifted the top, revealing the bracelet on the black pillow.

"Oh, Hayden. What did you do? It's beautiful." Meeting Hayden's eyes, she placed her hand on his cheek. "Isn't that sweet? Here, put it on me." She held out her arm and struggled to hold it still. Fastening the bracelet on her wrist, he cradled her arm with his hands to admire it on her.

"I love it, Hayden. Thank you so much."

"Happy birthday, Mom." Hayden embraced her.

"Hayden, I think the woman you marry one day is going to be the luckiest woman on this earth. You have such a big heart, even though you try to hide it from the world."

"I don't know if I'll get married, look at Dad."

"Hayden, look at me," his mother said with conviction. "You are not your father. You are warm, gentle, and strong."

"I'm not strong like him. I just stay out of his way and try not to piss him off so that he doesn't take it out on you. And that doesn't even work all the time."

"You think your father is strong, Hayden?" she asked. Hayden shrugged his shoulders.

"He's scared, Hayden—afraid of what people will think about him, of being himself, and of showing love and being vulnerable. He's angry because he doesn't understand the parts of himself he fears."

"I don't understand, Mom. That makes no sense," Hayden said, shaking his head.

"It doesn't today. But it will one day. When people make themselves bigger, it's because they're afraid they are too small—they avoid looking into themselves and instead find the faults in the world. Sometimes, they even take it out on the people who love them the most. The ones they are supposed to protect."

"Mom, why don't we leave? Let's move somewhere else," Hayden said, searching his mother's weary eyes.

"I'm working on a plan for us, Hayden. Right now, all I want is for you to have an amazing life. You are going to have choices—to do anything, move anywhere, to be free. That would make me so proud and happy. And don't give up on falling in love because that would be heartbreaking. I'm a mom, and I have a sense about these things. She's out there for you, and you'll know when you find the right one." She reached out and ruffled Hayden's hair with her hand, and Hayden nodded.

"Okay, let's play another hand, and don't even think about letting me win. I want to beat you in an honest game."

Hayden chuckled, "Fine, you're going down." They laughed, and Hayden dealt the cards.

He missed his mother and wished she was alive to ask for her advice about Brea—but as he looked out into the ocean, somehow, he knew she was rooting for them.

With the sun high and the temperature climbing, Hayden suspected it was time to meet Alonso. He checked his phone. It was noon. With his hands in his pockets, he turned and crossed the beach to venture out and finish the preparations for that evening. Tonight, there were no grand expectations—only his desire to see Brea smile.

CHAPTER FORTY

BREA

Following her final spa treatment, Brea lingered in the women's locker room to savor a rain water shower infused with eucalyptus mist. Over the course of the afternoon, she slipped into a state of divine contentment, having had a massage, facial, body wrap, and a manicure and pedicure. To end her spa day, a member of the staff ushered Brea to the salon.

Once seated in the salon chair, the hair stylist greeted Brea. "Ms. Staxon, nice to meet you. My name is Paola, one of our hair and makeup artists."

"Hi Paola. I'm in a bit of shock here. I have been in a near coma from all the treatments this afternoon, and now I'm at a loss what I'm doing here having my hair and makeup done."

"Mr. Botero instructed Alejandro that we are to prepare you for an 'elegant' occasion. What would you like for your hair and makeup?"

Brea exhaled. "I'm not sure. Something classic and romantic?"

"Hair up or down, and what color is your dress?" Paola asked as she played with Brea's hair and studied her reflection in the mirror.

"I'm not sure what I'm going to wear. I was waiting for Hayden to tell me where we're going."

Paola thought for a moment. "I'll be right back." Handing Brea a magazine, she hurried away, and then returned five minutes later.

"No need to worry. You're in my hands, and I know what to do," she declared with a broad smile.

"Why do I suspect you know something?" Brea asked, surveying the room and noticing several other staff members smile at her.

Paola smiled. "Just relax and let me work my magic."

Brea sighed, "All right, I'm all yours."

One hour later, Paola turned Brea's chair for the grand reveal. "Oh wow," Brea exclaimed. "I look five years younger. Can I take you home with me?" she joked, turning her head from side to side while admiring Paola's work.

Her hair was curled into a half updo with side-swept pieces pinned on the back of her head, and then swept over one shoulder. Her smoky-eye makeup and iridescent pink lipstick complemented the flush of pink and shimmer over her cheekbones.

"You look beautiful. I packed up the makeup to take with you. Now it's time for you to go—it's ten minutes to six."

"Thank you," Brea said, taking the white canvas pouch from Paola's hand. "It's been an incredible day. I don't have any cash, but I'd like to leave a tip for everyone."

Paola smiled and waved. "Everything is handled, go. You don't want to be late."

"Thank you all again," Brea exclaimed and hurried off. She would need to press her lavender sundress. It was the only piece she brought that could pass for an evening dress. Rushing down the path to her casita, she considered chastising Hayden—he should have warned her about tonight so she could have bought a dress earlier that morning in the hotel boutique.

Upon arriving at her casita, Brea pulled out her key card and swiped it. Entering, she froze—scattered throughout the room, someone had placed several vases of pink floral arrangements flanked by flameless lanterns on the tables.

Brea scanned the room, stunned. She went to the bedroom and saw a garment bag and several white boxes with black ribbons set atop the bed. With her mouth agape, she placed the makeup pouch and her purse on the desk. Tucked under the ribbon of the box was a card. She opened it and read.

"The resort cart will pick you up at six-fifty. Meet me at Casa 12 Supper Club, Hayden."

Brea chewed her bottom lip and pulled the zipper down on the white garment bag. Inside hung a dusty rose, silk off-the-shoulder gown with a side slit. In the two large boxes, buried beneath layers of black tissue paper, were a metallic clutch purse and matching high-heeled sandals.

In the last box she saw a large, black, square-shaped jewelry box. Opening the lid, she inhaled sharply upon seeing an elegant pair of diamond, rose gold butterfly climber earrings and a matching pendant necklace. Pressing her fingers to her chin, she sat on the edge of the bed. "Butterflies," she whispered.

Remembering the brooch, she hurried to the closet and pulled out the red cardboard box from her suitcase. Brea drew in a deep breath and opened it—a surge of emotion overcame her seeing the blue butterfly brooch, though she held back tears to preserve her eye makeup.

After removing it from the box, she fastened it in her hair, gathered and pinned behind her ear. Perhaps it clashed with her dress, but it mattered little—it belonged to her, and her heart belonged to Hayden.

Chapter Forty-One

Hayden

The Casa 12 Supper Club hosted exclusive events for select clients of the resort throughout the year, and as it happened, two special guests, Henry and Willa, attended annually to celebrate their wedding anniversary. With pleasure, they had extended an invitation for Hayden and Brea to join them that evening after Hayden had spoken with Henry for advice the previous night.

Though Hayden did not dance, Brea did, and he knew she would find the dimly lit supper club ambience and classic nineteen-forties décor charming. Gold-patterned wallpaper adorned the walls, and atop the polished wood floors sat black-and-white linen-covered dining tables paired with black velvet chairs. The center of the room held a large dance floor and a live brass band beneath a ceiling of numerous crystal waterfall chandeliers.

Hayden, having arrived early, found himself on the receiving end of a pep talk from Willa, reinforcing the idea that one should never give up on love. Grabbing Hayden's hand to wish him good luck, she then promised to keep her fingers crossed for him before Henry escorted her to their table.

At ten past seven, Hayden, dressed in a black suit and a matching dress shirt, waited on the edge of the dance floor for Brea. Though imperceptible to a casual observer, he shifted his weight from one foot to the other, awaiting her arrival. As the minutes passed, he worried Brea suspected his designs for the evening were to sway her decision to leave Adam, and she had thought against attending.

Hayden checked his watch, expecting she would have arrived by now. He glanced at the table where Henry and Willa sat with a slight shake of his head. Henry winked and pointed to the door. Hayden turned to see Brea enter the room, and his face relaxed into a broad smile. They locked eyes, and Brea paused in her steps. Hayden went to her.

"Hayden," Brea said when he stopped before her.

"Brea. You're stunning. I'm not kidding—you took my breath away."

"Thank you." Brea's cheeks flushed. She smiled and placed her hand over the pendant necklace. "And thank you for everything today—but this is too much—the jewelry. They're gorgeous, but I can't possibly keep them."

"Yes, you can," he replied. "When I saw them, I knew they belonged to you."

"Butterflies. You like butterflies, Hayden. Why?"

"They symbolize freedom and resurrection. I think those are themes we can both relate to."

Brea drew in a breath. "Thank you. I am—moved. All of this—no one has ever done something like this for me."

"Then I'm glad I solved that problem too on this trip. But it's early. I might have a few more surprises tonight, so don't thank me yet," he replied with a grin.

Brea nodded. "Of course you do. I just hope one of them isn't throwing me into the ocean in this dress."

"Well, let's see what kind of inappropriate contact there is during dinner. We have our rules, after all," he teased.

"I thought we didn't have any rules?" Brea replied, raising her eyebrows.

"Well, we have one for now," Hayden replied with a grin. He turned and offered his arm to escort Brea to their table. "By the way, we're not dining alone."

Brea scanned the elegant ballroom and smiled. "Really? Please don't tell me it's Greg and Julia from the cruise?"

Hayden laughed. "No, not them." Reaching their table, he cleared his throat to introduce her to Henry, dressed in a dapper navy-blue suit, a starched white dress shirt, and an elegant patterned silk tie. Henry rose from his chair to greet and welcome Brea.

"Brea, this is Henry and his wife Willa. They are celebrating sixty years of marriage tonight and invited us to join them."

With a glowing smile, Brea extended her hand to Henry and Willa. "Oh, that's wonderful! Congratulations. I'm so honored you're including us in your celebration. It's so nice to meet you both." Willa, radiant, dressed in a sequin silver gown, a striking diamond tennis necklace, and sizable pear-shaped drop diamond earrings, smiled and greeted Brea with a warm handshake.

Henry gestured to the table as Hayden pulled out Brea's chair. Once seated, Henry signaled to the server to bring the table a bottle of champagne. Hayden turned to Brea. "Henry founded a national real estate corporation, and Willa is a sculptor. They recently moved to Montecito."

"Yes, but with my arthritis, I had to retire. Now I teach and I'm publishing a book to document some of my most important pieces," Willa said.

Brea grinned. "That's incredible. I would love to see it after it's published. In the shop where I work, we sell many things, but our art, travel, and cookbooks are our biggest sellers. I bet my friend Hannah would love to include something like that in our stock."

"I'll keep that in mind," Willa replied with a wink. "You two make quite a pair. I hope to see you out on that dance floor after dinner."

Brea glanced at Hayden. Hayden spoke before she could tell Willa he did not dance.

"Of course," he replied.

Taken aback, Brea raised her eyebrows and turned her head to Hayden, though she remained silent. He winked at Brea and returned his attention to Henry and Willa. The champagne arrived, and the server filled their glasses.

Henry raised his champagne flute. "To the love of my life of sixty years. Willa, a love like ours doesn't bless everyone, and I'm damn lucky we found each other. I almost let you slip through my fingers once, but thankfully I was smart enough to win you back." Willa tilted her chin up as Henry leaned down to give her a kiss. In witnessing the tender moment, Hayden and Brea exchanged smiles.

"Cheers," the group toasted as they raised their glasses and sipped the crisp, dry champagne. Soon they fell into animated conversation, listening to Henry's stories about his and Willa's travels, the challenges they had faced with Henry's company, and the fascinating famous people they had met over the decades.

Hayden and Brea, riveted, then listened to Henry's account of having fought in the Vietnam War, the psychological toll it took on him and the tragic experience of losing friends in battle. Hayden glimpsed tears forming in Brea's eyes as Willa shared her personal account of her life throughout Henry's absence during the war, unknown if Henry would return home to her.

After enjoying their dinner, Henry and Willa rose from the table. Taking Willa's hand, he led her to the dance floor, leaving Brea and Hayden at the table.

"Hayden, is Henry your friend with the advice? You know, 'Love isn't complicated, people are complicated,' and so on," Brea asked, reaching for her champagne glass.

"He's a smart guy. What can I say?" Hayden replied as the server placed the dessert plates before them.

Brea chuckled and then gasped, "Oh, crème brûlée." She ate a spoonful and closed her eyes, savoring the sweet, creamy texture of the dessert enveloping her tongue. "Well, you outdid yourself tonight, Hayden. I think your mother is watching you, proud of the gentleman she raised."

"Not yet." Hayden stood and offered his hand to Brea. "Will you do me the honor?"

Brea smiled. "That depends. Does it count as illegal contact?"

"Not tonight," he responded, looking into her eyes and pushing banter and playfulness aside.

Her hand in Hayden's, she rose from the table, and he led her to the dance floor—their eyes met as they stepped in close to one another. Hayden placed one hand on her lower back and with the other, held her hand. They took one step to the side, and Brea followed Hayden's lead. Despite his lack of practice, he guided Brea across the dance floor with confidence, and to the onlookers, they made a captivating couple.

"Not bad, Hayden. For someone who never dances, I'm impressed," Brea complimented.

"I'm going to attempt a turn here in a moment, and I hope you and no one else gets injured. Here we go." Hayden lifted his arm to spin Brea in a slow turn. As she turned, his eyes caught sight of a familiar object in her hair. Stunned, he pulled back and paused. "What's in your hair?" he asked.

"The butterfly brooch. The one you gave me in the library at Harvey Slate," Brea replied as she held his gaze—his mind did not know what to make of it. Drawing her closer, again they danced.

"You still have it? You brought it here?" he asked, attempting to untangle his thoughts. Never had he imagined she kept it all these years, and the reason she wore it tonight eluded him.

"I kept it, but I buried it for years until today—because I made my decision." Hayden stopped dancing, held his breath, and searched Brea's eyes.

"I told Adam this morning I want a divorce. It's you, Hayden. I choose you, even though there really is no choice—it was always supposed to be us. It just took a really long time for it to sink in." Hayden raised his hands to cradle Brea's face, and behind her eyes, he saw what he needed to know and smiled.

"Brea, ask me again. I have the answer."

She shook her head and opened her mouth to speak, then shut it again, uncertain of the question.

"Hayden, what—"

"Remember what we used to ask ourselves—in your garage, after the diner in my car, at the beach that night when we woke up. Ask me again."

Brea searched her mind and lowered her eyes. A nuanced smile spread across her lips as she retrieved the question.

"Hayden, what are we?"

Hayden's smile widened, and he answered, "In love."

Brea nodded, and tears graced her eyes, hearing the simple truth they always knew but were too afraid to admit to themselves. It was incontestable—their love for one another had bound them together since the day they met.

Her lips stretched into a smile, and Hayden kissed her. Their kiss was an entity—an amalgamation of the tenderness and passion owed to their love, forgiveness of their mistakes, and the time that fate kept them apart. And as it always had been, when together, it felt as though they had come home, after the world had beaten them up and spit them back out.

Willa tapped Henry's hand. Pointing to Hayden and Brea on the dance floor as they kissed, she said, "Look at that, Henry.

You played a hand in that." Henry produced a half-smile and shrugged his shoulders.

"It wasn't me. It was fate." Willa tipped her head to the side, giving her husband a knowing look. Henry smiled wider. "All right, maybe I gave him a little nudge. They're good kids. A little stupid, but aren't we all?"

Chapter Forty-Two

Brea

To enjoy the night air, Brea and Hayden walked from the supper club to their casitas as Brea shared a humorous story of a famous writer Willa befriended when living in New York City in the nineteen seventies. Reaching Brea's casita, they admired the dense tapestry of stars stretching across the night sky until Hayden pulled Brea into his arms. "I'm almost scared to say it, but I'm happy," he whispered into her ear.

"So am I." After a tender kiss, Hayden wished her good night.

Brea's lips curved into a slight smile, and she shook her head. Opening her purse, she gave Hayden her room key and strolled to the door. He joined her, with eyebrows raised, and opened it for her. Brea slipped past him, set down her clutch on the console table and turned to face him. She beckoned Hayden to enter the casita with a slight nod before walking into the bedroom.

Hayden closed the door behind him, placed his hands in his pockets and hesitated about what to do next. Before he could speak, he heard Brea call his name from the bedroom. He crossed the living room and, upon seeing Brea leaning on the desk, paused in the doorframe.

Turning around, she placed her hand over the clasp of her necklace, gesturing for Hayden to unfasten it for her. Hayden went to her. After undoing the clasp, his fingers grazed the back of her neck. He lowered his head and with a gentle touch of his lips, kissed her shoulder.

Brea laid the necklace in the jewelry box beside the earrings, closed it and leaned back to press against Hayden's chest. Turning her head to the side, she whispered, "Leave the butterfly in my hair—I want to wear it while you touch me."

Hayden inhaled sharply and placed his hands on her arms. Brea pivoted around to face him, met his eyes, and slipped her hands under his dinner jacket. Her fingers lingered, savoring the feel of his toned chest. Sliding her hands upwards, she pushed it off his shoulders. Hayden removed it and set it on the desk.

He leaned down to kiss her and paused, leaving an inch of space between their lips. "Brea, I'm not expecting—"

Brea silenced Hayden by pressing a finger to his lips. "No more talking or waiting. I love you, and I want you to make love to me tonight." A delicate smile formed on Brea's lips—never had she been more certain of wanting something.

Hayden tipped his forehead against hers. "I love you," he whispered before he kissed her.

Their kiss fueled their mutual desire. Eager to feel the touch of Hayden's skin against hers, Brea untucked his shirt. The anticipation built as her fingers worked to undo each button from top to bottom. Once opened, she ran her fingers down his chest, and upon reaching his abdomen, circled his waist with her hands. Pressing her body closer, she dragged her lips across his chest and, reaching his collarbone, opened her mouth to kiss his neck.

Hayden closed his eyes and tipped his head back, giving Brea more access as she used her tongue to trail towards the base of his earlobe. The taste of his skin and the pressure of his hands on her back fueled her desire to go further.

Brea took a step back, lifted his hands to unbutton his cuffs, then slid her hands up his chest to remove his shirt. Enveloping Brea in his arms, Hayden kissed her and unzipped her dress. With two fingers he pushed the straps down her arms, and let the silk gown slip over her hips and collapse into a puddle on the floor. Wearing only pale-pink lace lingerie and high heels, she was a vision.

Seating himself in the desk chair, he removed his footwear and sat up straight as Brea stepped in between his legs. He gripped her waist and pulled her closer to kiss her abdomen. Lowering his hands to her bottom, he used his lips and tongue to trace down to the band of her panties and then along the length of them. Brea placed her hands on the back of his head and arched her back. The touch of his mouth on her skin below her navel evoked pulses of impassioned anticipation throughout her lower body.

Hayden rose from the chair and, with urgency, picked her up, and she wrapped her legs around his waist. He kissed her mouth with growing fervor, then moved his lips to her neck—a soft moan escaped from her mouth as she pressed her fingers into Hayden's shoulder blades.

Carrying her to the bed, he sat her down and knelt before her to remove her high heels. With a firm touch he gripped her bottom, slid her closer to him and kissed the tops of her breasts—her head fell back when he pulled down the fabric of the strapless bra to free her breasts and took one of her nipples into his mouth.

Brea released a soft exhale, fanned her fingers and pressed them into the mattress. Hayden's hands explored her back until finding the hooks of her bra. He removed it, dropped it on the floor beside him, and then returned his mouth to her breast. Hayden used his tongue and teeth to tease her, shuttling pleasure throughout her body—she was certain to orgasm with only a simple touch of his hand between her legs.

Changing course, his mouth trailed down her abdomen—he placed his hands on her knees and pushed, widening her legs further apart. With more access, he leaned down to kiss her inner thighs. His lips and tongue trailed to the edge of her panties and then brushed over the most intimate spot on her body—Brea's mouth dropped open, on the cusp of losing her mind with desire.

"Hayden," Brea cried out. His hands moved up the length of her thighs, then to her hips where he hooked and removed her panties. He watched her tilt her head back and her lips part, expectant and eager for his next touch.

Hayden rose to stand. Brea met his eyes, unbuckled his belt and then unfastened the button of his slacks. Hayden removed all remaining clothing and leaned down to kiss Brea as they moved back onto the bed in synchrony. He positioned himself over her, and Brea gripped his upper arms, firm and tense. Supporting himself with one arm, he used his other hand to explore the curves of her inner thighs. Feeling his touch between her legs, a breath escaped her lips. The erotic sensation of him teasing her with his fingers was too much to bear, and she was ready for him to be inside her.

"Hayden, please," she begged.

With his lips, he trailed along her collarbone and moved down to her breasts. He cupped one breast in his hand and teased her nipple with gentle pressure. His tongue took over the work from his fingers, and Brea let out another unrestrained moan.

With a light touch, he guided her left leg up, pressed her knee down, and entered her. Bringing his mouth over hers, he kissed her with an intensity and depth that matched the intense pleasure he felt as he pushed deeper until fully inside her. In unison they gasped, both feeling the exquisite sensation of their bodies joined together. Brea felt safe and comforted by the warmth and weight of Hayden's body on top of hers.

As the passion intensified, Hayden whispered her name, and Brea, abandoning her conscious mind, surrendered herself to the kindling pleasure she felt with every movement Hayden made within her. His right hand reached under her bottom and lifted her up, allowing him to penetrate deeper, and they both moaned upon feeling the delicious, exceptional heat spreading throughout their bodies. Brea wrapped her arms around Hayden's shoulders and, free of any inhibitions, allowed every sound of rapture to escape from her lips.

Unable to resist the urgency and tension, together they cried out and climaxed, clutching to one another in a firm embrace, their skin warm and damp. Making love with Hayden had been more than physical exaltation, but a fusion beyond what she had experienced before—it was eternal, honest, and irrefutable proof of the love they shared.

Holding one another until their breaths slowed and their bodies relaxed, Hayden moved to lie on his side beside Brea. She rolled over to face him, and they smiled at one another, eyes locked, placid yet euphoric.

"Brea."

"Hayden."

Hayden swept away a loose piece of hair that fell over her cheek as Brea closed her eyes and exhaled. Any other words were unnecessary. Shifting closer to one another, Hayden kissed Brea's forehead and took her hand in his. Neither of them wanted to sleep, but as time passed, it became difficult to keep their eyes open—it felt as though they had been awake not for one day, but for twenty years.

Hayden and Brea would drift off and then briefly wake to verify they were not dreaming and the other was still there. Eventually they fell asleep, at peace, against the backdrop of the ocean and the sound of the waves crashing onto the shore.

CHAPTER FORTY-THREE

HAYDEN

Opening his eyes, Hayden woke at dawn with Brea asleep beside him, peaceful and resplendent. Knowing she loved him brought him a level of fulfillment he never imagined possible. A second chance had blessed him, and although it had been an interminable wait, with the dawn, the world this morning seemed less cruel and cold.

Not wanting to wake Brea, he slipped out of bed and into his boxers. In the bathroom he scouted the extra hotel toothbrush, brushed his teeth, and then headed to the minibar to drink a bottle of cold water. He ambled to the patio doors, opened the curtains and stared at the ocean. It was still dark, but on the horizon, a streak of light blue signaled to the world the impending sunrise.

Lost in his meditation, he felt Brea's arms slide around his waist and press her cheek against his back. Lifting his arm, he pulled her around to face him, wrapped his arms around her, and kissed the top of her head. She had slipped into an ivory silk nightgown.

"This is when I think the ocean is the most beautiful, just before dawn. It feels as though there is so much possibility," Brea whispered.

"Sometimes it makes me feel uneasy," Hayden replied and held Brea tighter.

"Why?"

"Because I thought something similar the morning we woke up in my car at the beach. Then I went home, and everything fell apart."

Brea lifted her head to look at Hayden. "I think the universe has done enough to us. Besides, we can handle whatever it throws at us next."

Hayden smiled and leaned down to give Brea a soft kiss, hoping she was right—she had to be right.

"I'm going to wash up. Meet me back in bed," Brea said and slipped away.

Hayden returned to the minibar to grab a cold bottle of water for Brea, then returned to bed and covered himself to his waist with the blanket. Rolling onto his side, he propped up his chin with his hand, rubbed a finger against his lips, and replayed the events of the previous night in his mind.

It was not long until Brea reappeared, having washed off her makeup and let down her hair. Joining Hayden in bed, he turned to lie on his back for Brea to tuck in under his arm and lay her head on his chest.

"I think we should stay in this bed all day. It's our last full day here," Brea said with a forlorn tone.

"All right. Let's call Alejandro at the concierge desk and set up a meal delivery service for the day." Brea produced a stifled laugh.

"So, what happens now, Hayden? I'll stay with the kids at Hannah's until I find an apartment, and I also need to find a lawyer to figure out a temporary custody arrangement. Aside from that—how is this going to work with us?" Brea asked, playing with Hayden's fingers.

Hayden smiled. "No idea—I was hoping you would tell me." Brea groaned and tickled Hayden on his stomach. He squirmed and grabbed her hand. "Okay, seriously. I think we'll have to figure it out day by day, but to start, for the next few months on the weekends, I'll come to Ocean Crest Beach, and when Adam has the kids, you can be in San Francisco with me. And how about I change my flight to come back with you? We can tell Alex and Sophie I'm an old friend for now, and I'll help you move into Hannah's."

"That would be helpful—but for you to show up at the house with Adam at home would be a bad idea. I told him the bare-bones truth about this trip yesterday. He knows I'm here with a man, but for him to see you could be a disaster. Maybe you could stay at Hannah's and help us get set up at her place? I told her our story yesterday, and she knows all about you. She's supposed to pick me up at four at the airport. I'll let her know you're coming too."

"I'll have Ashley check to see if there's any space on your flight or I can book a private jet. I have many ways of entertaining you to make the time pass," he teased.

"And you know I would be a most willing recipient of your attentive efforts to distract me, Mr. Botero," she replied with a sultry smile, then frowned. "But Hannah has a Boxster. There won't be enough room for all of us."

Hayden laughed. "Oh no, as much as I would love you sitting on my lap again, I don't think it would work in her car. I'll tell you what, I'll rent a car and meet you at Hannah's. Look, our first hurdle. Together, nothing is unsolvable."

"Together—real life Brea and Hayden. Did you ever see that coming?" she said and sighed.

Hayden smiled. "I did not, but I'm happy the universe gave up torturing us and finally gave us a break."

"Took the universe long enough," she murmured. Closing her eyes, she pressed in closer to Hayden and a smile spread across her lips. She wrapped her leg around his, released his hand, and with her fingertips traced the length of his torso to his boxers. As she kissed his chest, she ran her fingers under the elastic band and then slid her hand under the fabric—she caressed his hip, then moved her hand to his inner thigh. Hayden groaned and tipped his head back.

"Should I stop?" she whispered.

"Hell no," Hayden replied, his voice hoarse.

Encouraged to press on, Brea kissed his chest again, using the tip of her tongue to tease him while pressing her fingers into his thigh. Feeling bolder, she moved her hand to his groin—he was firm and ready for her.

"Brea," Hayden whispered. Brea slid onto Hayden to sit astride him. Feeling the pressure of Brea atop his erection, moving her hips forward and back to tease him, an ache pulsed in his lower body. Overtaken by desire, Hayden sat up and pulled her nightgown over her head, thrilled to find she wore no panties. Brea cradled his head with her hands as he kissed her breasts, using his tongue and moving from one breast to the other. She pressed her lower body deeper into him, and he could not wait any longer.

Brea lifted herself up, and Hayden maneuvered to remove his boxers. Letting herself down gently, he entered her and they exhaled in exquisite relief from the intense ache they felt to join their bodies together. Hayden lay back against the pillows and watched Brea move her hips in a slow, undulating rhythm. Experiencing the unmatched feeling of Hayden inside her led her to abandon her inhibitions—she dropped her head back and let out a pleasurable moan. He was on the brink of climaxing watching her work her hips, but he wanted to witness her reach orgasm first.

Hayden wrapped his hands around her waist, and Brea accelerated her movements, possessed with an urge beyond any conscious control to feel the explosive release of the building tension in her body.

"Hayden, that feels so good," she cried out between breaths. Moving faster, she threw her head back, and lost in her body, her breaths became rapid and shallow. Hayden lifted his hips to penetrate her deeper, pushing her over the edge. Brea climaxed and cried out—Hayden let go and followed. He lifted himself to embrace her, and as they slowed their breathing, their heads fell onto one another's shoulders.

"Brea, I love you, I really do." Hayden whispered.

Brea pulled back, and after planting another kiss on his lips, met his eyes. "I love you, and I have a question for you."

"Yes?" he replied, focusing on her, still out of breath.

"What happened to the cinnamon gum?"

Hayden laughed and shook his head. "I never bought another pack after I lost you—couldn't do it. I think we're doing just fine without it, though."

Brea smiled and ran her fingers down Hayden's back. "Maybe, but what's the harm in doing a brief experiment to see if it increases the passion? Or you could try a little habanero again."

Hayden groaned. "No way, I'll buy the gum."

Brea kissed him again, and whispered, "Good choice."

Chapter
Forty-Four

BREA

Lying in bed with the television on, Hayden and Brea ate breakfast. After a second cup of coffee, Hayden proposed they take a shower, then walk on the beach.

"Are you joining me in the shower, or do you need to go back to your room?" Brea asked with a suggestive smile.

"Obviously joining you," he replied, seizing her foot. "At the rate we're going, I don't think we'll leave this room until we have to check out tomorrow." Hayden leaned his head down to kiss her ankle.

Brea inhaled, stretched her arms, and lay back against the pillows. "I wish we could stay another week." Hayden nodded in agreement while playing with Brea's toes, flexing them back and forth.

"Maybe we'll start a tradition like Henry and Willa. We can come back every year with Alex and Sophie," he suggested.

Brea smiled. "I love my children, but if we come back here, it's an adult trip because all I would want to do is stay in this room naked with you."

Hayden grinned. "Well, I can't say no to that. Come on, let's take a shower, then I'll go back to my room and change."

Rolling off the bed, Hayden went into the bathroom to warm up the shower. Once heated, Brea joined him.

They struggled to focus on the generally accepted goal of showering. Although difficult to keep their hands off one another, it was more a series of amusing distractions that prolonged the process. Hayden squeezed an absurd amount of shampoo onto Brea's hair, producing a prolific lather of soap that ran into her eyes, leaving her blinded and nearly knocking them off balance and slipping onto the floor. Afterward, Hayden teased he wanted to shave Brea's legs but they became distracted, like children, writing messages on the glass door with shaving gel.

Once their playful antics ceased, Hayden wrapped his arms around Brea. Giving her a gentle kiss, he turned off the water, and when Brea pressed her cheek against Hayden's chest, she could feel his heartbeat. As they held one another, water dripped off their bodies. Contented, Brea closed her eyes, blessed not only to have Hayden's love, but knowing that, most important, over the past week, she had begun to love herself.

❦

Hayden returned to his room to dress and to deposit Brea's jewelry in the hotel central safe. Brea dried her hair, made up her face, and dressed in a pair of ivory shorts and a matching linen wrap sleeveless top with the butterfly brooch fastened over her heart. Hayden knocked as she finished straightening up the bedroom.

Opening the door, she smiled seeing Hayden dressed in a white linen button-down shirt with the sleeves rolled up, navy shorts and a pair of sunglasses on his head. Brea's eyes swept over his bare forearms. The sight of him with a handsome smile on his face and his lucent blue eyes tempted her to pull him back into bed.

Hayden recognized that look. "If we don't take that walk, we never will—but you don't need to talk me into getting back into bed with you," he said, taking a step forward and hooking his finger into the band of her shorts.

Brea pressed her lips together and considered the delicious possibility of messing up the bed, having only finished making it when Hayden had knocked on the door. It was as though her body had catapulted back in time to her teenage self, full of unbridled hormones. With a smile, she cleared her throat. "Well, we have all day and night, so maybe we should get a little sunshine."

Leaning down to kiss her, Hayden pulled her in close and placed his hands on her bottom. "Let's set a one-hour time limit of outdoor time, then we'll come back here and finish what we started in the plunge pool the other day—bathing suits are optional."

Brea bit her lip and nodded. "I always knew you were smart, but now I'm certain you're a genius." She slipped her arms around his waist and nuzzled her face into the crook of his neck and shoulder.

"On second thought, let's shave it down to forty-five minutes for a walk, then we come back here," he said, closing his eyes while Brea kissed his neck. She laughed, stepped back to take his hand and pulled him onto the path.

As they walked to the beach, Hayden checked his phone. "I sent a message to Ashley to see about booking me on your flight if possible. She hasn't responded—must be busy at the office."

"Worst case, fly home and come back to me when you can."

Hayden halted his steps, and without warning, scooped Brea up in his arms. Taken by surprise, she let out a yelp, "Hayden!"

"Nope, I don't want to let you out of my sight, period." They looked into one another's eyes and kissed.

Brea chuckled. "Okay, put me down. We're going to become one of those couples that makes people want to throw up."

"Of course we will be. That's what I've been waiting for my whole life," Hayden teased upon setting Brea down on the ground. With a smile he reached out and ran his finger over the butterfly brooch before they turned to continue walking.

Although the midmorning temperature was hot, a soft breeze blew, and the sky was clear and the air dry. Reaching the beach, they removed their shoes and tossed them on the sand. Brea tugged Hayden to the foreshore, to the cooler, wet sand. While walking, they discussed their favorite spots to visit for when they would travel over the upcoming weekends to see one another—parks, bookstores, galleries, and restaurants.

"Hayden, I need a code name for you on my phone. I don't want Adam to know who you are yet. His family and friends are very wealthy and influential—I doubt they would do anything, but maybe it could cause a problem for you if they found out about you until things have settled down."

He nodded. "Sure, maybe think of a business, like dry cleaners or a car service."

Brea raised her eyebrows. "That's brilliant. Let me think a minute." She deleted their previous text messages and then deleted Allegra as his fake contact name. "Blush Salon—that's perfect."

Hayden narrowed his eyes. "Couldn't it be something more masculine, like—Al's Construction?"

Brea shook her head with a cheeky smile. "Nope, I like this one." Once finished, she silenced her phone to avoid disturbances for the rest of the morning.

They continued strolling down the beach, content and unhurried, pausing to gaze out at the water or to examine a shell or a pebble that had washed up on the shore. Brea tucked many into her pocket as she planned to give a small collection of beach treasures to Sophie and Alex. Both now thirsty, Hayden suggested they stop by the cafe for a drink and sandwiches to bring back to the casita.

Arriving in the lobby, Brea pulled Hayden's hand to hasten their steps to the cafe. Hayden handed Brea a bottle of sparkling water from the cold display case to drink while they scanned the menu and ordered. Planting a kiss on Hayden's lips, Brea excused herself to freshen up in the restroom while he waited in the cafe for their orders, and would meet her in the lobby.

Brea hurried to the restroom, and a libidinous smile spread across her face in anticipation of returning to the casita with Hayden. Before leaving, she rinsed her face with cool water, reapplied concealer and lip gloss, and spritzed on perfume. Studying her reflection, she smiled upon seeing her glowing complexion—the recent orgasms had taken five years off her face.

Clasping her hands in front of her, she exited, eager to return to Hayden. Halfway through the lobby, she froze, unable to breathe as though a large object had collided with her and knocked the air out of her chest.

Adam was in the lobby, staring at Brea, dressed in a maroon T-shirt and dark gray slacks. Behind him were two imposing men wearing identical black short-sleeved button-down shirts and pants. Stunned, she believed she had to be mistaken. She blinked and shut her eyes for a moment. Upon opening them, she drew in a shaky breath—it was Adam. A knot tightened in her gut. Approaching him, she opened her mouth, though no words came out.

"Brea," Adam said with eerie composure while running his hand through his sand-colored dark blonde hair.

"Adam, what are you doing here?" Brea uttered with difficulty.

"Bringing you home."

"Where are Alex and Sophie?"

"Still with my parents. They're fine. Excited to see their mother today."

Bewildered and with a slight shake of her head, Brea shut her eyes and reopened them. "I told you. I am not coming home early. Your showing up here is beyond—"

Adam interrupted her. "Brea, after you hung up on me, I spoke with my parents. We will not get a divorce. It's just—not going to happen."

"Adam—"

Before Brea could finish, Hayden appeared. Seeing her expression and the men before her, he placed the food and drinks on a table and went straight to them. The staff at the front desk, seeing the two large men behind Adam, sensed something was amiss and exchanged worried glances. Alejandro stepped out from behind the concierge desk to follow Hayden.

"Brea, what's going on?" Hayden asked with a concerned expression.

"Oh, and this must be the 'friend' who's been fucking with my wife's head and, probably, fucking her as well. Hope you had an enjoyable week because she's leaving with me right now, and you'll never see her again."

"No, I'm not Adam," Brea replied, steady and calm as she grasped Hayden's hand. Hayden held on to her hand tight.

"Brea, I'm not playing around. Follow me. I need to show you something."

"She's not going anywhere with you." Hayden stepped in front of Brea, ready to do anything necessary to protect her.

"Oh, it would be perfect if you threw the first punch. Let me introduce you to my friends. This is Arnauld and that is Sebastian. I brought them here, not to drag Brea onto a plane, but in the event they needed to take care of you. By the way, Brea—it's vulgar of you not to introduce your friend. And your name is?"

"Don't tell him your name," Brea replied in haste.

"I'm not backing down, and I'm not intimidated by these guys," Hayden announced and took a step forward. Alejandro intervened, stepping in between Hayden and Adam. He met Hayden's eyes and shook his head to warn Hayden to back down, knowing that it would be a fight Hayden would not win.

"That won't help her," he whispered to Hayden.

"Brea, follow me," Adam repeated, gesturing to an empty sitting lounge with a glass wall where they would be visible to everyone.

"It's all right, I'll be right back," Brea whispered to Hayden, then turned to follow Adam.

Alejandro tugged on Hayden's arm to bring him to the concierge desk with him. "Come with me, watch her, but come with me."

After taking several steps, Brea gripped her shaking hands and turned back to glance at Hayden once more. Adam flying to Mexico was an unexpected turn of events she had not considered. Perhaps she had been naive to believe he would let her go without protest, though with his having an affair, this dramatic attempt to retrieve her appeared excessive.

Upon reaching the lounge, an arrogant smirk spread across Adam's face, and in that moment Brea knew the truth—although his love for her had faded, in his mind, he owned her, and only he could decide whether to set her free.

Chapter
Forty-Five

HAYDEN

Tapping his thumb against his fingers, Hayden kept his eyes fixed on Brea from across the lobby. One of Adam's men eyed Hayden as he walked with Alejandro to the concierge desk.

"Señor Botero. Those men are locals—hired guys. I do not know how he found them, but they follow their own rules. If you try to hit that man or stop him, you will wind up in jail—or worse," Alejandro warned in a low voice.

"I'm not letting him take her—I can't lose her," Hayden replied as he observed Adam show Brea something on his phone. Brea's hands covered her face, and her head dropped. Crying and shaking her head, she turned to face Hayden and placed a hand on the glass to steady herself. Her handbag slipped off her shoulder and dropped to the floor. Adam grabbed her arm to turn her and held up his phone inches from her face.

Hayden took a reactive step forward, and Sebastian made an aggressive counterstep, ready to act if necessary. Alejandro grabbed Hayden's arm. "No! You cannot help her if you do something stupid here. If he takes her, you will need to go back to your country."

Unable to bear witness to Brea's distress and being powerless to help her, Hayden's face tensed. "Alejandro, see if there are any flights I can get on to any airport in Southern California as soon as possible, private or commercial—I don't care what it costs."

Alejandro summoned a bellman to join him. Whispering in his ear in Spanish, the man nodded and hurried out of the lobby through the front entrance. Brea opened the door of the lounge and took off running to Hayden.

Sebastian and Arnauld looked to Adam for instructions. Adam bent down to pick up Brea's handbag off the floor and followed behind her at a slow pace. He raised his hand and shook his head to allow her to pass them, then unzipped Brea's handbag, rooted through her purse and pulled out her room key card.

Reaching Hayden with tears streaming down her face, she fell into his arms. "He's going to take Alex and Sophie from me with an emergency court order, saying I'm unfit and having some kind of mental breakdown."

Hayden shook his head in disbelief. "That's ridiculous—he can't do that. I'll call my lawyer, and we'll fight it."

"He can. He has statements, letters from his parents, our nanny, and our friends saying I'm mentally ill, drinking, and a danger to my children. If I don't go with him, and give you up, he'll file it with a judge his parents know," Brea whispered, distraught. "I can't lose you, Hayden, I can't," she sobbed, pressing her face into his chest.

Hayden's mind raced—astounded by Adam's tactics to prevent Brea from leaving him. As Adam drew nearer, he knew he had little time left with Brea. "Go with him and get your kids. Do nothing impulsively. I'll figure something out."

"No," Brea cried out, and her knees buckled. Hayden held her up in his arms—he needed to maintain his composure for her.

"Brea, say goodbye," Adam announced from the center of the lobby with a callous expression. He had little patience for what he considered a pathetic and dramatic display of emotion. Handing Arnauld her key card, Adam told him the casita number he forced from Brea. "Go pack her things quickly and meet us at the car."

Hayden pulled back, cradled Brea's face with his hands and whispered. "Trust me. If any two people can find a way out of this, it's us. Right?" Brea nodded.

"To hell and back, remember?" Hayden said. Brea nodded again.

Adam walked to Brea and Hayden with Sebastian trailing behind him, and upon reaching them, groaned. "This is all so sweet, but we have a plane to catch. Sebastian, help Brea to the car. She's overwhelmed."

Sebastian gripped Brea's arm and pulled her back from Hayden. Holding Hayden's gaze, she mouthed, "Hannah, find Hannah." Hayden nodded. Sebastian tugged on Brea's arm again, pulled her through the lobby and guided her out the door.

Hayden's eyes followed Brea exit the lobby until she disappeared from view—he felt as though someone had brutally ripped away a piece of him. With Brea gone, Hayden's focus shifted onto Adam's smug face, and the pain he felt mutated to stone-cold anger.

Adam approached Hayden, then paused, keeping several feet between them. "I don't know who you are, or how you weaseled your way into my wife's head, but she's coming home with me, back to her family, and whatever you think you two had is done."

Haden stepped forward, confident in his restraint, though refusing to let Adam believe he intimidated him. In attempting to reason with Adam, Hayden softened his facial expression and stance. "Look, you know she isn't mentally ill. I know Brea has an incredible capacity to hide her sadness and pretend she's all right, but you must have seen how miserable she's been. If you care about her, why can't you let her go if that's what she wants?"

Adam rubbed his chin and sighed. "Yeah, that won't happen, because I know what she needs. You know, I suppose I should thank you when I think about it."

Hayden narrowed his eyes. "Thank me? For what?"

"I'll admit I was bored in my marriage. I screwed around, and that's on me, but now I know what to do to bring her back. And you should also know I don't like to lose, and I especially hate it when people try to take what belongs to me."

Hayden shook his head. "She doesn't belong to you. Do you really think she'll forgive you when you're blackmailing her? You've dug your own grave here." Attempting another angle to encourage Adam to see reason, he continued. "Think about Sophie and Alex. If you don't let her go, you are not only hurting her, but them as well. Brea deserves to be happy."

Adam advanced a step forward and a malevolent grin spread across his face. "Brea is so sweet, isn't she? Considerate, compliant—and so fucking beautiful. On the phone, she was begging me to fight for her, and look—I showed up. Believe me when I say she will forgive me. And when she does, I can't wait for her to wrap her legs around me and beg for me to make her come while I fuck her. I want you to picture that when you're on the plane going home to wherever you came from."

It was clear Adam's strategy was to bait Hayden into assaulting him—and it nearly worked. Hayden's body tensed and his hands clenched into fists for a moment before releasing them. The thought of Brea with Adam made him sick, but if he hit him, the hotel would have to call the police and there would be a record of Hayden assaulting Adam. That would not help Brea. Rather, it would favor Adam's case. Although difficult, he refrained from reacting and kept his eyes focused on Adam.

Disappointed Hayden had not taken the bait, Adam looked away, sighed, and took a step forward. "Listen to me carefully. If you try to contact or see her, Brea's the one who will pay the price. I know you don't care if you get hurt, but I know you care if she does." Adam turned to leave the lobby and called out over his shoulder as he strode across the floor, getting in the last word. "So be smart and stay the fuck away from her."

When Adam left, Hayden turned and slammed his hands on the concierge desk. Alejandro, having stepped away, returned after several minutes. "No commercial flights are available to Southern California today, but we know the driver, and he informed us they have a private plane at the airport flying to Santa Barbara."

"They're going to get their kids—damn it." That meant he did not know when they would be back in Ocean Crest Beach or how to find her. Hayden checked his phone. Ashley confirmed she had booked him on Brea's flight tomorrow. Frustrated, he rubbed his neck and searched his mind for what to do next.

"Hannah," he muttered to himself. Brea told him to find Hannah. The plan was to meet her tomorrow at the airport at four o'clock. If he could not reach Hannah before then, he would attempt to find her there.

Alejandro excused himself to make another phone call. Hayden, unable to understand the conversation, paced near the concierge desk. Upon hanging up, he shook his head. "No private Mexican jets are available either." Before Hayden could respond, another valet hurried to the desk and spoke to Alejandro in Spanish. Alejandro thanked him and turned to Hayden. "They just left for the airport. The driver will call as soon as they get on the airplane to take off."

"Thank you, Alejandro," Hayden said and shook his hand. "One more thing. Could you dial Mr. Fenniston's room?"

Alejandro searched his personal list of VIP clients, dialed the extension, and handed the phone to Hayden. After three rings,

Henry picked up. "Henry." Hayden's voice broke when he said his name.

"What happened, kid?" Henry asked.

"He's got her. Her husband came and took her."

"Meet me at the bar in fifteen minutes," Henry said and hung up the phone.

CHAPTER FORTY-SIX

HAYDEN

"Javier, you know what to do," Henry said. He patted Hayden on the shoulder and took a seat beside him at the lobby bar. "Tell me what happened."

Hayden tilted his head back and rubbed his eyes. The adrenaline had subsided, and now a feeling of empty desolation remained—he was powerless to help Brea, uncertain of her situation or how he could intervene. Amid sharing what happened, Javier, having witnessed the incident with Brea and Adam, placed two tumblers of Macallan 18 before them and informed Hayden and Henry it was on him. Hayden thanked him for the kind gesture.

Henry shook his head. "That's diabolical. For a man to threaten to take away a woman's children—that is one cold move. I think he's bluffing, banking on scaring the poor woman into submission."

Despondent, Hayden dropped his head into his hands. "I could never ask Brea to give up her children. She would do anything for them, even if it meant sacrificing her life and happiness for them."

"No, she wouldn't, you're right," Henry replied, tapping his fingers on the bar.

Hayden picked up his drink and took a large sip to steady his nerves. "I don't know what to do, Henry. He's a smart guy and an attorney. He has letters and witnesses lined up to lie for him, claiming Brea is mentally ill and a danger to her children. Brea has no one other than myself and her best friend. And what kind of witness would I make—the man who, according to Adam, 'brainwashed her.' If we had to go to court and tell them our story, they could very well believe I manipulated her."

"I agree. That wouldn't look good." Henry shook his head. "And he brought two hired guys with him? A man who needs to bring muscle to strong-arm his wife to come back to him is a weak man."

Hayden exhaled. "They were for me. In the event I tried to put up a fight or attacked him."

"You were smart, kid, not to take the bait. That's how you lose. This guy is thinking a couple of steps ahead—so, you have to be smarter and get ahead of him. Doesn't he know who you are? You're well financed with an army of lawyers who could back you and Brea to fight a big legal battle. But she could lose her kids for a while," Henry replied.

Hayden shook his head. "No, Brea was smart and didn't tell him. She was worried he might retaliate, and she even hid my number on her phone."

Henry chuckled. "Smart girl. So, you have an advantage then. Be patient, then hit him from behind when he isn't expecting it."

"Yeah, how am I going to do that? If I even try to contact her and he finds out, he said—he'd make her pay for it and I don't know what he's capable of doing to her." Hayden covered his mouth with his fist to compose himself.

"Well, then he can't find out. You're going to find his weakness. Think about it. It's like in business. I'm not ashamed to admit it—sometimes to get a deal through, I had to know who

I was playing against and use their flaws against them. It's like a game of—"

"Poker," Hayden said, finishing Henry's sentence. Hayden recalled playing poker on the beach with Brea, and an ache flooded his chest, picturing her wry smile after she won her first hand against him.

Lifting his glass to drink his scotch, Hayden paused. An idea came to him—the beginnings of a play formulated in his mind. Turning his head, he looked at Henry with a half-smile.

Raising his eyebrows, Henry said, "What is it, kid?"

"Henry, I think you may be the smartest man on the planet. Truly."

Henry pursed his lips and shrugged his shoulders. "That's what Forbes said, but I don't know their sources."

Hayden took another large swig of his drink. "I need to get out of here as soon as possible, but there aren't any flights today, commercial or private. I need to message my assistant and see if she can find a jet to get down here by tomorrow morning to take me to San Francisco."

Henry chuckled. "Kid, I can get a plane for you here in a few hours. You need a ride, you've got one."

Hayden raised his eyes to study Henry, moved that someone he knew for less than one week had played such a pivotal role in changing his life for the better. After all the pain in his life, one tragic outcome had been losing faith in the goodness of people—Henry was proof that there are people willing to help in ways one would never expect.

"Henry, if it weren't for you, I might have given up on me and Brea. I don't know why you helped me, but thank you."

A smile played on Henry's lips. "I'm an old-fashioned romantic, and a good romance never gets old, kid, no matter how many versions of the same story there are out there in the world. You two are good kids. You'll find your way back to one another, and if you need help, I'm here."

Picking up the scotch, Hayden drained it and as he stood, placed his hand on Henry's shoulder to say goodbye.

With a wink, Henry tapped Hayden's hand, and pointed over his shoulder. "Go, you've got work to do. I'll get you the details for the flight in fifteen minutes. And don't forget—I want to know how it all ends. But remember I'm old—I don't have unlimited time here."

Hayden laughed. "You've got it, Henry." He took off through the lobby to his casita. While jogging down the path, he called Ashley.

"Mr. Botero, you're all set for your flight tomorrow, and we can review your calendar for Monday if you'd like."

"Clear my calendar, Ashley, for the entire week. Call everyone to come into the office tonight at eight—the board, in-house counsel, and the executive team. We can videoconference with the board members who can't make it in. I'm getting on a plane soon and driving straight to the office."

"Yes, Mr. Botero. May I share with them the purpose?"

"Not yet. Get them together. And Ashley—"

"Yes, sir?"

"Find me a private detective for a personal matter."

"Right away, Mr. Botero." Hayden hung up the phone. It was a bold play, and alone it may not work, but it was a start. Upon reaching his casita, he dashed inside to pack and to wait for Henry's phone call.

Chapter Forty-Seven

Brea

After wiping her eyes with shaky hands, Brea inhaled slow, deliberate breaths to control her breathing. Sebastian, the man Adam had hired, stood by the car door after ushering Brea into the third row of the SUV—likely so she could not jump out of the car and run. Though she desired escape, she knew Adam had her trapped and would not hesitate to call the judge if she disappeared.

Wanting to see Hayden once more before they left, she craned her neck to look out the window, and hoped he could soon reach Hannah—he would need her help. In his hand, Sebastian held Brea's handbag with her cell phone inside. Brea knocked on the window to attract his attention, but he ignored her. Frustrated, she slammed her head against the headrest in disbelief at once again finding herself caged. Her agitated mind could not still, and feeling restless, she stretched out her arm to reach the car door handle. Adam exited the lobby, headed to the car, and she froze in place.

Adam, proficient in Spanish, spoke with Sebastian. Brea strained to listen, trying to pick up the thread of the discussion, but their voices, too muffled, made it impossible to understand them. They remained outside, waiting for Arnauld to return with Brea's suitcases from the casita.

The engine idled, and although the air conditioning cooled the car, beads of sweat formed on her forehead. With both hands, Brea cradled her neck and squeezed her arm muscles to discharge the tension she felt. She needed to focus her mind and formulate a clever plan to persuade Adam to let her go—she and Hayden had not found one another after twenty years, only to be ripped apart again.

The driver opened the trunk, and the chiming sound startled Brea. Arnauld tossed her suitcases in with little care as Adam opened the car door and climbed into the second row with Sebastian. Arnauld circled the car and scanned the area before sitting in the front passenger seat.

"Adam, how could you? How dare you threaten me?" Brea exclaimed, escalating the volume of her voice with disregard to the other passengers.

Without turning to look at Brea, Adam replied with an impassive tone. "We're driving to the airport. I know you're upset, Brea, but this guy messed with your head, and you're not well. We're going to get you help, and you'll see over time that the right thing to do is to come home to your family."

A surge of fury filled Brea. Adam's arrogance and callous disregard for her feelings astounded her. "Adam, what you have done is not something I'm going to get over. I'm not in love with you anymore, and you're blackmailing me to come home. You know I'm not delusional—I will never forgive you."

With a sigh, he turned to Brea. She fixed her gaze out the window, and fresh tears formed in her eyes. "Brea, look at me."

"No. I can't look at you. I don't know who you are, Adam," she replied, wiping her eyes.

"Yes, you do. I never lied to you, Brea, about who I am, and I know you. There is nothing wrong with moving on from your past and putting on a good face for your children. Your erratic behavior proves that something has corrupted your mind. And if you fight me, we can stop off at a mental health hospital here, and I'll check you in if you prefer that?"

"No! Please don't do that. I'm getting on the plane. I want to—okay?" she cried out. Pressing her trembling fingers to her lips, it felt as though the air had been sucked out of the car.

Adam softened his tone of voice. "Brea, look at me. You know I love you."

Brea shook her head. She had wanted Adam to say those words to her for so long, but it was too late. "You don't love me, Adam. You're trying to manipulate and control me."

Adam exhaled. "I told Kaylin it's over. I know I neglected you and I took our marriage for granted, but I found my way back to you. Something drastic was needed to get you away from that guy, and now I can find you the help you need. Can't you trust that your own husband knows you and wants to protect you—even if it's from yourself?"

She did not reply. Adam continued. "Take a step back and consider this—if you were confused and unhappy, how can you be certain this guy wasn't filling your head with bullshit to break up your marriage so he could get what he wanted from you?"

Brea turned her head to meet Adam's eyes. She had, without question, forfeited her autonomy and turned over control of her life to Adam because she had been too fearful to trust her own mind. But one thing was incontestable—an unshakable truth she knew with certainty—Hayden's love for her.

By studying Adam's face, she knew that arguing or attempting to reason with him would only result in failure. The sole path to freedom would be patience and a well-devised plan. Brea inhaled a deep breath, and a resurgence of will and determination filled her.

"Adam, I need my phone so I can call Hannah."

"There is no reason to call her. I called her just before I saw you in the lobby. I told her you're coming home early, having become sick in Mexico, and as a family, we decided you would resign from working at the shop."

"You did what? Give me my phone now!" Brea demanded.

Ignoring Brea, Adam continued. "I'm going to keep your phone to prevent you from doing something stupid, like trying to call your lover. Brea, I am not fucking around. All I need to do is call the judge, and I'll send Sophie and Alex to live with my parents."

Brea pressed her lips together, fearful of saying another word. A realization set in, and she shut her eyes. Believing she left Mexico early, Hannah would have no reason to go to the airport tomorrow—she hoped Hayden would meet her there. It mattered little—Hayden would find Hannah at Brine or track her down another way.

"So, are these guys coming home with us? Is part of your plan to keep me under surveillance in the house and lock me in the bedroom?"

"No, they're going to stay with us until we get on the plane, and then we're going to Santa Barbara to stay with my parents for a while. I'm not physically forcing you to do anything, Brea. You have a choice here. I only hope you don't make an irrational one and lose your children over it. I can't imagine he's worth that price."

Brea's hands clenched into fists, though she knew better than to surrender to her desire to assault Adam. Closing her eyes, she sank into her seat and leaned her head back on the headrest. Reflecting on her last moments with Hayden, his voice echoed in her mind. *"To hell and back,"* he had reminded her.

Placing her hand over the butterfly brooch, grateful to have a piece of him to keep with her, she willed it to give her the strength she needed until they found each other once again.

Chapter
Forty-Eight

Hayden

The jet landed in San Francisco at six o'clock. Hayden deplaned and hastened to the waiting chauffeured car. Having already changed into a gray business suit on the plane, he instructed the driver to take him to the office. On route, Ashley confirmed Gregory, chief operating officer; Peter, in-house attorney; Matthew, chief technology officer; Braden, CFO, and the members of the board via conference call, would be present in the executive conference room in one hour.

During the drive, Hayden called Gregory, Peter, Matthew, and Braden to explain the purpose of the urgent meeting. After arriving at company headquarters, Hayden had thirty minutes before the meeting and headed to his office—he halted mid-stride upon seeing Ashley setting up a hot meal for him.

"Ashley, you are amazing. Could you also grab me a cup of coffee?" he asked, sat down at his desk and opened his laptop. Ashley had booked a private plane to fly him to Ocean Crest Beach the following day in the early afternoon, and he did not want to waste time finding Hannah. It was too late today, but tomorrow he would try to call the store, aiming to reach her before takeoff. If not, he would be at the front entrance of the airport at four o'clock. The Brine website loaded, and Hayden scrolled through the homepage. In finding Hannah's last name, he wrote it down on a notepad.

"Here you are, Mr. Botero." Ashley placed a company porcelain mug of black coffee on his desk. Hayden smiled and thanked Ashley, dressed in a black tweed dress with her silver hair pulled back and pinned into a meticulous knot at the nape of her neck.

"Ashley, this woman, could you find a home address and a personal phone number? If you haven't already, I'll also need a car rental for tomorrow at the airport."

"Yes, anything else, Mr. Botero?"

"Ashley, are you ever going to call me Hayden? You've worked with me for over ten years?"

A tight-lipped smile appeared on her face. "I don't believe so. I'm old-fashioned. What can I say?"

Hayden nodded with a smile. Famished, he picked up his fork and ate a bite of the miso sea bass set atop a generous portion of soba noodles before him.

"Mr. Botero, may I comment on something personal?"

Hayden swallowed before answering. "Of course. What is it, Ashley?"

"You should take secret vacations more often. I'm not sure what the fire is right now, regardless, you look the best you have in years—there's a spark in your eyes."

Hayden's eyebrows raised. "You can tell that after seeing me for less than five minutes?"

"As you said, I've known you for ten years," she replied with a smile. On the verge of turning to leave, she paused and added, "Also, Miss Avery dropped off the keys to your residence and asked me to tell you she moved her things out. She requested I pass along a message—a rather profane one. Would you like me to relay it to you?"

Hayden rubbed his eyes and chuckled. "No, Ashley, but I'm sure it included something about what an asshole I am."

Ashley nodded and smirked. "In so many words."

Hayden thanked Ashley and swallowed several more bites of his meal before leaning back in his chair. Channeling his emotional stress into his hands, he clenched them into fists, and then relaxed them. To focus and steady his mind, he then inhaled a deep breath and visualized holding Brea in his arms at dawn that morning. In that moment, he knew they would prevail. He did not know exactly how—but he knew it. Grabbing the mug of coffee, he strode out of his office to join his executive team in the boardroom.

❧

Hayden boarded the jet for Ocean Crest Beach the following afternoon and would touch down at the airport at three o'clock. Exhausted and on edge, he had woken up early after a fitful night of sleep and despite two hours of exercise at the gym, his tension persisted.

Unable to reach Hannah, neither at the store nor on her personal phone number, he decided if Hannah did not appear at the airport as planned, he would drive to Brine. If she were not there, he would try the home address Ashley had uncovered.

After takeoff, Hayden opened his laptop to work. Concentrating felt near impossible. If the Board approved his proposal, it was a start, but the plan was half-baked—alone it would be inadequate to help Brea—and the manipulation and coercion Adam was certain to employ with Brea filled Hayden with mounting pressure to move at a rapid pace. To preserve his faith, he would need to remind himself that he and Brea were bound to one another, though at the moment a tenuous thread held their future together.

The attendant served Hayden coffee and offered to prepare his lunch. After declining the meal, Hayden asked the attendant to check if Brea's original flight was on schedule. Willing himself to focus on his work, he reviewed various files Braden had sent him, then replied to scores of messages needing his attention. It was not long before the pilot announced they were beginning their descent and would land within twenty minutes.

The flight attendant returned, informing him Brea's flight would land on time at three forty-five. Hayden checked his watch. It was twenty minutes to three. Gazing out the window, his eyes settled on the ocean forty thousand feet below—a vast blue-green splash of color beneath the cloudless sky. The view offered him a moment of relief from his preoccupied mind. "Magic," he reminded himself.

Chapter Forty-Nine

Brea

Mid-afternoon, Adam and Brea landed in Santa Barbara. Seated in the backseat of the Tandervon's chauffeured Mercedes, Brea tapped her fingers on the armrest, restless and eager to see Alex and Sophie, though dreading encountering Adam's parents, Mary and Allen.

"Adam, how could you lie to your parents about me? Your mother knows who I am as a person and as a mother. It's impossible she would think I'm unfit or dangerous."

"After a long discussion with my parents, sharing with them about your binges on alcohol, erratic behavior, and fleeing the country, my mother realized that the signs were there all along. First, there is your family history. I know you minimized your mother's mental health issues, but it's obvious she has serious problems and little awareness. And you said yourself that mental illness could be passed down."

Brea's eyes grew wide. Although there was truth in what he said, she found it abhorrent that he used her fear of turning into her mother against her. Adam, in making her question her own sanity, was taking a step too far.

"The last time we visited, my mother recalled you drank heavily and left Alex and Sophie alone in the pool with no adult supervision. Then she witnessed you grab Sophie's arm, hurting her, after she spilled orange juice on your dress. Oh, and Tina told me you came home from work two weeks ago, intoxicated and disheveled. Brea, how can we trust you wouldn't drive the kids after you've been drinking? Then you fled to Mexico with a strange man and began spouting off crazy things on the phone—that you were a different person."

Brea's mouth dropped open. Grabbing Adam's arm with a firm grip, she raised her voice. "Adam, none of that is true, and you know it. You are twisting everything or outright lying."

With a forbidding expression on his face, Adam turned to face Brea, removed her hand from his arm and then gripped her wrists. "Look at you—you're out of control. We're going to help you, Brea. There's a facility my mother researched where we can check you in for as long as it's necessary. If you do well, perhaps we can tear up the letters in the future—if you return to your old self."

Brea attempted to free her arms, but Adam was too strong. She closed her eyes and relaxed her body. "That won't be necessary, Adam."

Adam studied Brea before speaking. "We'll see. My parents will keep a close eye on you, so if I were you, I'd skip the dramatics or it will only go into another long letter for the judge." Adam released her wrists.

Clasping her hands together, she exhaled and adjusted her strategy to reason with him. "Adam, why can't you let me go? It's obvious you haven't loved me or wanted to be with me for years. This is ridiculous. Do you really want to stay married to me like this? I'll only hate you."

Adam reached out to place his hand on Brea's shoulder. Recoiling from his touch, he grabbed her upper arm and held it with an unyielding grasp. "Because you are my wife. You wanted me to fight for you, and I'm doing that. I will let no one take you away from me," he said, locking his eyes on hers. Inhaling a shaky breath, she turned her head away from Adam.

The car pulled to a stop in the courtyard of the Tandervon estate, and the driver stepped out to open Brea's door. Exiting the vehicle, she surveyed the beige Georgian-style stone structure with large black-framed windows. What Brea had once considered an elegant, luxurious estate home, she now perceived as an ominous prison.

Dressed in beige slacks and a white silk blouse, Mary, with her sleek blonde bob and flawless makeup, stood before the front door with her arms crossed over her chest and a sympathetic expression. With open arms, she beckoned Brea forward to embrace her, but Brea remained fixed in place—she opened her mouth to speak but remained silent and glared at Mary. Upon feeling the touch of Adam's hand on her lower back, she shut her eyes to compose herself, as Adam made a point of warning her not to be *"dramatic."*

"Come here, Brea," Mary said with a gentle, high-pitched voice, as though she were trying to coax a wounded wild animal to her side. "It's all right, come here," she repeated. Adam pressed firmly into Brea's back to nudge her forward.

Feeling as if her legs were submerged in a thick pool of honey, Brea walked slowly to Mary. Upon reaching her, Mary placed her thin, icy fingers adorned with several large cocktail rings on Brea's cheeks.

"You're exhausted, dear. Don't worry, I'll have Alice bring a light meal to your room. We're going to take good care of you here. The children are finishing up dinner, and I'll send them in to see you in a little while," Mary said.

Brea met Mary's eyes and forced herself to produce a tight smile. She refrained from speaking, knowing she would only fall apart or scream in Mary's face to call her a heartless liar.

"Adam, take her up to the bedroom so she can rest. Brea, we'll talk in the morning. I think it would be good for us to spend a little time together so we can chat, woman to woman."

Brea nodded, averted her eyes from Mary and fixed them on the marble sculpture over the portico, an angel looking over her shoulder with her eyes lowered. "Let's go, Brea," Adam said, and with his hand on her back, guided her inside.

After Brea passed by her, Mary lowered her voice and said to Adam, "You did the right thing to bring her back. She'll be all right. I've already made the necessary phone calls."

Stepping inside the foyer, Brea felt her chest tighten. It was difficult to draw in a deep, satisfying breath. Wanting her children in her arms, she turned to face Adam. "Sophie and Alex, I want to see them now."

"I'll bring them to the bedroom soon. Let's go." Brea clenched her jaw as she surveyed the black-and-white marbled flooring and the grand curved staircase with a gold railing. Adam stepped in front of Brea to lead her up the stairs. Following him in silence, they walked down the long hallway until reaching the bedroom where Mary roomed them on their visits.

Adam opened and held the door for Brea to enter the room. Mary had updated the guest room since their last visit with a linen king-sized panel bed, though the other furniture—the espresso end tables, matching dresser, and the antique secretary desk, remained unchanged against the backdrop of the wood floors, beige patterned wallpaper, and floor to ceiling carob-colored silk curtains.

Whipping around in an abrupt motion to face Adam, she exclaimed in a firm tone of voice, "I'm not sleeping in this bed with you."

Adam strode over to Brea and halted one foot before her, forcing her to take a step back, stumble, and knock into the dresser. "Brea, we are staying in this room together. I won't touch you tonight if that is what you're worried about. I want you to at least wash the scent off that guy in Mexico before we make love."

"That will never happen, Adam," Brea cried out.

"Brea, you are my wife. I gave up Kaylin, and you're giving him up. You will find your way back to me, but I have to warn you—I can be patient, but I have my limits. We won't discuss it tonight. Clean up, and after, I'll bring Alex and Sophie in. And keep it together. If you become overly emotional, you'll scare them."

"When are we going home? I don't want to stay here."

"In the middle of the week, maybe Wednesday. We need to set up a few things at home so we can monitor you," Adam answered.

Raising her eyes to the ceiling, Brea threw up her hands. "What? What are you talking about?"

"I let Tina go with a generous severance, and we'll have a new nanny. My mother has also hired a personal nurse to stay with us for a while. You'll meet her tomorrow. Since you will no longer work at the store with Hannah, you can focus on your health and the kids."

"Adam, you can't control my whole life—I won't make it. I won't let you trap me in the house," she said, her voice breaking from an overwhelming surge of desperation.

"It's not permanent, Brea. Only until you're back to yourself and I can trust you."

Brea sat on the bed and dropped her head into her hands. "Adam, I need my phone," she muttered.

Adam turned to leave, and before stepping out of the door, he replied, "No, you're not ready."

Once Adam closed the door, Brea's hand flew to her chest. Remembering there was a phone on the desk, her breath quickened, and she scanned the room. "Shit," she whispered, seeing someone had removed it.

Her body flooded with adrenaline, and her thoughts twisted into knots. Pacing the length of the room, she scoured her mind for various means of escape. Hayden had cautioned her not to do anything rash, but at the moment, she felt desperate and hopeless. A knock rapped on the door. Brea hurried to open it, hoping it would be Alex and Sophie.

"Hello ma'am. I'm here to unpack your luggage while you freshen up, and then Mr. Tandervon will bring the children in." Alice entered the room with Brea's luggage in hand, speaking in a cloying tone of voice.

"Could you bring in a telephone, Alice? I need to make a phone call." Alice paused in the center of the room.

"I'll see about that, ma'am. But Mr. Tandervon gave specific instructions that he did not want a telephone in the room."

Brea licked her lips. Closing her eyes, she nodded. "Of course."

Alice opened the door to the bathroom and gestured for Brea to enter. "There is a fresh bathrobe hanging on the door. I will unpack, leave your nightgown on the bed, and have the rest of your clothing cleaned and pressed, ma'am."

"Alice, you know me. Do you think I look unwell?" Brea asked with wide eyes.

"No, ma'am. Though you look tired," Alice answered before taking a wide step back and averting her eyes from Brea's. Brea inhaled and chewed her lower lip. Questioning Alice would be pointless—Mary would have instructed Alice that she was amid a mental breakdown and to avoid disturbing her further.

"Thank you, Alice. I'll go wash up now." Brea went into the bathroom and shut the door behind her. After turning on the shower, she walked to the mirror. Seeing her butterfly brooch, she placed her hand over it, drew in a deep breath, and then undressed.

Beneath the hot stream of water, she pictured Hayden holding her earlier that morning—closing her eyes, she nearly conjured the feeling of his arms wrapped around her. To survive, she needed to keep faith that they would prevail and overcome any subsequent hindrances conspiring to keep them apart.

Brea slipped on the plush white bathrobe after her shower and combed her hair. Returning to the bedroom, a tray with a bowl of yogurt and fruit sat on the bed. Although she had no appetite, she knew Hayden would tell her to eat to keep her strength up. She sat on the bed, ate several large spoonfuls of yogurt, and drank a glass of iced tea. The food did not sit well in her stomach, but even so she forced herself to eat several more bites, and then moved the tray onto the dresser.

Once dressed in her black silk nightgown, she sat on the edge of the bed to wait for Alex and Sophie. Ten minutes later, the door burst open, and her children ran into the room, jumping onto Brea's lap. "Mommy!" they cried out. Two pairs of little arms wrapped around her neck and shoulders. Tremendous relief and elation washed over Brea as she embraced her children and pulled them in close.

Tears formed in her eyes while kissing their plump cheeks and cupping their faces to study them intently. "Mommy missed you both so much, my babies," she whispered. Burying her nose in Sophie's hair, she inhaled, delighted to have them in her arms again.

"Mommy, come with us to our room. We have new toys, books, and Grandma gave me a pair of rainbow shoes with a bow," Sophie announced with exhilaration.

"And Grandma promised we can go to the stables tomorrow to ride the ponies again, and we can show you Marbles and Cotton, our favorite ones," Alex exclaimed.

"That sounds amazing. I can't wait to see you both on Marbles and Cotton. You are the luckiest, most incredible kids in the world," Brea said as she wiped away the tears sliding down her cheeks, then pulled Alex and Sophie in for another embrace. Looking over her children's heads, Brea noticed Adam standing in the doorway with his arms folded across his chest, his eyes fixed on Brea, and a cool smile on his face.

Sophie giggled. "Mommy, why are you crying?"

Brea smiled. "Because I missed you and I'm so happy to see you."

"That's right. Mommy missed you both so much—and she promised me she would never leave us again. She would give up anything to stay home with you because it would make her so sad if she had to go away and couldn't see you," Adam said. His smile widened as Sophie and Alex cheered.

Brea pulled her children close to her and shut her eyes, feeling her heart half-full and half-broken. She told herself to hold on and not to give up, but Adam knew her too well and how to manipulate her. It was true—she would never sacrifice her children for anything, even if it meant letting go of Hayden.

Chapter Fifty

Hayden

Nearing four in the afternoon, Hayden exited the executive airport lounge, rushed past the terminals, through the lobby, and out the main entrance. He stepped outside and scanned the length of the curb from left to right, searching for a Boxster or a woman matching what he could remember of Hannah's description. The crowds made it difficult to see the cars in the airport drop-off and pickup lane. Catching his breath, he felt alone and desperate, wishing he could have reached Hannah earlier in the day.

Turning right, he picked up his pace, dodging and side-stepping around the clusters of arriving and departing passengers in his path. Eyeing every car he passed, he grew disheartened. He halted his steps, seeing a young woman with blonde hair, though she appeared to be twenty-years old. To be certain, he asked if her name was Hannah, but she shook her head. He turned back in the opposite direction and checked his watch. It was five minutes after four.

Again, he hurried alongside the long stretch of cars parked by the curb. An elderly woman dropped her handbag ahead of him, and Hayden paused mid-stride to offer her help. Handing the woman her purse, she thanked him. He muttered, "You're welcome," as his eyes landed on a woman twenty feet ahead of him stepping onto the curb, dressed in an army green sundress with long blonde hair and a pair of sunglasses resting on her head. She appeared to be close to Brea's age—it could be Hannah.

The woman turned her head and noticed Hayden watching her. Their eyes locked, studying one another. Hayden jogged over to her, filled with hope. "Are you Hannah?" he asked.

She smiled. "Hayden?"

Hayden nodded, and an expression of relief spread across his face. He lowered his eyes to the ground for a moment before meeting her gaze again. "I didn't know if you would be here. I tried calling you this morning, but I couldn't reach you."

Hannah scratched her head. "Yeah, I lost my charger, and my phone died. I plugged it in on the drive over here and just now saw the missed calls from an unknown number—I figured it would be you. Brea isn't picking up her phone, and I don't know what is going on or where she is."

Hayden exhaled. "Adam came to Mexico and blackmailed her to come home with him."

Hannah sighed and shook her head. "Shit. I knew something bad happened when Adam called me yesterday, rambling that she was sick, coming home early from Mexico and quitting her job at Brine. I kept my mouth shut about everything—including you. She told me the entire story a couple of days ago, and yesterday, before Adam called, she sent me a 'top secret' text to tell me you were coming home with her. So, I came here in case you showed up."

Hayden blew out a sharp breath. "I'm glad you did. I have an idea to get Adam to step down, but it's only the start of a plan. And I don't know whether it will even work. Before Adam took her, she told me to find you. I think Brea thought that if we worked together, maybe we could figure out what to do."

Hannah rubbed her forehead. "Well, let's go. Do you have a car here?"

"I rented a car."

"Right. Pick it up, and we can meet at my place. Did you eat today?"

Hayden shook his head. "Not yet. My assistant found your address, so I have it."

"Okay, meet me there. There's a place near my house where we can eat and talk."

Hayden averted his eyes from Hannah to look at the ground. Although relieved to have found Hannah, his unease had only grown after hearing she could neither locate nor reach Brea by phone.

Hannah smacked Hayden on the arm. "Hey, snap out of it. I'm not a sentimental person, so I won't give you a hug and cry with you. Let's go."

Hayden chuckled and raised his eyes to meet hers again—he liked Hannah already. "Got it. I'll be at your place soon."

One hour later, Hayden met Hannah in her driveway. He parked and sprang out of the car.

"I'll drive, get in," Hannah directed. "By the way, you can crash at my place if you need to."

Hayden appreciated the offer. "Thank you, but I have a hotel room already booked for the week." Hayden climbed into Hannah's car. Once settled in the driver's seat, she backed out, hit the gas pedal with a heavy foot, and sped away.

"Whoa," Hayden exclaimed, taken by surprise. "You like to drive fast, I see."

Hannah laughed. "Sorry, I'll slow down." Hannah eased up on the gas, scoping Hayden clutching the armrest. If they had met under different circumstances, she might have teased him, but today she gave the poor guy a break.

"So, tell me what happened with Adam," Hannah said.

Hayden filled her in with the story, and once finished, they pulled into the parking lot of a weathered beachfront bar and grill—a shabby one-story building with wooden shingles and a large red sign over the door with gold lettering that read "The Pig and Bear Pub & Grill."

They exited the car, stepped out into the cool evening air and walked to the front door with the sound of gravel crunching beneath their feet. Hayden attempted to sidestep Hannah to open the door for her, but she waved him off and opened it for him instead. Raising his eyebrows, he followed Hannah inside.

"This place doesn't look like much, but the draft beer and burgers are the best in Ocean Crest Beach," Hannah proclaimed over her shoulder. Passing by a robust and tall server with a shaved head and myriad tattoos, Hannah gave him a high five. "Hey Barney, two draft beers, the big ones."

It was clear she was a regular as all the servers and bartenders appeared to know her, waving to her as she walked by and greeting her by name. Hayden surveyed the space. The pub comprised worn, stripped wood flooring and booths covered in cheap red vinyl. Otherwise, it was clean, and it had the classic vibe of an old beach bar, likely having first opened its doors for business fifty years ago.

Hannah led Hayden to a booth opposite the bar beneath a large framed poster of tropical birds perched on a palm tree. Within minutes of sitting down, Barney returned with two large glasses of draft beer and placed them down on red, square-shaped cocktail napkins.

"Barney, hold on a minute." Hannah pointed to Hayden. "Hayden, do you like burgers?"

Hayden nodded. He had little appetite, but he knew Brea would tell him to eat to keep up his strength. "Sure, that sounds good. Whatever you recommend—except nothing spicy." He made a mental note to tell Hannah the habanero story later.

"Two house burgers, extra cheese, medium well, and bacon, Barney." With a nod of his head, he hurried off to place their orders. Hannah took a sip of her beer, then leaned in with her arms folded on the table. "Hayden, I want to say something first. When I spoke with Brea on the phone, she sounded—genuinely happy. I've known Brea for a long time, and whatever is happening with you two is obviously something extraordinary."

Clasping his hands together on the table, he gave Hannah a slight smile. Hannah validating Brea's love for him was helpful and appreciated. "Hannah, do you have any idea where Adam's parents live? Brea had mentioned her kids were staying with them in Santa Barbara. I tried looking up his parents online, but I couldn't find an address or any phone numbers."

Hannah chuckled. "What are you going to do? Storm the compound and rescue her? That would be crazy and for certain backfire. From what I remember from the engagement party, that place is a fortress with security and staff. It's a good place to hide, Brea. This is all so crazy, though. I can't believe he has her under lockdown like this. He's always been uptight and controlling, but this is a whole new level."

Hayden leaned forward. "Tell me whatever you can about him. I need to figure out a way to break through to him or to use something against him. As I mentioned, I have a piece of a plan, but alone, it wouldn't be enough."

Pressing her lips together, Hannah sat back and thought for a moment. "He's your typical rich guy who had it all growing up. Brea was the trophy wife, gorgeous, who let him make all the decisions and never put up a fight. Except he hated her working in the shop, thinking it made her appear 'common' or rather, I think the words he used were 'beneath her.' He cared about her appearance, and when people told him how beautiful she was, he ate it up as though they were complimenting him."

Hannah ate a French fry. "I have to say though, Brea hid it well—how unhappy she was, even from me. Sometimes I could tell she seemed sad, but she always had an excuse—the kids kept her up, or they gave her a virus. Now it all makes sense. And I'm mad at myself that I missed it all."

Hayden sat back and exhaled. "Adam and my father seem to share some similar traits—controlling and egotistical, and yes, Brea is skilled at hiding her feelings." They drank their beer and sat in silence for several minutes, reflecting.

"Hayden, why do you love her? I mean, you went to all of this trouble to come back and find her, and it sounds romantic and all, but kind of insane. No offense, but I love Brea, and the last thing I want for her is to jump into another fire if she's able to get out of this marriage with Adam. She's been through so much, and your history with her—it's rather complicated."

Hayden could only reply with the one answer he knew to be true. It was simple and sentimental, but it was the truth. "True love. She's my soul mate."

Hannah did not react for a moment. Staring into Hayden's eyes, she broke out into a wide smile and slapped her hands on the table. "Shit Hayden. The way you just said that didn't make me want to vomit, so it has to be true."

He reacted with a stifled laugh. Barney delivered their burgers sitting atop a pile of French fries in red baskets and set them down. Hannah leaned over to grab the ketchup bottle at the end of the table, shook it and opened it. With a furrowed brow, Hayden watched as she poured an exorbitant amount of ketchup over her French fries.

"You want some?" Hannah offered, holding out the bottle to Hayden.

"No thanks, I'm good," he replied, then picked up a single French fry and ate it. The beer had relaxed him enough that some of his appetite had returned. They ate for several minutes before Hayden cleared his throat to ask Hannah another question.

"Do you think Adam ever hurt Brea? To be specific—did he hit her?" Hayden asked, clenching his fists under the table.

Hannah shook her head. "No, I don't think so. She never had injuries or bruises, nothing like that. I think he only enjoyed being in control, keeping her under his thumb like a beautiful doll he could parade around with. When they met, she would always say how she couldn't 'believe he chose me,' as though it was some type of honor to marry him or a once in a lifetime chance. I never thought they had much in common, but she seemed to love him. He was direct with her, that he was looking for a wife and wanted children, and she liked that he was transparent—an open book, so to speak."

Hayden continued to eat and listen, thinking to himself it resembled her relationship with Jaime in high school.

"She never dated much in college, and only had a few brief relationships after. There was always something wrong with the guy—she couldn't trust him, or she thought he was hiding something. I never knew where that came from until she told me what happened to her in high school with that disturbed scumbag, Cylis." Hannah paused and cleared her throat. "Then she told me about what happened with you in high school."

Hayden nodded. "There were a lot of reasons why she couldn't trust men. It nearly broke me that I was one of them for so many years."

"You can't go back there—stay focused on what to do now." Hannah cursed under her breath. "I still can't believe Adam is resorting to blackmail and lies to keep her. He should let her go. She's only going to hate him, and she'll never be happy being back with him this way."

"I know Brea, and she can bury things away to cope and survive. He's not wrong to assume that with enough time he couldn't brainwash her back into submission," Hayden explained with a resigned air.

"You know, for Adam, it's all about power and control. I mean, he cheated on Brea and neglected her for years. Then you, for example, came along and threatened to take away what he thinks belongs to him. So now he's digging in his heels. It's like a little boy on the playground who threw away his toy and now wants it back because another kid picked it up."

Hayden grabbed his beer and drained a quarter of it in one shot. "I think it would take something pretty big for him to back down," he replied, followed by a wave of hopelessness—his plan would not be enough.

"You know, with guys like Adam, image and appearance mean everything to him. He's a complete narcissist." Hannah paused and then suggested, "Maybe if someone threatens that, he'd reconsider blackmailing Brea."

Hayden lifted his hands, then slapped them down on the table. "So, what do I do? Tell on him to his friends?"

Hannah laughed. "They would never believe you, Hayden. You would have to be in their club to be a credible source. That would kill you right there, not that you're Brea's lover."

"Part of the club?" Hayden repeated, meeting Hannah's eyes as she drank her beer and nodded.

"Yeah, you know—in his circle of friends, a partner in his law firm, or one of the snooty rich people who think the Tandervons walk on water. Who you are has to hold weight to be believable or someone powerful enough he wouldn't want to cross," Hannah explained before taking another large bite of her cheeseburger.

Hayden sat back and grinned. "Hannah, what if I am part of the club, in a way?"

Hannah raised her hand. "Barney," she yelled out. She caught his eye and pointed to their beers for a refill. Turning back to

Hayden, one corner of her mouth lifted into a crooked smile. "All right. Lay it all out for me what you're thinking."

CHAPTER FIFTY-ONE

BREA

The following morning, Brea opened her eyes. She had fallen asleep on the armchair beside Sophie and Alex's beds. Rubbing the back of her neck, she sat up and licked her dry lips. Her mind felt foggy having slept poorly, restless and waking often from nightmares.

Both children were still asleep in their beds. Turning her head to glance outside the window, Brea estimated it was not later than seven in the morning. She stood to leave the room, careful to avoid tripping on the toys and books littering the floor.

While walking down the hall, a bout of dizziness hit her—she had barely eaten since the previous morning at the hotel. Pausing every ten feet, she leaned against a table or the wall until she felt stable enough to continue on. Upon reaching the bottom of the stairs, she crossed the foyer towards the kitchen.

The lavish formal living room on her left sat empty. She turned and peeked into the sitting room on her right, where Allen often met with his business associates or assistants. It was a large room with dark wood wainscoting, shelving holding endless volumes of leather-bound books, and richly shaded brown leather seating sets clustered atop a custom, imported Persian rug.

Brea was surprised to see Allen seated with his back to her in an oversized leather armchair, reading the newspaper. Hoping to avoid him, she backed away, but hit the door and made a loud knocking sound. Allen turned and saw Brea.

"Brea, we're glad to have you back," Allen said as he rose from his chair to greet her, dressed in a light-blue classic button-down shirt and black slacks. His salt-and-pepper beard was shorter since last seeing him at Easter. Approaching Brea, he outstretched his arms to rest his hands on her shoulders, leaned in and kissed her on the cheek. Brea's body tensed upon feeling his lips linger on her skin.

"Hello Allen, how are you?" Brea asked, the volume of her voice dwindling as she met his dark gray eyes, identical to Adam's.

"Perhaps you should change before coming downstairs, although I understand you had a rough couple of weeks. Don't fret, Mary will arrange everything to help you feel better."

Brea produced a strained smile and lowered her eyes, now self-conscious, dressed in her nightgown and bathrobe. Allen never failed to intimidate her with his broad-shouldered frame and stern demeanor.

"The children will be pleased to have you back with the family. I'm grateful we sorted out this whole mess quickly. Why don't you go back to your room and I'll send Alice up to help you this morning."

Brea nodded and turned to exit the room, though ignored his directive and continued on to the kitchen. Walking down the hall, she passed the staff office, the gym, and the informal family room with a large television and sofas where the children could watch movies and make arts and crafts.

Once entering the immense kitchen, Brea scanned the space and saw a member of the kitchen staff occupied with unpacking a delivery of fresh groceries in crates and cardboard boxes. An expansive island with a white marble counter sat in the kitchen's center, and along the walls, two large stainless-steel refrigerators and a wine cooler were built into the vast ivory cabinets and shelving. Through the pruned shrubbery lining the windows, a golden morning light entered the kitchen.

Seeing Brea enter, the woman gave her a warm smile. She had short, gray, shoulder-length hair, a stout body frame, and wore a white starched long-sleeved blouse and a black skirt. Brea searched her mind for her name.

"Good morning, Mrs. Tandervon. May I fix you something?"

Brea inhaled and turned her head to look out a large white-framed window overlooking a garden with rows of lemon trees. "Yes, some water, please."

About to turn, the staff member halted when Brea spoke again. "What is your name again? Forgive me, I forgot it."

"Elizabeth, ma'am."

"Elizabeth, yes, thank you." She turned to pour a glass of water for Brea. "Oh, and I'd love some toast, but I can make it myself," Brea added.

"No trouble, ma'am. I'll bring it up to your room if you'd like?"

Brea smiled. "Thank you, yes. Also, could I borrow your phone? My battery died, and there isn't one in my room. I just need to make a quick phone—"

"That won't be necessary, Elizabeth. I'll help Brea out with that concern," Mary's voice announced, standing behind Brea in the doorway.

Elizabeth returned to Brea and handed her a glass of ice-water. Brea's heart sank. She took the glass and turned to face Mary. "Good morning, Mary," Brea said.

"Brea, why don't you freshen up, dress, and then meet me on the patio for breakfast? We can have our chat. I had Alice place some clothing in your room, more appropriate than what I'm sure you brought on your vacation. There was a rack of sample items for the summer left here from my personal shopper, and although you lost a little weight since we last met, we're still about the same size," Mary said with a polite smile plastered on her face.

"Of course, thank you," Brea replied and hurried out of the kitchen past Mary, then down the hall. Once out of earshot, Brea cursed under her breath. Though fatigued, she jogged up the steps and strode down the hall to reach her room. Placing her hand on the door, she opened it and peered inside. From the doorway, she saw the bed had been slept in, but Adam was not in the room. Brea entered, drank her glass of water, and placed it on a small table by the door.

Adam coughed, startling her, and she swiveled around to see him in the bathroom doorway dressed only in his pajama pants. Brea averted her eyes from him. In the past she admired his athletic frame, but now the sight of his bare chest and arms filled her with a sense of unease, knowing his strength could subdue her.

"You fell asleep with Alex and Sophie?" Adam asked.

"I wanted to be close to them, but I didn't sleep well," Brea replied.

Adam kept his gaze on Brea. "Tonight, you'll sleep in here with me."

Raising her eyes to meet his, a sick feeling filled her stomach. She blinked away the tears that threatened to form in her eyes. "I need to take a shower and get ready. Your mother wants me to join her for breakfast on the patio."

Brea lowered her eyes and walked to the bathroom door, but Adam would not step out of the way. He lifted his hands and placed them on her arms. Brea attempted to recoil, but Adam gripped her with a firm hold, and she could not take a step back.

"I am not your enemy, Brea. Can you stop and remember something? We chose each other—we made vows. And most importantly, we have two children together. Do you really want to throw it all away? I have never hurt you. If anything, I have given you everything you wanted. I made a mistake, and I'm going to make it up to you. Could you try to think about that today?"

Brea continued to stare at the floor. Adam put two fingers under her chin and lifted her face to meet his eyes. Her heart raced, and fiery anger bubbled within her. Adam leaned down to kiss her, but at the last moment, she turned her head and his lips landed on her cheek.

Adam exhaled, released her arms, and stepped aside. "Think about it, Brea. I'll see you at lunch. We have guests coming—don't even think about acting out," he ordered as Brea passed him.

Once clear of the bathroom door, she closed it and locked it behind her with trembling hands. In her mind, she pictured Hayden's eyes and covered her mouth with her hand to muffle a sob. Brea inhaled slowly to calm herself—she needed to maintain her composure.

Wiping her eyes, a glimmer of hope bloomed—she could appeal to Mary. Perhaps she could explain everything to her and make her see reason. Although she was Adam's mother, she was a woman, and if she could recruit Mary to her side, it was possible she would talk to Adam on her behalf and advocate for her.

Brea turned on the shower and dashed to the sink to brush her teeth. Alice had arranged all of her creams, perfume, and makeup on the vanity table. To win over Mary, she needed to look flawless, confident, and then convince her of the truth of her sanity and that her and Adam's separating were in everyone's interest.

One hour later, Brea appeared on the patio, dressed in a pale-blue linen suit and an ivory camisole. She had blow-dried, waved her hair, and applied a full face of makeup. As she walked down the stairs and through the halls, she held her hand over the butterfly brooch fastened on the lapel of her blazer.

"Brea, you look lovely," Mary complimented, standing beside Alice on the patio. In her hand, she held the menu for the afternoon luncheon that would take place later for a select group of their closest friends. Mary waved Brea over to join her. Reaching her, Mary placed her hands on Brea's shoulders and kissed her on each cheek with a feather-light touch of her lips.

"Thank you, you as well," Brea replied with a warm smile, then seated herself at the table. Although not hungry, Brea thanked Elizabeth, who appeared and placed before her a poached egg with a side of fruit and toast.

"I'll have an Earl gray tea with cream," she said to Elizabeth, who nodded and set off.

"Brea, I'm sure you're thrilled to be reunited with your children. We spent an incredible week together, though they missed you and asked every day when you would return home. I'm relieved you made the right choice to come back."

Brea licked her lips and surveyed the patio to see if any other staff lingered nearby. "Mary, I love Alex and Sophie. I would never leave them. And as you know, they're not the problem—it's Adam," Brea said, maintaining tight control over her voice not to betray her anger.

"Brea, Adam behaved badly, but surely I'm not the only woman to tell you that husbands make mistakes. Men—and women, sometimes stray." Mary looked into Brea's eyes, confirming that she knew about Hayden.

"However, you have a family together, and a life together. You owe it to your children to forget the past and move forward. Adam wants everything to work out between you both, and I support him."

"Even if that means I'm miserable, and he is too? You would support us staying in a failed marriage only to keep up appearances."

Mary scoffed. "Brea, don't be dramatic. People stay married for many reasons, and you have little to complain about. Sometimes when you have everything, your mind is vulnerable. You become complacent and think about throwing it all away for a thrill or a fling. Use your brain. Some man manipulated you into believing a bunch of nonsense about love that does not exist in reality. What you have with Adam—stability—is real."

"Even if he has to lie and blackmail me, Mary?" Brea's voice teetered on the cusp of losing her temper.

"Brea. You are not well. I can understand why you felt the need to hide behind alcohol, but you're having a breakdown. I will not allow you to be around Alex and Sophie alone in this condition. Leaving Adam would be a confirmation that you are mentally unwell and, as a family, we will do what is necessary to protect the children."

Brea clenched her hands into fists on her lap. "From me?"

Mary tilted her head to the side. "Yes, Brea, from you. I have hired a wonderful nurse to stay with you for the following month, perhaps longer, if needed. She'll lighten the load for you at home and take care of you while you recover. In addition, there is a facility I would like you to consider signing yourself into. They have an opening on Friday. It's a wonderful program that could help you rest and straighten out some of these disturbing and distorted thoughts you have been having."

"Mary, I don't have an alcohol problem, and I'm not mentally ill. I'm in love—genuine love. And I'm ready to be with this man—someone I should have been with from the beginning."

Mary sighed. "Brea, I think you're farther gone than I realized. I'll call the facility and tell them we'll sign you in Friday morning."

"No! Don't do that. Please don't do that, Mary," Brea pleaded, failing to steady her voice as tears appeared in her eyes.

"We could go through the courts—if necessary, Brea. I am prepared to go as far as we need to for my grandchildren, though I would like to avoid the whole mess if possible."

"Okay, I don't need that. I promise. Let's see how things go over the week. All I want is to be with Alex and Sophie."

"And?" Mary asked, staring into Brea's eyes.

Brea swallowed as her throat tightened. "And Adam," she replied.

Mary inhaled and picked up her fork. "Good girl. Now eat something. If you develop an eating disorder, we'll have another issue to deal with."

Brea lowered her eyes to her plate and dabbed the tears falling down her cheeks with her napkin. She lifted her fork, speared a strawberry, and placed it in her mouth. With her free hand, she placed it over her brooch.

Mary's eyes flickered over to Brea. "That's a lovely brooch. Is that a family heirloom?"

A wave of panic stormed through Brea—she should have packed it away rather than worn it. "Yes, it belonged to my grandmother. I found it a long time ago in her attic."

Mary's eyes narrowed, and then a smile appeared. "Wonderful. Well, then you understand that tradition and family matter the most. Eat, Brea. With our guests joining us this afternoon, I hope you'll be cheerful and welcoming—and I expect you to put your wedding ring back on."

Brea nodded and continued to eat. Holding onto her belief that she could figure out an escape became more difficult after speaking with Mary—Adam would not be the only obstacle she and Hayden would need to overcome.

Chapter Fifty-Two

Hayden

Having remained in Ocean Crest Beach, Hayden had hoped Brea would have returned home by now. Every evening, Hannah called the house and drove over to ring the doorbell, though it remained empty. It was now Wednesday evening.

In the mornings, Hayden occupied himself with remote work in his hotel room, a modest one-bedroom suite in a beach-front boutique hotel with generic décor, but it was clean and quiet. Once free, he spent the afternoons in Hannah's office at Brine, researching family law firms and legal articles related to contesting emergency custody orders in California. When the door chime rang, Hayden's breath would catch in his chest, and he would crane his neck out the office door to see who came in.

Hannah told him that if Brea came to the store, she would enter through the back. Regardless, he could not stop himself from verifying it was not her, and when seeing a customer enter, his heart sank with disappointment.

In the evening, Hayden would return to his hotel to have a drink and push the food around his plate until ultimately abandoning his meal to sit on the balcony. With every day that passed, he grew more despondent that Hannah could not reach Brea. Worse, the private detective he had hired to look into

Adam and his family failed to turn up anything that could be useful to use against him.

Ignorant of Brea's whereabouts, the strain took its toll on Hayden. He would wake from vivid and perturbing dreams throughout the night, and over the days he felt himself growing more irritable and short-tempered. Last night he dreamt Cylis had kidnapped Brea while they slept in her casita in Mexico. The dream felt so real that he woke up startled, perspiring with his heart racing, and could not fall back asleep.

His only comfort in the morning was going to the gym and running on the treadmill. The speed and repetition of his movements followed by lifting weights could temper his agitation for a while, but the relief would never last long. Earlier than morning, he nearly cracked, resolving that once in front of Adam again he would resort to physical violence if needed. In those weak moments, Henry's words would echo in his mind. He needed to be smart and play Adam's game if they wanted to win and liberate Brea.

Having been away almost two weeks, Hayden would need to return to San Francisco soon. His board requested to meet in person regarding his proposal, and there were other projects and obligations requiring his presence. Ashley checked in with him daily to see about booking the jet to fly him home, though he stalled, finding it impossible to leave until he knew where Brea was. As long as he was in Ocean Crest Beach, he would be nearby when she returned, and if she needed him.

Seated on the balcony, Hayden watched the ocean. Hit by a wave of drowsiness, his eyelids became heavy, and he closed his eyes. An ache filled him, picturing Brea lying beside him after making love for the first time. Hearing his cell phone ring, his eyes sprang open. He stood and hurried into the room. Upon seeing Hannah's name, he answered with his heart pounding.

"Hayden, they're back. I drove by the house, and Adam answered the door. He told me Brea was still sick and that I couldn't see her, but when I left, I saw her peeking through the living room curtain. I couldn't stop and signal to her because Adam watched me until I drove off."

Hayden leaned against the desk. "All right, when are you going back?"

"I told Adam I would come by tomorrow, but he doubted she would be ready to see me. Then he reminded me that Brea had to quit Brine and she would need to stay home to rest for a long time. This is worse than I thought—he's going to isolate her completely."

"So how will you be able to get to her? Other than my breaking in and carrying her out on my shoulder, I don't know how to reach her. She won't sneak out and risk Adam taking the kids."

"Hayden, I think I need to play this from a different angle. If I come in declaring he needs to let her go, then he'll block me out of her life. But if I come in on his side, I can get close to her."

"How are you going to do that if he won't even let you in the house?"

"Flattery. It worked before with him when Brea wanted to work in the store, and I think I can do it again."

"Okay, I'll stay and wait until you can get her out of the house," Hayden replied.

"Hayden, you need to go back to San Francisco and push the plan forward on your end. I'll call you when I get somewhere with Adam. You need to be patient. I don't know how long it will take for me to see her, and Adam might watch us the whole time. Trust me, all right?"

Hayden exhaled and paced the room. It would be difficult to do what Hannah asked of him, but she was right. It would not be useful for him to sit around in a hotel room.

"All right. I'll fly out tomorrow morning. Call me when there's a way for me to contact her."

"Okay. Good luck in San Francisco. I'll be with her, Hayden—soon. I promise I'll watch over her."

"Thanks, and if you can, when you see her—" Hayden paused and looked up at the ceiling. "Tell her I love her."

"I will, goodnight."

Hayden felt hollowed out, and his temples throbbed after hanging up the phone. He sat on the edge of the bed and sent Ashley a message to book the jet and to inform his team he would return tomorrow. Sleep would not be possible knowing Brea was nearby. He sprang off the bed, grabbed the keys to his rental car, and hurried out of the hotel room.

After stopping at the hotel café to buy a sandwich and a bottle of water, he walked to the valet stand for his car. He tossed the plastic wrapping into the garbage can, finished eating and drank half the bottle of water. When the car arrived, he tipped the driver and sped away, careful not to drive recklessly despite his agitation.

Fifteen minutes later, he killed the front lights as he slowed near Brea's house, and parked across the street. The lights were on inside. He was unfamiliar with the home's layout, though Hannah had mentioned that the living room and guest room windows were visible from the front.

Studying the house, he figured the long row of large windows on the right was the living room and the set of three windows to the left of the front door was the guest bedroom. There were lights on in both rooms. Hayden gripped the steering wheel and hoped Brea had moved into the guest bedroom. Although it would change nothing he felt for her, he could not bear to think about Adam coercing Brea into being intimate with him—but he knew she might not have a choice.

Hayden watched the windows, willing Brea to glance outside. Even if she could not leave, perhaps she would see the car and somehow feel that he was nearby. Hayden did not know how long he sat there until he drifted off to sleep. At midnight, he woke.

Turning his head to glimpse the house, he saw all the lights switched off. Rubbing his eyes, he drank the rest of his water, and waited several minutes until he felt alert enough to drive. He turned on the engine and with one last look at Brea's home, drove off.

Chapter Fifty-Three

Brea

Upon concluding breakfast on the patio with her mother-in-law, the nurse Mary had hired for Brea arrived. Alice led Brea to Mary's office, a large room on the second floor, which Brea seldom visited.

Brea entered the room, and her eyes swept over Mary's ivory, stone executive desk, set atop a curved gold base. The built-in white shelves housed various collectibles, and on the beige-painted walls hung black-and-white framed photographs from celebrated twentieth-century documentary photographers. In the center of the room, four teal, tufted, button-accented chairs encircled a low table similar in color and style to Mary's desk. The nurse stood beside one chair, holding her hands clasped together at her waist.

Brea fixed her eyes on the nurse, dressed in black cigarette pants and a short-sleeved green silk blouse. She was a late middle-aged woman with shoulder-length dark brown hair, brown eyes, and a long narrow nose, with a formal stance and a stolid air about her.

"Mrs. Tandervon, good morning. My name is Sandra. It is nice to meet you," she said in a rich, deep voice. With an outstretched arm, she invited Brea to have a seat across from her.

"Hello," Brea replied in a petulant tone of voice, folded her arms over her chest, and sat in the chair.

"I would like to start with the purpose of our visit. Your husband and mother-in-law asked me to spend some time with you this morning. They tell me you have experienced some mental health struggles. Symptoms that have progressed over these past several weeks."

Brea refused to speak. She released an audible exhale and stared at the gold clock sitting on Mary's desk, knowing the nurse had been told lies, nothing more.

"Please allow me to pour you a drink. Would you like tea or coffee?" Sandra gestured to the sterling silver carafe of coffee and a blue porcelain tea service set upon a silver tray on the table between them.

"Tea, please." Brea replied. "I'm fine. I'm not ill. There are reasons why the past few weeks have been difficult."

"I understand. Here you are." Sandra placed the teacup on a saucer and placed it in front of Brea. "Well, Mr. Tandervon asked that I keep a close eye on you over the following month and recommend some treatments for you. There is no shame in receiving help when one is mentally unwell. I would also like to share that it is not uncommon for someone with a mental health condition not to recognize it—I understand that is the case with your mother."

Brea eyed Sandra with a hostile glare before lowering her eyes to study the teacup on the table. It was insupportable—a mental health evaluation with a nurse who had received false information and, with no doubt, was well compensated to do Adam and Mary's bidding.

Sandra continued, tilting her head an inch to the side. "You are fortunate. You have resources and a caring family that loves you. They will do everything they can to help you. With hope, you'll be back as you were in no time. Only you need to put your trust in them, and me."

Brea shook her head, laughed and turned her head to look out the window. She did not have it in her this morning to feign interest in speaking with Sandra nor to entertain the idea that Adam and Mary "*loved*" her.

"I would like to be transparent with you, Mrs. Tandervon. Your family has asked for my professional opinion on whether we will need to coordinate with a physician I work with to petition for guardianship. This would allow your husband to oversee and decide on your mental health and medical care. That would include his having the right to sign you into a facility if needed. If I cannot have a thorough evaluation, it will make it difficult for me to say that you have the ability to consent—"

"No, that isn't necessary. I'll cooperate," Brea said, interrupting Sandra.

Over the following hour, Sandra interviewed Brea, asking her a host of questions regarding her mother's mental health history, how much alcohol Brea drank, her sleep and eating patterns, and a constellation of symptoms she may have experienced either recently or in the past. Brea lied about the severity of her mother's condition and denied having any mental health symptoms, though Sandra appeared skeptical of Brea's answers.

"One more thing, Mrs. Tandervon, you will need to sign this form." Sandra removed a piece of paper from a folder and placed a pen on the table before Brea.

"What is this?" Brea asked, ripping the paper from Sandra's hand. Scanning the form, she read at the top, "*Consent for Mental Health Treatment and Medications.*" Brea shook her head. "I'm not signing that," she said, placing it on the table.

Sandra lifted her hands off her lap and clasped them together, continuing to hold Brea's gaze with expressionless eyes. "If you will not voluntarily sign the consent form, then my recommendation will be that we pursue involuntary—"

Brea inhaled sharply and interrupted Sandra again. "Fine." Picking up the pen, she signed the form and handed it back to Sandra. Sandra then handed Brea another form to allow disclosure of all information to both Adam and Mary, and Brea signed it as well.

Sandra took the form from Brea's hand and smiled. "We are finished for the morning. I will formulate our treatment plan, and we will begin as soon as I speak with Mr. Tandervon."

Brea hurried out of the room and slammed the door behind her. She strode down the hallway, and Alice appeared behind her and followed Brea to the family room where the children were watching a movie, waiting for Brea to walk with them to the stables to ride the ponies. Brea shook out her hands and produced a smile, pushing aside any thoughts of the nightmare she would endure for the near future.

That evening, Sandra appeared in Brea's room with a glass of water and a white pill. She directed Brea to take it, informing her it was a medication for her mood and it might make her drowsy. Adam stood in the doorway, monitoring to ensure Brea swallowed it.

In the following days, Brea had little to no privacy. Sandra stayed close to Brea unless Adam or Mary was with her. To Brea's annoyance, when the Tandervons were not entertaining, Sandra served her meals on a tray in the bedroom, supervised her with the children, set up her baths and clothing, and provided her with her nightly medication. If Brea pushed back, Sandra threatened to inform Adam and Mary that her behavior had devolved into *"oppositional and erratic acting out."*

When the Tandervons entertained, Brea had no choice but to plaster a smile on her face, dress impeccably, and socialize with the stream of friends who visited the estate for lunches and dinners. Adam and Mary watched her, and if she failed to perform to their standards, she feared they would send her to the mental health facility Mary had threatened her with. As long as she looked beautiful and exhibited gracious behavior, she could remain silent and ponder ideas for liberation.

Although she did her best to remind herself Hayden was out there, working on a plan to help her, the days passed, and a sense of hopelessness consumed her. Brea could feign composure and pleasant manners while Mary and Allen entertained, but keeping a smile on her face while forced to endure Adam touching her in front of their hosted company had proved to be a sizable challenge. He would wrap his arm around her waist or shoulders and take liberties to kiss her on her lips or rub her back.

In the evening, he would undress in front of her and insist she join him in bed at ten o'clock. He did not force her into any form of sexual intimacy, but lying beside him left her unsettled and made it difficult to sleep. Sleep-deprived, Brea grew more irritable during the day, and her mood only lifted when able to spend time with Alex and Sophie.

Unable to sleep, Brea would stare at the ceiling and think of Hayden, wiping away her tears and replaying her most treasured memories of them together in Mexico. On Monday night, Brea glimpsed Adam's phone on his nightstand. If she moved with stealth, she could swipe it and call Hannah. She waited until Adam fell asleep, then with painstaking, slow movements, sat up in bed.

Glancing over her shoulder to ensure Adam still slept, she inhaled and held her breath. Upon standing, he grabbed her wrist, startling her.

"Where are you going?" he mumbled.

"To the bathroom. I'm bleeding. Started my period," she replied.

Adam released her wrist. It was a good lie. He did not know that on her birth control her periods cycled every three months and it would afford her several more days of avoiding sex with him.

They arrived home late Wednesday afternoon in Ocean Crest Beach, with Sandra moving in for the time being into the guest room. Although Brea was all but a prisoner, she felt relieved to be back in her own home. Once the children had fallen asleep, she settled into the living room to write. Fearful Adam or Sandra could use what she wrote against her, Brea wrote with clever wording to conceal the poem's true meaning.

Brea sat in the living room for two hours when she glanced at the clock and sighed, seeing it was ten. She rose and switched off the lights. Humiliating and infuriating, if she stayed up past ten, Sandra would fetch her and escort her to the bedroom like a child.

Before leaving the living room, she strolled over to the window to peer outside. The street was empty other than one car parked across the street. Brea sighed and tipped her forehead on the glass—she longed to go for a walk in the night air. Anger as well clung to her sadness, having witnessed Adam tell Hannah several hours ago that she was still sick and he would not allow her to visit. She was desperate to reach Hannah and find out if Hayden had found her.

With no phone or access to a computer, she could not consult a lawyer or much less research what rights and options she would have if she fled, and a judge awarded Adam full custody of Alex and Sophie. One night, feeling desperate, she briefly contemplated driving herself and the children after midnight to a police station. She knew that domestic violence shelters existed, though she did not know if they would accept her, claiming Adam was blackmailing her without proof.

Shutting the curtain, she left the living room to check on Alex and Sophie before returning to her bedroom. She would have poured herself a drink if she could have, but Sandra had advised Adam to remove all the alcohol from the house, and he obliged. She checked on Alex first, smiling upon seeing his hair sticking up in various directions as he slept. Brea smoothed his forehead and leaned down to kiss his cheek before checking on Sophie.

Brea entered her bedroom, dressed in the navy silk nightgown and matching robe Sandra laid out for her earlier. Adam sat propped up against the pillows on their light-gray king-size upholstered bed, dressed only in his boxers and reading a book.

"The new nanny arrives tomorrow so you can meet her. Her name is Naomi. My mother called the best agencies, and they highly recommended her. She has worked with many high-profile families and is very discreet."

Brea ignored Adam. "Am I allowed to have any friends, Adam, or would my having someone else in my life other than yourself violate your conditions?" she asked with an edge to her voice.

"I never said you couldn't be friends with Hannah. She's coming back tomorrow to visit us. I'll stick around during her visit, though, to make sure you behave." Brea clenched her jaw. It was intolerable, but she was helpless to do anything about it.

"Come here," Adam directed and set down his book. He handed Brea her medication, and she glimpsed an extra pill in the white cup.

"What is this, Adam? There's another pill in here."

"Something to help you sleep." Brea stared at the pills. "Brea, take it," he said, handing her a glass of water.

She swallowed the pills, one by one, then sat on the bed's edge with her back facing Adam and stared at the taupe and gold abstract painting hanging above the oak dresser. A minute later she felt Adam place his hands on her arms and pull her onto the bed to lie down. Lying flat on her back, he untied the belt of her silk robe.

"Adam, stop," she said and pushed away his hands. He grabbed Brea's hand. "Brea, look at me. I will not rape you." When he said the word "rape," she winced. "I'm only going to help you get comfortable and show you that you can trust me."

Brea closed her eyes. "I don't want you to touch me at all."

Adam exhaled. "Are you still thinking about him? It doesn't look like he's made any effort to find you. Look at how far I'll go to fight for you. Where is he now? He got what he wanted from you and now he's disappeared."

"No. You could never understand what I have with him. He will always do the right thing to protect me. It's a type of love you don't understand because you aren't capable of it, Adam," she replied, raising her voice.

"What will it take to put this behind us?" Adam asked, his voice calm and steady. With his fingers, he traced her cheek, then lowered his hand and placed it on her abdomen. "Don't you remember what it's like to make love to me, Brea? You used to wrap your arms around my neck and tell me you loved me."

Brea shook her head as a tear fell down her cheek. "Adam, please let me go so I can make the choice for myself." She closed her eyes and tipped her head back, hoping it would help her to inhale a deeper breath.

"I will not let you go back to him. You aren't in the right frame of mind, and you haven't slept in days. Can you please just let me hold you? Maybe you'll remember what it was like years ago." Adam reached over and wiped the tear that had fallen down Brea's cheek. He leaned over to his nightstand and opened the drawer. "Brea, open your eyes and look at this."

Opening her eyes, she turned her head to see what Adam held in his hand—it was a photo of Brea holding Alex as a newborn, with Adam beside her. They were looking at one another, radiant, after the photographer had snapped a candid photo of them.

Brea took the picture from Adam's hand. She remembered the joy she felt that day holding Alex, soft and tiny in her arms, when she believed her life was perfect. Brea's lips formed a slight smile. She wiped away another tear and met Adam's eyes.

"Brea, you need to sleep. You have circles under your eyes, and you look pale. Think about the kids—Sophie is worried about you. She asked me today if you were turning into a 'ghost'."

That garnered Brea's attention—it was what she used to say about her own mother. Shaking her head, Brea held the photograph close to her chest. "I don't want to be a ghost," she muttered to herself, and in that moment, she resolved to do better, try harder for her children and conceal what was happening from them.

As Adam watched Brea, the corners of his mouth turned up, pleased he made a small yet palpable breakthrough. He felt a newfound assurance, certain that he would bring her back to him. All he needed was time, and she would forget about her week in Mexico. He had nine years of history with Brea over this other man, and tonight he felt certain he would win.

Adam slipped his hands under the fabric of her robe, pushed it off her shoulders and removed it. He lay back, pulled Brea onto his chest and kissed the top of her head. Brea trembled as Adam ran his fingers down her back.

"Does that feel good when I touch you, Brea?" he asked. His desire for her stirred, though he knew restraint and a slow, cautious approach would be necessary to win her back.

Brea did not resist. "I don't want to be a ghost, Adam," she whispered.

Adam rubbed her back. "Go to sleep. I'm here."

"I'll be good. I won't be a ghost," Brea mumbled several times, drowsy and feeling as though she were floating out of her body. Tomorrow, she would be stronger for Alex and Sophie. She could not frighten them—they needed her to be the mother she never had. Her eyes grew heavy, and she soon fell asleep.

⁂

Brea's eyes opened, but she struggled to stay awake until twenty minutes passed. Surveying her room, she saw she was alone, rolled over and checked the clock on the bedside table. It was nine in the morning. With effort, she lifted herself up to sit. Her head felt heavy, and she braced herself with both hands on either side of her body on the mattress. Alex and Sophie were certainly awake by now, though the house was silent.

By the bay window, Brea glimpsed her robe draped on the chair. Shifting her legs off the bed, she sat on the edge and waited until she felt steady before standing. She trudged to the chair and slipped it on before crossing the length of her room and stepping into the hallway. Still exhausted, she yawned, despite having slept the most she had since Mexico.

"Good morning, Mrs. Tandervon," Sandra said upon seeing Brea enter the kitchen. She pulled back a kitchen table chair and gestured for Brea to have a seat. Brea's irritation returned upon seeing Sandra. "I heard from Mr. Tandervon you slept through the night. That is excellent news," Sandra remarked and placed a plate of toast and scrambled eggs on the table before Brea.

Brea scoffed and with a hostile tone replied, "Because he's blackmailing and drugging me—and so are you." As the words escaped her lips, Brea regretted it. She squeezed her eyes shut and pressed her fingers to her forehead. Sandra gave Brea a tight-lipped smile, pausing before speaking.

"How about some tea or coffee?" Sandra asked.

"Tea, please," Brea replied. "Where are Alex and Sophie?"

"They went to the park with Mr. Tandervon. They should be back in an hour. Go ahead, eat some breakfast," Sandra encouraged and poured the hot water from the kettle into a mug.

Brea lifted her fork and took a bite of the eggs. Attempting to recover from what she said earlier, she produced a smile. "They taste good, Sandra, thank you." Brea stared at her plate and forced herself to eat another two bites.

"How about we try some soup for lunch today? I will make the broth from scratch," Sandra said while moving about the kitchen.

"I don't care, Sandra." Brea wanted to pretend she was her old agreeable self, but she could not muster the energy this morning. She tossed her fork onto the table and sat back in her chair. Even after sleeping through the night, she only found herself more resentful and frustrated with her circumstances.

Appearing at her side, Sandra placed a mug of tea beside Brea's plate, circled the table, and seated herself opposite Brea. Brea avoided looking at Sandra and fixed her gaze out the patio doors.

Sandra reached out and patted Brea's hand, but she withdrew it abruptly at Sandra's touch. Glimpsing Sandra's reaction, she knew she had made another mistake, which did not bode well for the report Sandra would give Adam about her behavior.

Brea picked up her tea and blew on it before taking a sip. It was cooler than expected and sweeter than usual, but it tasted good. Thirsty, she drank the entire cup in several large gulps.

Rising from her chair, Sandra brought Brea the newspaper to read and refilled her tea. Making light conversation, Sandra asked Brea about any craft projects or games they could plan for the children once the new nanny, Naomi, arrived. A little over half an hour passed when Adam returned home with the children.

Although eager to see Alex and Sophie, a wave of profound drowsiness hit Brea, forcing her to rest her head on the table. She felt Adam's arms wrap around her and lift her up. "Come on, Brea, I'll take you to the bedroom," he whispered in her ear and carried her through the kitchen.

Before leaving the room, Adam paused to speak with Sandra in a low voice—she could not hear what they said. Sandra remained in the kitchen to clean up and watch over the children. Brea heard dishes clinking in the sink as Adam carried her down the hall. Her body felt weightless, and she laughed, though she did not know why. Adam smiled at her. "It's nice to see you happy, Brea."

Adam laid Brea on the bed and covered her up to her waist with a blanket. He rubbed her cheek with his thumb, then leaned down to give her a kiss on her forehead. "Do you love me, Brea?" he whispered.

She mumbled, "Adam," unable to open her eyes, then fell asleep.

Brea woke in the middle of the afternoon upon hearing the bedroom door shut. Her eyes fluttered open, and she felt as though a thick layer of foam had wrapped around her brain. A folding table held a meal tray with a grilled chicken salad beside the bed. A guttural groan escaped Brea's mouth upon finding it took a monumental effort to sit up and remain so on the edge of the bed—she felt too dizzy to stand.

Her mouth was tacky, and her lips felt dry. A glass of iced-tea sat on her tray, and she drank the whole glass down. Although she had no appetite, she needed to eat, otherwise Mary would push to check her into the facility. The chicken was difficult to chew, and her mouth could not quite respond to her brain's command to move. A quarter of the salad through, she gave up to lie in bed again.

The fatigue enveloped her like a weighted blanket, lulling her back to sleep. It was difficult to hold on to any line of cohesive thoughts as everything felt scattered and loose. A memory of Hayden standing on the dance floor at the supper club flitted through her mind, and Brea questioned whether being with him in Mexico had truly happened or had only been a dream. Hearing her children's laughter echo in the distance, she drifted off to sleep.

Chapter Fifty-Four

Hayden

On Friday morning, the board of Hayden's company voted to move forward on acquiring Pltanix, the mid-sized software company with innovative technology that brought Hayden to Ocean Crest Beach over a month ago. Though he welcomed the news, Hayden could not celebrate as there had been no promising updates regarding Brea.

Checking in with him daily, Hannah had no luck seeing Brea for two days. It was now Saturday late in the afternoon, and his restlessness felt near unbearable. Pouring himself a glass of water, he sat on a barstool at his kitchen counter and stared at the clock on the microwave.

Hannah last spoke with Hayden the previous evening. Yesterday, a woman, who she presumed was a newly hired housekeeper, Sandra, had refused her entry into the home, telling Hannah that Brea was too ill for visitors. After asking if she could see Adam instead, Sandra informed her that Adam was busy with the children and unavailable to speak with her. Hiding her frustration, Hannah changed her strategy and lied.

"I'm so concerned about Brea, and I know her family would like to come take care of her. I'll call her parents and see if they

can send out her cousin. But if I could see Brea, it might save her a trip. "With a polite nod, Sandra informed her she would pass the message on to Adam.

Hayden's cell phone rang. He picked it up with a swift hand, seeing it was Hannah. "Hannah, did you see her today?" he asked without saying hello.

"Hayden, it's not good. She looked terrible—I've never seen her like this. Adam called earlier—my bluff worked, and he invited me over. The housekeeper is actually a private nurse, and when she walked Brea into the living room, I almost fell over. She could barely walk and was like a shell of herself. Adam kept saying she was getting better, but all Brea could mumble was, 'I'm fine, I'm not a ghost.' Hayden—I think she's being drugged."

Overwhelmed at having seen Brea so altered, Hannah paused a moment to collect herself before continuing. "And Adam stood behind her the whole time with his hands on her shoulders, and the nurse sat next to her. It was—disturbing."

Sinking into his chair, Hayden stretched his neck back to look at the ceiling. "Hannah, I'm coming back and getting her out of there. I can't sit here and do nothing—I have to get her now." Hayden's voice wavered. "Hannah—he's hurting her."

"Hayden, I'm upset too, but we can't just break in and kidnap her. We could get arrested, and we'll lose our chance to help her. It's not all hopeless—there is some good news. After the nurse took Brea back to her room, I sat with Adam for a while and fed him a bunch of bullshit about how lucky Brea was to have him. He said she's having a breakdown and paranoid he's trying to take the children from her. I told him I would come every day to convince her she's safe with him—he bought it, and I'm in."

Hayden sniffed and composed himself. "Good. So, what do I need to do?"

"Don't panic, okay? Can you do that?"

Looking around the room, he inhaled. "Yes," he replied.

"Good, here's what I'm thinking. Let me talk it through with you."

CHAPTER FIFTY-FIVE

BREA

Water. Perhaps a pipe had burst, and sheets of water were cascading down the walls and pooling onto the floor. The noise was loud, intrusive, and jarring. Brea's eyes flickered open. No, she heard running water coming from the bathroom. With tremendous effort, she rolled onto her side. Her body ached as though she had run twenty miles. Beside the bed, there was a tray with breakfast and a cup of tea. Disoriented, she rubbed her eyes, confused about what day it was and for how long she had slept.

"Hello?" she called out.

A woman familiar to Brea appeared in the doorway of her bathroom. "Mrs. Tandervon, good morning. You have had quite a bit of rest. Today, we are going to get you outside for some fresh air. How does that sound?" she asked, walking to the bedside and seating herself on the edge of the bed.

Brea rubbed her neck and searched her mind. "I don't know—my entire body hurts. I know you. Your name is—"

"Sandra, I'm your nurse."

"Of course, yes. I'm having difficulty thinking," Brea mumbled.

"That is because you have been in bed for so long. You have slept for three days. Your friend Hannah is coming by in a little while to visit. Such a lovely woman, and she is so concerned about you."

"Hannah?" Brea replied. It was difficult to grasp a solid thought. "Did I see her yesterday or the day before? Or maybe it was a dream?" she asked.

"She came by yesterday, but you were still quite ill," Sandra replied. Brea closed her eyes, trying to remember, but drew a blank. All she could retrieve was a garbled image of Hannah sitting on the sofa in her living room. She knew she wanted to see her, but she could not recall for what purpose.

"Where are the children?" Brea asked, struggling to articulate her words.

"In the backyard, playing with Mr. Tandervon. He will be so pleased to see you awake. For the past several days, he would not leave your side. All right, after you eat, you will take a hot bath, then I will help you dress and style your hair."

Brea looked into Sandra's eyes, searching for something, but she did not know what. "Adam?" she whispered aloud. Her thoughts were too muddled, and she wondered if she were dreaming.

Sandra smiled. "Let me help you up for some tea and break-fast. I prepared oatmeal topped with fresh berries and sliced almonds." Holding Brea's hands, Sandra helped her to sit up on the edge of the bed. Brea's eyes drifted to the tray. She studied the white porcelain bowl of oatmeal—something about it gave her pause. A thought or a memory, obscured by a thick haze, struggled to break through to the surface.

"I don't think I like oatmeal. I'll have eggs," Brea replied in a monotone voice as she pressed her fingers to her cheeks to inspect her face, confused why moving her lips and mouth felt so taxing.

"No, you will have the oatmeal. It is better for you," Sandra insisted as she moved about the room to select an outfit for Brea.

Brea did not have the energy to argue and picked up the spoon. Lifting her arm, she felt as though she had a weight tied around her wrist. She ate a spoonful with a raspberry on top and chewed it with extraordinary effort. Bringing the cup of black tea with cream to her lips, she drained it. Still thirsty, Brea next drank the entire glass of orange juice, swallowed two more bites of oatmeal, and then set the spoon on the tray. "What happened to me? Why am I sick?" she asked Sandra.

"Your body only needed a good rest to help clear your mind," Sandra replied, then returned to Brea's side to help her stand and led her to the bathroom. After removing her nightgown, she held onto Brea's arm to steady her while stepping into the marbled alcove tub.

"I don't need help. I can manage," Brea said, self-conscious of her nudity.

"Nonsense. I have seen it all, and you are still weak. I do not want you to fall down." Brea nodded. Sandra shampooed Brea's hair, rinsed her off, and instructed her to lift her arms and legs, one by one, to shave for her. The duration of time Brea sat in the bathtub felt interminable, but she had little will nor clarity of thought to ask Sandra to help her step out of the tub.

Entranced, Brea stared at the water and bubbles. Everything was strange—her surroundings, what she could see of her body, and the sound of her own voice. "Can I see Sophie and Alex? I don't want them to get sick, though."

"Of course. First, we will dry you off." Sandra gripped Brea's hand and arm as she stepped out of the tub, then Sandra wrapped a towel around her. "And after styling your hair, I will help you with your makeup. Mr. Tandervon is looking forward to seeing you healthy and restored to your former self," she added and led Brea to her vanity table.

Once groomed, Sandra helped Brea into her clothing, a beige linen skirt and a light-blue silk camisole. As time passed, Brea felt her motor control improving, and she examined her reflection in the mirror. She saw herself, but she felt nothing—it was as though her brain had been removed, washed clean, and returned to her skull. Without warning, Sophie and Alex burst into the bathroom.

"Mommy," they cried out. Sandra scolded them not to shout or they could frighten their mother. Brea smiled, reached out to touch Alex and Sophie's cheeks and then pulled them in close for a kiss. Although she felt oddly detached, seeing her children inspired a moment of joy.

"My babies," she whispered. Brea stood, took Sophie and Alex's hands, and walked with them into her bedroom. The children chattered, talking over one another to express their excitement that their mother was feeling better and could play with them again.

"Sandra, what day is it?"

"Sunday."

Brea sat on the bed with Sophie and Alex on either side of her. She wrapped her arms around them and kissed them on their foreheads. "I have an idea. Let's go to the park today and have a picnic," Brea suggested.

Sandra tilted her head to the side. "That may be possible tomorrow. Today is the trip to the science museum, and Mr. Tandervon mentioned taking—"

Adam appeared at the bedroom door. "Brea, I'm hoping you're feeling better."

Brea turned to Adam, handsome and dressed in navy-blue slacks and a fitted white dress shirt. She was unsure why, but seeing him in the doorway with a wide smile troubled her. "Yes, I'm better, Adam," she replied, searching her mind for why she felt uneasy. Adam and Sandra exchanged glances, and she stepped aside.

Adam strolled over to Brea and cupped her face with his hands. Tilting her head up, he leaned down and kissed her. Alex and Sophie giggled. He scooped up Sophie, placed her on his lap and sat beside Brea. "Look how cheerful everyone is today. Everything is back to normal," he proclaimed.

Brea studied Adam's face, unable to decode the odd feeling that something was off. Abandoning her efforts, she asked, "Adam, can we take the children to the park and have a picnic today?"

"Of course," he replied and gestured for Sandra to take the children with her out of the bedroom. Ushering Alex and Sophie out of the room, Brea heard them ask Sandra if they could help pack the picnic as they ran down the hall.

"You look so beautiful, Brea. I think you're much better after getting some rest," Adam said, running his finger along her collarbone. He pushed her hair off her shoulder to kiss the base of her neck.

"Does that feel good, Brea?" he whispered, then kissed her on the mouth.

Brea closed her eyes. "Yes," she answered, despite feeling uncertain that was the truth.

Adam kissed her shoulder and placed his hand over her heart. "I've missed you," he whispered in her ear. Brea inhaled a deep breath—something felt wrong. Opening and lowering her eyes, she fixed them on her wrist, and an image of a heart drawn in ink appeared in her mind—something stirred in her brain.

Imperceptible to Adam, Brea shook her head, though it was more of a vibration rather than a movement. She had dreamt of Hayden sleeping beside her in a room by the ocean. No—it was not a dream—it was a memory. The wall in Brea's mind cracked and collapsed, and all her memories of Hayden and Mexico shook loose. With wide eyes, Brea sucked in a sharp breath and stopped herself from saying Hayden's name out loud.

Adam placed a hand on her knee, and her heart beat with force in her chest. Kissing her neck with increasing intensity, he slid his hand up her thigh under her skirt, pausing when Sandra knocked on the door and announced that Hannah had arrived for her visit. Brea sprang to her feet and dizziness overcame her—Adam caught her by the waist and steadied her.

"Be careful. You've barely walked in days. Put one foot in front of the other and take your time. Hannah will wait for you," he instructed. He wrapped his arm around her waist and led her out of the room. In the doorway, Adam turned Brea to face him and kissed her once again. "I'm glad you're getting better, Brea," he said with a satisfied grin.

Brea forced a half-smile onto her face before averting her eyes from his. Adam gripped her hand and walked with her to the living room. Seeing Hannah, she pulled her hand out of Adam's and flew to embrace her best friend, light-headed and falling into her arms, but Hannah held her up.

"Whoa, I missed you too," Hannah said in a gentle voice and hugged her. Adam followed close behind Brea, his goal being to monitor the interaction. The three of them sat, Brea next to Hannah on one sofa, and Adam seating himself opposite them.

"You look great today," Hannah complimented. "So—rested."

"Thanks, I feel better," Brea replied and searched Hannah's face, hoping to decipher whether Hayden had found her.

"I am so grateful Adam brought you home early. You were so sick, and he took such good care of you. He was so worried—we all were," Hannah exclaimed, taking Brea's hands in hers, and turning her head to flash Adam an exaggerated smile of admiration.

Brea felt Hannah press her finger twice into her palm. Glancing at her hands, then meeting Hannah's eyes again, she knew it was code for something. Perhaps Morse code? Regardless, Brea would not know how to interpret it, but she now knew Hannah was there to help her, and it filled her with immeasurable hope.

"I understand why you need to step away from the store," Hannah said while shaking her head. She pressed her finger into

Brea's palm twice again. Twice. Brea could not understand what that meant.

Brea replied. "It's for the best. I've been away from the kids for so long and with being sick—I'm sorry, Hannah." Hannah pressed a finger once into Brea's palm. Brea blinked with confusion.

"Don't apologize. Adam, don't let her feel bad. She needs to be home with you, Sophie, and Alex. I was too selfish keeping you for as long as I did. You are so lucky to have Adam. Never forget that." Hannah pressed twice into her palm. Brea suspected twice meant she was lying, though still uncertain.

"Adam, if Brea is up to it, I need her to come by the store tomorrow to pick up her things and help me out with those order and payment files you organized for me. I wouldn't even know which files to bring over here. I was so confused last week. I need her to run it all by me or I'll be in big trouble. Brea can bring the kids since we'll be closed. They love the shop." Hannah pressed one finger into Brea's palm.

Brea shifted her hopeful gaze to Adam and remained calm to convey it was his decision, and she would defer to him. Adam considered the request and tapped his fingers on his knee. "Sure, as long as Sandra is with you. And no computers or phones, Hannah. Everything needs to be on paper."

"Of course. I'll leave my laptop at home." Hannah pressed into Brea's palm twice.

Brea licked her lips and spoke. "I think I can manage with the children. This way, Sandra can have a break."

Adam narrowed his eyes, and his lips drew into a tight line. She should not have pushed back. To recover, she smiled and backtracked. "Of course, it makes more sense for Sandra to help me. You're right, Adam." Hannah pushed a finger into Brea's palm three times.

Adam rose from the sofa. "All right, it's settled then. Hannah, can I bring you a drink? You take your coffee black with sugar if I remember correctly?" he offered.

Hannah beamed at Adam. "Yes, thank you! Brea, can you clone your husband and give him to me? He's so thoughtful." With a self-satisfied grin, Adam turned towards the kitchen.

Rolling her eyes, Hannah turned to Brea. Hannah whispered, "I know everything." Brea nodded. Hannah mouthed, "Hayden found me."

Brea pressed her lips together as tears formed in her eyes. Hannah mouthed, "Shh."

Adam would sense something was amiss if they did not speak. Brea swallowed. "Did that small credenza table ever sell, Hannah? The one with the walnut stain?"

Hannah smiled. "Yes, I shipped it out a few days ago." Then she mouthed, "He says he loves you."

Brea wiped away a tear spilling down her cheek. "I'm so happy to hear that," she said, maintaining control over the tone of her voice not to betray any emotion.

Adam was on his way back to the sofa with Hannah's coffee. "Be strong," Hannah mouthed.

"Thanks, Adam, ugh, I'm so jealous Brea snagged you." Hannah picked up her coffee cup and took several sips before shifting the topic over to a new man she was dating, hoping Adam would become bored with the conversation and leave them alone on the sofa again. After ten minutes of prattling on, Hannah gave up, realizing Adam had no intention of leaving her alone with Brea.

"So, what are you two up to today? It's gorgeous outside," Hannah asked.

"A picnic and a trip to the park with the kids," Brea replied.

"Well, that sounds perfect. So, I have to head out. I have to run to open up the shop, but I'll see you tomorrow, Brea. Come by around noon."

The three of them rose from their seats. Hannah embraced Brea, then gave Adam a kiss on the cheek before she left the room. Adam turned to face Brea. She cleared her throat. "Adam, I need a few minutes to use the restroom before we go."

Reaching her bedroom, she hurried into the bathroom, shut the door, and sank to the floor with trembling hands. Although relieved Hannah had found Hayden, Brea was terrified now knowing what Adam and Sandra could do to her—it was clear they had drugged and sedated her for days. Brea pressed her hands to her forehead and drew in a deep breath to calm herself. Adam and Sandra would know something was wrong if they saw she had been crying.

Brea redirected her thoughts. She did not know if Hannah and Hayden had a plan yet, but having seen her best friend, and hearing Hayden's message provided her with the lifeline she needed to keep her hope alive. And having regained her composure, she would need to conjure an excuse or a plan to divert Adam later that night—a headache, falling asleep early on the sofa, or even faking an injury. Adam's sexual advances would only become more insistent as time stretched on, and the idea of being intimate with him made her feel ill.

"Mrs. Tandervon, do you need anything?" Sandra asked, tapping on the bathroom door.

"No, I only have a slight headache. I'll be fine." Brea lifted herself off the floor and hurried to the toilet to flush it. Pausing before the mirror, she checked her makeup and there were no smudges or streaks.

Brea opened the door with a polite smile. A cup of tea sat on the tray next to the bed. "No thank you, Sandra. I'm very full. I'll go find Sophie and Alex." She hurried past Sandra and went out the door. Now that her mind was clear, she would refuse the tea or dump it out, knowing Sandra could lace it with drugs.

As she walked down the hallway, she reminded herself to play her part today so Adam would not have a reason to cancel her visit to Brine tomorrow. Above all, she would need to oust Sandra, and, if possible, call Hayden. Brea closed her eyes at the thought of hearing his voice and pressed her fingers to her lips.

When she reached the doorway of Sophie's room, she paused for a moment and watched her children playing on the floor before joining them. Brea plopped down beside them, and Sophie jumped into her lap. Wrapping her fleshy arms around Brea's neck, she looked up into Brea's eyes. "Mommy, you look happy," she said. Brea buried her nose in Sophie's curls. "I am happy, baby. So happy."

Chapter Fifty-Six

Brea

Brea's eyes fluttered open the following morning, and she sighed. The sight of the breakfast tray beside the bed did not fail to irritate her. To circumvent Adam last night after dinner, Brea laid her head down on the kitchen table and complained of a migraine and nausea. Adam instructed Sandra to skip Brea's medications, carried her to the bedroom, and put her to bed. To Brea's relief, though he removed her clothing and covered her with a blanket, he did not otherwise touch her and left her alone to sleep.

The sight of the smoked salmon made Brea's stomach turn, but if she ate nothing, Sandra would inform Adam. She picked up a plain piece of toast, took a bite and carried the cup of tea to her bathroom sink. Dumping it out, she hurried back into her bedroom and set it on the tray before leaving her room to find Sophie and Alex.

She checked their rooms, and finding them empty, searched the house. Sandra greeted Brea while tidying the kitchen with an acknowledging smile.

"Mrs. Tandervon, you are up earlier than usual. The children are outside, and Ms. Naomi will arrive later this afternoon after we return from visiting your friend at her shop. Did you eat your breakfast?"

Brea walked over to the patio doors, peered out and saw Alex and Sophie in the backyard playing with a soccer ball. After watching her children through the glass for a moment, Brea inhaled and turned back to Sandra. "Yes, I'm feeling better. I ate some toast, thinking it would be best not to overwhelm my stomach. I'm excited to see Hannah today at the shop."

"Only if you eat some more. Have a seat at the table, and I will cut up some fresh fruit and prepare another cup of tea for you."

"I would like coffee this morning. I'll need the extra help to focus on Hannah's paperwork. With cream, no sugar, Sandra."

"Yes, of course."

"I was thinking, Sandra. Later this afternoon, could you lay out my backless navy dress with the halter top? It's Adams favorite." Brea lied, but she wanted Sandra to believe that she was free of any paranoia or ill feelings towards Adam. Somehow, she would need to find time alone with Hannah, and she had a hunch the only way that would happen is if she could fool Sandra into believing she was returning to her usual self.

Sandra replied, "That sounds lovely. Mr. Tandervon will be so pleased. I will see to that once you finish eating." Brea raised her eyes to smile at Sandra and saw her slip something into the pocket of her apron with a swift motion of her hand.

Brea cleared her throat. "I'll have that coffee black. I changed my mind."

"Yes, Mrs. Tandervon." Brea watched Sandra pour a fresh cup of coffee and bring it to the table for her.

"And let's style my hair down today. It's the way Adam likes it," Brea added. Sandra opened the refrigerator door to pull out the strawberries and blackberries. Picking up the newspaper, Brea glanced at the front page, flitting her eyes back and forth to watch Sandra as she washed and arranged the fruit on the plate.

Sandra set the dish before Brea and sat in the chair opposite her. Picking up her fork, Brea pierced a strawberry and ate it.

After swallowing, she cleared her throat and pasted a pleasant smile on her face.

"Sandra, I know little about you, and you've been by my side all week. Where do you come from?"

"My family is from Illinois," she replied, further straightening her impeccable posture.

"And how long have you been a nurse?" Brea asked.

"Twenty-six years. I have worked with many esteemed families of equal caliber to the Tandervons."

"I can tell you are—skilled. It's as though you brought me back from the dead," Brea said and flashed a warm smile.

"Yes, well, we will see how you progress. It is still quite early, Mrs. Tandervon."

Brea backed off. If she appeared too eager, Sandra would become suspicious and report it to Adam and Mary. "I'll trust you and follow your lead then," Brea replied, feigning a humble air.

Sandra rose from the table. "I will see to that dress while you finish your coffee. Perhaps it would be wise to step outside and get some fresh air with the children."

"Of course, I will," Brea answered, lowering her eyes to the table and then raising them to watch Sandra exit the room.

Brea clenched her fists and let out a forceful exhale once the sound of Sandra's steps faded down the hall. Walking over to the sink, she dumped out the remaining coffee and set the mug into the sink. She lowered her head for a moment before pivoting in a half-circle to take a cold bottle of water from the refrigerator. Cracking it open, she drank its contents down.

Before opening the patio doors, she grounded herself with a deep breath and stepped outside to join the children in the backyard. Seeing Brea, Alex and Sophie ran into her outstretched arms. Brea fussed playfully over them until Sophie grabbed Brea's hand to show her the painted rocks she and Naomi had made for their rock garden. Seating herself on the grass, she pulled Sophie onto her lap and handled the rocks one by one to examine them as Sophie described to her what she had painted.

Alex joined them after a little while, sat beside Brea, and laid his head on her shoulder. "I'm glad you're doing better, Mommy. When is that scary lady going to leave? I don't like her—she doesn't let us play with you that much."

Brea smiled. "Soon baby. Mommy's getting better, and then she'll be gone forever. And guess what?"

"What?" Alex and Sophie asked at the same time.

"We are going to visit Aunt Hannah today at the store, won't that be so much fun?" Alex and Sophie cheered.

"Can you buy us a present at the toy store?" Sophie asked. Brea's mouth dropped open—that was a great idea.

"Absolutely. And you know what, ask Aunt Hannah about the ice-cream shop too—and don't let her say no. But it's a secret. Wait until we get there, and then ask her again and again until she says yes," Brea replied with a wide smile. Turning her head, she glimpsed Sandra inside, standing behind the patio doors and watching Brea with a sober expression.

❧❦❧

After an early lunch, Sandra drove Brea, Alex, and Sophie to the arts district. Brea directed her to the Brine store parking lot to park in a reserved space. Hannah's Boxster sat in its usual spot.

The children, animated and enthusiastic to see Aunt Hannah, chatted throughout the entire drive and as soon as they exited the car, both ran to the back door and burst into the store shouting her name.

Hannah ran to meet Alex and Sophie in the center of the shop and wrapped her arms around them. "Oh my goodness, wild children in my store. I don't know what to do with them other than to pick them up and spin them around!"

Out of the corner of her eye, Brea observed Sandra scan the shop, likely searching for any telephones. Hannah scooped up Sophie in her arms and grabbed Alex's hand to show them a puzzle she had bought for them to take home. Brea sat in a chair and made a dramatic show of dropping her head into her hands.

"Sandra, I feel lightheaded. Could I have the water we brought?" Upon reaching Brea, she pulled out a sealed plastic bottle of water from her purse and handed it to Brea.

The children followed behind Hannah, holding the puzzle box. "Mommy, can we get an ice-cream at the shop down the street?" Alex asked.

"I don't know. Sandra, did they eat enough lunch? I'm too lightheaded to walk at the moment, but perhaps you can take them if you think they deserve a treat?" Brea asked as though she relied on Sandra's opinion to decide.

"Yes, but we should stay in the shop for now. We can all go together later. I am not to leave Mrs. Tandervon alone with anyone."

"No!" Alex and Sophie cried out and carried on.

Hannah laughed. "Kids, I'll tell you what. I'll go with you and Sandra so we can let your mommy have a moment to rest. Your dad would not want me to take you out alone on such a busy street without another grown-up to keep you safe. Sandra, I'll lock the back door behind us. It's a double-cylinder deadbolt, and I have the only key. Once I lock the doors, no one can leave, and she'll be alone in the shop. The front door has an internal padlock, as you can see, for extra security."

"Is there a telephone in the store?" Sandra asked.

"You know the wiring is so old it went out a few days ago, and I have the company coming tomorrow. I'm having all the store calls directed to my cell phone." Hannah held up her phone, then returned it to her pocket.

"Where is the telephone?" Sandra asked.

"Over here." Hannah ushered Sandra to the checkout counter and plopped the landline phone on the table. Sandra picked up the handset, satisfied there was no dial tone.

"And the computer?"

Hannah nodded. "As Adam asked, I left it at home. All the paper files are stacked near the cash register." Sandra glanced at the children, whining and fussing, then studied Hannah's face and inhaled.

"My treat for ice-cream. And I'll even take them next door for a toy!" Hannah exclaimed, and Sophie and Alex cheered at an ear-shrieking volume. Brea feigned pain and winced, covering her ears. "Sandra, please take them. I can't take the noise," Brea cried out.

Sandra scanned the shop once more and determined it would be acceptable to lock Brea in the store alone, and she agreed to take the children out with Hannah.

"Brea, when you feel up to it, if you could go through those files and reorganize them for me. Oh, and jot down some notes about when I need to make those payments to the book supplier and the steps for that complicated shipping company we have to use for international orders. Brea shut her eyes, rested her head against the wall behind her, and nodded.

"All right, kids, let's go so your mom can rest and do a little work." Hannah took Alex and Sophie's hands to lead them out, and Sandra followed.

Brea shook her head once they were out of sight. How was she going to get any time alone with Hannah? This was going to be more difficult than expected. A moment later, Hannah ran back in past Brea.

"I'll be right back. I forgot my sweater," she called out. Watching Hannah run to the counter and grab her sweater,

Brea shrugged her shoulders and lifted her hands, exasperated. Hannah pointed to the office. A large painting covered the door. Gesturing for Brea to move the painting, she mouthed, "Go in."

Hannah took off to the back door. Brea waited to make sure she had locked the door before rising from her chair to walk to the office. Although now trapped in Brine, Brea remembered the other phone in the office. Hannah was a genius—she had sabotaged the phone at the checkout counter. Brea could call the operator to find Hayden's office number and reach his assistant.

Hurrying, she moved the painting and opened the door. Her heart stopped beating, and she cried out, nearly collapsing upon seeing Hayden seated on the desk. Hayden sprang from the desk to stand, and a look of relief swept over his face.

Brea flew into Hayden's arms with tears flowing down her cheeks. He wrapped his arms around her and pulled her close. "You're here—is this real?" she asked between breaths.

"I'm here," he replied, his voice packed with emotion as he pressed Brea to him and kissed the top of her head.

They pulled apart, elated. Hayden placed his hands on Brea's cheeks to pull her face closer to him, kissed her on her mouth, and then on her forehead. He wiped away her tears, and they laughed—seeing him again was everything.

"I heard you talking out there, and we don't have a lot of time. Hannah will send me a message when she's coming back, but we should hurry to be safe. Are you okay? Is he hurting you?" he asked, searching her eyes.

"Not in the way you think, but they made me sign a form to take medications. They think I had a mental breakdown, or it's another lie they tell themselves to control me and justify the blackmail. The nurse Adam's mother hired is giving me drugs to make me sleep or when they think I'm acting paranoid. She gave me so much I slept for three days. And I can avoid Adam only for so long. He's getting impatient, and wants me to be my old self—to touch me and have sex. It's horrible, Hayden," she said, shaking her head. Hayden embraced her again as fresh tears pooled in her eyes.

"Tell me what you want to do, Brea. We could leave now. I'll take you back with me to the hotel, and we'll hire lawyers to fight the emergency order. It could take some time, and from the lawyers I spoke with, we can't just take Alex and Sophie with us and disappear. You could get into trouble. But if we tell the court he's blackmailing and drugging you—"

Brea shook her head. "No, I signed forms consenting to take medications, and his family knows a corrupt judge—maybe even more than one. I have no proof he's blackmailing me, and they have too many witnesses on their side willing to lie and testify. Worse, if I bring Adam to court with those allegations and the court deems us both untrustworthy, my mother-in-law could receive custody of Alex and Sophie. It's too risky—we need another way, Hayden. I can't leave them behind."

Hayden shut his eyes and kissed Brea's forehead. "Okay, listen to me. Do whatever you have to do to get through this. I love you no matter what happens with Adam—just survive until we can get you out."

"I know I have to go back, but I don't know how much more I can take. They're watching me all the time, and they won't let me use the phone or the computer. Adam and Mary threatened to put me in a facility if I don't comply or get better."

"That will not happen—I won't let it." Hayden picked Brea up by her waist and seated her on the desk. Moving the desk chair to sit before Brea, he placed his hands on her hips, and looked up to meet her eyes.

"I miss you. It's torture not being with you," she said as Hayden tipped his forehead onto Brea's abdomen. Brea ran her fingers through his hair, then lay her head on top of his.

"For me too. I try to remember you swimming in the ocean and how happy you were that day outside the cabana. It pushes me to keep going," Hayden said.

"I think about you eating the habanero shrimp," Brea teased, and they both chuckled.

Hayden pulled his head back, looked into Brea's eyes, and replied with a solemn expression. "I'd eat ten of them if it could get you and the kids out of there right now." She leaned down and as she kissed Hayden, found her strength and resilience bolstered with the touch of his mouth against hers. When they pulled apart, he took Brea's hands in his and played with her fingers. "Brea, we came up with a plan, but we're going to need you to pull it off. It's the most important part, and it won't be easy."

"Anything. What do I have to do?" Brea felt no fear, only hope.

Hayden explained and reviewed the detailed instructions. He frequently glanced at his phone, anticipating a message from Hannah warning him of their return. Once finished, Brea repeated back to him what she needed to do, then Hayden told her that when Hannah pressed into her palm, once meant *"yes"* or *"keep going,"* twice it meant *"no"* or *"I'm pretending,"* and three times meant *"be careful."*

He pulled Brea onto his lap, and they embraced. "If you need to leave, I'm hiding a phone and cash in a black waterproof bag behind the pink rose bush under your living room window tonight. My number, the hotel where I'm staying, my assistant Ashley's number, Hannah's number—it's all in there. The four-digit code is your birthday, month and date. Do you have your house keys?"

"Yes, I think so." Brea stood to retrieve her purse from the floor where she had left it beside the chair. Returning to the office, she pulled out her keys.

Hayden took them from her hands. "Just the house key. Which one is it?"

Brea pointed to it. Hayden took it off the keyring and put it in his pocket. "If I need to, I can get in and get you out. Do you have outdoor security cameras?"

"No, only the interior alarm. The code is Alex's birthday, eleven twenty-two," she replied.

Placing his hands on her cheeks, Hayden tipped his forehead to hers. "I have to go. Hannah gave me a copy of the store keys. I'll lock the door behind me."

Brea shook her head and wiped her eyes. "I can't say goodbye to you, Hayden. I can't watch you leave."

Hayden smiled. "It's not goodbye. With us—there's no such thing."

"I love you," Brea whispered.

"I love you," Hayden replied, kissing her on the forehead and closing his eyes. "Remember, take everything Hannah gives you back to the house with you. It's on the counter in a blue gift bag."

Pulling back to look at her one more time, he smiled. "We're almost there. We don't give up, right?"

Brea shook her head. "No—never again." Hayden cradled Brea's face with his hands and kissed her. She took a step back and lowered her eyes to the floor as he turned and left. Brea stood fixed in place for several minutes, feeling as though a piece of her had walked out of the office with Hayden.

Pushing aside her feelings as she had little time, she stepped out of the office, replaced the painting over the door, and hurried to the checkout counter, where the blue bag sat. Looking inside, she saw everything Hayden told her she would need to pull off her part of the plan. She set to work, hiding what she could in her bra or purse, and leaving the remaining objects Sandra would believe were her belongings in the bag.

Taking a pad of square-shaped notes and a pen, Brea opened two of the paper files. Seating herself on the stool, she scribbled fake notes, days of the week, and random numbers to make it appear as if she had been working on the files.

Five minutes later, Sandra returned with Hannah and the kids. Sophie and Alex each held a large shopping bag and ran to show Brea their new toys. "We had too much ice-cream, and we made too much noise," Sophie announced with pride.

Brea laughed and hugged her children. "I think I organized everything for you, Hannah. Let me show you." Sandra strolled around the store, peeking inside various books and examining small decorative objects while Brea and Hannah hovered over the files.

With Sandra's guard down, Hannah and Brea wrote messages back and forth to one another on a notepad, confirming the plan. They both continued talking about irrelevant bills and files while writing.

Hannah wrote, *"If you pull it off, convince Adam to let the kids sleep at my house Wednesday night."*

Brea scribbled, *"Any ideas how?"*

Hannah smirked, then wrote, *"Time alone-to seduce him. You can't have the kids in the house for what you want to do to him."* Brea sighed with wide eyes.

Hannah then added on the notepad, *"Get rid of her too, less risk of something going wrong."*

Brea shook her head and wrote, *"I can't have sex with him."*

Hannah smiled and wrote, *"Be creative. You won't have to if the plan works."* Brea exhaled and rubbed her forehead. Hannah wrote again and pointed to what she had scribbled to emphasize her message. *"It's an act. Own your body and take back control."* Meeting Hannah's eyes, Brea and Hannah exchanged a fleeting smile.

"We need to be going, Mrs. Tandervon," Sandra announced.

Brea inhaled a deep breath and brightened her expression. "Yes. Sophie and Alex, let's go. When we get home, we can have a snack, and then open up your amazing new toys."

The children ran to Brea. "Give Aunt Hannah a hug and don't forget to say thank you," she reminded them. Alex and Sophie took turns embracing Hannah and thanked her.

"Oh, don't forget your things. I know you'll want your picture frame," Hannah said, handing Brea the blue bag. Sandra intercepted the handover to peek inside the bag. Satisfied upon seeing the picture frame and a water bottle, she turned it over to Brea.

Sandra and the children walked out first. Brea turned to embrace Hannah. "Thank you, I love you," she whispered into Hannah's ear.

"It's going to work. Remember, you're just acting a part," Hannah replied and squeezed Brea before she let her go. Brea left the store and as she walked to the car, surveyed the parking lot and wondered if Hayden lingered nearby. Though she longed to see him again, knowing he was in Ocean Crest Beach was enough to give her the comfort and strength she would need to battle her way out of hell and find her way back to him.

CHAPTER FIFTY-SEVEN

BREA

Adam returned home from work at seven o'clock. Before leaving, Naomi bathed and put the kids to bed early while Sandra prepared dinner and set the table for Brea and Adam. Excusing herself, Sandra left the kitchen to return to the guest bedroom.

Brea, dressed in her navy sundress with a deep V-neck, sat in her chair at the kitchen table. Hearing Adam's footsteps approaching, her eyes fixed on the picture frame from the blue bag set upon the center island opposite the kitchen table. Adam entered the kitchen and paused upon seeing Brea seated at the table. "Well, you look stunning, Brea."

Rising from her seat to face Adam, she smiled. "Thank you, Adam." She turned to serve the meal Sandra had left in the oven for them. Stepping behind her, Adam placed his hands on her shoulders, moved her hair, and kissed the back of her neck.

"I'm a patient man, Brea, but seeing you tonight, I think I'm at my limit waiting for you to be ready to make love," he whispered and caressed her arms.

Brea turned around with a cool smile. "Why don't you have a seat, and I'll bring you your dinner."

Adam's eyes swept over her dress and paused at the plunging neckline. "Sure." He loosened his tie and seated himself at the table. Brea moved about the kitchen to plate the meal, paused, and shook out her hands to steady them while Adam checked messages on his phone.

With their plates in hand, she returned to the table, leaned in close, and grazed his shoulder with her arm as she placed his dish before him. Adam rubbed her lower back, then sat back and exhaled. "We'll go to bed early tonight," he said with a grin.

Brea sat in her chair, inhaled a deep breath, and replied with a smile, "Let's eat." She met Adams' eyes and watched him pick up his fork to take a bite. Mirroring Adam, Brea did the same and told him about her day with the children. Her heart raced, and her hands continued to tremble. She steadied her voice for what she needed to say next to move the plan forward.

"I've been thinking, Adam, things are better now. I would like to have my phone, and I think it's time you destroyed the fake letters from the witnesses saying I'm a danger to the children."

Adam sighed, lowered his eyes to his plate and continued to eat. "We're not there yet, Brea."

"I think you're bluffing, Adam," she responded with a haughty air.

Placing his fork down, he brought the glass of water to his lips and drank a good portion of it before he replied. "Brea, I don't bluff."

"If you file for emergency custody, I'll be able to convince the judge that I'm neither mentally ill nor an alcoholic because it's the truth. I will also tell the judge that you're holding me prisoner, and that you and Sandra coerced me—I mean blackmailed me—to take away my children unless I take medication and stay with you."

Adam laid his hands flat on the table and leaned in, calm, and spoke with an assertive tone of voice. "Brea, you don't have a lawyer, and I know the system. Not to mention several judges in my pocket that my father knows well and compensates to make sure things go our way. Don't fuck around, Brea—you would lose."

"I could tell everyone your parents paid off a judge. You're breaking the law, and the state will disbar you."

"I would love to see you try to prove it, Brea. No one would believe my unhinged wife, who, by the way, also tested positive a couple of days ago for narcotics and sedatives in a blood test we drew while you were sleeping. I have letters signed by half a dozen witnesses stating that you're broken and a danger to Alex and Sophie."

"You're lying about everything. Those letters are all lies, Adam," Brea exclaimed, raising her voice.

"So what, Brea? It's all stacked against you. The truth doesn't matter—what I say matters. Clearly, you should not have missed your medication last night, or it isn't working. Sandra will need to make some adjustments tonight."

"You're giving me medicine I don't want or need. I just want a divorce—why can't you let me go?" Brea shouted.

Startling her, Adam abruptly stood and slammed his hands on the tabletop. He strode around the table, grabbed her chair and forcefully turned it to face him. Brea froze, eyes wide, and with her heart pounding in her chest, met Adam's livid eyes.

"Brea, keep your voice down. You're not leaving me—get that out of your head. You have one more chance, or you're going to the facility. We will get you conserved, and I will put you away whenever I want to because you belong to me."

Brea shook her head. "I'm sorry, Adam," she cried out. Seeing Sandra enter the kitchen, Brea sprang out of the chair, intending to run out of the room, but Adam was too quick—he grabbed her arms and restrained her.

"Sandra, medication now," Adam instructed. Nodding, she hurried out of the room.

Adam pulled Brea into his chest and wrapped his arms around her. Although she resisted and attempted to wiggle out of his arms, his strength overpowered her. "Listen to me, Brea, one chance. I don't want you to bring any of this up again." Brea braced herself, knowing Sandra would dose her with strong medication.

"I'm sorry, I won't ever talk about it again, I promise. I'll do whatever you tell me to do—I'll go to the bedroom with you. Please, I don't need any medicine."

Upon Sandra's return, Adam pulled Brea closer to his chest to keep her arms still. Pinching a muscle on Brea's arm, Sandra injected a syringe full of clear liquid. Brea cried out, "No, please don't." Adam continued to hold her against him.

"Sandra, check on the kids and then clean up the kitchen. I'll take care of Brea." Sandra nodded and left the room. Brea felt lightheaded and sank into Adam's chest. Bending at the knees, he placed one of his arms under Brea's legs and lifted her up.

"Brea, we were making such progress. It could have been an exceptional evening. Why did you have to lose control of yourself?"

"I'm sorry, Adam. I'll be good, I promise," Brea mumbled.

"We'll see about that," he replied. Adam carried Brea into the bedroom and laid her on the bed. Her limbs felt heavy, and she had difficulty keeping her eyes open.

"Please let me go," Brea mumbled as Adam shut the door and dimmed the lights.

Seated beside Brea on the bed, he slid his hands behind her neck to unfasten her necklace, removed it, then undressed her and covered her with the bedsheet. He exhaled and ran his hand down her back.

"Brea, we're going to try again tomorrow when you're calm and you see things my way." Adam leaned down, kissed her shoulder, and Brea slipped away into the darkness.

Chapter Fifty-Eight

BREA

B rea rolled onto her back and struggled to open her eyes. They felt leaden, and sweat dripped down her forehead. She had dreamt of being with Hayden in her garage in Black Harbor, but they were grown, not teenagers. Holding hands, they sat side by side in silence on the damp concrete floor, bathed in an amber-orange glow as they watched the sun rising through the windows.

After wiping her forehead, she rolled her head to the side and opened her eyes. Sandra sat beside the bed in a chair, dressed in a brown silk blouse and tan trousers with her hands folded in her lap. Brea's blurred vision made the room hazy, and her tongue and cheeks felt raw and dry.

"I need water," she whispered. Sandra handed Brea a small glass of water, and she drank it down.

"It may take you a little longer to wake up today, but you will feel better soon, Mrs. Tandervon. We have made progress, I assure you. Last night was only a minor setback." Sandra leaned over to run her hand over Brea's forehead—she smelled of earth—a blend of moss and sandalwood. "Mr. Tandervon is expecting you to be seated in the dining room tonight at seven-thirty for a formal dinner. I will return to check on you in a little while and bring in some lunch. Then you can visit the children after I help you dress."

Brea fought to wake up, but her body felt weighted down, and her eyelids could not stay open for more than several seconds. Sandra pulled the shades halfway up to let in more light. Brea rolled over, finding the bright light irritating.

An hour passed, and Brea felt strong enough to lift herself to sit on the bed. Her temples throbbed. She needed a pain reliever, though she could not trust Sandra to fetch some for her. Brea exhaled, recalling that in her vanity drawer she kept a bottle of anti-inflammatories. She placed her hand on her chest—the heart pendant necklace she had worn from the blue bag last night was missing. Her breath caught in her chest as her eyes darted around the room. Seeing it on the nightstand, a wave of relief washed over her.

Brea braced herself, and with a gentle push of her hands, rose from the bed. Once she felt steady, she grabbed the necklace off the table and took one step forward. Although fatigued, she could walk without dizziness. She slipped on her robe and went to the bathroom.

Seated at her vanity table, she opened the center drawer and placed the necklace into a white cardboard box. After dropping two pain relievers into her mouth, she ambled to the sink and cupped her hands under the faucet for water to swallow them.

Peeking into the bedroom, she checked to ensure Sandra had not returned. Brea then hurried to the bathroom window, unlocked it, and opened and shut it once, to test whether it made excess noise. There were no creaks or rattles. Reassured, she returned to the sink to brush her teeth and wash her face.

"You should have waited for me, Mrs. Tandervon—you could have fallen," Brea heard from the doorway.

"I needed to use the bathroom, Sandra."

With a sigh, Sandra waved her hand. "Come, I have your tray by the bed."

Brea followed her and sat on the bed's edge while Sandra moved the folding table with the lunch tray in front of her. It was another grilled chicken salad and a bowl of mixed berries.

Sandra seated herself in the chair near the bay window to monitor Brea while she ate. Brea kept her eyes fixed on the tray and ate in silence, preparing herself for the night's plan.

Throughout the day, Brea occupied herself with the children in the backyard, playing tag, drawing pictures with Sophie, and helping Alex build a new Lego set. After the children ate dinner, she gave them a bath and read them fables in Alex's bedroom until Sandra interrupted, informing her it was time she dressed for dinner. Brea styled her hair, leaving it down with voluminous waves, and then slipped into a red strapless chiffon floral dress with a deep side slit paired with gold high-heeled sandals.

"I will put the children to bed, and dinner will be ready shortly, Mrs. Tandervon," Sandra informed her from the bathroom door. Brea thanked her, finished applying her mascara, and took a sip from the Brine water bottle she had filled from the refrigerator water dispenser. She planned to avoid anything Sandra offered her to drink and would perform impeccably tonight to avoid any injections or strong medications.

"I'm ready," Brea replied and rose for a last glance in her full-length mirror. Brea relaxed her shoulders and drew in a slow breath to calm her nerves.

"You look lovely, Mrs. Tandervon," Sandra complimented.

"Thank you. I feel much better. The extra sleep helped," Brea replied with a placid smile and crossed the bedroom. Brea ventured down the hall and entered the dimly lit dining room—an attempt on Sandra's part to create a romantic ambience set against the backdrop of the damask beige wallpaper, taupe wainscoting, and wooden floors.

Brea surveyed the cream-colored concrete dining room table, set with their formal tableware and a round crystal vase holding an arrangement of mixed pink dahlias. With a light touch, she ran her fingers over the cool surface of the table, remembering how she had agonized over whether to purchase it because of its size and weight.

Sandra poked her head in for a final appraisal as Brea settled into a beige linen Parsons chair. Her gaze landed on a bottle of white wine in an ice bucket and one wine glass set before Adam's plate.

"Sandra, why is there wine on the table?"

"Mr. Tandervon requested it," she replied before returning to the kitchen.

Tipping her head back to stretch her neck, Brea inhaled a deep breath. She was living a nightmarish Victorian-era novel, overdressed, trapped, and forced to sit at the dining room table while waiting for her husband to arrive home—her life's outcome would have been unbelievable to her fifteen-year-old self. Hearing the front door open and Adam's foot-steps in the hall, she straightened in her chair. He paused upon entering the dining room.

"Brea."

Rising to meet Adam, she adjusted her stance and shifted her leg to peek through the dress's slit. "Adam, I'm happy to see you," she replied. Adam studied Brea—her dress, posture, and expression. He took several steps closer, and as he looked into Brea's eyes, the corners of her mouth made a slight upturn.

"You look beautiful. I hope you're in a better mood tonight," he said with a guarded demeanor.

Brea tilted her head to the side with a broad smile. "I am. Yesterday was a tough day, but I slept well last night, and I had a wonderful day with the kids. How was work?"

Adam placed his hands on Brea's waist and pulled her close to him. "Great, but I have some work to finish tonight after dinner."

Brea leaned in to kiss Adam with a light touch of her lips. Adam pulled back to study her face. She dragged her hands across his chest, leaned in, and kissed him again. He relaxed, kissed her with passion, and wrapped his arms around her to pull her in closer. Releasing her, Brea smiled and turned to take her seat at the table as Sandra appeared to serve the salads.

"Sandra, please bring a wine glass for Brea." Sandra nodded and left to fetch the glass from the butler's pantry. Brea glanced at the bottle of wine and then fixed her eyes on Adam with a puzzled expression.

"You can have one glass tonight," he said, registering Brea's confusion.

"As long as you feel it's all right," Brea replied with deference.

Sandra returned, poured the wine, and exited once again. Raising her glass, Brea licked her lips first, drawing Adam's attention to her mouth before taking a small sip. He smiled and lifted his fork to eat his salad.

Brea watched him eat for a moment before she picked up her fork. "Tell me about your day, Adam."

Adam shared in great detail a time-consuming intellectual property dispute that had demanded his full attention for days. The conversation then shifted to personal news regarding their friends, updates about which private schools their children had gained acceptances to, and salacious gossip regarding a friend of his from law school. Their social circle circulated a story that his political aspirations shattered after an alleged arrest for trafficking an underage girl across state lines.

Brea listened, occasionally leaning her head to the side to push her hair off her shoulder or running her fingers across her collarbone to draw Adam's attention to the tops of her breasts. Finishing the main course, braised short ribs, whipped potatoes, and balsamic glazed carrots, Adam sat back in his chair with his glass of wine in hand to observe Brea. Although pleased with her behavior and thrilled with her choice of dress, it was clear he was uncertain if her pleasant comportment was genuine.

Sipping her wine, Brea met Adam's eyes. Sandra entered the dining room with dessert set upon a wooden tray—almond pear tarts dusted with powdered sugar and topped with sweetened mascarpone cheese.

"Adam, could I ask you for something?" Brea picked up her fork to eat a bite of dessert once Sandra exited the room.

"Yes," he replied, pouring himself another glass of wine.

"I would like Sandra to take me out shopping tomorrow."

"What would you like to buy?"

"A new dress."

Adam rubbed his chin and raised his eyebrows. "Don't you think you have enough clothes, Brea?"

Brea's eyes flitted to the side, and she shrugged her shoulders. "I would like to wear something special tomorrow night."

"Tell me, what is special about tomorrow night, Brea?"

Brea inhaled and leaned forward to afford Adam a clearer view of the curves of her breasts. "I don't want to say it out loud. Sandra might overhear."

"I'd really like to know, Brea," Adam said with his eyes lowering as she leaned forward. Brea rose from the table and went to Adam, pausing beside him as he pushed his chair back. After seating herself on his lap, she crossed her legs, picked up his free hand and set it atop her knee.

Brea leaned in closer to Adam. "For you. I want a new dress to wear tomorrow night so we can celebrate a new chapter in our lives. Then, I want you to take it off, and make love to me."

Adam shifted beneath her. "Brea, are you trying to manipulate me?"

"No," she replied, placing a hand on his chest and parting her lips.

"I'm suspicious, Brea. Last night you went crazy."

"That was yesterday," Brea whispered, brushing her lips against Adam's cheek, then lowered her head to kiss his neck. Placing her hand on his thigh, she shifted her bottom from side to side several times. Adam's mouth opened and he let out a breath.

"I realized the truth today. You were right, Adam. He was a liar and only wanted to use me and break up our marriage. I almost ruined my life over him, and he never even tried to find me—but you saved me. You've shown me how much you love me by fighting for me, and when I woke up this morning, undressed in bed, all I wanted was for you to be there with me, touching me, making love to me."

Brea arched her back and pressed her bottom deeper into Adam's lap. He groaned and dragged his hand up Brea's thigh as he spoke, "We don't have to wait until tomorrow."

"I can't make love to you the way I want to with the children here. I want it to be special. The kids asked me if they could do a sleepover at Hannah's. Why don't we ask her? She hired someone new at the store already, and she promised Alex and Sophie she would take them to the zoo. They could go the next morning."

Adam pulled back in an abrupt motion, and Brea startled. Adam pinched Brea's chin and looked into her eyes, searching for something to confirm that what she told him was sincere. She held his gaze and smiled. He nodded. "Fine."

"And I'm not comfortable with Sandra here. Could you give her the night off, put her in a hotel, and she can come back in the morning before you leave for work?" Brea gripped Adam's upper arms with her hands, moved her lips to his ear and gently licked and teased his earlobe with her teeth. She paused and whispered, "Then I can be as loud as I want to."

"Sandra will stay in the guest room. She would leave us alone," Adam replied in a low voice. Brea knew all he needed was a nudge to cave.

She felt Adam firm beneath her, rolled her hips, and continued. "Adam, tonight, I want you to watch me touch myself. And tomorrow, when you're at work, I want you to think about my hands all over my body. Then, when we're alone in the house tomorrow night, make love to me in our bed, and then again on this table the next morning."

Adam kissed her. "All right. I'll let Sandra know tonight. I'm done with dinner. Let's go to the bedroom." Brea stood, and Adam grabbed her hand to lead her down the hall. She slipped past Adam into the bedroom and pulled down the zipper on her dress. Adam followed her in and shut the door.

⁂

Seated on the edge of the bed, Brea slipped on her robe. Her efforts to hold off Adam succeeded. Adam, exceedingly aroused, stimulated himself to climax in little time while watching Brea touch herself. Even though Brea struggled with her performance, she persevered, reminding herself of the end goal—freedom.

Adam kissed Brea and, with a smile, left the bedroom to work in his office. It was half past eight. Brea hurried to the bathroom and locked the door behind her. Sandra would knock on the bedroom door soon to check on her, and she would need to hurry.

Brea pulled out a small black trash bag from the bathroom sink cabinet. She emptied the water bottle, dried it, and placed it in the bag along with the necklace she wore the previous night. Last, she added the picture frame from the blue bag with the photo of herself and the kids Hannah had inserted. Tying the bag shut, she pressed her ear to the bathroom door—she heard no sounds coming from the bedroom.

Satisfied, she hurried to the window and opened it. She out-stretched her arm to drop the bag onto the ground—startling her, a hand grabbed her wrist. Brea stifled a laugh, then leaned her upper body out of the window. "Hayden. You almost gave me a heart attack," she whispered.

Crouched on the ground, Hayden looked up at Brea and took the bag from her hand. "Sorry, couldn't help it," he said with a devilish grin.

"Stay down. Adam is in his office on the other side of the house, but the nurse is coming in any minute. I put the picture frame and everything else in the bag. I hope they worked," Brea whispered. Hayden rose, wrapped his hands around Brea's face, and kissed her, long and deep.

"Do you ever follow instructions?" Brea whispered when he pulled back from her.

Hayden smiled. "Nope. And that was worth it. It always is." Hayden and Brea tipped their foreheads together and sighed. "Are you all right?" he asked.

"I will be soon. Go. Be careful. I love you, and tell Hannah Adam will call her about the kids sleeping over at her house tomorrow." There was a knock on the bathroom door.

"Mrs. Tandervon?" Sandra's voice called out as she knocked on the door again.

"Coming, just a minute," Brea replied. She glanced over her shoulder before turning back to Hayden and whispered, "He even agreed to sending the nurse to a hotel." Hayden placed a hand on Brea's cheek, and she placed her hand over his.

"Brea, you're amazing. I've said it before. You're stronger than you think—maybe now you'll believe me." Across her lips stretched a wide smile. Hayden kissed her again on her mouth. "Mrs. Tandervon, please open the door." Sandra's voice repeated.

"Yes, I'm coming, just a minute." Brea looked into Hayden's eyes.

"I love you," Hayden whispered. He grabbed her hand, kissed it, took off and disappeared from sight.

"Mrs. Tandervon, are you all right in there or do I need to call Mr. Tandervon over?"

"Coming," Brea called out as she closed the window and hurried to flush the toilet for a credible alibi.

CHAPTER FIFTY-NINE

HAYDEN

Driving back to the hotel, Hayden called Hannah to relay Brea's message. "I got it," Hayden announced once Hannah answered.

"Great, that's a relief. If it worked, then it all comes together. There's no going back now, Hayden."

"I know. And she looks better—stronger. Adam is going to call you to arrange watching Alex and Sophie tomorrow night. I don't want to get my hopes up too much, but I think we have a strong shot."

"Adam already called me. I'll pick up Alex and Sophie at four. He's expecting me to take them to the zoo the following morning, so we're all set with the kids. Let me know if anything changes."

"All right, we'll talk tomorrow. Goodnight." Hayden hung up the phone and placed it in the cupholder.

The idea of Brea being alone with Adam in the house the following night unnerved him. He knew what Brea needed to do, and the risk of something going wrong was high—worrying was unavoidable. He planned to drive to the house and park across the street after sunset in case she needed him.

If everything went according to plan, Brea would flash the porch light five times and repeat it twice after a pause. If something went wrong but the plan was still in play, she would follow the same pattern though flash the light twice, and if there were no flashes by ten o'clock, he would come into the house and do what was necessary to break her out.

The stakes were high, and if the plan failed, there would be no choice but to fight a contentious legal battle, risking her separation from the children and the defaming of her reputation. They hoped it would not come to that.

Arriving at the hotel, Hayden pulled into the valet circle and grabbed the black trash bag before exiting the car. He handed the keys to the valet driver and hastened his steps through the lobby, eager to see if Brea had pulled off the most critical part of the plan.

With his confidence bolstered, his appetite returned, and upon entering his room, he called room service and ordered a hot meal. Hayden seated himself at the desk, opened his laptop, took a deep breath and set to work. In two days-time he hoped to have Brea and the children free. Henry told him to be smarter—all his hopes banked on the fact that he had been.

Chapter Sixty

Brea

The following afternoon, Brea returned home from shopping, greeted Alex and Sophie at the door and promised to play with them after unpacking her purchases. Hannah would arrive at the house to pick up the kids at four o'clock, and Sandra would drive to the hotel once Adam returned home from work that evening.

Sandra unpacked the groceries and then assisted Brea in the kitchen to prep the meal. The dinner menu comprised braised duck breasts in a red wine reduction, scalloped potatoes, and mushrooms with butter, shallots, and parsley. For dessert, she had bought a hazelnut dacquoise with a salted caramel ganache.

Brea joined her children, and they settled on the living room floor to play a board game until it was time to pack their bags. Alex and Sophie followed Brea down the hall, bursting with enthusiasm in anticipation of Hannah's arrival and her promise that they could make as much noise as they wanted, indulge in an ice cream sundae bar, and construct a pillow fort on her couch. They spoke over one another as Brea listened and laughed, unable to get a word in between their delightful chatter.

A wave of bittersweet emotions washed over Brea while packing Sophie's bag. She had loved Adam, and although their marriage had crumbled and she now saw the true nature and severity of his narcissism, still, he had given her the most precious gifts—Alex and Sophie. A permanent connection would remain with him. It would be difficult to find her way to forgiveness—but, in her heart, she hoped one day he would acknowledge his disastrous mistakes with Brea, apologize, and find his way to becoming a better man for the sake of his own soul and future.

At four o'clock, Hannah rang the doorbell. Sandra greeted her at the door and led Hannah down the hall, where she found Brea building a tower of magnetic blocks with the children in Alex's bedroom. Brea rose to embrace her.

"Ready?" Hannah whispered, holding Brea tight.

"Hope so."

"Kiddos. Who is ready for Aunt Hannah's amazing fun sleepover party with no parents and no rules?" Hannah bellowed with exuberance. The children cheered and jumped into the air with outstretched arms. Grabbing the packed bags, Hannah and Brea followed Alex and Sophie, bounding down the hall and then running out the door to the large SUV Hannah had rented.

"You know, Hannah, maybe after tonight you'll reconsider having kids. It isn't too late to change your mind," Brea teased, glimpsing the oversized car in the driveway.

Hannah laughed. "Not a chance in hell."

Brea enveloped Sophie and Alex in her arms and sprinkled kisses on their cheeks. She held them for longer than usual before helping to load the car with their bags and strapping them into the car seats. Sandra watched from the front door.

Before climbing into the car, Hannah pulled Brea in for another embrace and whispered in her ear, "You have the power tonight, don't forget that. Adapt and be one step ahead." Brea nodded, remained fixed in place and waved to the kids as Hannah backed out of the driveway.

Sandra waited for her in the doorway, and upon reaching the house, Brea met Sandra's eyes, drew in a breath, and smiled. With the children gone and under Hannah's care, she could now focus on the coming night, and there would be no time for tears or doubts. Brea would surrender herself to playing her part for the last time—she could not change history, but she had the courage and will to shape her future.

At a quarter to seven, dressed in her robe, Brea arranged the final touches on the dining room table while Sandra packed her overnight bag. Brea straightened the ivory placemats, inspected the sterling silverware for smudges, and then lit the pillar candles flanking the cappuccino rose centerpiece. With ten minutes left, she needed to dress before Adam arrived home.

The prepared meal was set in the oven to warm. Entering the kitchen, she placed two champagne flutes on the island counter, opened the bottle, and set it in the ice bucket. After a final survey and a deep breath, Brea hurried to her bedroom.

Earlier at the lingerie shop, she bought a nude lace strapless plunge bodysuit with a garter belt—this was not her style, but tonight demanded a costume that was provocative, elaborate, and laborious to remove. Brea tucked the tiny plastic vial she would need later into a bra cup, then leaned over to ensure it remained fixed in place.

Seated before her mirror at the vanity table, she touched up her eye makeup and dabbed perfume behind her ears. She ruffled and then sprayed her hair, styled with curls cascading down her back. A knock rapped on the bathroom door.

"Brea, I'm home," she heard Adam say.

"I'm almost ready, Adam. Meet me in the living room. I just opened a bottle of champagne on the counter," she replied, staring at her reflection in the mirror.

"All right. Sandra left for the hotel. We're alone."

"I'll be out in a minute," she called out and ran her fingers over the butterfly brooch beside her perfume bottles. Brea pressed her hands together, squeezed them tight, and released them. After another glance in the mirror, she stood to dress.

With tremulous hands, she undid the zipper of the silver crystal beaded dress with a sweetheart neckline and off-the-shoulder draped sleeves. Brea slipped it on and then stepped into her high heels. Turning, she checked the mirror to ensure the short skirt hid the lace welts of her stockings and the straps of her garter belt.

Walking down the hallway, Brea shut her eyes and placed her hand over her heart. Before entering the family room, she dropped it to her side, paused and smiled at Adam dressed in a dark gray suit, seated on the plush ivory sofa with his legs crossed. His mouth opened and his lips curled into a smile, pleased with Brea's sultry appearance.

He rose to his feet and went to Brea. "I will not make it through dinner. You look incredible, so sexy."

Brea ran her fingers through her hair before draping her arms over Adam's shoulders. "Let's not rush the evening. I have a surprise planned after dinner for you, and it will be worth waiting for, I promise."

Adam kissed her before pulling his head back to speak. "All right, I'll play along, but no promises. All I could think about today was watching you last night in the bedroom. You were so hot."

"I can't wait for you to make love to me," Brea whispered, looking into his eyes.

An arrogant grin spread across his face. Adam took a step back—now certain he had won, and she was his. "I'll pour us some champagne," he said and turned to walk to the kitchen island counter. Brea followed.

Adam lifted the bottle out of the ice bucket. "What is this champagne, Brea? I've never seen this before."

"The sommelier recommended it. The price was ridiculous, but I thought it was worth a splurge for tonight," Brea answered. She slid between Adam and the counter, then traced the length of his belt with her fingers.

Adam groaned. "If your plan is to drive me crazy, Brea, it's working."

She kissed him on the cheek and stepped away as Adam poured the champagne and then handed her a glass. "To a fresh start," Brea toasted, raising her glass to Adam and taking a sip. "Have a seat at the dining room table. I made dinner myself, and I want to serve it to you. You don't have to do anything tonight until I've slipped out of my dress."

Adam exhaled and, with one hand, caressed Brea's bottom before he turned to walk out of the kitchen. Brea grounded herself with purposeful breaths as she removed the food from the oven and plated the meal. Entering the dining room with plates in hand, she served Adam.

"This looks delicious. You have always been a fantastic cook, Brea," he complimented.

"Save room for dessert. One surprise is that I picked up one of those espresso machines we always spoke of buying but never did. And I stocked up on those imported Italian espresso beans you love—decaf of course, for tonight."

"You thought of everything, Brea," Adam replied, pleased that Brea was doting on him. Brea smiled, and while they ate, she shared with Adam her plans to sign Alex up for a soccer league in the fall and her thoughts on whether to run for a spot on the parent board at the kids' private school for the school year.

Seeing Adam's glass empty, Brea rose to retrieve the champagne bottle from the kitchen. She returned, and as she stood beside Adam to refill his glass, he placed a hand on her hip. "Only one more glass, Brea, AJ called me just as I pulled into the driveway. He invited me to a last-minute meeting tomorrow morning, and I can't be late."

Brea flashed Adam a seductive smile and replied, "Of course. But tonight, I only want you to focus on me." Adam chuckled, shared with Brea the events of his day, then spoke of a substantial investment property his father was considering purchasing. Once finished, Brea stood to clear the table, leaned down, and kissed Adam before picking up his plate. Adam patted her bottom before she turned to prepare dessert and Adam's espresso.

In the kitchen, Brea checked the time. Her heart pounded as she opened the cabinet to pull out the beans, and then from her bra cup she retrieved the small vial of liquid sedative Hayden gave her at Brine. With a swift hand, she filled the dropper and dispensed the dose Hayden had instructed her to use into the espresso cup. She hid the vial behind an opaque jar in the cabinet.

Once brewed, she brought the espresso to Adam and set it before him with the dessert plates. "I'll be right back with dessert." Adam smiled and finished his glass of champagne. Brea took the flute and the champagne bottle with her to the kitchen. Setting them down, she placed her hands on the counter, squeezed them into tight fists, then shook them out to steady herself. With careful attention, she transferred the hazelnut dacquoise onto the dessert dish.

"Brea? I'm growing impatient," she heard Adam call out from the dining room. After scooping the fresh whipped cream on top, she placed the knife under the dish to carry with her. Returning to the dining room, her eyes shot over to his espresso cup—it sat untouched.

"Here you go," she said and sliced the cake, hoping Adam would not notice her trembling hands. Brea met Adam's eyes. He tilted his head and fixed his gaze on her as she set his dessert plate down. She produced a smile though her heart ran rampant in her chest. On the verge of turning, Adam grabbed her wrist, startling Brea so that she dropped the knife on the table. He pushed his chair back and placed a hand on her hip to pull her closer to him.

"Brea," he said, maneuvering her between his legs with an indecipherable expression. "Lift the skirt of your dress up." Brea's breath trapped in her chest.

"I was hoping we could have dessert first, then move into—"

Adam shook his head. "Lift your dress, Brea," he directed. Breathing faster, she placed her hands on the hem of her dress and pulled the fabric up slowly.

Adam grabbed her wrists and stopped her. Upon revealing the straps of the garter belt, he smiled. "A garter belt. I thought I saw the straps when you walked into the kitchen. So hot Brea. More to look forward to later," he said, releasing her. He pulled down the skirt of her dress and patted her on the hip.

Brea let out a stifled laugh and inhaled—she swore she nearly fainted from having held her breath. Returning to her chair, she sat, cut herself a slice of cake, and transferred it onto her plate. Adam ate half of his dessert, brought the espresso cup to his lips, and after taking a small sip, set it down. He met Brea's eyes watching him intently.

"Is it too hot?" she asked with a steady voice.

"No, it's fantastic." Adam picked it up again and drank it down. Brea blew out a small breath and ate a bite of her cake. The clock started now—it would take twenty to thirty minutes until the drug would take effect.

She would need to prolong dessert for as long as possible. Brea reminded Adam of a conversation they had the previous month regarding updating Sophie and Alex's bathrooms. She prattled on about the various design details, styles of fixtures, and colors.

"Now that I'll have more free time, should I call our contractor to have him come by the house for an estimate?" she asked after exhausting the topic.

"Of course. I'm glad your focus is back on our home and family, Brea," Adam said.

Brea affected a coquettish expression. "Adam, I'm so happy you forgave me. Being at home and not having the pressure of working will be so helpful. I want only to make you happy."

"If you are back to your old self, then I'm happy, too. I can't eat another bite, Brea, and I'm done waiting." Adam leaned forward and clasped his hands together to let Brea know he was ready to move on to the next phase of the evening.

Brea set down her fork and rose from the table. Pushing her hair to one shoulder, she went to him. Adam leaned back in his chair, and his smile faded as Brea sat on his lap. Placing her hands on the back of his head, she leaned in and kissed him, prying open his mouth with her tongue. Adam groaned and gripped her hips, growing more aroused from their kiss. Brea pulled back.

"I'm going to fix my makeup and freshen up. Meet me in the bedroom in five minutes."

Adam wiped the corners of his mouth and nodded as Brea rose and left the dining room. Brea hurried down the hall and into the bathroom. She checked the time and estimated ten minutes had passed since he drank the espresso. If her timing was off, she would need to adapt—surrendering her body or her mind to Adam would never happen again.

Locking the bathroom door behind her, she sat at her vanity table and waited until she heard Adam enter the bedroom, and the sound of objects being placed on the nightstand. She checked the clock again. Another ten minutes had passed. Brea drew in a deep breath and raised her eyes to look into the mirror. "To hell and back," she whispered.

Brea opened the door and paused. Adam sat in the upholstered chair beside the bay window with his legs crossed, dressed now only in his button-down shirt and slacks. From the dresser, she picked up the remote and began her pre-selected music playlist.

Turning, she went to Adam and, upon reaching him, knelt down on the floor before him and raised her eyes to meet his. With a gentle touch, she uncrossed his legs and pushed his knees apart to make space for her. Her hands moved up his thighs and over his chest as she slowly unbuttoned his shirt. Reaching the last button, she opened his shirt and leaned in to kiss his neck. She gripped his thighs and with her lips and tongue trailed down his abdomen. Adam tilted his head back and exhaled.

Brea smiled, placed her hands on Adam's knees and rose. She held out her hand for Adam to join her. Though flustered, he continued to play along and allowed her to lead him to the bed where she removed his shirt and placed it on the nightstand.

With her fingers, she traced the length of his arms, then moved her hands to undo his belt. Pulling it off, she stepped away, dropped it to the ground, and pointed to the bed for him to lie down. Adam sat on the bed and lay back against the pillows to watch Brea's seduction routine. The song she had selected for her dance began. Adam would only have the patience to watch Brea for five minutes at most—she would need to stretch out the routine for as long as possible.

Adam watched Brea as she swayed her hips, turned, and un-zipped her dress. She paused halfway, slipped her arms out of the sleeves, and glanced over her shoulder. Adam, entranced, was enjoying Brea's sensual striptease. Running her fingers through her hair, she piled it on top of her head, and let it tumble down her back.

Stretching her arms in the air, she rolled her hips, then un-zipped the rest of her dress. She held the top of her dress against her chest and turned once again to face Adam. Bending from the waist, she dropped her head to the floor and slowly straight-ened while sliding one hand up her leg. Brea let the top of her dress fall and pushed the fabric down her hips, pausing to drag her fingers over her abdomen, before sliding off the dress.

Adam's mouth opened at the sight of Brea dressed only in the sexy lingerie and high heels. Brea continued to dance until Adam made a move to sit up. Shaking her head and wagging a finger at him, he paused, and lay back on the bed. To make a show of taking off her thigh-highs, she placed her leg on a stool and unhooked the straps of her garter belt one by one—Brea estimated that twenty-five minutes had passed since Adam ingested the laced espresso.

After stepping out of her high heels, she rolled down the stocking on each leg. Observing Adam, her heart skipped—he did not appear drowsy yet. Brea whipped around to face the wall, continuing to dance as her eyes darted around the room and her heart pounded in her chest. She lifted her eyes to the ceiling and inhaled—she could not stall much longer.

Turning to face Adam, she pasted a sensual smile on her face. Adam watched her, though unless imagining it, his facial expression appeared more subdued. He raised his hand, beckoning Brea to join him on the bed.

Brea shook her head and smiled. It was difficult to take in a deep breath as she swayed her hips and slipped off the garter belt—the only article left to remove was her lace bodysuit. Sliding it down her breasts and hips, she removed it, leaving her nude and out of time.

Adam's eyes closed, then opened again—he now struggled to keep them open. Brea walked to Adam at a slow pace and, upon reaching the base of the bed, climbed onto the mattress to straddle him.

"Touch me, Adam," she said. Lifting his hands to her waist, it was clear his arms were losing tone. Adam closed his eyes and moaned as Brea rocked her hips over him—he was fading fast. She stopped moving, and his head fell onto his left shoulder.

Placing his arms on the bed, she waited, frozen in place. He did not stir. She sighed with relief, slid off him, and sat on the bed's edge for several minutes. Once confident he was unconscious, she rose to remove his slacks. It was difficult to wiggle them off his hips, though with patience, she removed them. She paused again, ensuring he was in a deep sleep before removing his boxers. Taking slow, light steps, she tossed the garments onto the chair, then hurried to the dresser to slip into her nightgown.

Brea checked the time—it was five minutes after nine o'clock. Hayden would be waiting for her signal to ensure everything went according to plan. She hurried into the living room and flashed the porch lights five times, counted to five, and repeated the sequence twice. After scurrying to the windows, she opened the curtains to peer outside. Hayden's car was parked across the street, and upon seeing Brea at the window, he flashed the headlights three times. Brea smiled, pressed one hand against the window, and with the other, blew him a kiss. Hayden flashed the lights again, and she laughed. After a minute, Hayden drove off.

Racing to the kitchen, she emptied the remaining champagne into the sink and placed the bottle in the recycle bin. Knowing that mixing sedatives and alcohol could be deadly, she intentionally purchased alcohol-free champagne that morning and scratched off the zero percent alcohol print from the bottom of the label.

Brea then retrieved the vial of sedative. She washed it with soapy water and opened the cabinet under the kitchen sink, where she kept essential oil bottles of various shapes and sizes. After filling it with several drops of lavender oil, she tucked it in the tray with the others. Last, she washed the espresso cup, placed the plates from the counter in the dishwasher, and blew out the candles in the dining room.

When back in her bedroom, she exhaled, relieved to find him still deeply sedated. From the nightstand, she grabbed Adam's cell phone and powered it off. Although Brea struggled, she pulled the comforter and flat sheet from beneath Adam, removed the extra pillows under his back and covered him to his waist.

After slipping out of her nightgown, she climbed into bed beside him, fixed her eyes on the ceiling and placed her hand on her chest. With her part of the plan concluded, the rest was in Hayden's hands. All Brea could do was wait.

CHAPTER SIXTY-ONE

HAYDEN

Dressed in a navy wool suit, a light-blue shirt, and a striped tie, Hayden sat at the head of a mahogany table in a large conference room. He thanked an assistant as he placed a pitcher of water and a hot cup of black coffee before him. On his left sat Braden and Matthew, and on his right, Peter and Gregory, all having flown down last night to join Hayden for the meeting.

At nine-thirty, a group of two men and a woman entered the room. Hayden and his team rose from the table. The older gentleman stepped ahead with a warm expression on his face and outstretched his arm for Hayden to shake his hand.

"Mr. Botero, welcome. We're thrilled you're here this morning and honored you're considering us to represent your software company," the elder gentleman proclaimed with fervor. Dressed in a gray pinstripe suit, a starched white shirt and a solid navy tie, he had a full head of white hair and sharp eyes.

"It's a pleasure. We are very interested in hearing more about your firm today. I have with me Braden Morrisson, CFO; Gregory Joren, COO; Matthew Marconwood, CTO; and Peter Lewis, our in-house attorney," Hayden replied with a handshake and a smile.

"I'm Arnold James Vanderman, the firm's Senior Equity Partner. I have already spoken extensively with Peter to review the letter of intent regarding your offer to acquire Pltanix, which, as you requested, I handle with the utmost confidentiality, solely with my most senior and experienced partners beside me, Serena James and Christopher Flornworth. I must apologize, however, the attorney—"

"My apologies, AJ, for running late. An urgent call kept me." Adam hurried into the conference room, dressed in a black suit, a light-gray shirt, and a classic gray houndstooth tie. He halted in the middle of the room, seeing Hayden at the head of the table, flanked by his team. Adam turned his head to the side, paused and wiped his mouth with one hand, before joining his partners at the table.

"It's all right, Adam. I was only making the initial introductions. This is one of our illustrious attorneys, Adam Tandervon, whom you requested be present here at the eleventh-hour yesterday evening, having heard of his stellar reputation and skill with negotiations. Adam, this is Mr. Hayden Botero, CEO of BoteroX Software."

Hayden extended his hand to Adam. "Adam, pleasure to meet you." Adam walked to Hayden and shook his hand.

"Glad to meet you. I appreciate you including me this morning for the interview," Adam replied with a steady voice and maintained eye contact.

Hayden let go of his hand and held up a finger. "You know Adam—I think we may have met once before. You look familiar to me," he said with a grin spreading across his face.

Adam managed a tight smile. "I don't think so. Pleasure to meet you all the same."

With a slight head tilt, Hayden inhaled and replied, "Well, my mistake then." Adam turned, straightened his blazer, and went to his seat. Before seating himself, he glanced back at Hayden.

Hayden exhaled and spoke. "Let's get to it. My company would like to acquire Pltanix, a mid-sized software company located here in Ocean Crest Beach. There are many reasons, however, foremost being their outstanding engineering talent and cutting-edge software technology, that would add significant value to my company. I have board approval, have met with the Pltanix executive team several times, and they are receptive to an offer. On the advice of my in-house attorney, we would like a local corporate legal team to negotiate and represent BoteroX Software. We'll need a seasoned team of mergers and acquisition attorneys with around the clock availability and unparalleled experience to ensure a smooth and legally sound transaction. Mr. Vanderman, we would like to hear about your firm and what you could offer my company to secure the deal."

"Of course, and please, Mr. Botero, call me AJ." Hayden nodded and gestured for him to proceed. AJ spoke on behalf of the partners to review their experience in similar acquisitions—risk mitigation, ensuring regulatory compliance, strategic structuring, protection of company interests, common pitfalls of negotiations they overcame in previous acquisitions and an overview of stumbling blocks they could foresee.

Hayden locked his eyes on Adam periodically as Peter and Braden jumped in with questions and clarifications over the following hour and a half. Adam, uncomfortable, remained silent unless someone directed a specific question at him.

When both teams paused to write notes, Hayden spoke. "You know, Adam, I know why you're so familiar to me."

Adam pressed his lips together, looked up and met Hayden's eyes. "Sure, tell me," he replied in a clipped tone of voice while tapping his pen on the table.

"I went to high school at Harvey Slate Prep with your wife. I saw a photo of the two of you on our alumni website. Brea Staxon."

AJ chuckled and sat back in his chair. "Well, isn't that something? The world is getting smaller and smaller. His wife's name is indeed Brea, a lovely woman. Perhaps this is a sign that this firm is the right one to represent your company."

Hayden smiled. "I do like to think of my company and the people I work with as family. Family, reputation, and trust are things I value. You know, Adam, I have the photo here on my phone. Let me show it to you."

Removing his phone from his pocket, Hayden rose from the table and walked to Adam. "This will only take a minute," Hayden said to the group as he handed Adam his phone. Adam glanced at AJ, and fixed his eyes on the screen.

"Just press that button and it will pop up," Hayden instructed.

Adam pushed his chair back to angle the screen out of view from Serena, seated on his left. He inhaled, focused on the screen, and pressed the button. Clenching his jaw, the color drained from his face. He hit the button after watching the screen for several seconds, then raised his eyes to meet Hayden's with an icy glare.

"Yup, that's us. Small world," Adam said with a tight-lipped smile, aware that everyone in the room had eyes on him.

"Yeah, that's a nice photo. I'll email you a copy, Adam." Hayden plucked his phone out of Adam's hand. About to turn, he paused and looked back at Adam. "Should we put it up on the big screen over there so everyone can take a look?"

Adam chuckled and sighed. "No, let's save that for another time."

A half-smile stretched across Hayden's lips. "Sure." He placed his phone in his pocket and returned to the head of the table.

AJ clasped his hands together. "Mr. Botero, I expect that if you choose us to represent you, we will successfully secure this deal. Peter informed me that your assistant reserved a table for lunch at Sovereign Prime Steakhouse with myself, Serena, and your team. The cars are waiting downstairs, and we will continue this discussion over lunch. I'll leave you with your team for a break, and we can all reconvene downstairs in fifteen minutes."

Hayden shook AJ's hand, then crossed his arms in front of his chest. "You know, AJ, there are some unique challenges here we'll be facing with this acquisition, and since Adam is just joining in, how about he sticks around for another ten minutes with me so I can get to know him a little more? If one of your partners could give my team a quick tour, I'd appreciate it."

AJ nodded. "Fantastic idea. Adam, we'll talk after lunch. Mr. Botero, I'll see you in the car." Adam drank half his glass of water, then rose from his chair as the room cleared out. They waited until the door shut behind the group to speak.

"You think you're pretty fucking smart, don't you?" Adam said, his tone of voice laced with palpable hostility.

Hayden shrugged his shoulders. "I've been told I am. I think I am—"

Adam cut Hayden off. "How did you get the video of me and Brea? Did you break into the house, or did Hannah do it?"

Hayden sighed, crossed his arms, and strolled to the window. A faint smile touched his lips as he remembered kissing Brea by her window after she had given him the trash bag with the recording devices.

"That detail isn't important. What is important, Adam—is that you know you're fucked. I watched that video five or six times, and it was—disturbing. You're admitting to blackmailing Brea, bribing a judge, and the tape caught you restraining and drugging her against her will with injectable medication. Now, I'm not a lawyer, but based on that video, false imprisonment charges and sexual extortion are possible as well. Those are a lot of crimes, Adam. I'm sure you don't need me to tell you this, as you're an attorney, that even though it was a secret recording, it would be admissible as evidence."

"What are you planning to do with the video?" Adam asked, folding his arms over his chest.

Hayden turned to face Adam. "That depends on you. I have an email drafted to AJ and your partners with a link to the video, and now that you know who I am, you know that I'll help Brea fight you in court, and you would eventually lose. Although I suppose you should be most worried about criminal charges at this point. You mentioned your father has judges in his pocket too? Not a good outcome for him either."

Adam lowered his head and rubbed his eyes. "What do you want for the video? You want me to give you Brea?"

Hayden shook his head and scoffed, "You still don't get it. She isn't your property—you can't give her to me."

Adam took a step forward and raised his voice, his composure on the edge of shattering. "Fine, so what do you want?"

Hayden stepped closer to Adam, pausing several feet before him. "Let her go so she can make her own choice and stop threatening to take the kids from her. I'll hit you with everything I've got if you ever bring that up again or tarnish her reputation," Hayden stated plainly.

Adam chuckled arrogantly. "You know, Hayden, that's your name, right? How can you be certain she even wants you? She told me the other night that she gave up on you. I believe her words were, 'He lied to me to break up our marriage and never tried to find me.' She also told me, referring to you, that I saved her from ruining her life."

Adam glanced out the window, and a sordid smirk spread across his face. "And as I told you she would, she begged me to make love to her last night. Put on a sexy dress and lingerie for me. Brea wasn't thinking about you last night while she stripped down naked to fuck me."

A knowing smile spread across Hayden's face. "I'll bet it was—a memorable experience."

Adam's eyes narrowed as Hayden continued to meet his gaze, realizing Brea had manipulated him—it was all an act, and he fell for it.

Hayden's expression shifted—he was tired of playing games with Adam and wanted the matter settled. "Adam, what are you going to do here? You have five minutes to decide or my assistant is sending out the email and it will only be a matter of time until it circulates to your friends, family—and of course all the legal authorities as well—we don't want to forget about them.

"Fuck it. Take her off my hands," Adam spat, turning away from Hayden and running his fingers through his hair.

The assistant knocked on the door. "Mr. Botero, they're waiting for you downstairs."

"Thank you. I will be down in just a moment." With a nod, the assistant hurried off.

Hayden turned to Adam. "Make the call."

Adam shook his head, ripped his phone from his pocket, and called Sandra. "Let Brea out. She's free to do whatever she wants. I'll send a car to take you to the airport and back to my mother's house." Adam hung up the phone.

"You'll hear from the divorce attorney soon for temporary custody arrangements. Brea will be fair. She knows you love Sophie and Alex and you're a good father to them." Hayden paused before leaving, casting another glance at Adam. "Oh, and I'll let AJ know we decided it would be best that you aren't involved in the acquisition. After all, it's better to keep business and friendship separate, wouldn't you agree?"

Hayden gave Adam a clipped smile. Placing his hands in his pockets, he walked out of the conference room, leaving Adam behind as he sat in his chair to reconcile the fact that he had underestimated Brea, lost, and never saw it coming.

CHAPTER SIXTY-TWO

BREA

S eated beside her suitcases on the bed at half past ten, Brea replayed the earlier events of the morning in her mind. Adam had opened his eyes at a quarter to nine and pulled Brea in close to him, ready to have sex.

"What time is it?" Brea whispered.

I don't care," Adam replied, pulling down the sheet to expose Brea's chest and then sliding on top of her. Brea turned her head to look out the window.

"It must be well after eight. Look how bright it is outside."

Adam glanced out the window and grabbed his phone off the nightstand. Seeing it powered off, he checked the time on the nightstand clock and cursed. "Shit. Brea, get me a clean suit and a shirt while I take a shower. I'm going to be late."

"Sure," she replied with a cool demeanor. Adam sprang out of bed, and Brea called out after him, "Adam, last night was amazing. You were incredible." She covered her mouth to hide her smile.

"It was, I just—let me get ready," he called out from the bathroom with confusion.

Brea watched the minutes pass on the clock. Restless, she stood and left the bedroom to walk through her house. It was hard to believe—the dramatic shift of her life's core in less than one month's time.

Strolling through the expansive rooms, her fingers grazed over the furniture pieces she had painstakingly chosen—the upholstery colors, fabrics, materials, rugs and paintings, all of which she agonized over as though the fate of humanity hinged upon those decisions. Now, they mattered little, and she was ready to leave them behind. After everything that happened over the years, she recognized her mother had been right all along, *"They're only things, Brea, things don't matter."*

Indeed, her dream home housed beautiful objects and pleasant memories—but it was not enough. Brea suffered for decades believing she had no voice, that suffering in silence would save her from herself, and that she did not have the strength or resilience to survive if she experienced pain. It was a lie she had told herself—a lie that no longer served her. Within her, alongside her pain and fear, there was strength buried inside her all along. To truly live—all she needed was to believe in it.

Entering the kitchen, Brea paused. Sandra stood at the island counter, dressed in a beige sleeveless shift dress, preparing a late breakfast for Brea. Brea took a deep breath and approached the opposite side of the counter from where Sandra stood. Before she spoke, she observed Sandra for a moment.

"Why do you work for these people, Sandra? I hope you realize you're not helping anyone—you're hurting them for money. And it's an insult to people who are in pain and to the ones out there with good hearts who hope to help them."

Sandra met Brea's eyes with a cool expression. Brea studied them, hoping to find some evidence of humanity, but behind her eyes stood an erect wall—impenetrable.

"Mrs. Tandervon, often people do not know or do what is best for them. They live in their minds, in a fantasy that is not compatible with reality, searching for a happiness that does not exist. Would you not agree that is harmful?"

Brea pressed her lips together. "Maybe it isn't a fantasy. Maybe it's hope. Without that, what's the point? What do we have left?"

Sandra sighed. "Hope is an illusion, a dangerous idea, and when what someone hopes for does not materialize, the devastation takes its toll—drinking, depression, anxiety, and despair. I believe you understand what I mean."

"It took me a long time to see it, but I think what we feel isn't the enemy. It's the pretending—avoiding what we feel—that hurts us. If we embrace the pain, the disappointment along with the joy, then we are living."

Sandra sighed. "Mrs. Tandervon. You are so fortunate. If you do not resist and accept your life here, it will be beautiful and simple. Like a wonderful dream."

Shaking her head, Brea replied, "No. I want my life, flaws and everything, in one complicated, tragic, crazy, but beautiful package. If I make mistakes, and I'm lucky enough to wake up tomorrow, I'll make a new choice and keep going. If someone hurts me—I will heal. I used to be afraid of the world, but I'm not anymore. I'm not afraid of Adam, and I'm not afraid of you."

Sandra knitted her fingers together and set her hands upon the counter. "Mrs. Tandervon. Please go rest in your room, and I will bring in your tray soon, or we may head down the road of another injection."

Drawing in a breath, Brea straightened her posture and took a step forward. Placing her hands flat on the counter, she looked into Sandra's eyes. "I'm going to leave this house today—because I decided to—no matter what is waiting for me on the other side of the door. I'll handle it, and I'll survive.

"Mrs. Tandervon—"

Brea would not allow Sandra to finish speaking.

"So, I will give you the chance to let me go and do the right thing. And if you try to stop me, I'll try my luck at fighting back today—and maybe beat the shit out of you."

Sandra's eyes widened, and her mouth opened. Brea smiled and turned on her heels to leave the kitchen. Waiting for permission to leave was no longer necessary—Brea was already free. Her biggest enemy had been her own mind for too many years, but today it became her ally. Grabbing the car keys off the hook by the door, she replaced them with her wedding ring, went into her bedroom, picked up her bags, and left her dream home and seemingly perfect life behind.

Chapter Sixty-Three

HAYDEN

Arriving at Hannah's two-story beach house, Hayden saw only Hannah's Porsche parked in the driveway. He sprang out of the car and stepped into the street to look for Brea's car. Not seeing it, he sprinted to the door, unlocked it, and bounded into the house. Several times he had tried to reach Hannah after leaving the restaurant, but she did not answer her phone, and a sense of unease crept into his chest.

"Brea?" he called out in the foyer. He removed his blazer and tie, then dropped them on the upholstered bench. There was no reply. Hayden checked each room on the ground floor and continued to call her name. His heart raced, worried something had gone wrong—everyone was supposed to meet at the house according to the plan. "Hannah?" he bellowed and jogged up the stairs to the second floor to check the bedrooms—they were also empty.

As he stood in the bonus room Hannah used as a workshop, Hayden tore his phone out of his pocket and checked to see if there were any messages—there were none. He opened his recent call list to find Hannah's number. On the verge of pressing the call button, he glimpsed a white piece of paper taped to the glass doors leading out to the balcony. He went to the door and braced himself for the worst.

Various scenarios flashed through his mind—perhaps Adam had called someone to take the children and forced Brea to return with him to Santa Barbara. He held his breath, pulled off the note, and opened it. *"Hannah took the kids to a movie. I'm on the beach, Brea."*

Hayden tipped his head back to look at the ceiling, exhaled, and shook his head as relief blanketed him. He crumpled the note and dropped it on the floor. Opening the glass doors, he stepped onto the balcony and saw Brea on the beach, dressed in a long pale-pink sundress, gazing at the water.

"Brea, are you trying to give me a heart attack?" he called out to her with a broad smile stretched across his face.

Brea turned around, smiling and shielding her eyes from the sun. Seeing Hayden on the balcony, she called out, "What is this, Romeo and Juliet?"

Hayden laughed. "Yeah, it kind of is—but without the tragic ending. And now, I'm certain the universe finally gave up on torturing us."

"Well, it certainly took its time—so come down here and give me a happy ending," Brea replied with a mirthful smile.

He raced down the steps to meet Brea on the beach as she strolled across the sand to meet him halfway. They paused with several feet of space between them and smiled, savoring the moment of their reunion.

Brea swept her hair over her shoulder and dropped her arms to her side. "It's been twenty-five years since we first met in the library, Hayden. Did you ever believe that our story would end like this?"

Hayden closed the distance between him and Brea. Reaching her, he cupped her face in his hands. "Believed—not every day—but I always hoped it would."

He kissed her, and everything they overcame to be together became a piece of the past, relevant, but all the same history. Hayden pulled back, looked into Brea's eyes and added, "And this isn't an ending, Brea. It's just the way it should have been from the beginning."

Brea nodded—it was the undeniable truth. Hayden leaned in and kissed the girl he always loved, both of them relieved they had come back home into one another's arms. And in a world, savage though beautiful, where both joy and sorrow coexist, it was a kiss inspiring hope that true love is real, evil will never prevail, and an earnest love story is always worth hearing.

Chapter Sixty-Four

Hayden and Brea, 18 Months Later

"We're going to be late," Brea exclaimed, glancing out the window of the chauffeured car. It was nearly four o'clock. Having lingered at the salon with Hannah and Allegra, the girls had lost track of the time drinking champagne and laughing as they shared memories and stories from the past.

Six months prior, Brea and Hayden had moved into their new home in Ocean Crest Beach after Brea's divorce decree and Hayden's company had relocated. The court had granted Brea primary physical joint custody of Alex and Sophie, and although they adored Hayden, their transition to their new lives had not been without difficulties and adjustments.

It was not perfect—it was flawed, humbling, and messy, but they dealt with the challenges and mistakes as best they could and embraced the imperfection of their lives with the humility and grace it deserved.

Adam and Brea communicated only during weekend drop-offs or when making important decisions concerning the children. Brea had been fair and more forgiving of Adam than others would have been in her shoes, but for her own sanity and her soul, and with the help of her therapist, she continued to strive towards freeing herself of the things in her past that could drown her.

Once they had settled into their new rhythm, Hayden encouraged Brea to reach out to Allegra. Overjoyed and floored by Hayden and Brea's story, it was not long before their families had formed a close friendship. Allegra lived in Portland with her husband and three children though, to Brea's elation, they planned to move to Southern California in the coming year.

And Brea, feeling rather bold, had resumed her writing and was editing a book of poetry she hoped to publish. Her collection of poems, titled *Stolen Nights*, detailed her and Hayden's story.

Some evenings, when Brea and Hayden lay in bed, exhausted from a chaotic day or after making love, Brea would read Hayden one of her poems. One of his favorites, "Forgiveness," Brea had written about the night when they almost lost each other decades ago. It was dark and sad, yet hopeful and true, written in Brea's authentic, unfiltered voice.

"We'll be fine. What's an extra ten minutes after twenty-six years?" Allegra said, reassuring Brea and exchanging a warm glance with Hannah. "By the way, Hayden wanted to make sure you opened this just before we arrived." Allegra handed Brea the mysterious large white box tied with an ivory ribbon that she had carried with her since the morning.

Brea's eyes widened. "I have been dying to know what is inside this box all day."

Hannah handed her a card. "Read this first. Hayden's precise instructions."

Opening the envelope, Brea pulled out the card, and inside it sat a white folded piece of paper. She read the card first. *"Brea—the day we first met, I fell in love with you exactly as you were. Please wear this today. Love, Hayden."*

Brea opened the box and peeked inside. Pulling aside the tissue paper, she laughed, and tears formed in her eyes.

"No," Hannah and Allegra cried out.

"Your makeup. We're going to kill him," Allegra exclaimed.

"Okay, okay, I'm fine," Brea said, reassuring her best friends.

She opened the folded-up paper from the card. Scanning it first, she saw the date written on the top right corner—it was the poem she had asked Hayden to write when they were in Mexico. Brea shook her head, stunned, and read.

> *"I followed amber eyes in a library*
> *To find out what made her smile*
> *In a world that could be cruel*
> *It brought us together and broke us apart*
> *Time and time again*
> *But the universe always knew*
> *We were bound together like pages in a book*
> *She stole my heart in the stacks*
> *And I knew that day, real love was true*
> *Now, us, and our story, belong there too."*

Brea closed her eyes and pressed two fingers against her lips. Allegra took the paper from Brea's hand and read it aloud. Even Hannah, who proclaimed herself anti-sentimental, could not stop the budding tears in her eyes as Allegra finished the last line.

The car slowed to a stop, and Brea smiled upon seeing Henry waiting for her on the curb. He took a step forward to open the door and held out his hand for her. Placing her hand in his, she exchanged a joyful glance with Henry. "You look beautiful, my dear. He's waiting for you inside. Are you ready?" Henry asked.

"Yes, but there's one thing left I need to do before we go in," she replied and turned to her friends.

Hayden and Alex, both dressed in light-gray wool suits, stood beside one another in the Ocean Crest Library Botero Rare Volumes Wing. The violinist and cellist began to play, signaling that the bridal party had arrived, and Hayden drew in a deep breath. Alex nudged Hayden's arm. He gave Alex a wink, then swept his eyes over his and Brea's friends seated in two rows of white wooden folding chairs—Willa, Braden, Ashley, Matthew, Gregory, Peter, Allegra's husband Michael, and their children. They smiled at Hayden before angling themselves in their seats towards the center aisle.

Sophie led the way, adorned in an ivory chiffon dress and scattering pink rose petals as she walked the length of the aisle. Behind her, Allegra appeared dressed in a blush pink cocktail dress, followed by Hannah wearing a full-length gown in the same color. Upon witnessing Hannah wipe a lone tear meandering down her cheek, Hayden gave Hannah a playful nod. She reached out and squeezed Hayden's hand before taking her place.

The guests rose from their chairs as Brea entered on Henry's arm, and the musicians played the song Brea and Hayden had danced to at the supper club in Mexico. A wide smile stretched across Hayden's face, seeing Brea engulfed in an oversized ivory sweater, three sizes too large for her, over her wedding dress. Brea and Hayden laughed as their eyes met.

Brea and Henry stopped before the officiant. Henry turned to Brea, kissed her hand, and placed it in Hayden's. It was a tender moment, a powerful silent gesture, with no need for spoken words. With a nod, Henry took a step back and turned to take his seat beside Willa.

Hayden and Brea turned to face one another. "It's perfect," Hayden said and tugged at the hem of her sweater.

"I've been dreaming of wearing this dress for months, Hayden. I would like for everyone to see it."

"It's symbolic," Hayden replied with a grin.

"What if I promise to wear it, and only it, tonight?" Brea whispered, raising her eyebrows and flashing a seductive smile.

"Now you're talking," he whispered.

Hayden let go of her hand. "Arms up," he directed. Brea smiled and raised her arms. Hayden pulled off the sweater and tossed it on an empty chair, revealing a simple ivory silk spaghetti-strapped gown with a draped bodice, and in her hair, she wore her blue butterfly brooch. Everyone clapped and laughed. Hayden wrapped his arms around Brea and kissed her.

"Not yet," the guests cried out.

Hayden laughed and looked into Brea's eyes. "No rules, right?"

Brea shook her head. "Never."

Ignoring the surrounding noise, Brea and Hayden embraced and kissed again. They had both been through hell, made it back, and they were together, as it should have been from the beginning and was always meant to be.

ABOUT THE AUTHOR

Ella Khort is an adult fiction novelist publishing her first two novels, *Locked Away* and *Unlocked*. Her writing draws inspiration from themes of second chances, love, the complexities of the human mind, and resilience. Outside of writing, she enjoys spending time with family, cooking, and painting.

Instagram: @ellakhortauthor
Facebook: Ella Khort Author
Substack: ellakhort.substack.com